Wrapped
up in
You

Carole
Matthews

sphere

SPHERE

First published in Great Britain in 2011 by Sphere
This paperback edition published in 2011 by Sphere

7 9 10 8

A CIP catalogue record for this book
is available from the British Library.

ISBN 978-0-7515-4509-8

Typeset in Sabon by M Rules
Printed and bound in Great Britain by
Clays Ltd, St Ives plc

Papers used by Sphere are from well-managed forests
and other responsible sources.

MIX
Paper from
responsible sources
FSC
www.fsc.org FSC® C104740

Sphere
An imprint of
Little, Brown Book Group
100 Victoria Embankment
London EC4Y 0DY

An Hachette UK Company
www.hachette.co.uk

www.littlebrown.co.uk

Hello!

Whether you've chosen it for yourself or have been given this book as a Christmas present, I just want to say **THANK YOU** so much for picking up *Wrapped up in You*. I hope that in among the chaos that so often comes with this time of year, you find the time to take a break from the madness and dip into my seasonal gift to you. So, go on – open that tin of Celebrations you've been keeping for yourself, curl up on the sofa with a glass of something suitably festive, kick back with a few chapters and enjoy some quality 'me' time. You deserve it.

I wish you a very merry Christmas and a happy new year. I hope that this season brings you all that your heart desires, and more.

Love Carole ☺ xx

Also by Carole Matthews

For my dear uncle, Thomas Hunt.
14 August 1927–31 January 2011.

Chapter 1

Mrs Norman comes in to see me at Cutting Edge at ten o'clock every Friday morning without fail. She likes to look nice for the weekend as she goes ballroom dancing on Friday and Saturday nights at the Conservative club and, since Mr Norman died two years ago, she's on the lookout for a new man. Someone neat. Someone who doesn't drink. Someone exactly like Mr Norman. Life alone, she reminds me every week, is not all it's cracked up to be. Tell me about it.

Methodically, I comb her age-thinned hair into neat sections and put the last of the rollers into her old-fashioned, brick-set hairdo. I'd like to do something radical to her hair that would take a few years off her and maybe help her snare that elusive man. Put on a bit of honey-coloured mousse to warm the silver grey perhaps, or cut it so that it sweeps forward and feathers onto her face. But Mrs Norman will not be swayed. She knows what she likes – tight sausages of curls and a can of lacquer to hold it in place – and has had the same immovable hairstyle for the last ten years that I've been doing it.

Mind you, if I didn't work in a hairdressing salon, perhaps I'd stick to the same cut too. As it is, I let the juniors practise on

1

me with varying degrees of success. Now I am a block-coloured brunette, a rich chocolate brown the colour of my eyes, with a chippy pixie cut. But I have had many incarnations in the past twenty years. I think this suits me more than some of my other styles (the curly perm was a memorable mistake) as my face is small, heart-shaped and my skin pale. I haven't embraced the whole fake tan thing – way too much trouble. Plus, who wants to smell like a rotting apple every time you apply it?

'How's your love life then, young Janie?' Mrs Norman asks as she breaks into my musings. She asks me the same question every single time I do her hair. I'm constantly disappointed that I have nothing to report.

I raise my eyebrows at her. 'I could ask you the same.' My client is seventy-five and, frankly, sees a lot more action than I do at forty years her junior.

She giggles at that. 'Men these days.' She shakes her head in despair and I narrowly avoid stabbing her with the sharp end of my tail comb. 'All they want is sex, sex, sex!'

I do hope not at Mrs Norman's age.

'That Viagra has a lot to answer for. There used to be a natural time when interest in "things like that",' she mouths that bit into the mirror, 'used to wane. But not now. Oh no. They expect to still be *doing it* until they're ninety. Twice a night.' More head shaking. 'All I want is someone to take a turn around the dance floor with me and perhaps share a nice meal or two. I don't want the *Last Tango in Paris*.'

She makes me smile. I hope when I'm her age I have as much go in me. Come to think of it, I wish I had as much *now*. Finishing off the set, I tie a pink hairnet over the top. 'Let's get you under the dryer.'

Mrs Norman picks up her handbag and follows me towards

the back of the salon to where our two dryers are. I sit her down and find some magazines for her. She likes the more lurid ones, chock full of gossip: *Closer*, *Heat* and *Now*.

'Are you all right?' I ask as I lower the hood towards her.

She nods.

'Cup of tea?'

'I'd love one.' Then, as I turn to go to the staffroom to find a junior to make it, my client unexpectedly takes my hand and squeezes it. 'You'll find someone,' she says. 'A lovely lass like you.'

Yeah, right.

'You should come ballroom dancing with me. It's not all old fogeys, you know. They'd be like bees around a honey pot with a young thing like you.'

'Are there any spare men then?'

'Mostly spare women,' she concedes sadly.

The story of my life. 'I'll get you that tea.'

In the staffroom, I can't find any of the juniors. They're probably all out at the back of the salon having a sly smoke, as Nina and I once would have been, so I make the tea myself. Our staffroom is not glamorous. There are row upon row of hair dyes and supplies, stacks and stacks of towels, piles of coats mouldering damply now that the weather has turned cold and wet, and the usual amount of tat and paraphernalia associated with teenage girls. Our owner, Kelly, keeps threatening to make us clean it all up but, thankfully, she never follows through.

Kelly only bought the shop a couple of years ago or, more accurately, her rich boyfriend did. I think Phil Fuller thought it would give her something to play with while he was busy being an 'entrepreneur'. For that, I read 'small-time crook' or something else similarly dodgy. Our boss is only twenty-seven while her boyfriend is thirty years older than her. I wonder if she would still be with him if he wasn't a millionaire with cash to flash. She's tiny, pretty and blonde. He's a portly, red-faced bloke with a beer belly like a bowling ball and a penchant for gold chains and bracelets. Would I content myself with a man like that? I wonder. How is that a perfect match? Yet they seem to get along well enough.

Nina follows me in, plonks herself down next to a pile of towels waiting to be folded and picks up a magazine to flick through. 'Mrs Norman trying to sort out your love life again?'

I laugh. 'Of course.'

Nina Dalton is my best friend. She and I go back a long way. We were friends all through senior school from the age of eleven and it was no coincidence that we both went into hairdressing. All those hours we spent doing each other's hair in my bedroom didn't entirely go to waste as my parents had feared. We've worked here together since we were both starting out as juniors many years ago. I had a Saturday job to start with and when I went full-time, I persuaded the then owner to take Nina on too. Now I'm sure she's one of the main reasons I've stayed here so long. My friend is the polar opposite to me and has gone down the high-maintenance, white-blonde road and has to have her roots done every couple of weeks, usually by me. She's a blue-eyed beauty with an enviably curvy figure whereas I'm boyish, straight up and down.

Nina reaches into her bag and pulls out an apple. Since she gave up smoking, my friend chain-eats fruit in an attempt to keep her curves in control. But then she also embraces chardonnay wholeheartedly as a fruit-based drink and immediately undoes a lot of the good work.

Despite its optimistic moniker, our salon certainly isn't the most cutting-edge one you'll ever come across. We're based in a lovely little courtyard of shops just off the High Street in Buckingham, a middle-of-the-road place that is the county town of this area. Very charming in its own way but, admittedly, not Beverly Hills. We compete with another much more trendy salon here that *should* be called Cutting Edge, but isn't. We do our fair share of hair extensions and celebrity lookalike cuts for the younger crowd, but our main clientele are the Mrs Normans of the world with their wash-and-sets and their regular perms.

It's nice enough in here. We had a much needed makeover not long ago and now we're all matt mocha walls with chocolate chairs and silver-gilt-framed mirrors at each station. Instead of the scruffy lino, a new marble-effect floor was put down and all our towels are coordinated in shades of brown and cream. The clients seem to like it.

Perhaps it shows a lack of ambition that I'm still here after all this time and haven't thought to go chasing fame and fortune in one of the London salons. But it wouldn't do if we were all like that, would it? I might not be setting the world alight, but I'm happy. Ish.

'She does have a point, Janie,' Nina says, munching her apple as I clatter about with cups. 'You've been on your own for a while now.'

'I like being on my own.' I don't really. I hate it. But my long-term partner, Paul, and I split up nearly a year ago and, I don't know, I just can't face that whole dating scene again. I'm thirty-five and I'd just feel bloody silly starting all over with someone new. You sort of get past it, don't you? I'd hoped that once I was into my twenties, 'dating' would be a word that wouldn't trouble my vocabulary again. It's not as though anyone has asked me either. There are no hordes of attractive, available men beating a track to my door so the problem has never arisen.

I lay out Mrs Norman's tray (white china cup and saucer, stainless-steel pot and tiny milk jug) and pop on a few of those individually wrapped caramel biscuits that she likes so much. Kelly says the clients are only to have one each – portion control – but to me, customer service isn't always about balancing the books. I remember a time when Mrs Norman had very little joy in her life and those few biscuits managed to bring a smile to her face every week. You can't put a price on that, can you?

'We need to do something about it, Janie Johnson,' Nina says decisively and I turn my attention away from caramel biscuits and back to my friend. 'Get you out a bit more. Find you a hot lover with pots of cash and a Ferrari.'

'Yes,' I say without enthusiasm.

'Gerry must be able to lay his hands on a spare bloke somewhere.'

The last person on earth I'd want meddling in my affairs of the heart is Nina's husband, Gerry. Mrs Norman, bless her, is bad enough.

I wish everyone would realise that I'm OK like this. I don't want excitement. I don't want change. I certainly, absolutely, most definitely don't want another man in my life.

Chapter 2

Mrs Silverton is next on my list. She is the Barbara Windsor of Cutting Edge. A glamorous woman of a certain age who adds a bit of colour to our lives by wearing fake fur coats, copious costume jewellery that jingles as she walks and a mahogany-hued perma-tan. This is a lady who's independently wealthy as she owns a chain of racy lingerie shops in the area. Her husband is ten years younger than her. Mrs Silverton is a 'cup full' sort of person and not just in the underwear department. Today she's in for a full head of highlights and a blow-dry. I've already mixed her colours.

'You're looking well,' I say as she shrugs off her coat and sits down.

'Just got back from safari, love,' she tells me. 'The Maasai Mara in Kenya. Bloody marvellous.'

I don't know what hairdressers would do without holidays to talk about half of the time. It's the standard opener with new clients, a fail-safe for those awkward quiet moments when the conversation dries up. Christmas is a godsend on that front too, although this year, it's rushing up far too quickly for my liking. It's October already, which means that the festive season is just

7

around the corner. People love to talk about their plans. It'll keep me going with inane chit-chat for weeks.

With Mrs Silverton there's never a shortage of conversation, whatever the time of year. She's always just been on holiday, whether it's Marbella, Mexico or the Maldives, or she's just about to go on one. Mrs S and toy boy spouse have travelled the world in luxury.

Cristal, the youngest and most hip of our juniors, comes and lounges next to me, handing me the foils in a state of trendy tedium.

'Africa should definitely be on the list of the one hundred places you *have* to go before you die,' Mrs Silverton expounds.

'Hmm,' I say and take another foil from Cristal. 'It sounds wonderful. I'd love to go there.'

'You should do it.'

'I've got two weeks' holiday left and I have to take it by January or I lose it.' Frankly, I'd rather forgo the holiday and take the money but Kelly doesn't work like that. Use it or lose it is the company policy here so I haven't even bothered to ask. I'll probably just take a few days off here and there, do some bits on the house that desperately need attention and get on top of my Christmas shopping.

'It's lovely and warm at this time of year. The perfect time to go.'

Just as Mrs Norman tries to sort out my love life, Mrs Silverton tries to encourage me to travel the world. Travel expands the mind, she says. I should open myself up to different cultures. It's very liberating, she says.

The trouble is wherever I've been has turned out to be exactly like England with sunshine. To be fair, I haven't been abroad all that much. Paul only liked to travel spontaneously

8

when football matches were involved. Like everyone else, we went for our obligatory two weeks to the Costa del Sol, Ibiza, Majorca, Lanzarote – where everyone speaks English and eats egg and chips and drinks British beer. I never went abroad because I particularly liked it, just because it's what people do.

Paul and I were together for seven years. The seven-year itch we used to laugh, until, of course, he left me for someone else just as we were about to slide comfortably into eight years. A divorcée, older than me with two small children to boot. I think that's what hurts the most. If he'd gone off with some taut and high-octane youngster like Cristal, I could have understood it more. Perhaps. As it was, I thought we were in it for the long-term. Marriage had been mentioned. More than once. Though we'd never quite got around to it. We'd even talked about having a family together but Paul had never been keen and it didn't seem all that important to me either.

Were we happy together? I don't know. We rubbed along well enough. Paul worked hard as a self-employed plumber and liked to play hard too. Most nights he went to the pub and at the weekends he played rugby for the local team. I did aerobic classes if I couldn't think of any way to avoid them, saw Nina sometimes for a drink or a pizza and watched a lot of soaps on television. There was no floating on clouds, but no major fire-works either. We didn't argue, we didn't make love all that much. When he left, life continued pretty much as it had.

'We took a balloon flight across the African plains,' Mrs Silverton continues. 'I'm telling you, if you want romance, that is the thing to do.'

Do most people live in a state of heightened romance? I don't think I ever did with Paul. He wasn't that sort of bloke. Who is? Other than Mrs Silverton's husband who is always surprising her with something marvellous. There was never any impromptu whisking me away to Paris or Rome. It would have had to coincide with some football match or other to make it worthwhile in his book. But did I miss that? Not really. To be honest, I never did anything romantic or spontaneous for him either. We weren't that sort of couple.

My experience of loving and living with someone was pleasant, but not overly so. My experience of living without him is pretty much the same. I wonder sometimes if I've ever really been in love. Did I move in with Paul because I truly loved him or simply because he was the only person who had asked me and I thought 'why not?'. I read in these slushy novels about passions that have never touched me. I watch romantic films and can't relate to them at all. My heart has never fluttered, my knees have never gone weak, my appetite has never deserted me in the face of love. Perhaps they're all just selling us a myth that keeps us borderline discontent with the men in our lives.

Before I settled down with Paul, I'd dated some nice guys – not that many, I suppose – but no one really set my heart on fire. I could have quite happily lived without any of them. And did. When I think of my friends, of the girls and boys in the salon, none of them seem particularly overjoyed with their partners either. Nina and her husband Gerry are hanging by a thread most of the time and she's getting to the point where she can hardly move without Gerry's say so. Kelly and Phil rarely socialise with anyone else as he seems to like to keep her all to himself. The boys, Tyrone and Clinton, are always having a major blow-up at the drop of a hat and while Cristal and Steph are single, their lives are far more complicated than I could ever cope with.

Also, I see all of life beneath my scissors in here. The

wannabe marrieds, the happily marrieds, the unhappily marrieds, the adulterers, those hoping to be adulterers, the resolutely single, the reluctantly single, the still looking for Mr Rights, the just divorced, the many times divorced, the ones who vow to never marry again and then do. Is there really such a thing as perfect love?

I realise that Mrs Silverton is still talking about the wonders of her holiday and that I've drifted away. Snapping my attention back to her, I smooth bleach along the final strand of hair and wrap it neatly in foil.

'All done.'

'Things we go through to look beautiful.'

It's worth it, I think. It's worth it for Mrs Silverton as she seems to be greatly loved.

'Here.' She hands me her iPod touch. 'Have a look at these. There are just a few photographs on it. My husband took over a thousand pictures! A thousand! Everywhere you looked there was something spectacular to snap. The light is perfect for photographers.'

So, not wishing to offend her, I take the gadget and slip it into my pocket. I set the timer for half an hour and retreat into the staffroom for a well-earned break during a gap between clients. It's mad busy today but I shouldn't complain as business has been slow over the last six months, recession and everything, and Kelly thought, at one point, that she might have to lay one or two of us off or get rid of a couple of the juniors. Now that the amount of clients through the doors has once again picked up, we're all hanging on in there.

In the staffroom, all I want is peace and quiet for a few minutes. Instead I find that Cristal is crying loudly. Nina has her arms around her and is shushing her softly.

'What's wrong?' I whisper.

'He hasn't phoned yet?'

'Who?'

'The man she slept with at the weekend.'

'Oh. How long has she been going out with him?'

Nina gives me an old-fashioned look and says over Cristal's head, 'She only met him on Saturday. They spent the night together. She thought he was The One.'

'And now she hasn't seen him for dust?'

Renewed sobbing from Cristal. 'I thought he loved me.'

'Can't you call him?' That's what modern women are supposed to do, right?

'I can't remember his name,' she sobs again.

I shrug at Nina and she shrugs back. I don't dare point out that in my day we used to call that a one-night stand and if you were stupid enough to do it, you knew that you'd never hear from him again.

Nina reads my mind. 'It was different in our day.'

Too right, I think, even though 'our day' didn't seem all that long ago. Things change too quickly, if you ask me. How would I fare now? I didn't sleep with Paul for months when we first met and there wasn't any pressure to. What would I do if someone I didn't know wanted to get me into bed on the first date? Even the thought of it makes me shudder.

'I need to look at these,' I say, showing Nina the iPod. 'Photos from Mrs Silverton's latest trip.'

'Lucky bitch,' Nina concludes. 'Who does she think she is? Bloody Judith Chalmers?'

'Who?' Cristal wants to know as she sucks in another sob.

I flick to Mrs Silverton's photos. Stunning scenes of immense, cloudless blue skies flood the small screen and take my breath away. I don't think that I've ever seen colours so vivid. Scanning with my finger, I take in shots of lakes pink with the wings of thousands of flamingos, wildlife so close that you feel you could reach out and touch it, the dazzling monochrome madness of zebras, the sad soulful eyes of lions, plains stretching as far as the eye can see, dotted with artistically sparse trees.

'Wow,' I say, half out loud.

'Let's have a look,' Cristal says, sniffing now.

I show her the screen.

'Where is it?'

'The Maasai Mara.'

Her face registers boredom. Perhaps not enough discos. 'Where's that then?'

'Kenya,' I say. 'Africa. Mrs Silverton's just been on a safari.'

'I've always fancied going there,' Nina says, 'but Gerry says he'd be bored.'

In my humble opinion, way too much of Nina's life is influenced by what Gerry wants and doesn't want. Greedily, I scan more of the photographs. I don't think I'd be bored. I think that I've never seen anywhere quite as beautiful.

Then a pinger goes. 'That's Mrs Silverton cooked,' I say and go to take out her foils.

Chapter 3

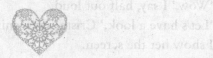

'Come to ours for dinner,' Nina begs. 'I knocked up a spag bol before I came to work this morning. It'll only need reheating and there's plenty to go around. We can open a nice bottle of plonk too.'

'I'm fine,' I say. 'I just want to go home and put my feet up.' My legs are throbbing from being on my feet for hours and I keep trying to put off the day when support tights begin to sound like a fine idea.

'You shouldn't spend so much time alone,' she insists.

'I have a wild night in front of the telly planned.'

My friend tuts at me.

The truth is that I'm not very keen on Nina's husband and try to spend as little time with him as possible. Sometimes Nina's not very keen on him either.

If I want to see Nina out of work, then I try to make sure that we go out on our own. Whenever Gerry's around, Nina can't get a word in edgeways and he's the world's best at ignoring everyone else's viewpoint. He's too much like hard work in my book. I don't say anything though, what friend would? I just try to support her as much as I can when the going gets tough.

They've been together since they were teenagers and have been married for about fifteen years. They've no children – needless to say, Gerry's choice. Nina would have loved to be a mum. Instead they have two dogs of indeterminate breed, Daisy and Buttons, who are the apple of Nina's eye.

Frankly, I don't know what she sees in Gerry any more. He's always been loud, opinionated and he's not getting better as he grows older. What happens to middle-aged men to turn them into grumpy old buggers? When he was a teenager, I have to say that he was quite a looker, the heartthrob of our year. Nina was a much-envied young lady when she caught his eye. Now the same Gerry, while still a handsome man who can turn on the charm like a tap when he wants to, more often than not has the personality of a bad-tempered wasp when it comes to Nina. Their marriage is not exactly the stuff that dreams are made of. He seems to give out just enough to keep her hanging on in there. Which is not what it should be about, surely? But then Paul and I were hardly Burton and Taylor so I'm not one to talk. So for the sake of our friendship I've never mentioned my misgivings to Nina and, even though I might have given up on the idea of ever warming to Gerry years ago, I tolerate him as best I can.

'I'm definitely going to get him to fix you up with someone,' Nina warns. 'This can't go on.'

'Please don't,' I beg. I know what Nina's like when she gets a bee in her bonnet.

The other thing about Gerry is that he constantly leads Nina a merry dance. Twice she's caught him out having affairs with other women and twice she's taken him back, but I wouldn't trust him as far as I could throw him. In all honesty, I'm not sure that Nina does any more. It's a mystery why she sticks with

15

him at all. She says she doesn't want to fail but I don't think it's her that's doing the failing.

'I'm fine. Really,' I assure her. 'Absolutely fine. A quiet night in is just what I need.'

'You have too many quiet nights in, woman.' With that, she tuts, but lets me pack my bag and go home on my own.

I kiss her on the cheek. 'See you tomorrow, hun.'

'Yeah. Unless I win the lottery,' she mutters. 'Then I'll be outta here.'

Funny, it's the only way I can see myself getting out of here too.

My drive home takes me about fifteen minutes. When Paul and I split, I bought myself a little cottage called, enterprisingly, Little Cottage, in one of the villages that's halfway between Buckingham and the encroaching metropolis of Milton Keynes. When I say little, I mean *little*. But it's mine. All mine. Paul and I had rented a furnished place all the time we were together, which made parting quite painless. There was no home to sell, no valued possessions to bicker over, but suddenly on my own again, I wanted to feel settled, put down some roots.

We'd always lived in the town but I decided I wanted something different, more rural. After much trawling around the area, I picked out Nashley as top of my list of ideal villages. A month later and this house came onto the agent's books. It took all of my meagre savings to put a deposit down on this place and I have a mammoth mortgage which is quite daunting to face on my own. Still, every night when I turn the corner or, like on this cold October night, the beams of my headlights illuminate Little Cottage, my heart squeezes. The village is as tiny as my home. There's a quaint pub, a much-used village hall, one shop-cum-post-office that's always under threat of closing and, well, not much else. There's a scattering of twee thatched houses around the green, a small duck pond with suitably pretty ducks, and on the outskirts there are a few bigger houses – one that used to be the rectory to the medieval church and a very stately Manor House.

A lot of the people who live here were born and bred in the village, the rest are incomers like myself. A few are city types who commute to London every day and are rarely seen, especially in the winter months.

I park up outside the house and breathe a sigh of relief. Now it's just me, my cat, Archibald the Aggressive, and no one else to worry about.

My cottage is on the far left, the end one of a terrace of three. The front door opens straight into a minuscule living room with low, low beams. Original. I'm only five feet, three inches tall and yet I feel as if I permanently have to duck. There's not a straight wall, floor, door or ceiling in the whole place. The fireplace, complete with a gorgeous wood-burning stove, takes up most of one wall. A sofa, a comfy armchair and my telly are shoehorned into the rest of the space. There's a separate dining room, also small, that was added as an extension some time during the seventies. I couldn't hold a banquet in there but you can at least stand upright. The kitchen is slightly bigger and higher too, with room for a small table. There's a utility room that was originally the outside loo, but someone knocked the wall down and now it houses my washer and dryer as well as doubling up as a bit of an office. Upstairs there's one bedroom and a bathroom. That's it. But it suits my needs and I adore living here.

Opening the door, Archie winds around my feet mewing pathetically. Don't let that cute look fool you though. My cat

17

would have your arm off as soon as look at you. Very few people get through his door and don't lose some flesh to Archibald. He likes nothing better than to lurk on top of the kitchen cabinets and then pounce on the shoulder of unsuspecting visitors and sink his teeth into their neck. I'm thinking that he might have been a vampire in a former life or is currently training to be one.

He was a feral cat when I met him. Perhaps he was once someone's pampered pet who, out of choice or out of necessity, was living rough in the fields at the back of my cottage. Perhaps he simply sank his fangs into soft skin once too often and was banished. I got used to him prowling my small garden, deftly and stealthily picking off the sparrow population. When I started to put down food for him in an attempt to keep the birds off the menu, he tentatively edged nearer to my back door. A few months later and he was brave enough to come into the house. Now he lives here and happily curls up on my bed at night but it's not a joke that I have a 'Beware of the Cat' sign on my front door. Strangers send him into a hissing, spitting frenzy.

'What's up, puss?' I bend down to stroke him. 'Been bored at home all day?'

I bet he's hardly moved from the side of the radiator where his basket is now installed. This cottage may have set me back a fortune to buy it, but due to its inordinately small size, it costs very little to run. Relatively. There still always seem to be more bills than there is cash to pay them.

Before I think to feed myself, I tend to Archie's needs. I have learned that any delay in can-opening leads to severe lacerations to the lower leg. Sometimes I wonder whether he is entirely grateful for my unconditional love and hospitality.

In the freezer, there's a macaroni cheese ready meal and I

slide it into the microwave. As a token nod towards healthy eating, I fling together a salad. Even though it's a weeknight, I pour myself a glass of red wine. I was ridiculously busy at the salon today and think I deserve a treat.

After I've finished my meal, Archie takes up residence on my lap and we're settling down for an exciting night's viewing when there's a knock at my door. Instantly, I know who it is. My neighbour has developed his own 'signature' knock, so that I don't have to peer through the spyhole to see who it is.

I open the door and, sure enough, Mike is standing there. Miserable Mike, Nina calls him. But he isn't miserable, he's sad and I think there's a world of difference.

'Come on in, Mike.' He does so and instantly fills the living room.

Mike Perry lives in the house next door to mine. Not the one joined to me, but a slightly bigger, detached cottage to the left. Six months ago, his wife just up and left him. No reasons given, no explanations, no build-up to it. He thought they were perfectly happy. She clearly didn't. One night he came home from work to find their suitcases were gone, along with all of Tania's clothes and the contents of their bank account. Five years of marriage down the pan, just like that. A 'Dear John' letter on the coffee table told him that she'd never really loved him and was leaving 'to find herself'. I hope one day that she finds out that she's a selfish cow. In my book, Mike is one of the nicest men you could hope to meet.

He was great when I moved in here alone, helping out with small DIY jobs that needed doing, fixing leaking taps, oiling squeaking doors, carrying heavy objects, doing the kind of things that men do best. Since Tania's been gone, I've tried to return the kindness by being a shoulder to cry on for him.

'You said you'd cut my hair,' Mike reminds me.

'Ah. Yes, of course.' That's my telly watching up the spout for now. Archie glowers at Mike, now that his rest has been disturbed, and skulks off to the bedroom in a mood.

'If you're busy, it doesn't matter.'

'Do I look busy?' I chide. 'It'll take me two minutes to get my stuff together.'

You have to help out a friend in need, don't you? Otherwise, what's the point?

Chapter 4

'Did you eat dinner yet?' I ask when we're in the kitchen.

'I picked up a sandwich on the way home.'

'You can't keep living on sandwiches for ever, Michael Perry.' I give him a mock scowl. 'You'll waste away. Sometimes you have to venture back into the kitchen.' Says she, who lives on pinged dinners for one.

'I did take the liberty of bringing this though.' He holds up a bottle of red wine.

'I've already started.' I show him my half-empty glass.

'Celebrating?' He looks worried. 'I haven't missed your birthday or something?'

'No.' I sigh. 'Just glad to get through the day.'

'Well, I have some good news,' he states. He puts the bottle on the table and claps his hands together. 'Pour me a glass while I go and wash my hair and then I'll tell all.'

So Mike runs the gauntlet of Archibald, who could well be lying in wait to pounce on him on the landing, and quickly washes his hair in my bathroom. Then he comes to sit on the chair that I've dragged into the middle of the kitchen, under the light, and I throw a clean towel around his neck. He's not a bad-looking man, Mike. He's slim, tall and has a nervous, boyish charm. His face is open and kind, honest. His hair is thick, brown and is desperately in need of a cut.

Feeling as if I have failed in my hairdressing services to him, I take out my scissors. 'Good grief, I had no idea there were latent curls in here. When did I last do this?'

'Weeks ago,' Mike admits.

'I hadn't noticed how long it was getting.' I start to snip.

'I've been busy,' my neighbour says. 'Big shake-up at work. Luckily, I came out of it unscathed. In fact,' he picks up his glass and holds it aloft, 'I've got a promotion.'

'Brilliant news!' I pick up my glass too and we toast him.

'It means I can work from home now. I'll be travelling quite a bit but just in the southern region. When I'm not on the road, my office will be here.'

'Nice.'

He clears his throat. 'I'll be around a lot more.'

Up until now Mike has had some terrible commute to Oxford or somewhere every day. He leaves at ungodly o'clock in the morning and is rarely home before nine. Perhaps that's one of the reasons Terrible Tania upped sticks and left. You never know, do you? It's hard to maintain a wonderful relationship when one of you simply, even through no fault of your own, isn't there. Anyway, she was always a bit too glamorous for Nashley, and probably for Mike. I could see her more in a penthouse apartment overlooking the Thames or something, on the arm of an investment banker.

'That's great. Things are really looking up for you.' I know that he still misses Tania every day but now, maybe, he can start to move on.

'I thought I might even risk dating again now that I'll have a bit more free time.'

I snort. 'You're braver than me.'

'Do you know any available ladies who wouldn't mind taking on a wounded soldier?'

'I'm sure you could have the pick of the single girls in my salon but it would be like throwing you to the lions. I couldn't do that to you.'

'Doesn't sound like my kind of thing. That's part of the problem. The modern woman terrifies me.' He shakes his head and gives a mock shudder. 'It would probably be better if it was someone I knew already. As a friend, sort of.'

'Keep your head still.' I snip some more.

'Ever thought of putting your toe in the water again?'

'Me?' I laugh. 'Not likely. I'm quite happy as I am. Relationships seem to be so complicated now and I just don't need it.'

I think of Nina and Gerry and decide that kind of relationship's definitely not for me. Then there are the other girls in the salon. Their love lives are tangled enough to keep a soap opera going for years. I often wonder if the template for modern relationships comes from too much watching of *EastEnders* and *Hollyoaks*. Poor Cristal, who sleeps with a different bloke every weekend and falls head over heels in love with every one of them, is just the tip of the iceberg. There's Steph who has a list of married lovers longer than my arm. Then we've got two lovely gay guys in the salon, Tyrone and Clinton, but they're both green-eyed monsters and their relationship is best described as fiery as they both have roving eyes and, quite possibly, wandering hands. And don't even get me started on the lives that some of my clients live. Believe me, one day I'm going to write a book about it. All that drama, that heartache, it's not for me. I'm quite happy on my own.

'Keeping Archie happy takes up all my time,' I continue.

'Perhaps we'll just grow old and single together,' Mike suggests.

'Perhaps we will,' I agree. 'Now,' I hold up my mirror, 'short enough for you?'

Chapter 5

'I'm not interested,' I say to Nina. 'I told you.'

'He's nice,' she wheedles as she peels a banana, one of her twenty portions of fruit a day that have replaced her twenty ciggies a day. 'It would be just one lickle-ickle date.'

I breathe out an exasperated sigh. Nina, against all my wishes, has coerced her cheating husband into fixing me up with a blind date. 'How does Gerry know this bloke?'

'He works with him.'

'Have you met him?' Is he anything remotely like Gerry? is what I really want to ask. Because if he is, then I want to run for the hills. I can manage without a controlling bully in my life no matter how charming he is, thanks very much.

'Yes, of course,' Nina says.

'When?'

Now she looks shifty. 'I can't quite remember. It must have been at one of the office parties.'

'So he didn't leave a lasting impression on you.'

'Well . . .'

'I don't want to do this, Nina. I told you.'

'Is he married?' Steph is in today. She only works part-time at

25

the salon, preferring to do a bit of mobile business for her own clients during the rest of the week, cash in hand.

'Divorced.'

Steph wrinkles her nose. 'You should only date married men, like I do,' she offers. 'No hassle. See them when you like, dump them just as easily. No strings. All you have to do is call them when you want a bit. Fuck buddies are definitely the way to go.'

I think that is the single most depressing thing I've ever heard. 'What about the sisterhood?'

'What?' Steph says.

'Never mind.'

'For goodness' sake, Janie. It's just a date. A glass of wine, dinner, a bit of convivial chit-chat. Nothing more. I'm not asking you to donate a kidney to him.'

'What if he tries to snog me?'

'I don't think anyone has used the word "snog" since the eighties.'

'I'd give him a go.' That's from Steph.

'I'm sure you would,' Nina says archly, 'but I'm not asking you. This is a date for Janie.'

Steph tuts.

'Say yes, Janie, and Gerry can fix it up for you in five minutes. What harm can it do? You can't spend your life hanging out with Miserable Mike,' my friend advises.

'He's not miserable . . .'

'*He's sad*,' we say together, as we have done many times before. That makes me laugh.

'He's not miserable,' I reiterate. 'He's very kind.'

'That has to be one of the worst things you can say about a bloke surely? "He's very kind",' she mimics.

Cristal comes in. 'Your next client is here, Janie.'

Thank heavens for that. I leave Nina to her fruit frenzy and her impromptu dating agency and her rubbishing my neighbour, and rush out of the staffroom seeking a bit of peace with Mrs Vine and her cut and blow-dry.

I take a deep breath before I say, 'Hello, Mrs Vine. How are you today?'

'Rushed off my feet, love. Glad to come in here for a sit down.'

'Just need a tidy up?'

My client nods. 'Do your worst.'

So I get Mrs Vine shampooed by Cristal and then set to with my scissors.

'How's things with you, Janie?' she asks. 'No man on the scene yet?'

'Not yet,' I say.

The worst thing about being a hairdresser is that your clients tell you everything, things that you wouldn't believe, and what's more, you feel obliged to open up to them in return. Every single one of my clients knows about my break-up with Paul and now it's open house on my heart.

I think about Nina's attempt to set me up. Perhaps it wouldn't be a bad idea to go on a date, just to see if I can still do it. Plus it would keep my clients happy. They wouldn't all worry about me so much if they thought I was making some effort to find a bloke.

Last night Miserable Mike and I watched a film together after I'd cut his hair. We polished off the bottle of wine while engrossed in *The Bourne Supremacy* – not for the first time. Matt Damon seems to be the only person who sets my pulse racing these days. This film-watching thing is a habit we've sort of slipped into, Mike and I. Two or three times a week, we'll watch something together. We're company for each other. It's not exciting. It's not taxing. Is there anything wrong with that? We're just being supportive of each other. Mates. That's all.

'You want to think about that internet dating,' my client says. 'It's all the rage, these days.'

I can't think of anything worse. Shopping online for a stranger, some stranger than others from all that I've heard.

'You could have yourself a little bit of fun like that.'

Why does everyone think that I need 'fun'? Do I really look so unhappy? It won't only be Mike they're calling miserable soon. I start to comb Mrs Vine's hair and then stop. 'Could you just hold on for me one second?' I ask. 'I'll be right back.'

Marching to the staffroom, I stand in front of Nina. 'Do it,' I say. 'Fix me up with him.'

My friend looks at me open-mouthed. 'You're not serious?'

'I am. Perhaps it will stop everyone from hounding me. Tomorrow night,' I instruct. 'Before I change my mind.'

Nina is so stunned that she puts down her bunch of grapes and scrabbles in her handbag. 'I'll phone Gerry now.'

'Good,' I say and then stomp back to Mrs Vine.

'Everything all right, love?'

'Yes, fine,' I tell her as I comb through her hair. 'I've got a date tomorrow night.'

In the mirror, I don't know who looks more shocked, her or me.

Chapter 6

I have four dresses laid out on the bed and I'm wearing another one. A demure black number, just above the knee, scooped neck but not too low.

'What do you think?'

Archibald opens one eye and appraises me lazily.

'Sad, single cat woman goes on hot date?' I check myself in the mirror. How can I lose a few pounds by eight o'clock? 'Is this the right look?'

My cat yawns. I hope that my outfit doesn't produce the same reaction in my date.

'I don't want to send out the wrong signals,' I reason with my feline friend. 'If I sex it up too much, he'll think I'm easy. If I go in jeans and a top, he'll think I can't be bothered to make the effort.'

Archibald stretches out, flexing his claws and burying them into the duvet. If I ever brought a man back here I'd have to get new bedding as this lot is slowly shredding due to Archie's attentions.

'Help me,' I implore. 'I need advice.'

Then comes Mike's familiar knock at the door and I hurry down to answer it, aware that the clock is ticking away and that

I'm due at a trendy wine bar in Milton Keynes in less than half an hour.

'Wow,' my neighbour says as I fling open the door. 'You look amazing.'

I stand and smooth down my dress, palms clammy. 'You really think so?'

'Hell yes.' He ruffles his newly cut hair and frowns. 'Special occasion?'

'Hot date,' I tell him, puffing out my breath uncertainly.

My neighbour looks taken aback, as well he might. It's a bit like the Pope announcing that he's going to a lap dancing club. Mike's face darkens further. 'Who with?'

'No idea,' I admit. 'For reasons best known to myself I have allowed my mad mate to fix me up on a blind date.'

Now Mike looks completely shocked. 'You're kidding me?'

'No.' I glance at my watch. 'And I hate to hassle you but I'm going to be late and that's never a good start.'

'No,' Mike agrees, still perplexed. 'No, it's not.'

'Are you sure the outfit's OK? I've been asking Archie but he's useless.'

'Well, I'm no Gok Wan.'

'I don't want to give off the wrong signals.'

Mike is suddenly serious. 'If you're trying to say that you're a stunningly beautiful woman that any man could fall in love with, then the dress works.'

'Thank you,' I say awkwardly. Me and compliments are not a ready mix. A simple 'you look OK' would have done. 'I'd better be going. What was it you wanted?'

'Nothing,' he says with a shrug. 'Just at a loose end again. Thought we might do another film? I've got *Young Victoria* on DVD.'

Mike knows that I'm a sucker for my historicals. Now I'm torn. I'd much rather stay at home and have a quiet night in with him watching a film than put myself through this torture. Actually, at this particular moment I'd rather have my fingernails torn out than go on this date. I think about calling the mobile phone number I've been given, along with the name of Lewis Moran, so that I can pull out. But then I think that's rude and I was brought up to be polite and nice. However much I'd like to, I can't leave Lewis in the lurch. I'd hate for someone to do that to me.

'Tomorrow,' I say to appease Mike. 'Let's do it tomorrow. Then I can fill you in on all the gore.'

'I could cook dinner or something,' my friend offers hesitantly.

'No, don't worry. I'll eat and then I'll come round later. Nineish?'

'It's a date,' he says, and we both laugh uncomfortably.

Then he registers that I'm fidgeting. I still have my jewellery selection to make and, already, my time is running out.

'I'll go,' Mike says. 'Leave you to it. Have fun.'

'Wish me luck.'

'Yes,' my neighbour says as he turns to head home. For the first time in months he does look miserable and my heart goes out to him. What awful timing that I'm going out for once. 'Good luck.'

And, as this is my first date with a new man in over nine years, I think that I'm going to need it.

The Blah-Blah Bar is already busy when I arrive. I am thirty-five years old and am standing at the door, scared to go in by myself. Ridiculous, I tell my inner wimp. Women row the Atlantic single-handedly these days, they base jump, they free climb, they run countries. Walking into a bar unaccompanied is not that difficult.

I steel myself and go inside. My courage only falters slightly when I see that everyone else in here is under twenty-five. Where do women of my age go to socialise when they want something sophisticated? I wouldn't mind coming here with a bunch of the girls from the salon, this is just up their street, but as a venue for a date? Who chose this? Was it Lewis Moran or was this Gerry's idea of fun? That should worry me and it does.

This place is, apparently, retro and is done out in purples and oranges in psychedelic patterns. The music is sixties, the volume very much now. Go-go dancers dressed in knee-high boots and silver shift dresses that skim their bottoms gyrate at head height in cages suspended from the ceiling. I can see their matching silver knickers without even trying.

Scanning the bar, I can't see anyone who fits Lewis's description. According to Nina, he's tall, dark and handsome. That could apply to about a dozen men in here. Unfortunately, most of them look young enough to be my son, when actually I am hoping for someone who looks old enough to be my date. Taking the one empty seat at the bar, I eventually manage to catch the barman's eye for long enough to order a drink. Even though the Blah-Blah Bar has a scintillating list of cocktails that I've studied extensively, I order a Diet Coke as I'm driving.

Sitting self-consciously on my stool, I sip my cola and try not to look as sad and lonely as I feel. Ten minutes pass and I've nearly finished my drink. One glass doesn't last long when it's all you've got to concentrate on. I'm being jostled and I don't want to order anything else to drink as it took so long last time. Another ten minutes and I begin to wonder if Lewis is going to show at all. I try texting the number I've been given but there's no response. Now I don't know what to do with myself. I can't even sit properly. Should I cross my legs or just keep them together? And my arms, they're no better. If I cross them, do I look defensive and unapproachable? Then again, I don't want to be approached by anyone other than the person I'm waiting for. This dress was a bad idea. I look dated and frumpy in among the trendy tunic and leggings brigade.

Half an hour now and I'm more than certain that I've been stood up. The first date I've summoned up the courage to go on in years and the bastard hasn't even had the courtesy to show. I haven't been stood up on a date since I was about fifteen and believe me, it's no easier now than it was then. Tears prickle my eyes, but I think that I will not cry over this. A man will not get me in this state, let alone a man I don't even know. Wait until I tell Nina, perhaps then she'll stop bullying me into another blind date.

I pick up my handbag and head for the door. I'll be home

well before nine. Perhaps Mike will still be up for that film and we can laugh about this together. Then I can have a few glasses of therapeutic grape juice and not think about it any longer.

Pushing my way through the crowd, I'm almost at the door when a hand catches my arm and spins me around.

'Hey,' he says. A short, balding man is standing in front of me. I have no idea who he is. He leans in close and shouts at me, 'Are you Jemma?'

'Janie,' I offer.

'Oh, right. That's what I mean,' he says. 'I'm Lewis,' he gives me a smarmy smile, 'your date for this evening.'

'I was just going home,' I tell him.

He looks a bit put out by that.

'I've been waiting for half an hour.'

'Got caught on the internet,' is his explanation. 'You know how it is.'

Not really, I think, but that's all I'm going to get by way of an apology. Clearly Lewis Moran has not been going through the agonies of preparation that I have subjected myself to.

Not that looks are everything, but I'd be perfectly entitled to complain under the Trades Description Act about this one. I'm just thinking how I can tell him that I'm still planning to go home as he's not quite the image I had conjured up when Nina said he was tall, dark and handsome, when he increases his grip on my arm and drags me back towards the bar.

'Vodka and tonic,' he says to the barman. Lewis is texting on his phone as he orders while I stand there like a lemon. 'Make that a double.' He nods in my direction. 'One for you?'

'Diet Coke please.' Why is it that things come out of your mouth before your brain has time to censor them? I should have said, no thank you. I should turn on my heels now, cut my losses and go home straight away, but I'm transfixed by the awfulness of this.

'Not planning to let me get you drunk and take advantage of you then?' Lewis laughs raucously.

'No,' I tell him. 'That's not what I had in mind.'

His phone beeps to say that he has a message. 'Twitter,' he says. 'Bloody great fun. The people you meet on here.' Eventually his attention drifts back to me. 'So how do you know old Gerry then?'

'I work with his wife, Nina.'

'What are you then?'

'A hairdresser.'

'Bet you give a nice blow job, I mean blow-*dry*.' More laughing.

Already I want to kill him. And then kill myself. 'Look,' I say, 'I haven't had a date in a long time . . .'

'What? Pretty girl like you?'

'Out of choice,' I supply. 'This isn't really my scene.' I look at the young kids in the bar, the go-go dancers, the retro décor that I remember too well from my parents' home.

'Knock that back and then we can go somewhere else.' He downs his vodka and nudges my elbow, nearly spilling my Coke all down my hateful dress.

'Come on.' My date heads towards the door again, barely suppressing a burp on the way. 'We can go to the Jarman's Hotel, then if you change your mind about letting me take advantage of you, we haven't got far to go to my place.'

Ha, ha, ha.

35

Chapter 8

We walk the few hundred metres down to the hotel but even with a change of venue, the evening does not get better. The mood here is more mellow but it clearly doesn't rub off on me. My blood pressure is ratcheting up by the minute.

'I was going to get you roses and stuff,' Lewis informs me as we sit in a secluded leather booth, 'but we're both old enough to know better. Right? You don't have time to waste on all that romance shit at your age. Every woman over thirty is watching their weight so chocolates are a no-no. All those calories, eh? Waiter!' he shouts.

It's hard to keep my mouth from dropping open. A young man comes over to us.

'Double vodka and tonic for me. Coke for her.'

'Diet Coke please.'

Lewis raises his eyebrows as if he's perplexed by my choice. The young barman raises his eyebrows as if also perplexed by my choice, but not necessarily of drink.

My date, and I am using that term loosely, texts as he talks. 'You can waste a lot of time wining, dining, all that rubbish, only to find that you're not compatible and you're a grand down on the deal. Know what I mean?'

Not really. But my contribution to the conversation doesn't actually appear to matter.

'I've dated every Tammy, Debbie and Harriet,' he says, clearly one of his favourite jokes. 'It's so easy now, isn't it? Pick 'em up off the internet. Have you given that a go?'

Again the absence of my reply isn't registered.

'Lot of weirdos out there.' Lewis pulls a scary face.

That I can believe.

'Vegetarians. Swingers. Bunny boilers. Goths. I've had them all. Not many "normal" women on the old worldwide web.' He makes quote marks with his fingers.

Don't you hate it when people do that?

The waiter returns with our drinks and looks at me with pity. I mouth at him, 'Kill me,' and he grins in return but doesn't put me out of my misery in a humane way and instead returns to the bar.

'I'm not asking for much,' he says. 'I'm an easy-going bloke. That's what everyone says. Life and soul of the party. All I want is someone with their own teeth and hair. And *huge* bangers.' Much laughing as he mimes enormous breasts for the benefit of the rest of the bar it seems. 'Someone who likes football, though not an Arsenal supporter. And I like a woman who doesn't mind picking up her fair share of the bill.'

He glances towards his rapidly emptying glass. I'm assuming, then, that this round is on me.

'So? What can I tell you about me?' he breezes on. 'I'm successful in business. Less so in love.' More laughing.

I wonder why.

'I'm in IT.' He smiles, self-satisfied, as if a round of applause is about to ensue. I wonder if he thinks that is somehow equivalent to being in counter-intelligence for the CIA. Somehow I believe that he does.

'I've got my own house. Four bedrooms, detached in Woughton Lea.' He leaves a space for me to be impressed. 'Managed to salvage something from my divorce. Had a bloody good lawyer who hid most of my money from the ex.' He's obviously very pleased with his guile. 'I like foreign travel. I've been to Thailand twice this year.'

Strangely, that doesn't surprise me. Given a flowered shirt and bad shorts, Lewis is the type of man who would have 'sex tourist' written all over him.

'I've got a Legend yacht moored at Southsea marina. Forty-two foot. I like to call it the Lurve Boat.' Now his laugh is really beginning to annoy me. 'How many men can tell you that?'

Being disadvantaged in the looks department is no big thing if you have a personality to compensate for it. Lewis, unfortunately, doesn't.

'How would you like to *come* on my boat?' He leers at me, clearly amused by his innuendo.

Frankly, I can't think of anything worse.

'I've got an Audi TT too. I like to embrace my inner boy racer.' Ho, ho, ho. 'I usually leave it up here and get a cab home but if you're not on the lash you could drive us back to my place. I've always got a spare toothbrush on hand if you fancy staying over.'

Then he winks at me. Truly, he does.

Do I seem to be so desperate? How can I be giving off any encouraging vibes when I haven't said more than three words for the last hour? How can he think that I like him when every fibre of my being is telling me to go home and scrub myself all over with a hard bristle brush just from sitting next to him?

How can there be men in this world who are so seriously lacking in charm? If I stay here any longer, then I will know his entire life story while he knows nothing about me beyond that I'm a hairdresser.

I've been brought up to be nice, to be polite, to be kind to small furry animals, but I just can't do this. It's not me.

'Can you just excuse me for a minute please?' I say.

'Little girls' room?'

'Yes.' I ease myself from the low-slung sofa that does little to disguise Lewis's businessman's paunch.

'Hurry back.' He gives me a little wave and then, before I'm a step away from him, returns to his texting.

I see the sign for the restrooms and head in that direction. As I pass the bar, I see the young waiter who served us. 'How much do we owe for the drinks?'

He tells me the damage and checking that Lewis can't see me, I hand over the money and a nice tip. 'Is there a back way out of here?'

'I'm afraid not,' he says.

Damn. I'm just going to have to be brave and face Lewis. All I have to do is tell him that this just isn't working for me and go home.

Chapter 9

Five minutes' reprieve in the ladies' loo should give me time to think of something pleasant to say to extricate myself. I slip inside and close the door behind me and breathe a sigh of relief. There's no one else in here and I'm just glad to be alone. A date with Lewis is like being cursed with tinnitus – there's a constant irritating noise in your ears.

I wash my hands, fiddle with my hair and reapply my lipstick just for something to do. Then I notice that there's a big, well, biggish window at the far end of the room. I look down at myself trying to work out the proportions. Could I get through that? I wonder. My bottom in particular could well be a problem. It might be a tight squeeze but surely I could manage. Then I could slip away into the night and Lewis would be none the wiser.

Needs must.

I double-check that the cubicles are empty – which they are – and then go to the window. Thankfully, it isn't locked and I'm sure with a bit of judicious wriggling I could fit through it. Just think Archie getting through cat flap, I tell myself.

Slipping off my shoes, I pull a little padded stool up to the wall and then stepping onto it, I haul myself up onto the windowsill and open the window. Ooo. The ladies' room is only on the ground floor but the land falls away beneath the window and it looks a little bit higher than I'd imagined. The window overlooks a walkway that goes between a few bars and, at this time of night, there's a gaggle of happy revellers wandering back and forth.

Sticking my top half out of the window, I ease and squeeze and wiggle until I'm half in and half out. Now I'm definitely like a fat cat beached on its cat flap. I hear my dress tear but who cares? A ripped frock is a price worth paying to get out of here without being bored to death. Now I'm dangling above the walkway.

'Hello!' I shout to the many girls walking by below me, oblivious to my plight. 'Hello!' I risk waving my arms.

Eventually a group of about six hefty hen party ladies in bright pink tutus and DayGlo leg warmers stop to look up at me. 'All right, love?'

'Can you give me a hand getting down please?' I ask.

'Course we can. What the fuck are you doing up there in the first place?'

'Escaping from a bad date,' I explain.

'I've had a few of those,' the chief ballet dancer explains. 'Know the feeling. You don't want to break your neck though. Chuck us your shoes.'

So doing as I'm told, I throw the shoes that are in my hand and she catches them.

'Good job. Now lower yourself down. We've got you, love.'

Heart beating faster, I ease myself off the window ledge, my knees scraping on the brick wall, and sure enough, I feel the secure hands of the ballet dancers grab my legs and hold me aloft. They all totter one way and then the other and a bizarre disco version of *Swan Lake* springs to mind. Yet within a minute, and true to their word, they manhandle me down to the ground.

'Thank you,' I say. 'Thank you so much.'

'You're welcome, love.' I'm thinking that this is the bride-to-be as she has a pink tiara and a short veil on her head. 'It's too early to go home. Come with us.' She throws her arms around me and it's like being cuddled by an octopus, although a very drunken one.

I look down at my torn outfit, the one I took so much time over. This dress will only ever now hold bad memories for me. 'I don't think I'm dressed properly.' All I want now is a cup of tea and a hot bath. 'But I'd love you to have a drink on me.'

'There's no need for that. We had to help a sister in distress.'

'Please, please.' From my purse I produce a twenty-pound note. 'Get a couple of bottles from me.'

The bride ballet dancer hugs me.

'I hope you'll be very happy together.'

'We will,' she says, all teary with alcohol-based emotion. 'We bloody love each other. We bloody love each other, don't we Kylie?'

'We do,' a girl with a number one haircut agrees and they melt into each other's arms.

Oh. OK.

'We bloody love each other,' they chorus together.

'I wish you all the luck in the world,' I say, quite choked now.

At least these ladies have managed to find their soul mates, I think. And then, before my date twigs that I'm missing, I slink away into the night.

Chapter 10

When I pull up outside Little Cottage, the lights are still on inside Mike's house next door. What shall I do? Give him a knock, see if he's available for some tea and sympathy? Perhaps I'd be able to laugh about this, find my hideous evening hilariously amusing if only I had someone to share the sorry tale with.

It's not late, it's barely past ten. I start up Mike's path and then I see the living room light go out and a few seconds later, the bedroom light goes on. Seems as if my neighbour has decided on an early night. Sensible man. I should do the same thing. Nurse my wounded heart alone.

I backtrack and trudge to my own cottage instead and let myself in. As soon as he hears the key, Archie comes down the stairs, complaining bitterly about being left alone. He gives me a love swipe as I pick him up to cuddle him, before he allows himself to be mollified with his favourite fish treats. I think these are the equivalent of giving him some Class A drugs as they instantly send him into a stupor of drooling ecstasy. If only I could find a food treat that would do the same for me.

I have some tea and toast as the promised dinner clearly

never did and, it seems, was never likely to materialise. None of that 'romance shit' for me. After that I go and soak in a hot bath, pouring in some of my favourite jasmine and honeysuckle foam to soothe my mind and body and rid my nostrils of the smell of Lewis Moran's overpowering aftershave. Archie sits on the floor next to the bath expectantly. My cat has a taste for scented bath suds and so I hand feed them to him in a languorous if regular fashion, and he laps them up appreciatively. If he feels his supply doesn't come quick enough there will invariably be painful repercussions.

'Why do I put up with you?' I ask him. 'You do nothing but abuse me and all I do is love you unconditionally in return.'

He answers my question with a series of embittered miaows and I wonder who has treated him so badly in the past that it has scarred his tiny feline heart.

I think of my date tonight, reminiscing thoughtfully, but not in a pleasant way. What is wrong with men these days? Did Lewis Moran – should read Moron! – really think that was the way to behave when you first meet someone? I couldn't get away quick enough. In my mind I had played out how my date would go a dozen times. I thought there might be some initial awkwardness, then perhaps a little chemistry, some friendly conversation, a companionable and delicious dinner, maybe a bit of tentative flirting, perhaps even a shy kiss. Never once did I imagine that I would feel compelled to jump out of a powder room window into the arms of waiting lesbian ballet dancers simply to escape the torture.

I'm not a hopeless romantic. I'm not expecting a knight in shining armour. I'm not thinking that I'm going to be swept off my feet or that we're going to go riding into the sunset together. But if I'm ever brave enough to risk dating a man again, and at this moment it seems highly unlikely, then I would like to be treated nicely.

After my bath, I slip on my fleecy pyjamas and slide into bed. Archie pads around deciding which of his thirty-two sleeping positions he's going to adopt first. Usually he ends up in my hair at about four o'clock in the morning. I read a few pages of some romantic claptrap that I'm becoming deeply disillusioned with before my eyes start to grow heavy. By eleven o'clock I turn out the light and snuggle down for the night. I feel Archie wedge himself in the back of my knees and, in the silence, start up a motorbike-style purr.

Is this it? I think as I stare into the enveloping darkness. Is this it for the rest of my life? In bed at eleven with nothing but a cantankerous old cat for company?

Without wanting them to, tears squeeze out of my eyes. I'm not happy alone. No matter how much I try to convince myself that I am. I'm lonely. I want someone to love. Someone nice and normal. Is that really too much to ask?

Chapter 11

I stagger into work the next day, feeling punch drunk. I slept fitfully last night, waking in the wee small hours to feel sorry for myself all over again. I even had a little cry into Archie's fur, which he wasn't best pleased about.

Just wait until Nina hears about my disaster. I'll have her grovelling all day. She might even donate some of her best fruit to me and normally she's very reluctant to part with it in case she leaves herself short.

Some of the girls like to race in late in the morning, leaving skid marks on the floor of the salon, arriving in the nick of time just seconds before their first client is due. Nina and I are old school. We get here early, set out the tools of our trade on our station, start the day with a leisurely coffee and a chat. In the days when we were vaguely rebellious teenagers and used to smoke, we'd enjoy a cigarette together too. Now the cigarettes are gone (a long time ago for me, more recently for Nina) but the coffee remains. Today, however, I feel like I need a restorative brandy in it.

Sure enough, my friend is already in the staffroom when I swing in. She's giving a bunch of grapes some grief.

'Hello! Hello!' she says brightly. 'Love's young dream.'

'Yes, very funny.' I throw down my bag and strip off my coat. 'You won't be so keen to fix me up on any more blind dates when you hear about this one.'

Nina looks puzzled. 'I *did* hear about it.'

That makes me whirl around, even though whirling is never advisable at this time in the morning. 'What?'

'Lewis phoned Gerry first thing this morning to crow about it, then Gerry stuck me on the phone to hear it all over again. You've reduced the man to a gibbering wreck. He thinks you're ... what were the words?' Nina strikes a thoughtful pose. 'Adorable. Divine. Delectable.'

Lewis knows words like that? I thought he was irrevocably stuck on shag and shared bill.

'Never,' I say.

'True. As God is my witness. He was raving about you.' My friend winks knowingly at me as she pops a grape into her mouth. 'Seems you made quite an impression, little lady.'

I purse my lips. 'Interesting.'

'Did you like him?'

'Not that you'd notice.'

'Aren't you going to see him again? Sounds like he's mad for you, hun.'

'Just mad, I'd say.'

'I'm taking it that you didn't see this date going off in quite the same way that he did?'

'He didn't tell you about the part where I jumped out of the powder room window and into the arms of a waiting lesbian ballet dancer to avoid his tedious, odious company?'

'Er ...,' Nina says. 'No. No, he didn't mention that part.'

'It's true,' I say with a sigh. 'I couldn't bear him for a minute longer, Nina. For my own sanity, I legged it.'

'Let me make our coffee.' Still looking slightly shell-shocked by my revelation, she jumps up to make our brew. 'Sounds like you need it.'

I flop into a waiting chair. 'He was awful, Nina,' I confess. 'I know you did it with the best intentions, but what were you thinking of?'

My friend has the good grace to laugh. 'God, I'm sorry,' she says. 'I had no idea. By the sounds of it I thought you'd been swinging on the moonbeams of love or some shit. What went wrong?'

'What went right is a shorter list.' I sigh then launch into recounting the tale of my dating hell. 'He was late for a start. Half an hour, at least. When he did turn up, he was clearly intent on getting roaring drunk. There was no dinner in the offing, he made that patently clear. I learned everything I needed to know about him and more within about ten minutes, yet he still doesn't know a thing about me. He made it obvious that he wanted me to pick up half the bill and then, once he was thoroughly pissed, trot back to his place for a quick one.'

'Ugh,' Nina concludes.

'Very ugh,' I agree.

'Well, he's desperate to see you again.'

'I have no idea why. It was a disaster. An *unmitigated* disaster.' I put my hands over my eyes. A touch melodramatic I know, but I feel the situation warrants it. 'I'd be quite happy if I never laid eyes on him again in my entire life.'

'Ah,' Nina says. 'There might be just one little problem.'

Now I sit up straight.

'When you said he didn't know a thing about you,' she says, 'that's not exactly true.'

'Oh, Nina.'

'I know, I know,' she offers, defending her crime before I've even been told what it is. 'He was just so convincing. I thought the feelings were mutual. I'll swear I heard wedding bells ringing in the background.'

'Oh, Nina,' I say again.

'I gave him your address,' she confesses. 'He said he wanted to send you flowers.'

I hang my head.

'I'm so sorry, Janie. What a twat I've been.' She gives me a consoling smile and offers me a conciliatory grape. 'But look on the bright side. At least you might salvage something out of the date. By the time you get home I bet a pound to a penny that there'll be a whacking great bouquet of red roses waiting for you.'

This from the man who told me all that 'romantic shit' was a complete waste of time? This is bad. Very bad.

'I do hope not.'

'Just say thank you politely and then you'll never have to see him ever again.'

There is that. Lewis Moran doesn't seem to be the type of man who would pursue his intentions when they're not wanted. He looked to me like someone who would like an easy lay, he's not one for the chase. Thank goodness for that, I think.

'Janie,' Nina ventures, 'where exactly did the lesbian ballet dancer come into it?'

'You wouldn't want to know,' I reply, knowing that being in the dark will drive my meddlesome little friend to distraction. 'You *so* wouldn't want to know.'

Chapter 12

'You're not yourself, Janie,' Angie Watson observes. 'Everything all right?'

It's true. I've been out of sorts all day.

'I'm fine,' I lie. 'Just a bit tired.'

Angie is one of the few clients who is younger than me. She comes in every six weeks for a cut and highlights. Her hair is shoulder-length and she likes it straightened after I've dried it. I've been doing her hair since she was about fourteen and a sulky teenager. Now she's a beautiful young woman with a slender figure and an ever-changing list of boyfriends. I don't even try to keep track of their names now.

'Isn't it about time you had a break?' Angie suggests. 'You haven't had a holiday this year yet, have you?'

'No.' I stroke the GHDs through her silky tresses. 'The colour's come up nicely.'

'Yeah.' She admires herself in the mirror.

While Angie Watson is glowing with health and happiness, the reflection of my face is white and dark shadows bruise my eyes. I couldn't look any more like I need a holiday.

'I've had a lot of expense with the cottage.' It's just so much harder managing on my own. I knew it would be in theory, but in practice the pressure of bill-paying is relentless. I have to watch every penny now. Not that I was extravagant before, I've always been Mrs Careful, but now all the bills are down to me and me alone and, unlike most of my contemporaries, I'm terrified of being in debt. Every month is a balancing act worthy of the Cirque du Soleil.

'You should treat yourself,' Angie urges. 'There's nothing like a bit of foreign sunshine to put a spring in your step.' We both look out of the big window at the front to see the rain pouring down in the courtyard. 'I try to escape Christmas every year by jetting off somewhere hot.'

If I remember rightly, I think Angie has had about three holidays this year, each of them with a different bloke, and she certainly has a lot of spring in her step. I would do well to listen to her.

'You never know, you might meet the man of your dreams out there,' she teases.

Better than going to Blah-Blah Bar and meeting the man of your nightmares.

'I wouldn't know where to go,' I admit.

'You need to go a bit further afield to catch the rays at this time of year. You should give somewhere a bit exotic a go like the Caribbean or Thailand.' My client shrugs. 'You should just jump on a plane. You've no commitments, no ties. The world is your oyster.'

Angie is the sort of person who always has a few pairs of shorts and some flip-flops ready to throw in a case at a moment's notice. I've never been like that. I'm not the spontaneous sort. I like plans. I like to prepare myself. I'm not the jetting-off kind.

'How's the boyfriend?' I ask.

'Dillon's wonderful,' she sighs.

I don't think it was Dillon six weeks ago when I last did her highlights.

'He could be *The One*,' she intimates.

But he won't be. Poor Dillon will only last until Angie next comes in for a blow-dry. By then, and I'd stake my life on this, Dillon and Angie will have 'grown apart' and some other Mr Wonderful will be *The One*.

I only want one, I think, not one every six weeks. Just the one man would see me right.

Chapter 13

It's still bucketing down with rain when I leave work. I'm not the only one who has been subdued today. Nina has been quiet too. She's been most solicitous towards me all day, even graciously offering me her last banana on our tea break. Clearly she's feeling very guilty about her lack of matchmaking skills. She also tried to persuade me to have dinner at their house again, but I declined. I so didn't want Gerry picking over my dating disaster with the glee that he was bound to demonstrate. No doubt he would blame it all on me for being 'uptight' rather than admitting that he has a twat for a friend.

I'm glad to get away at six o'clock. The clocks have just gone back and the nights have gone from drawing in to downright dark in one fell swoop. I've been busy all day long so I haven't had much time to dwell on my predicament but now, as I listen to Michael Bublé lamenting that he still hasn't met me yet, it's playing on my mind. I'm also dreading finding that the promised flowers have actually been delivered when I get home.

Sure enough, when I swing up to Little Cottage, my headlights pick out the glisten of rain-soaked cellophane wrapped around a bouquet of roses. 'Christ on a bike,' I mutter to myself.

Parking up, I reluctantly leave Michael and the cosy warmth of my car and walk in the rain to my front door. I have my key ready and, en route, pause only to whip up the bouquet as the torrent flattens my hair. It's enormous. A dozen or more of those beautiful long-stemmed Emperor roses in blood red. I dash into the house, banging the door against the rain. Then I take in my room. 'Oh no!'

From the frantic cheeping I can hear, clearly a bird has come down the chimney while I've been out at work. There's a tell-tale flurry of soot spread across the rug and, no surprise here, a trail of Archie's footprints takes the silky dirt across the cream carpet, along the back of the sofa and both cushions, up the curtains, dappling across the wallpaper and then they disappear into the kitchen. Scattered all over the room are remnants of feathers and little piles of panicked bird droppings. One of my favourite vases is broken on the tiles by the door. A plant is upturned and the pot, a pile of soil and the broken foliage lie on the floor. Some of my ornaments have been knocked off the fireplace and are smashed in the grate.

It seems that Archie has been zealous in his pursuit of our uninvited visitor.

'Archie!' I shout. This time my cat doesn't come to greet me.

Shaking my head, I go through to the kitchen. At the window, a starling is scrabbling at the glass, beating its wings in terror against its own reflection. I'm amazed there's anything left of it, given Archie's past form. Usually I find a bit of bloody goo and a beak. He must have seriously OD'd on cat treats last night if he wasn't hungry enough to munch on our guest.

Glasses and plates are broken on the draining board, shards of crockery litter the tiles. The contents of the pasta jar are scattered over the worktop. More bird poo. Everywhere. Up the front of the cooker, the fridge, on the bread bin. Amidst the mayhem and squawking, one creature lies peaceful and untroubled.

Archie, snoring like an orchestra tuning up, is prostrate in the middle of the kitchen floor, clearly exhausted by his earlier exertions.

'Oh, Archibald,' I sigh, at which my cat jumps and turns to give me a scowl.

'How dare you disturb my nap, lady,' his facial expression says. 'Can't you see I've been busy while you've been out enjoying yourself at work all day?'

'Now I'm going to have to spend the next two hours or more cleaning up this mess, Mister.'

'Don't you forget my dinner,' his glower warns.

Then I realise that I'm having a conversation in my own head with my cat and think that way danger lies.

Madly, the bird beats its wings again. There's no way I can deal with this alone. I hate flapping things and, more particularly, I hate them in my kitchen. Finding my mobile, I punch in Mike's number on my speed dial.

'Hi,' he says when he answers, and the kindness and solidity in just that one silly word almost reduces me to tears.

'Mike,' I say, trying not to sob. 'I've got a bird trapped in the house. Could you pop round and give me a hand?'

'I'll be right over,' he says and hangs up.

Putting my bouquet down on the table, I stare at it as I wait for Mike to make my home bird-free so that I can roll up my sleeves and set about returning my house to some semblance of order once again.

Not a moment later and Mike knocks at the door.

'Woaw,' he says when he sees the state of my living room.

'Archibald's handiwork.'

'The mark of the cat.'

'Quite.'

We go through to the kitchen and see that the bird is still fluttering wildly.

'Shush, shush,' Mike coos at our feathered friend. 'Everything will be fine.'

He advances slowly on the bird making soothing noises, uttering calming words. The bird's wings beat slower and slower until, eventually, he flops exhausted on the windowsill. Even I'm relaxing. While the bird is momentarily settled, Mike advances softly and cups it gently in his hands. It makes a vain attempt at flapping again.

'Open the back door please, Janie,' Mike says steadily. 'Keep Archie inside. This little chap might well need a rest before he flies away and I don't want Jaws here chasing after him for a farewell chew.'

'Good point, well made,' I say and go to grab the feline fiend.

But Archie is having none of it. Seeing that his fun is about to be thwarted, he makes a mad dash at Mike as I go to collect him in my arms and, claws extended, runs up my neighbour's leg to have a final flail at his deadly foe. Perhaps he's regretting nodding off on the job now.

'Archie!' I scold. Making a grab for the cat, I snatch him from Mike's leg and the scream he emits tells me that the tearing of flesh is involved. 'Naughty cat. Naughty, naughty cat.'

Small droplets of blood from two neat circles of five puncture wounds start to seep through Mike's jeans. Archie's lips curl in a smile.

'The door. The door!' Mike shouts. Somehow he still has his grip on the bird.

My friend is through it without hesitation and dashes into the garden, Archie in hot pursuit. But I, for once, am smarter than the cat and as Mike hits the grass, I slam the door causing Archie to do a quick bit of back-pedalling or end up with a flattened face. He howls in protest as his exit is cut off.

Peering out of the glass, I watch as my neighbour tenderly lifts the totally traumatised bird into the lower branches of my now winter-bare cherry tree. I can almost feel its tiny heart beating from here.

Mike comes back to the door and, keeping Archie away with my foot, I let him inside. My neighbour dusts down his hands.

'Nice job,' I say.

'All in a day's work as a superhero,' Mike quips.

'How are the wounds?'

He looks down at his stained jeans. 'I'll live.' He gives a mock wince. At least, I'm assuming it's a mock wince. 'I think.'

The blood is oozing nicely into the denim.

Shaking his head, he addresses my cat. 'Man, you've got claws like Freddy Krueger.' He wags a finger at the unapologetic Archie. 'No dinner for you tonight, young man.'

My cat gives him a smug look that says, 'Oh yeah? Watch this space.' When he turns to me, the sweetest, most innocent face is reading, 'Didn't I do a great job, Mummy, protecting our home from intruders?'

'Not that easily,' I say to Archie, trying to sound stern.

The cat skulks off, acknowledging that the humans are ganging up on him and that, temporarily, he is beaten.

Chapter 14

'Thanks so much, Mike. I don't know what I'd do without you. Can I make you a cup of tea or something?'

'You get the kettle on,' he suggests, 'while I start cleaning up this mess.'

'Oh no, you can't do that. You've helped me out enough.'

Mike spreads his hands. 'I've got nothing else planned, Janie. A bit of action with a J cloth seems quite attractive comparatively.'

'You're very kind.' As I go to make some tea, I see him casting a wary eye over my bouquet. 'I suppose I'd better put those in water.' I pick up the roses and lift them into the sink, which I fill with water. The perfect vase for them is smashed on the living room floor, so another container of some sort will have to be pressed into hurried service.

'I guess the date was a roaring success.'

'Er . . .' I'm not really sure how to answer that. 'In my mind it was a hideous experience never to be repeated. I'm not exactly sure how the rose-sending has come to pass.'

'Seems as if your date didn't feel the same.'

'It would appear not.' I busy myself with the cups. 'I was

home so early that I was going to knock, but just as I came up your path, your light went off.'

'Oh,' Mike says. 'Bad timing. Typical of my luck.'

'It didn't do me any harm to have an early night.'

Mike goes to the cupboard where I keep my cleaning materials, and pulls out a pack of J cloths and a disinfectant spray. Clearly he knows where to look, having helped out in more than one domestic emergency.

'Will you see him again?' he asks over his shoulder.

'No,' I say adamantly. 'Never.' Not as long as there is breath in my body.

I hand over Mike's tea and sip my own. I'm starving but I can't contemplate dinner until all this is tidied up. 'That's me done with dating. One toe in the water was enough. It was cold and scary in there.'

'You shouldn't be put off by one bad experience,' he advises. 'Not all men are the same. There are some nice guys out there.'

'I don't have the energy to find one, Mike,' I confess. 'I don't think I believe in love any more.'

'It can be hard to bounce back from a knockdown.'

'We both should know,' I say, acknowledging that it is still a very short amount of time since his wife left him.

'I felt that I did everything I could for Tania,' he tells me, nursing his cup as gently as he held the bird. 'And still it wasn't enough.' He shrugs. 'Women are a complete mystery to me.'

'Men are a mystery to me.'

'What a pair of sad sacks we are,' Mike says with a weary laugh.

'Let's get this cleaned up and then I'll treat you to a Chinese if the Hong Kong Garden will deliver.'

'It's a deal.' Mike puts down his cup, arms himself with a

cloth and starts wiping down the fridge and the cooker front with well-aimed squirts of disinfectant.

I head into the living room with the vacuum and dust pan and brush, and clean up the soot, broken glass and china whilst muttering 'That bloody cat' over and over to myself. Mike, on the other hand, whistles a very pleasant rendition of The Feeling's 'Love It When You Call' while he works. There's just something so comforting about having him around and not having to deal with all this myself.

An hour later, and there is very little evidence of my domestic devastation left. Everything is, once again, looking shipshape. Coast clear, Archie takes the opportunity to creep down the stairs and wind himself around my legs, purring in an ingratiating manner.

'I suppose you think it's dinner time?'

He purrs in agreement.

Mike appears at the kitchen door. 'Doesn't sound like a bad idea for us either. It's all clear in here now.'

'Here too.' I show off my housekeeping skills with a twirl. 'The menu for the Chinese is in the top drawer. Pick whatever you like. The only thing I'm not keen on is chilli beef.'

'I remember that,' Mike says with an easy smile.

I follow him into the kitchen and nearly trip over the cat en route, who is heading full tilt towards his bowl, lest I forget him in the excitement.

'Wow,' I say when I see what Mike has been up to. Every inch of my kitchen sparkles. 'I don't think my kitchen has ever been so clean.'

'I'm glad all my hours of watching How Clean is Your House? weren't wasted.'

'Kim and Aggie would be very proud of you.'

He grins as he calls the Hong Kong Garden and orders the food.

I, in the meantime, think about feeding my spoiled brat. Archie is on the newly disinfected kitchen windowsill, craning to see the cherry tree, tail flicking in anticipation. When I look at the tree myself, the bird is still sitting there, but he looks like he might live to fly another day. 'Don't even think about it, buster,' I warn Archie.

I shake out some biscuits into his bowl and with a last evil glance in the bird's direction, he jumps down to concentrate on his legitimate meal.

When Mike hangs up, he says, 'They couldn't deliver for forty-five minutes and I'm starving. I'll just nip out and get it.'

'I'll warm some plates while you're gone. A beer?'

'Oh yes,' Mike says with longing in his voice.

Pulling a twenty from my purse, I hand it over to him.

'There's no need for this,' he assures me.

'I'd still be tidying up if it wasn't for you. It's the least I can do.' It's my last twenty, so I can't really afford to be so rash, but Mike's help has been worth every penny.

Reluctantly, Mike puts the money in his pocket. 'I'll be back in ten.'

When I hear the front door close, I flick the oven on and then get out a couple of plates to put in it. I set the table and find glasses for our beer.

The doorbell rings a second later and I think that it must be Mike having forgotten something, so I rush to answer it. When I pull open the door, standing there in the pouring rain is Lewis Moran, every woman's dating nightmare. My mouth falls open.

'Hi,' he says, huddling under my porch. 'Just saw a bloke

leaving your place.' There's a frown on his brow. 'Boyfriend you didn't mention?'

'Er . . . er . . . no,' I stammer in reply, wondering exactly what it's got to do with him. 'Neighbour.'

He looks relieved. 'Thought I had competition for a minute.'

'What?'

'Roses?' he says. 'Did you get the roses?'

'Yes, thank you.' I'm thinking, would it be really bad form to hand them right back to him?

'And?'

'They're lovely.' I suppose that I should have texted him right away, but with the bird-down-the-chimney incident, I confess that it didn't even cross my mind.

'We could discuss this inside.' He glances up at the strident rain and then stares past me into the cottage.

I still can't quite grasp that he is standing here on my doorstep or why.

'This isn't a good time,' I say calmly.

'Oh?'

I could offer him an excuse if my mind could come up with one quickly enough. I take a deep breath. There's no point beating about the bush with this man. 'The roses were a very nice gesture,' I repeat. The phrase 'romance shit' pops into my head again, unbidden. 'But I'm afraid that I felt we didn't have very much in common.'

Lewis laughs his annoying laugh. 'We got on brilliantly.'

At what point? I wonder. 'I jumped out of a toilet window rather than have our date continue,' I remind him.

'That was hilarious.'

'It was desperation.'

'I like a woman who plays hard to get.'

'I'm not playing at anything, Lewis. I've decided that I don't want to date. Anyone.' But most of all you. 'I'm sorry.'

'You're an amazing woman,' he says.

'And you're a ...' Conceited. Annoying. Obnoxious. Self-centred. Thick-skinned. '... man.'

Lewis leans on my doorframe and gives me a louche smile. 'So when can I see you again?'

Not until hell freezes over. Not until Katie Price becomes a nun. Not until Jonathan Ross speaks without a lisp. Not in a million, trillion, squillion years. Never.

'I've just told you, Lewis.' I find myself speaking to him as if he's a small and irritating child. 'I don't want to see you again.'

He smiles. 'Is this part of the master plan?'

'I have no plan, master or otherwise. I just don't want to see you again.'

Before I can do anything about it, he reaches in and kisses me full on the mouth. I want to splutter and spit.

'Now tell me you don't want to see me?'

'I don't want to see you,' I manage to say through my mounting rage.

He points a finger at me and backs into the rain. 'I don't give up easily,' he says, before he gives a jaunty spin on his heel and sprints towards his car.

The Audi TT he bragged about last night is slammed into reverse, and he flicks his headlights at me as he drives away into the night.

'Yak,' I say and wipe my mouth on my sleeve. But my hands tremble as I close the door and I remind myself to use my spyhole in future.

Chapter 15

Ten minutes later, Mike comes back with our Chinese meal. I busy myself with the plates and dishing out the hot food from all the little foil dishes. When we sit down, I glug back my beer.

'Everything all right?' Mike says as he tucks in. 'You look all done in. Has Archie's avian adventure taken its toll on you?'

I think about just saying 'yes' but then I realise that honesty is probably the best policy. My visit from the bombastic Lewis 'The Moron' Moran has shaken me up a bit. I didn't really want him knowing my home address and I could crown Nina for giving it to him. The village is quite remote and the lane is pitch black at night. I don't like the idea of someone being able to track me down.

'My date from last night turned up,' I tell him. 'While you were collecting the food.'

Mike looks suitably surprised. 'Here?'

'Yes. I didn't give him my address, but my friend did so that he could send the roses.'

'Friend?'

'Nina. She probably thought she was doing me a good turn, and I hadn't had the chance to tell her how awful he was.'

'Persistent chap.'

'Yes,' I muse. 'A bit too much so. The strange thing is that on the date he just talked about himself constantly and my presence was largely irrelevant. Now he seems to have decided that I'm some wonderful elusive woman who's playing hard to get.'

Mike laughs and it reduces my tension. I find myself laughing too.

'What a nut job,' he says.

'I couldn't agree more.'

'Don't let him get to you,' he advises. 'He'll soon lose interest. That sort always do.' He eyes me over a prawn cracker. 'It's the quiet, unassuming ones who don't give up.'

'Yeah, right.'

We giggle like kids over the rest of the food and by the time we've settled on the sofa to watch *Angels and Demons* on DVD, with Archie curled between us, the loathsome Lewis has long been forgotten.

Still, when I show Mike out with a grateful peck on the cheek, it's nearing midnight so I take particular care to deadlock the door behind me and, call me paranoid, I check the back door twice as well.

Despite my anxieties, when I slip under the duvet and cuddle down with Archie, my fear dissipates and sleep finds me instantly. So it's quite a shock when my mobile phone starts to ring at two o'clock in the morning. I pick it up and see that the display shows 'caller unknown'.

'Hello?' I say tentatively. 'Who's this?'

But there's no answer at the other end, just an interminable silence. I say nothing else and hang up. A moment later, I hear an engine start and the arc of headlights illuminates the bedroom.

Jumping out of bed, I fly to the window, but I'm too late to see what type of car is departing at full speed along the lane.

It has to be Lewis Moran. Who else could it be?

I slip back into bed, glad that Mike is only a stone's throw from my window. If I screamed and screamed he would hear me and then I think, it would be a better idea if I just phoned him.

When I first moved in here, sleeping solo for the first time in seven years, I was a nervous wreck at night. Not used to being in a double bed alone, I chased myself around, getting tangled up in the duvet, and I spent half the night punching pillows. Every single sound would wake me up and it took me weeks to get used to the settling of the ancient wooden beams, the clanking of unfamiliar plumbing and the pinging of modern central heating. The hooting of the owl in the oak tree across the road used to spook me, as did the theatrical rustling of the trees. Now I find all of those sounds comforting and soothing.

It's only late-night silent phone calls that put the wind up me now. Pulling the duvet higher around my neck, I eventually doze off again only to be woken by a second silent phone call at four a.m. After that, I turn off my phone, but sleep dodges out of reach and by the time the alarm goes off at seven o'clock, I'm gritty-eyed and irritable and very, very tired. The fact that, at some point in the night, Archie puked in one of my comfortable working shoes does nothing to improve the start to my day.

At the salon, I tell Nina about my visit from Lewis The Moron and my nocturnal phone calls.

'Creepy,' she says. 'What a wanker.'

'Couldn't have put it better myself.'

'Did the roses turn up?'

'Yes. Now I wish I'd told him to stick them where the sun doesn't shine.'

'I'll get Gerry to tell him to lay off. I'm really sorry about this, Janie. I had no idea he was a psycho.'

'Are you and Gerry OK again?'

Nina shrugs. 'Sort of. You know what it's like.'

But do I? My relationship with Paul wasn't awful, but neither was it marvellous. It was just there, existing without very much input from either of us. Could we, with some effort, have turned it into something much, much better? There are times in my life when I wonder why I ever split up with Paul and then I remember that it wasn't my choice, and contrary to the more usual reasons for leaving, it was an older, more divorced model who signalled the end for us, so it's no good dwelling on that now.

All my appointments this morning are absolutely full, so I cut, blow-dry and perm my way to lunchtime feeling grumpy and worn out and, despite the fact that I have a fledgling stalker, very unloved.

Chapter 16

I usually send one of the juniors out at lunchtime to get me a sandwich from the deli just down the road, but today I could do with a bit of fresh air to wake me up. I grab my handbag from the staffroom. I've only got half an hour for lunch today – my first proper and very welcome gap between clients. 'Anyone want anything?'

There are a few orders for chocolate bars that I scribble on a piece of paper, otherwise I'd forget by the time I reach the shop. Nina wants some more fruit from the greengrocer's. The bagful she gets through each day is nearly half empty and it's clearly making her edgy. You don't want to be caught dangerously low on fruit.

'I'll have pears,' she says. 'No apples. Maybe plums. Or grapes.' When I start to tap my foot, she concludes, 'Just get me what they've got.'

As I walk out of the salon, I glance up and there, right across the courtyard, leaning on a wall, is Lewis. I look around. Surely, *surely* he can't be waiting for me? Before he sees me, I duck back inside.

'Cristal.' I wave the junior towards me. 'Can you get this

order for me from Deli Delights, and pop to the greengrocer's for Nina and get her some fruit?'

'Yeah, sure,' she says and shuffles off in her vest top, shorts, bare legs and UGG boots. I stifle my inner old biddy and refrain from asking her if she shouldn't put something warmer on as it's November and bloody freezing.

Back in the staffroom, I sit down next to Nina.

'That was quick,' my friend observes.

'I didn't go,' I tell her. 'Guess who's standing outside the salon?'

'You're having a laugh,' she says when I tell her who I've just spied.

'Someone is, but I'm afraid it isn't me.'

'Is it definitely Lewis?'

'Definitely.'

'Come on.' She pulls me out into the salon and we sneak behind the reception desk. Crouching down, we peer around the corner of it and into the courtyard.

'It *is* him,' Nina confirms, as if there was some doubt in my mind. 'Let me go out there and give him what for.'

'We can't prove he's done anything wrong, Nina. He's just lurking.'

'We could call the police.'

'And what would they do?' I sigh. 'I'm assuming the phone calls were from him, but I might be wrong. It could just have been a wrong number, or someone playing a prank.'

She tuts at herself. 'I should never have given him your damn address.'

'A lesson learned,' I console. We retreat back to the safety of the staffroom.

'Janie's got a stalker,' she tells the boys.

'Want us to take him down for you?' Clinton offers.

For the record, Clinton couldn't take down Iggle Piggle.

'You're OK,' I assure him. 'Just get Gerry to have a word with him, Nina.' I feel as though she bears some responsibility for getting me out of this situation, having been the one to drop me in it in the first place. 'Tell him I'm not available. Tell him I've got herpes, AIDS, terminal cancer, no money.'

'Don't joke about things like that,' Nina says.

'Tell him that I've run away with Johnny Depp then.'

'That's more like it.' Nina nods approvingly. 'Although, knowing you, you'd find some reason to turn the Deppmeister down.' Then she leans her head against my shoulder and looks up at me. 'I feel sad that you've given up on love, Janie.'

'I haven't given up on love,' I protest.

'You're still young,' she continues. 'You're lovely. Don't close your heart.'

'I haven't closed my heart, but neither do I want to *open my legs* to some arrogant arsehole ten minutes after I meet him for the price of a Diet Coke. That's not what love is about to me.'

'I think the era of chivalrous romance is long dead. Perhaps you should change your perception.'

'I'd rather be on my own than go through *that* on a regular basis.' I flick my thumb in the general direction of Lewis Moran.

'Don't give up,' Nina pleads. 'Please don't give up.'

'Are you desperate for me to have a relationship like you and Gerry?' It's a low shot and I know it.

Her face darkens and she sits up. 'I know we're not love's young dream,' she says, 'but we rub along OK. Most of the time.'

Nina and Gerry don't 'rub along OK'. They bicker constantly, and that's when they're not throwing crockery at each other. Gerry goes walkabout on a regular basis and then Nina stomps out of the house, threatening never to return.

My friend has spent many a night on my sofa, under my spare duvet, calling Gerry all the names under the sun and vowing never to go back to him – only to have forgotten all about it by the next day. Her husband must know how to say all the right things because after a few empty promises, she always decides to toe the line again and falls into his arms once more. Is that what true love is? Is it really blind? Are you inexplicably drawn to that other person, whatever their faults and flaws? When your head says you should leave, does your heart constantly overrule it?

My lunch arrives and I eat it morosely. There is definitely something deep within me that doesn't want to shuffle off this mortal coil without having experienced all-consuming and passionate love. How sad would that be? Is a life worth living that hasn't climbed those giddy heights? To get to the end of my time and never have come close to the ecstasies that are the stuff of life itself; the pain and the glories that make the world go round? My parents still held hands in their seventies and said that they loved each other every single day. Once my dad had gone, my mum followed him not long after. Life without him, she said, wasn't worth living. To still feel like that after forty-odd years together has to mean something special, right? That kind of love would work for me too.

While I'm pondering the joys of a lonely life ahead, Cristal pops her head around the door. 'Mrs Silverton's here.'

'I'll be with her in just two minutes.' My client is going to some posh function tonight and is having an up-do in honour. I'm thinking a sophisticated chignon – a big step away from her usual, more casual look.

I pop to the loo and wash my hands, studying myself in the mirror. The view isn't getting better. A terrible vision stares back at me. I'm gaunt, pale, washed-out. What am I going to do with myself? Tears spring to my eyes and I wipe them away with a piece of pink toilet roll. Nina comes in and finds me snivelling.

'Oh, hun,' she says and takes me in her arms and gives me a hug. Perhaps that's the thing I miss most: physical contact. I don't mean just sex, but hugs, cuddles, the comfort of someone's arms around you. 'Don't cry.'

'I don't want to die alone and have never loved,' I wail.

'Of course you won't, you silly thing. Do you think I'd let that happen?'

'No.'

'Wipe your eyes,' she instructs. 'Brave girl.' My friend strokes her thumb under my eyes, wiping away traces of mascara tracks. 'Don't let one bad experience with that tosser put you off.'

'No.' I'm going to give myself hiccoughs if I'm not careful. I try to pull myself together. This is ridiculous. It's just because I'm tired.

'Auntie Nina will sort it all out for you,' she promises. 'Now, put your best professional face on.'

I nod. Then, before I start crying again or feeling any more sorry for myself, I go out to see Mrs Silverton.

My client is already seated and I plaster a smile onto my face as I approach her. Glancing nervously out of the window, I'm glad to note that Lewis is nowhere to be seen.

'All ready for your big night?' I say to Mrs Silverton.

'Can't wait,' she says. 'I had a Fake Bake tan yesterday and my nails done this morning.' She shows me her fingers so that I can admire them.

'Let's get started then.'

'Oh,' she says, 'before we do, I brought that brochure for you.'

'Brochure?'

'For the safari we went on. You said you fancied it.'

Did I? Perhaps I was just making chit-chat, although, admittedly, her photographs did look utterly fabulous.

'Oh, lovely,' I say politely. 'I'll have a look through that.'

'Take it home with you,' she tells me, pushing the brochure in my direction. *Safari in Style*, it says on the front. 'I don't want it back.'

'Thanks.' I smile to myself. Mrs Silverton is well-intentioned but does she really think I'm likely to be jetting off to Africa?

Chapter 17

Mid-afternoon, and it's Clinton's turn to pop his head around the staffroom door. 'Man for you at reception, lady,' he says to me brightly.

My heart sinks. 'Did he say who he was?'

'No.' Clinton gives me a wink. 'Handsome though.' Then he disappears back to his client.

Surely it can't be Lewis Moran given that description? Or perhaps Clinton was being facetious.

Tentatively, I open the staffroom door and risk a peep out. How I wish Nina was here to back me up or send out as my envoy, but she's popped out to the post office to dispatch a friend's card in time for her birthday. I'm amazed to see that it's not Lewis standing there and even more amazed to see my ex-boyfriend, Paul, leaning casually against the desk.

This is a man I haven't clapped eyes on for months. Months and months. In all the time we've been apart, I've only bumped into him a handful of times and we're always genial to each other. I took a step away from our usual circle of friends when we split up, and when I moved to Nashley, I had no reason to see him regularly as I didn't go near our old haunts. Now it seems strange to see him waiting there as he used to do so often when we were together.

As long as it's not the dreaded Mr Moran then I feel safe enough to risk coming out of the staffroom, so I scuttle across the salon in Clinton's wake.

'Paul?' I say as I near the desk.

My ex is staring out of the window and, as he sees me, he smiles somewhat sheepishly. 'Hi,' he says. 'Just thought I'd drop by.'

'Oh.' Now? I think. Why now? I try to give him a thorough appraisal without looking as if that's what I'm doing. The past year has been kind to him. There might be a few more grey hairs, and there's a definite softening of the waist, but the extra weight suits him and clearly his new love is a better cook than me. 'It's nice to see you.'

He runs a hand through his hair, perhaps conscious that I'm not his hairdresser any more either. 'Got five minutes for coffee?'

'Not really.' My answer sounds too apologetic. 'I've got another client in ten.'

'I just wanted to tell you something.'

I shrug.

'Not in here.'

'OK. Just let me get my coat.'

I nip back to the staffroom and slip on my jacket. Weird thoughts flash through my mind. Has it all gone wrong with his new partner? Has he suddenly realised that it was me he wanted all along? Is he anxious for us to give our relationship another try?

Paul's hand goes under my elbow as he escorts me out of the door. Then neither of us knows what to do. There's nowhere to sit near the salon, nor is there a place to take shelter, so we end up walking around the corner and leaning on a wall just outside the pretty florist's shop. Workmen are busy putting up the Christmas decorations on the lampposts and, if I tried, I couldn't feel less Christmassy. The weather is bitter and Paul, in the absence of gloves, blows on his hands. I cross my arms in front of me as the wind whips around us. There's an alarming fluttering from my stomach but I can't tell if it's because I still have feelings for this man or whether it's because he's just turned up out of the blue.

'How are you?' Paul asks. He looks as if he regrets coming now.

'Fine,' I say. 'Absolutely fine. And you?' It's strange how conversation can become stilted between two people who once lived together for seven years.

'Yes,' he says. 'Good. Everything's good.'

Then there's a moment that goes on too long where neither of us say anything, but my mind still races on. If Paul asks me to give it another go, what would I do? Is that what I want? Would the danger be that I jump back into a relationship just because it's familiar? Is that better than being alone?

I'm starting to shiver now. 'What did you want to talk to me about?'

He takes a deep breath. 'I just wanted to tell you that Trudi and I are getting married.' Paul shuffles his feet.

'Oh.'

'I thought you should know,' he says. 'I thought you should know from me and not hear it from someone else or see it in the local paper.'

'Thanks,' I say, struggling to control my voice from the shock of finding out that my ex has well and truly moved on. He 'didn't come to see me because he was having second thoughts or because he'd decided that I was the love of his life. Quite the opposite. 'That was very thoughtful of you. Congratulations. I hope you'll be very happy together.'

'We are,' he says, and then I notice the proud smile on his face. 'She's having a baby, Janie. *We're* having a baby.' He looks like he might want to run up and down the High Street, telling everyone that he meets.

'Really?' More reeling inside. 'That's marvellous. I'm pleased for you.'

'Are you?' he asks. 'Are you really?'

'Of course. We've both moved on. You and I are old history.' I try a tinkling laugh but I can't summon one.

'I thought about asking you to the wedding. It's Christmas week. But then ...' He tails off.

'I'm not around Christmas week anyway.' The lie is out of my mouth before I can curb it. 'I'm going away.'

'Where to?'

'Africa.' Where the hell did that come from?

'Wow.' Now my ex is the one to be impressed. 'That's very adventurous for you.'

I shrug. 'I decided I'd like to see the world.' Why am I lying my head off to him? I haven't even been for a day out to Bognor Regis since we split up. Do I feel that inadequate just because he's getting married and starting a family? Yes, I think I do and you don't know how pathetic that makes me feel. 'It sounds as if everything has worked out well for you.'

'It has,' Paul says. 'It's brilliant.' Then he looks guilty about effusing too much about his new life. 'I should never have done what I did to you. It was wrong of me. Stupid. Things between us, they weren't that bad.'

'No, but we were never absolutely crazy for each other either,' I point out. 'Seems as if it was for the best.'

'Yeah,' he agrees reluctantly. 'Trudi's a great girl. You'd like her.' I see the love in his eyes for her and I know that I never saw them shine like that for me. 'So? What about you?'

'I'm a different woman now.' I'm not, I think. I'm exactly the bloody same and that pains me to admit to myself. This announcement – his marriage, his child – has hurt me more now than when we actually split up. It's as if it's suddenly flagging up all that I haven't achieved.

'Africa's meant to be wonderful.'

'Yes, so I've heard.'

'None of that for us for a long time.' He looks as if he really doesn't mind that. Family holidays in Cornwall or Wales in a caravan for the next ten years will suit Paul down to the ground. He adopts a casual air. 'Are you with anyone?'

'I'm seeing someone,' I tell him. 'Lewis. He's called Lewis.' I don't tell Paul that I'm only seeing him in my nightmares. 'It's early days, but he's a really great bloke.' I should have sliced out my own tongue rather than say that.

'That's good.' My ex looks relieved.

I glance at my watch. 'I'm going to have to get back.'

Paul touches my arm. There's a tenderness in it that we never had in our relationship and I wonder if this new woman has made him a softer and more caring person. Or perhaps it's because he's about to become a daddy. I look at him sadly. Will he turn out to be The One That Got Away? Should I have loved him more? *Could* I have loved him more? What if we'd been more romantic, more loving? Can you force that into a relationship? Doesn't that sort of thing occur naturally if you both feel it? What if there's no one else in my life that matches up to

Paul? The small taste I've had of what else is on the market doesn't leave me with much hope.

'You know if you ever need anything, Janie, you only have to ask me.'

'I'm fine,' I assure him. 'Honestly.'

'If you're sure?'

'You'll have to let me know when the baby's born.'

'We're expecting a little girl. Next March.' Again, the glow of pride.

Perhaps if we'd had children together, Paul and me, things might have turned out differently. 'That's wonderful.'

He pecks me on the cheek. 'Have a great time.'

'Yes.'

'In Africa.'

'Africa?' Then I remember. 'Oh, yes. Africa.'

'I'll see you around, Janie.'

'Yes. Lovely. Give my love to . . .' But Paul is already out of earshot.

I scuttle back to the salon and lock myself in the loo and cry.

Chapter 18

When I get home that night, I lock the front door and pull the curtains shut before I do anything else. Well, after I fuss over the cat, of course. Otherwise blood would have been spilled.

I'm exhausted and not just because I've been on my feet all day. Emotionally, I feel drained too. Seeing Paul was a shock and, whether I like it or not, the news of his impending marriage and fatherhood has left me feeling empty and lonely. The whole world is moving on while I stand still. I think part of the trouble with being alone is that every problem is magnified, simply because you have no one else to share it with. Every decision has to be your own. Usually, I cope quite well. Today, it's worn me down.

'What shall we have for dinner?' I say to Archie and even that makes me choke up again. Talking to my bloody cat – I'm going madder and becoming sadder quicker than I'd hoped.

Archibald headbutts the cupboard where his food is kept. I wonder if it's tedious living on dried biscuits and whether that's why he still harbours a yearning for mouse entrails and birds' heads.

His look says, 'Get a move on, bitch.'

When I've fed the cat, I opt for a frozen lasagne and open a bottle of red to go with it. While it's cooking, I polish off a glass. Drinking alone is a bad thing too and it's something that I don't usually do during the week. I normally try to last out until the weekend, but over the last few weeks my willpower has been slipping and I've been having a few glasses even on school nights. Sometimes it's the only thing that hits the spot.

The roses that arrived yesterday are still in my sink and now I can't bring myself to cut open the cellophane and arrange them artistically. More than ever, they seem tainted, a poor parody of what they are supposed to represent.

A night on my own stretches ahead of me. There was no sign of life at Mike's house when I got home and, idly, I wonder where he is. Out somewhere working late maybe. I could just call his mobile, see if he's OK, but then I tell myself I can't always be calling up Mike when the slightest thing goes wrong. He can't for ever be my fall-back plan. The man must have a life of his own.

As I sit at the kitchen table and sip my wine, Archie winds himself around my legs and I start to relax – even though it's wise to be wary of the tips of claws being drawn. Pulling Mrs Silverton's brochure out of my bag, I start to flick through the pages. *Safari in Style*. That was obviously what planted the lie about Africa in my mind. Pathetically, I did take some small pleasure in making Paul look suitably shocked. Is it so unlikely that I'd go travelling on my own? Am I that boringly pre-dictable? Yes, I probably am. Hmm. The holidays look fabulous. Glossy photographs of acres and acres of vast African plains, luxury lodges, upmarket camps and photogenic animals fill the pages.

The microwave pings and my lasagne is bubbling and ready.

Picking through the pasta offers me more succour and another glass of wine doesn't go amiss either. The pages of the brochure are enthralling.

'Look at this.' I show the page to Archie who has climbed onto the table to inspect what I'm reading. The face of a lion with a full mane fills half of the page. 'One of your lot,' I tell him. 'He'd give you a run for your money.'

Archie doesn't argue.

When I've eaten, I wash up my plate and go through to the living room and put some wood into the log burner. Mike was, as usual, fabulous and went to collect some more for me a couple of weeks ago and now I probably have enough piled up in the wood store to see me right through the winter.

Curling up on the sofa, I tuck my knees beneath me. This home is my sanctuary. I feel safe here and I'm so lucky to have good neighbours – not just Mike. The couple on the other side of me, Lyn and Martin, are always happy to help out or chat over the garden fence. Paul and Ali at the end of the terrace are a great couple too, though they both work in London in crazy high-powered jobs and aren't often at home. I carry on flicking through another few pages of the brochure. This looks very tempting. Then there's a rap on my door and my blood freezes.

I know who it is without even going to have a look. Despite myself, I go to the door and peer through the spyhole. Sure enough, on the other side, Lewis Moran is standing there, hands jammed in his pockets. He's whistling to himself. I put my back against the door. There's no way I'm going to open it for him. I don't want him lunging at me again and trying to kiss me. He'll be able to see the lights through the window, but there's no welcome here for him tonight. I'm only glad that I thought to draw the curtains earlier so I know that he can't look inside.

Lewis raps again. 'Janie.' He tries to lift the letterbox to shout through it, but it jams against my bottom. 'I know that you're in. Answer the door. I just want to talk to you.'

Making sure the door is bolted – which it is – I quietly tiptoe away. I go and sit on the sofa, huddling at one end, hauling Archie onto my lap.

'Have dinner with me,' Lewis pleads as he stands outside my home. 'A drink. What harm could a drink do?'

Does he seriously not appreciate how awful the last time was? How, even as an out-and-out lie, could I possibly have told Paul that I was seeing this man?

I grab a cushion and fold it over the top of my head, pulling it down so that it covers my ears and blocks out the sound. A second later, my mobile starts to ring and I don't even need to check who the caller is. I let the call go to voicemail. It rings again, two, three, four times.

'I won't give up,' Lewis shouts and then, thankfully, I hear his footsteps retreat down the path.

Dashing to the window, I pull the curtain back a fraction and watch his figure head to his car in the darkness. He turns and gives one last look at the cottage and I quickly duck back in case he sees me. But he doesn't and, a moment later, he's roaring off into the night again. I groan to myself. One awful date, and now the man sees me as some sort of challenge?

Back on the sofa and, of course, I can't settle. I think about a film and dismiss the idea – something romantic or sentimental and I'd be off bawling again. Anything with a high body count or gore and I'd never sleep. What am I going to do? How am I going to get rid of my unwanted suitor?

Then it hits me like a bolt out of the blue. I could go away. Perhaps I wasn't just bullshitting Paul. Perhaps it was my subconscious leaping in to suggest what I really need. I could leave all this hassle behind. Why not? There's not a massive surplus in my savings account, but there is some money put away for a rainy day. And this feels like a rainy day to me.

I chew at my fingernail. I could, I suppose, get a cheap deal to Majorca or Ibiza or somewhere like that. All safe places that I've been to before. Or I could go wild and step out *into* the wild. I glance down at Mrs Silverton's brochure and my lips curl into a smile. I could actually go to the place I told my ex I was going to. Africa.

Chapter 19

'You're doing *what*?' Nina looks at me, horrified.

'I'm going to Africa. On safari.'

We've slipped out of work for fifteen minutes and are having a quick coffee in the Costa across the road from Cutting Edge. I bagged the big leather sofas for us by the window. Clearing a small square in the condensation with the tip of my finger so I can see out, I peer at the flurry of early snow that's falling. The flakes are tiny, fluttering to the ground. It's not settling but it still makes it look pretty out there. I wonder if we're in for a long winter.

'Fuck me,' Nina says, shaking her head. 'Who put that crazy idea into your head? Is this something to do with seeing Paul?'

'Sort of,' I admit. I didn't get the chance yesterday to tell Nina about his announcement. I turned my phone off last night to thwart unwanted callers, so I didn't get her dozen texts asking me to ring her. 'He's getting married, Nina. They're expecting a baby.'

'Bloody hell.'

'I had to tell him something good that was happening in my life.'

'So you said that you were going to Africa?'

'Yes.' My cheeks are glowing pink as I confess. I fail to mention the lie regarding Lewis or the fact that he came to my house again last night.

'You could have told him something better,' she muses as she toys with the froth on her cappuccino.

'Like what?'

'Like you were shagging George Clooney or something.'

'It had to be something believable.'

'And you going to Africa is any more believable?'

'Mrs Silverton's just come back from there. She was raving about it. Yesterday, she brought the brochure in for me to have a look at.'

'We could have gone to Spain for a few days or something. Just me and you.'

'Kelly wouldn't let us have the time off together in the run-up to Christmas. She wasn't that happy about me going on my own, but I've got to take the holiday or I'll lose it. So she had no choice but to let me book it.' Just as well, as a few clicks on the internet last night and I'd got everything in place. 'I'll phone all my clients this afternoon and, if they want to, move their appointments to you.'

'You can't go to Africa on your own,' Nina whines.

'I'm not going on my own,' I reason. 'It's a group holiday. There are going to be five of us.'

'You might hate them all.'

'I might,' I agree. 'But it's only for a week.' I didn't want to risk Kelly's complete wrath by booking two weeks off at the busiest time of year. Plus, I thought it better not to completely empty the Johnson coffers by going for any longer.

'Gerry's going to Thailand for a stag weekend,' my friend

complains. 'This would have been my chance to get back at him. What's good for the goose . . .'

'To Thailand for a *weekend*?'

'Tell me about it.' Nina rolls her eyes. 'I can't imagine what he's going to do there.'

I can. All too well.

'When we got married, it was a couple of pints down at the local pub with a few mates the night before the wedding,' she continues. 'Now, the send-off is a major event in itself. Costs as much as the bloody wedding!' Nina sips her coffee. 'The bride is going to the Seychelles for a week with ten of her girlfriends. Something so lavish used to be the honeymoon. I don't really know her, so I wasn't invited. More's the pity.'

There's no way that her dear husband would have let her go anyway, despite what he might be getting up to himself.

'Gerry went to school with the groom so he's got the perfect excuse to clear off and have some fun.'

'Come to Africa.'

Nina snorts. 'Not likely.'

'Why?'

'What do I want to go to Africa for?'

'The scenery is stunning. The wildlife looks amazing. From Mrs Silverton's pictures, it looks as if you can get right up close to it.'

'Lovely.' Nina doesn't look like she thinks it's lovely. 'Wildlife.' She puffs out a disgruntled breath. 'You can see all that in a zoo.'

'It's not the same though, is it?'

'No. It's not likely to eat you in a zoo.'

'It'll be different.'

'It'll be boring. Why don't you swap it for a beach holiday, then I'd come? We could have some laughs.'

'I've booked it now,' I remind her. 'Besides, I don't want a beach holiday. I did that for years with Paul and never really enjoyed it. You should be pleased for me that I'm trying something different.'

'This is about getting away from Leery Lewis too, isn't it?'

I sigh and stir my cappuccino. 'Partly,' I admit. 'He came to my house again last night, Nina, banging the door down, shouting through the letterbox. Then he was ringing and ringing me.'

'Oh God,' my friend says. 'No wonder you turned your phone off. What a prat. Let me send Gerry round to kneecap him. He won't bother you again then.'

'I just thought if I went away for a week, by the time I came back he'd have realised I'm not interested and will have moved on.' And Paul will be married and will have also moved on.

'So? If I can't talk you out of it, where exactly *are* you going on this harebrained jaunt? Tell Auntie Nina all.'

'I'm going to the Maasai Mara.'

'My geography isn't all it might be,' Nina says. 'Where the fuck's that?'

'Kenya,' I tell her. 'I've booked a Premier Adventure.'

'That sounds expensive.'

I shrug in agreement. 'It wasn't cheap.'

'And what does a Premier Adventure get you when it's at home?'

'I'm staying in a luxury camp.'

'A tent?' Her look of horror returns with a vengeance. 'With lions running loose?'

Now it's my turn to look horrified. 'I don't think they're going to be running loose around the camp.'

'Don't you?' she says. 'I'd have checked the small print.' Then, 'Who's going to look after Archie?'

'I'm sure Mike will do it. If not, he'll have to go into a cattery.'

'Yeah, right,' Nina says. 'That cat could chew through iron bars. Either way, he's not going to be happy.'

She's right. Archibald the Aggressive will definitely make his displeasure felt but, me, I'm looking forward to it already.

Chapter 20

It's bonfire night and I've agreed to go with Mike to a fireworks party at one of the neighbours' houses just down the lane. A few rockets have ripped across the sky already and Archie, like the majority of cats, is terrified of them. By now he'd normally have flattened himself into impossible proportions and crawled under the sofa in the lounge, which has a gap of about two inches, where he'd stay until the noise had died down. Currently, he's sufficiently distracted not to have retreated. I've baked a tray of chocolate brownies which are cooling on a rack, ready to be popped into my biscuit tin to take with us. Archie is sitting beneath them trying to decide whether cats might like to eat them and how many.

'Don't you dare,' I chide and he gives me a catty mouthful in return.

My trip is fast approaching – just one week to go – and I've yet to tell Mike or ask him whether he'll be available for Archibald-sitting. He's been working away this week and I haven't seen hide nor hair of him. I've started to put a few bits and pieces together, ready to go in my case. I've ordered money from the bank and my visa arrived back from the Kenyan embassy just this morning. Excitement and panic are rising steadily in tandem. Mrs Silverton is stoked that I'm following in her footsteps and has been giving me lots of useful tips.

While I'm pulling on my warm furry boots, Mike knocks at the door. Even though I'm sure it's his 'special' knock, I check the spyhole first. Lewis's pursuit of me hasn't abated, despite Gerry having had words with him, apparently. Seems as if he can't control his friend as much as he controls his wife. Nina says that if it carries on after I come back from Kenya then I should think about going to the police. But why would they care? Lewis is an annoyance, but I don't think he's harmful. He calls me several times a day, but I never answer the phone to him. Every couple of nights he will turn up at my door, sometimes he leaves chocolates, once a pink teddy with an I ♥ YOU embroidered on its chest, other times he might leave a note begging for a date. Occasionally, I see him lurking in the courtyard outside the salon, but he never comes in. Does that warrant enough to go to the police? If he starts putting dog poo through my letterbox or sending abusive texts requesting to see me in my underwear or something, then I might reconsider, but I'm still just hoping he will get tired of chasing someone who simply isn't interested and will find some other unsuspecting and less choosy female to love him.

I let Mike in. There's a box of fireworks tucked under his arm. 'Ready and raring to go?' he says, clapping his hands together. I'm assuming he means to the party, but it could equally apply to my trip.

Mike is all wrapped up in a padded North Face jacket, jeans and boots, and he has a colourful Peruvian *chullo* on his head. It's knitted in red, white and yellow wool, the ear flaps ending in gaudy red tassels.

'That's a bit fancy for you?'

'Bought it when I did the Inca Trail a few years ago,' he explains, giving me a twirl of his tassels. 'It was flipping cold up in the Andes at night. Saw me in good stead, this hat. It's been stuck at the bottom of the wardrobe ever since. Tania wouldn't be seen dead with me in it. One of the few benefits of not having a wife any more.' He tries a laugh. 'I can wear whatever I like now, so I thought it was time to give it an airing. It's a bit risqué for the good folks of Nashley. Do you think Mr and Mrs Codling-Bentham will let me into their garden wearing it?'

'I'm sure they will.' I smile. 'It suits you.'

Mike looks doubtful.

'I didn't know that you were the adventurous type,' I tease him.

'I used to do all kinds of things like that.' He gives a sad shrug. 'Before I met Tania, of course. I've been to the Himalayas, Bhutan, South America, India – all over the place. It wasn't her kind of thing.'

'That's a shame.'

He shrugs. 'I might get back to it one day.'

'I'm about to go on an adventure of my own,' I confess.

Mike looks up, surprised.

'I've just booked a holiday to Kenya. I'm going on safari for a week.' I pack the brownies into the biscuit tin as I tell him and then shrug on my coat. 'Luxury camp in the Maasai Mara.'

My neighbour is speechless.

'Don't look at me like that,' I warn. 'I know I'm a hairdresser, but we don't all have to go to Benidorm for our holidays. I'm striking out, trying something new.'

'What's brought this on?' Mike says, sounding perplexed. 'You never mentioned that you were thinking about going away.'

'It's only for a week,' I laugh. 'Not six months. Are you ready?'

'When you are.'

I kiss Archie on the head. 'Go and get under the sofa,' I advise. 'We'll be back before you know it.'

If my cat could give me the finger, he would.

We head out into the cold night. The sky is glittering with the red and green and gold of rockets bursting. Our breath hangs in the air as we walk side by side down the lane.

'It was a spur of the moment decision,' I explain as Mike opens the Codling-Benthams' garden gate and, together, we turn into their path.

Mr and Mrs Codling-Bentham live in the Manor House of the village – an old, grand home of mellow Cotswold stone. It stands adjacent to the church on the other side of the rectory and together they form a slice of olde-worlde England. We don't have a Lord and Lady here any more but if we did, the Codling-B's would make perfect candidates. Happily married for over fifty years, they have a string of children spread out across the globe doing wonderful jobs in the diplomatic service, the forces and television. Now they are revered in the village as an institution and not only because they open their marvellous grounds to the rest of the villagers on every occasion that it is required: winter, Christmas church fayre; spring, hog roast and barn dance; summer, barbecue; and tonight, fireworks party.

A couple of dozen of the neighbours are already here, which is practically the entire population of the village. There's a bonfire halfway down the garden giving off a good blaze. Beside the house on the terrace, there's a table laid out with a tureen of hot soup and garlic bread. The vicar is barbecuing sausages and from the kitchen, there's the mouth-watering smell of jacket potatoes and chilli. I'll certainly look forward to some of that later. I hand over my chocolate brownie contribution and Mike goes to put his fireworks on the growing pile.

When he returns, Mike launches straight into, 'It's nothing to do with this prat who's bothering you, I hope.'

'Well ... partly.' I try to look unconcerned, as if it doesn't bother me as much as it does.

Then Mr and Mrs Codling-Bentham greet us and press polystyrene cups of mulled wine into our hands. The spices smell wonderful and the warm alcohol packs a punch.

'Tot of brandy in there,' Mr Codling-Bentham says, explaining the potency of his brew. 'That'll warm your cockles.'

'It's a long time since I've had my cockles warmed,' Mike says as we walk away, giggling.

'Then tonight is your lucky night.'

We go and stand by the blaze so that we can feel the warmth on our faces. The cold is already trying to nip at our fingers and toes. 'You know, Janie, next time this bloke turns up you should give me a call. I'll be straight round and have a word.'

'I don't want to involve you in my troubles, Mike. You do more than enough for me already. Besides, I did have some holiday to use up too.' At this point I could tell him about Paul getting married and the baby, but what purpose would that serve other than to make me look like a sad old spinster who no one wants?

'I would have come with you.'

The thought never crossed my mind to ask Mike to accompany me. If I'm honest, the first thing that occurred to me was, would he look after Archie? Is that bad? I wouldn't like to think that I was taking Mike for granted. 'I didn't even think about it.'

'Did you book it online? I could try to get on the trip tonight. If you'd like that, of course.'

'It would be fab,' I say. Having Mike by my side would be a great comfort and we get along so well. 'I'm going next week. Why not come too?'

'Damn,' he says and he gives a little frown that's incongruous with his colourful hat. 'So soon?'

I nod.

'I'm away at a conference for work during that week. There's no way that I can miss it, not now I'm going to be the boss. Any other time wouldn't have been a problem.'

His face looks troubled in the firelight and, strangely, it's nice to have him concerned about me going off to an unknown country all by myself.

'Is there any possibility that you could change it? I could go any other time between now and Christmas.'

I shake my head. 'We're mad busy over the next few months. My boss has really only let me go because she couldn't do anything else.'

'That's a shame,' Mike says. 'A damn shame.'

It is, I think. I would rather have liked him to come along on holiday with me – and not only because his camera skills are a lot better than mine.

Someone starts to light the fireworks and a shower of silver sparks lights up the hydrangea bushes and the maple trees. Mike rubs his hands together. 'Looks like I'm going to be required to do man things.'

'You go and do that,' I say. 'I'm going to try to make a serious dent in this mulled wine. It's going down rather well.'

'Save some for me,' he instructs and then he's off, joining the other men in making explosions. Why is it that boys never grow up?

Then I watch the display over the Codling-Benthams' garden, lighting up the rolling Buckinghamshire countryside, oohing and aahing along with everyone else. And all thoughts of Africa go right out of my mind.

Chapter 21

Now I'm stressing. I've got so much still to do and any minute now, any *second* now, I've got to leave for the airport. Mike is already here and waiting to drive me down there. Currently, he's throwing anything manky out of the fridge for me. I've had to sit on the lid to get my suitcase closed and I have no idea what's in there.

'Aren't you going to need these?' Nina asks, holding up my GHD hair straighteners.

'I don't think there's any electricity, Nina.'

She looks at me disbelievingly. 'How are you going to do your hair?'

'Perhaps the lions won't mind if I go *au naturel* for the week, eh?'

'I still don't know why you can't go to Ibiza,' she mutters under her breath. 'Well, if you're not going to need these ...' She tosses my straighteners aside. 'Then you'll definitely need these.'

Nina throws a couple of packets of condoms down on the bed and shrieks with laughter. Just then Mike walks in and I feel a fire start in my face.

'She needs to have a brilliant holiday, Mike, doesn't she?'

I hurriedly pick up the condoms and then don't know what to do with them.

'With lots of booze and rampant sex,' my friend adds.

Mike looks alarmed. 'Not *too* much rampant sex.'

His face says that he'd rather I didn't have any rampant sex at all and, to be honest, I agree with him.

'There will be no rampant sex, Nina,' I say sternly as I secrete the condoms in my bedside drawer. 'It's not going to be that kind of holiday.'

'*Is* there any other kind of holiday?'

'I'm going to learn about a different culture and look at some lovely wildlife – I hope. That's all I want.'

'Have fun, love!' she says, rolling her eyes.

Mike looks as embarrassed as I feel. 'Fridge is all cleared,' he says. Archie mooches in behind him looking miserable. 'We'll be all right without her. Won't we, fella?'

My cat complains vociferously.

'I might kip here, on the sofa, a couple of nights,' Mike says. 'So that he's not on his own.'

'You don't need to do that. Really. He'll be fine.' Archie won't be fine. He'll make sure he isn't. For the first few days, he'll play the drama queen and refuse to eat and act as if he's fading away. Then he'll wrap Mike around his little finger and forget that I'm gone at all. That's cats for you.

This is the first time that I've been away by myself and, the truth of it is, I'm now anxious. I'm going to be part of a small group though, and I can only hope that they'll all be nice. Then I remind myself that it's only for a week and, even if I hate them all on sight, I only have to put up with them for seven days. And if they hate me on sight, vice versa. Now I desperately wish that Mike was coming on the trip with me.

'All done with your case?' my neighbour wants to know.

'I think so.' I chew my lip, worrying that I've forgotten something critical.

'You can buy anything you've forgotten,' Nina advises.

'I'm not sure that there'll be many shops out on the African plains,' I remind her and wonder, as Nina clearly is as well, why I haven't opted for the safety of Spain.

Mike hefts my case with a heartfelt puff. 'Feels like you've got the kitchen sink in here.' Then he heads out of my bedroom, down the narrow stairs and out to the car.

'Miserable Mike fancies you,' Nina whispers as my neighbour's back retreats.

'He does not,' I insist.

'Does too.'

'He's just nice.'

She nods in agreement. 'You could do worse.'

'When you call him Miserable Mike?' I remind her. 'And tell me I spend too much time with him?'

'Perhaps I got him wrong,' she admits. 'He does seem quite sweet and not nearly so miserable now that he's over his wife.'

Is he over her? Maybe he's starting to get back to normal once again. It's like a grieving process – I should know. I might not have been head over heels in love with Paul, but his leaving still hit me like a body blow. And Mike adored the very ground that Tania walked on. Once that person has gone, it takes some adjusting to, particularly when every fibre in your body still wants them to be there. Mike was a mess when she left and, understandably, very miserable. It's nice to see that he's now back on his feet again and that I was able to help him in some small way.

'We're going to be late, Janie,' Mike calls from the bottom of the stairs.

'Looks like this is it,' I say to Nina.

'Please take these.' She grabs the condoms again and shoves them into my handbag. 'Just in case.'

I roll my eyes at her, but don't argue. It's easier that way. Then together we clatter down to the living room.

Scooping the reluctant Archie into my arms, I kiss his nose. 'Be good,' I tell him as he wriggles against my cuddle like a surly teenager. 'Mike will be looking after you. Don't bite or scratch him. It's not nice.'

My cat looks at me as if to say he'd never consider such a crass idea.

I lock the door and Nina stands at my gate as I jump into the front seat of Mike's car.

'Case is in the boot,' he says. 'Have you got your passport, ticket, money?'

Quickly, I double-check. 'Yes.'

'Condoms?' he teases.

Obligingly, I flush. 'Yes.'

He laughs at me but he'd probably be appalled to know that I do actually have them.

'Then let's hit the road.'

We pull away and I wind my window down to wave at Nina who is jumping up and down and generally making a fuss.

'Come back safely,' she shouts. 'And remember, I want to hear about lots of shagging!'

The postman, who is coming the other way, wobbles on his bike.

It's raining and it's cold. Mike is a steady driver and we negotiate our way through the M25 traffic without too much pain and an hour and a half later, we arrive safely and promptly at Heathrow's Terminal Three.

He whips into the Short Stay car park and insists on accompanying me into the terminal, carrying my luggage all the way.

'Flight's up on the board,' I say. 'Nairobi, Kenya. Desk twenty-six.'

My neighbour walks me to the appropriate check-in desk and waits with me while I queue and deposit my over-stuffed bag. Then we have a quick coffee together at a scruffy, crowded Starbucks to calm my nerves before I go through to the departure lounge.

We stand at the last security barrier – the place where Mike has to go home and I take my first step alone into uncharted territory. I get my plastic bag of toiletries out of my hand luggage in preparation for the tedious security checks.

'Well,' Mike says. There is a catch in his voice. 'I'm going to miss you.'

'I'm going to miss you too,' I agree. And as I say it, I realise how much I really am going to be lost without this reliable man who's always close at hand for me.

The crowds push around us. 'Don't worry about Archie,' he says. 'I'll look after him.'

A tear springs to my eye and it's not just for my stroppy cat.

'Maybe when you get back,' Mike says tentatively, 'I could take you out for a nice dinner or something.'

'That would be lovely.'

'I mean properly,' he adds shyly, in case I've missed his meaning. 'Not just as neighbours. Not just as friends.'

'Oh,' I say, having completely missed his meaning. 'Oh.'

With that, he grips me awkwardly in a bear hug and squeezes

101

me in his arms. 'Come back safely to me, Janie Johnson,' he whispers in my ear. 'Come back safely.'

'Yes,' I hear myself say in a dazed way. 'Yes.'

Mike breaks away from me. Holding me at arm's length, he gazes at me as if trying to record every contour of my face, and they must surely be registering surprise. Then he kisses me soundly on the cheek, turns and after a final wave, walks away, leaving me slightly gobsmacked at the gate.

It seems that my friend, Nina, might well be right. Mike fancies me. I smile to myself. And it feels quite nice.

Chapter 22

The sun, which is stronger than I've ever known, is already flaying strips off my skin. It's just past nine in the morning and the temperature is climbing steadily. The air tastes different here – of dryness and dust. Eight hours after leaving London and two hours after leaving Nairobi, the robust four-wheel-drive minibus I'm in stops at a roadside curio shop called, rather optimistically, Harrods Africa.

This African version of the world-famous department store is a shack made of rough planks of wood, nailed haphazardly together in the approximate shape of a garden shed. The walls are laden with wooden carvings for sale – scary African masks, slender giraffes, bowls in gleaming olive wood, blue gum and ebony. The floor around the shack is stacked with more carvings, this time made from smooth soapstone in delicate shades of cream and green and pink. Brightly coloured woven blankets in scarlet reds, lurid pinks and shades of orange are strung up on a wire that's hanging on the door alongside small goatskin shields.

The group pile out of the minibus and we all buy cups of sweet milky *chai* and stand on the balcony – also randomly

103

created from bits and pieces of wood – that precariously juts out from the escarpment. We look out at the stupendous view of Africa's Rift Valley, a vast geological fissure that stretches all the way down from the Red Sea to the Zambezi river. The place that's often known as the cradle of man, the place from where all human life is said to have begun. I feel that this is my first proper glimpse of the Africa I had envisaged. The landscape is immense, ancient. In all of my life, I've seen nothing quite like this before. Nothing so vast, so primal. It's a million miles away from Nashley and its twee little cottages and neatly trimmed hedges. The cerulean sky is all-encompassing, the ochre plains stretch out to infinity and beyond. In the far distance, enormous mountains rise up to meet the rare powder puff of clouds. A long weary sigh escapes my lips. I'm here. I'm finally here. I want to laugh and cry at the same time. I'm both exhausted and excited.

After a few minutes of rest, the driver ushers us back onto the bus. We still have a long, long way to go before we reach the Maasai Mara. Another five hours or more, dependent on the condition of the road, the driver tells us. I settle back in my seat and let the scenery pass by me.

As we travel through shanty-town villages, ramshackle houses, shops painted in bright colours to advertise mobile phone networks, zebras and gazelles graze by the side of the road and herds of goats wander aimlessly into our path, risking the wrath of our driver who toots his horn furiously but doesn't slow down. The further we go, the bumpier the road becomes until, at the bustling touristy town of Narok, we turn off to the only road which leads into the Maasai Mara.

My travelling companions are not as fearsome as I imagined. There are just five of us. A young couple, Sean and Maura, also on their first trip to Africa, Pat, a single lady, older than me, and an elderly man, John, who has already set his sights on her it seems.

We jolt and buck along the baked yellow-rock road, etched with deep grooves from the traffic that has passed this way before us. Children from the villages, with dirty faces and heavenly smiles, run out to greet us, keeping pace with the bus as best they can to wave and call out their names to us. Occasionally, we stop to let a herder guide their skinny cattle across the route from one barren-looking field to another. The Maasai Mara, our driver tells us, hasn't seen a drop of rain for nearly two years and now water is a scarce and much needed commodity.

Another two hours of bone-breaking, spleen-shattering, jaw-juddering driving and we're travelling along flat open plains dotted only with acacia trees. The rutted road disappears and all that remains are dirt tracks etched into the land with no visible signposts except those that nature has provided. Vast herds of wildebeest wander across the reserve and I think, if I see nothing more for the rest of my trip, then even this has far surpassed my dreams of what Africa might be like.

The driver still navigates skilfully and soon, after our long, beautiful and bumpy journey, we see two crossed spears in the ground and bounce happily into an area of grassy scrub. Kiihu camp. My home for the next seven days.

As we park, a couple of zebras grazing in the shrubby bush lift their heads and give us the once-over, then trot away as the van door opens. Tired, we're helped by smiling staff to unload our bags. It's late afternoon now and every muscle in my body aches, first of all from being stuck overnight on a plane for hours, and then ricocheting around a bus like a marble in a tin can for the best part of the day. But when I see the camp for the first time, my spirits lift and I forget all my aches and pains.

The large olive green tents are arranged in a loose circle around the perimeter of the camp. In the centre, there's a campfire and to one side there's even a vast living room tent for relaxing.

I'm taken to my own tent by the driver and, inside, there's a double bed, a proper loo and a shower. This isn't camping, it's glamping, and right now I'm very grateful for it. My bed is covered with a large colourful blanket and there's a thick cotton rug on the floor. Behind the bed is the luxury of a dressing table and stool and beyond that is the bathroom area. The knot of anxiety in my stomach starts to uncurl.

The driver moves on to help someone else and leaves me with my unpacking and my comfortable bed beckoning. I don't really know where to start, so I kick off my trainers and lie back on my bed, taking a moment's rest.

A minute later, I feel a shadow cross my face and I open my eyes, jerking awake immediately from the half-sleep I was happily drifting into.

And there he's standing. My first glimpse of a Maasai warrior. The man at the opening to my tent is tall, amazingly so – easily six foot four or more. He's slender, rangy, but I've never seen anyone with more muscle or sinew in my life. His head is shaved and his skin is as dark as the olive wood I saw earlier – a rich burnished brown. A red cotton tunic covers his body and his neck is draped with colourful beaded necklaces. He wears more bracelets on his wrists and ankles. Around his hips is tied one of the now-familiar traditional blankets in bold red and orange stripes. His feet are bare and in his hand is a stick that's nearly as tall as he is. He is stunning, beautiful.

I sit up, flustered, and fuss with my hair. 'Hello.'

When he smiles at me, a dazzling white smile, eyes twinkling, I feel something inside my heart twang. I have never seen a man quite so imposing and so proud.

'*Jambo*. Hello.' The smile widens. Then he reaches out a hand to grasp mine. It is cool, dry and the strength in his fingers is tangible. 'I am Dominic, Mrs Janie Johnson,' he says softly in a lilting voice. 'I am a Maasai warrior and I am here to look after you.'

'Thank you.' I smile shyly in return and think that if I have Dominic, my very own Maasai warrior, to look after me then I never need fear anything ever again.

Chapter 23

We sit on the veranda of my tent in two director's chairs. 'You must not go anywhere without me,' Dominic stresses. 'I am here to protect you and keep you safe.'

I can barely hear what he's saying, I'm so transfixed by simply looking at him. His movements are so elegant, graceful.

'Whenever you want me,' he continues in his impeccable English, 'you must make a noise.'

That makes my attention snap back. 'A noise?'

'Yes. Do not come out of your tent alone. Do not walk on the plains alone. Stay in the short grass, never the long grass.'

'What happens in the long grass?'

'That is where the lions sleep.'

'*Lions?*'

'Yes.'

My mouth has gone dry and I gulp gratefully at the glass of pineapple juice that has been brought for me.

'The minute you call me, I will come to you.' Dominic sits back in his chair. 'Now. Tell me your sound.'

'My sound?'

'All Maasai have a sound. When we call it, our loved ones

will know us wherever we are. If we are lost, if we need help, we make the sound.' He looks to see if I understand, but clearly sees a blank and, perhaps, even vaguely terrified expression. 'This is my sound.' He makes a high-pitched call that ends with a click. 'Now you will know me wherever I am.'

He looks at me expectantly, waiting for my sound, and I suddenly feel ridiculously tongue-tied and British. A sound. It can't be that difficult to think of a sound.

Eventually, I dig deep in my brain and then I whistle a passable impression of the Counter Terrorism Unit telephone ringtone from the series 24. If Dominic doesn't come running to my aid then perhaps Jack Bauer will although at the moment, I'm thinking that Jack Bauer would be a pretty poor substitute for a Maasai warrior.

Dominic studies me seriously. 'That is a good sound,' he says. 'Now I will always know you.'

'It's from a television show,' I explain pointlessly. 'A very good show.'

He nods to indicate that he understands. Though I think perhaps that he doesn't.

'There are animals all around the camp,' Dominic goes on, now that he has my sound marked. 'Lions, hippos, hyenas, warthogs. They are very dangerous, Mrs Janie Johnson. We must get very close to them so that you can take lovely photographs, but not close enough to let them eat you.'

'That would be good,' I agree breathlessly, even though I haven't been running.

Then Dominic throws back his head and laughs out loud and it's a wonderful, uninhibited sound. 'You should not worry so much, Mrs Johnson.'

He can laugh. As a Maasai warrior he's probably used to

lions on the loose. As a hairdresser from the Home Counties, I'm not. The only wild animal I'm used to is Archibald the Aggressive. When I booked to stay in a tented lodge, albeit a luxury one, I didn't really think through the fact that there would be animals – wild ones! – running around just outside my door. Or that I wouldn't actually have a door. Or walls. Just fabric. Thin fabric. Between me and lions and hippos and hyenas and warthogs.

Then Dominic stops laughing and is serious again. 'Do not make a frown. I will protect you.'

'Thank you,' I breathe.

And that doesn't even begin to encompass just how very, very grateful I am to have my own Maasai warrior to guard me.

Chapter 24

As the sun is starting to set, we all go back to the van and head out for a short game drive while dinner is prepared. The other driver has disappeared into the working part of the camp and now Dominic takes over as our guide. I notice that even the men in the party gape in awe at this proud warrior.

'Sit here, Mrs Janie Johnson,' Dominic instructs, patting the seat next to him. Doing as I'm told, I slip into the front alongside him while the others pile into the back of the bus.

'Are you happy?' he asks us all with a broad grin. 'Because if you are happy, then I am happy.'

We assure him that we've never been more happy – and I, for one, mean it. Then we set off with purpose, the bus bumping over the unforgiving ground. Our first foray out on the plains with the intent of seeing the local wildlife has begun in earnest.

The roof of the bus has been lifted so we have an excellent viewing area. It's still hot too, so the faint breeze it provides is very welcome. Dominic steers the bus expertly through the ruts and furrows as we cover the hard-baked uncompromising African land.

'All this,' a sweep of Dominic's arm takes in the landscape, 'should be covered in grass as tall as wheat.'

There's nothing but dust and scrub.

'We are very much needing the rain,' he says, a worried frown on his handsome face.

I think that we could send him some spare from England. It seems so unfair that we complain bitterly about having too much rain when the Maasai Mara is so very desperate for it.

'It is called a game drive,' Dominic tells us, 'because it is a *game*. Our game is to find the animals. Their game is to hide from us.' Then he gives us one of his hearty laughs.

Yet within minutes, we spot a dozen or more giraffes, their silhouettes unmistakable, even to the untrained eye, on the horizon. There's a range of sizes from the enormous male down to the cutest baby. We head towards them and then follow them at a respectful distance until they reach a copse of acacia trees where they stop to graze, oblivious to the pop-eyed, open-mouthed people in their thrall. We sit and watch them for half an hour as they go about the business of existing in this harsh climate, snapping photographs, but mostly just gazing. Then Dominic swings the bus around.

'Now we will play our game again,' and he drives us further into the plains.

We pass a warthog and four babies as they race across the ground, the mother stopping to give us a hard stare before she goes off running after her babies again. Then there's an ostrich trotting, wings flapping, beside us. Dominic points out half a dozen different species of gazelle – Thomson, Grant, impala – all with their distinct markings. A group of banded mongoose scamper across the great plain, playing together, nibbling on some tasty morsel they've uncovered, wisely scurrying home before the predators come out to play.

Then we come to another shady copse and there, beneath the

112

trees, three lionesses are dozing happily, resting before their evening's exertions. As the van approaches, one of them raises her head and checks us out and then has a good stretch and returns to her cat nap. It reminds me of Archie stretching out in front of the fire – only on steroids.

'They're magnificent,' I whisper to Dominic.

'Yes,' he agrees. 'Soon they will be hungry again.'

Now I'm worried that the windows of the bus are all open. Could a lioness get inside? Depends quite how hungry they are, I suppose.

But this is certainly a sight to behold and I never expected to be at such close quarters to a lioness, let alone three at once. So we sit and watch as the sun sinks lower and lower until, finally, we're rewarded by the sight of the lionesses stirring. They all sit up, groom themselves, yawn, stretch and eventually, as one, all stand up and slowly head out for the night's hunting.

Dominic reverses the van and their curiosity is piqued. They wander alongside of us, matching our leisurely pace, so close that my camera is useless. I can hardly believe my eyes. Three lionesses are within a metre of us. Then they turn away and wander off into the night, no doubt to put some fear into the heart of the wildebeest population.

'Are you happy, Mrs Janie Johnson?' Dominic asks.

'I'm very, very happy.'

'Good.' He gives me his trademark grin. 'Because when you are happy, I am happy.'

Chapter 25

It's past seven when we return to the camp. The last of the sun has gone and the temperature has dropped considerably. Someone has closed up my tent and a hot-water bottle has been slipped between the sheets of the bed. I enjoy the hot shower that's provided by a bucket above a rainshower head, and I'm glad to wash the dirt and dust from my skin and hair.

My clothes are filthy and crumpled from all the travel. It feels nice to finally be able to change into my clean jeans and a jumper. I brush through my wet hair and then leave it to dry naturally. I've brought some moisturiser that I slick on, but I've abandoned my make-up for the week – apart from a flick of mascara. A girl has to have one luxury.

Then I stand at the opening of my tent and, feeling self-conscious, make my 24 ringtone noise. Immediately, Dominic appears out of the darkness. His red blanket is tied around his shoulders now, his tall stick still clasped in his hand.

'It is cold tonight,' he says. 'Are you wrapped up in warm things, Mrs Janie Johnson?'

'Yes, I am,' I assure him. 'And please, it's Janie. Just Janie.'

'Then, Just Janie,' he smiles, 'you must come and sit by the fire with me.'

He offers me his arm and then escorts me to the campfire that is now blazing away, sending sparks into the all-encompassing blackness. The canopy of stars is simply stunning. A circle of chairs has been put around the fire for us all. My travelling companions are already there, drinks in hand, admiring each other's digital photographs. There's a bottle of red wine on the table and Dominic offers me a glass which I gladly accept.

I lift my glass when he gives it to me and say, 'To Kenya, to the Maasai Mara and to all its inhabitants.'

Dominic laughs. 'That is very kind.'

'Aren't you joining me?'

'I do not drink alcohol, Just Janie. A Maasai warrior must always be alert to danger.'

'Do you live far from here?'

'This is my land,' he says proudly. 'When we have visitors, I live here in the camp. All the time. When there is no one here, I go home to my village. It is only ten kilometres to walk. Not far.'

'You speak excellent English, Dominic.'

'I speak my own dialect, Swahili and English. We learn all of them from the age of two. I know many bad English swear words, Just Janie.'

'The first thing anyone learns in any language.'

'Lovely jubbly,' he says, laughing.

Then dinner is served and we move to a long table set out under the stars. We're all given plates of grilled meats and rice with beans and dishes of fragrant greens. Hurricane lamps provide romantic lighting. Once again, I find myself seated next to Dominic. Sean and Maura are quite engrossed in themselves and the two older travellers, Pat and John, seem to be getting along just fine together.

'You're not eating?' Everyone else is served, but Dominic has nothing before him.

'Maasai warriors do not eat, Just Janie. We still live on a traditional diet of milk that is fermented then mixed with the blood of our cattle. I drink this at six-thirty in the morning and again in the evening. It makes our bodies strong.'

'That's it?'

He shrugs. 'Sometimes I will take a little meat or *ugali* which is like your porridge. That is all we need.'

'I can't imagine a life without chocolate.'

He smiles indulgently at me. 'In many ways, your life is very different to mine I think.'

'Oh, goodness me. So different,' I agree. 'My life is really boring.'

'I cannot believe that.'

'It is.' I shrug. 'I live in a nice village, but it's not wild like this. I work as a hairdresser, which I quite like, but it's nothing special. Then I go home at night and watch television. I like films,' I say, then realise that this sounds particularly lame. I should say something to make my life sound more interesting, but I can't think of a single thing. I'm talking to a man who is as exotic as the wild animals on the plains, who is as different to me as chalk is to cheese and whatever I say will make me sound as dull as dishwater in comparison. 'This is the first time I've ever really been anywhere different,' I confess. 'This holiday, coming here by myself, this is the most daring thing I've ever done. If I'm honest, I feel a bit out of my depth.'

'I think that you are a very interesting person.'

'Really?' That makes me laugh. Me, interesting? 'I'm not,' I assure him. 'I don't know that much about the world.' Or anything, really.

'Then I will be very happy to share my small part of it with you.'

'Thanks.' I smile shyly.

'*Asante*,' he tells me. 'Thank you.'

'*Asante*,' I repeat.

When we've eaten, we retire to the warmth of the campfire again. But Sean and Maura don't last long before they're feigning yawns and retiring to their tent and soon, Pat and John take their leave too and head their separate ways. It's been a long and tiring day but, somehow, I don't want it to end. Dominic and I are alone again under the stars. I'm feeling mellow after good food and two glasses of wine.

Dominic produces a traditional Maasai blanket. 'This is a *kanga*,' he tells me, as he wraps it around me. 'Now you are a Maasai.'

'Thank you.'

'*Asante*,' Dominic reminds me.

'*Asante*,' I copy again as I stroke the blanket and snuggle into it. 'It's very beautiful.'

'*Karibu*. You are welcome.'

We sit silently for a moment until Dominic turns to me. 'May I ask you,' he says, 'where is your husband? Why is he not in Africa with you?'

'I've never been married,' I explain.

He looks surprised at this. 'Maasai women marry at a very young age. It is not the same in England?'

'No, no. We tend to put it off for as long as we can at home.' I think that's a joke, but I'm not so sure these days. 'It must be a mistake on the booking form that I'm down as Mrs Johnson.'

Truth be known, I probably pressed the wrong button on my computer when I filled in the details and ticked the wrong box. 'I was with someone. For seven years. But we never married.'

'He was your husband in everything but name?'

'Yes, I suppose so.'

'But why were you never his wife?'

'I don't know,' I admit. 'I don't think that we loved each other enough.'

Dominic falls quiet while he considers this.

'He left me for someone else over a year ago,' I add, not sure why I'm telling the story of my failed love life to this handsome stranger.

'That is a very bad thing to do,' he concludes.

Shrugging my shoulders, I say, 'It was probably for the best. He's happier now.' It reminds me of Paul's impending marriage, of the child on its way, of how I have been left behind. 'I think I am too.'

'There is another man?'

I think of Mike, my friend, my neighbour, and his halting, uncertain and very unexpected kiss at the airport. What will happen with Mike when I go home? Will we pick up where we left off? Will things be different between us? Will we have that dinner date and suddenly see each other in a different light? It's too complicated to think about myself, let alone explain to anyone else.

'No,' I say. 'No other man.' The conversation has dwelt on my inadequacies for too long so I ask, 'Do you have family, Dominic? A wife? Children?'

He shakes his head. 'This necklace,' he lifts the strands of colourful beads around his throat to show me, 'this is the necklace of a married man. I had taken a wife,' he says, 'when I became a warrior. That is our way. That is what we must do. Our marriage was arranged by our parents when we were very small. We were very happy together but my wife, she died two years later during the birth of our child. The child, a boy child, died too.'

'I'm sorry to hear that.'

Now it is Dominic's turn to shrug. 'It is the way of Maasai men to take a great number of wives. But I find that I cannot, Just Janie. It is the way of my people, my culture, but it is not my way.' Dominic throws another log on the fire and the sparks fly up. 'My daddy has four wives. That is a good thing. A man must have many cows and many wives and many children to be a rich man. I have many cattle, Just Janie. I could afford to buy many wives. I should have many children. That is important to my people. Now I wear the necklace of a married man, but I live alone.'

'Perhaps you're just not ready,' I suggest.

'It has been a long time. That is seen as weakness.'

'Not where I come from.' I smile at him in the darkness.

He returns it. 'We have talked for a long time. Now you must go to bed or you will be too tired for your day.'

I stand and go to walk away.

'You must let me take you home.'

Oh, God. The lions. How could I forget that?

So he escorts me to my tent and once we're beyond the light of the fire, I can hardly see an inch in front of me whereas Dominic is still foot-sure. His hand under my elbow comforts and steers me. Eventually, we reach my tent and I sigh with relief. Together, we stand on the veranda in the pitch darkness.

'Thank you, Dominic. *Asante*.'

'*Karibu*. You are most welcome, Just Janie.'

119

Then there's the most fearsome noise that vibrates through the night air, shattering the silence. It rumbles under the ground and strikes terror in my heart. I resist the urge to jump into Dominic's arms. 'What's that?'

He laughs. 'It is our lady lions. Do not be afraid. They are just telling everyone that they are out on the town. They are far away yet.'

'How far?'

'Two kilometres.'

'That sounds very near to me.'

'Soon they will be near.'

'They're coming this way?'

'Yes.' Dominic nods. 'Lie in your bed and enjoy the sounds of the night. You will be safe, Just Janie. I am here.'

And I know, just *know*, that I'm not going to get a wink of sleep.

Chapter 26

I force myself to undress. If I'm going to get eaten by a lady lion and her friends then I'm not entirely sure I want to be in my pyjamas while they do it.

Ridiculously, I make sure that my tent is securely zipped up – as if that's going to save me from a marauding pride of hungry lions. Then I slither down in the bed, sweating and not just because the hot-water bottle in here is still scalding. I've never camped before, even in a posh tent, and I'm not sure that doing it alone – particularly for the first time and, more particularly, for the first time surrounded by lions and such – is the best idea.

Reluctantly, I turn off the light. The blackest, blackest pitch black I've ever known fills my vision and I check that I have actually got my eyes open because I can see nothing, nothing at all. I'm very glad that I gave the tent a thorough bug inspection and didn't find anything with copious legs before I settled down.

Sitting around the campfire, the crackling of the flames and the spitting of the logs, plus the low murmur of conversation coming from Dominic and me, helped to disguise the many noises of the African bush at night. Now, right outside my tent, right by my head, I can hear something moving slowly through the scrub, chomping at the bushes as it goes, and it sounds like something big.

'Christ on a bike,' I mutter to myself as I lie there frozen with fear.

Then something lands on the roof of my tent and I can hear its footsteps pattering about. It sounds like it's the size of an elephant and could crash through the canvas at any moment. Do lions climb trees? I'm sure they must. Haven't I seen that on one of those David Attenborough stylee programmes? I sit up and grip the blankets around me, resisting the urge to turn on the light once more.

The lions roar again. It isn't the theatrical roar of the MGM lion, but a low feral growl designed to strike terror into the heart of all who hear it. And it works for me. Terror, in my heart, struck! It's a roar that says, 'Don't mess with me, I'm the King of the Beasts.' This time they sound close, right outside the tiny perimeter of scrubby brush that does little to separate us from the vast fearsome plains. That's when I crack and switch my light back on.

A moment later, I hear a familiar voice outside, but it still makes me jump out of my skin. 'Just Janie?' Dominic says. 'Are you happy?'

I think about saying, 'I'm fine,' but I can't actually speak, so instead I leap out of bed and unzip my tent. As I do so, I see Dominic emerging from the darkness. Simply seeing his calm presence standing there, wrapped in his cheery blanket with his sturdy stick to hand, makes me feel better instantly and my sick terror subsides. My protector looks at me with concern.

'I'm not used to the noises, to camping,' I babble. 'I'm frightened.'

'Do not be.'

'There's something on the roof of my tent.'

'It is a gennet,' he explains. 'They are very pretty. Like your domestic pussy cats at home.'

If it's anything like *my* domestic pussy cat at home, then I know that I should be afraid, very afraid. It could come and rip my head off.

'It will not harm you.'

'But it sounded so big.' And fierce. With sharp pointy teeth. I lower my voice. 'And there's something chomping outside my tent. I can hear it breathing and its stomach rumbling.'

'Ah,' he says with a smile. 'This is a hippo.'

'A hippo!' I shriek. 'Aren't they *massively* dangerous?'

'He is gone now,' Dominic laughs. 'You are not yet used to the wild animals, Just Janie. If you leave them alone, they will not hurt you. Enjoy their presence.'

'OK.' Even to my ears, I sound doubtful.

At that moment, the bushes rustle and I grab Dominic's arm. He puts his fingers to his lips, asking me to keep quiet. Seconds later and two tiny deer tiptoe into the camp and trot across by the dying embers of the campfire before disappearing into the bush at the other side.

'Dik-dik,' Dominic tells me. 'Very pretty?'

'Beautiful.'

'You were not frightened?'

'No.' I laugh at myself. 'I feel silly now.'

'Do not feel silly. This is very different for you.'

'Thank you,' I say. 'Thank you for being understanding.'

'*Hakuna matata*. No worries. I will stay here,' Dominic assures me. 'On your veranda. I will be right outside your door all night.'

'You'll sleep here?'

'Maasai warriors do not sleep. The day does not start with the heat of sun or end with the twinkling stars – it flows like a river for us. Our job is to guard the village, our women and our cattle. In the darkness, like the animals, we are awake and watchful.'

'So you'll sit here all night? Right here?'

He sits in one of my director's chairs. 'Right here.'

'All night?' Doesn't hurt to double-check, just in case there's a misunderstanding in translation.

Dominic nods. 'All night.' He sets his stick down and puts his hands on his knees. 'Good night, Janie.'

'Good night, Dominic.'

I retreat to my tent and zip it up tightly. Then I slip into bed and settle down under the covers. Lying still, I let the sounds of the night envelop me again. Something whoop, whoops and my stomach tightens.

'That is a hyena.' Dominic's soft voice comes through the fabric. His head is right next to mine. If it wasn't for the canvas of the tent, I could reach out and touch him. 'It is a fluffy dog.'

Fluffy dog, I think. Fluffy dog.

Then it all goes quiet again. The gennet patters about on the roof of my tent and now it makes me think of Archie. My body is so tired and this bed is very comfortable. Heaviness settles on my eyelids.

'Dominic?' I say sleepily.

'I am here, Just Janie.' His voice is low and soothing. 'I am here.'

'Just checking.' And with that I sink into sleep.

Chapter 27

Dominic brings me tea at five-thirty in the morning. 'Did you sleep well, Just Janie?'

I smile at him as I rub a hand through my hair, wondering just how tousled it is. 'I did. Thank you again, Dominic.'

'*Hakuna matata.*' He stands and looks down at me in my bed, his features soft in the dawn light.

I want to say more to him, to explain to him just what a comfort he was to me in the dark night, but I can't find the right words. I feel like a different woman just having him near me.

'If you are happy, then I am happy,' he says as he pours my tea. 'Today we start our game drive in half an hour. We will take a picnic breakfast. This is good?'

'Sounds fabulous.'

As planned, half an hour later we're all in the minibus again, heading off into the Maasai Mara. I take my place at the front near Dominic while Sean and Maura, Pat and John sit in the back and it seems natural that I do so. Is it my imagination or is there a special bond between Dominic and me this morning? His warm smile seems to be just for me and I'm sure that there's even more of a twinkle in his eye than there was yesterday.

We follow a winding herd of wildebeest meandering towards the Mara river, the last stragglers of the massive annual migration to the Serengeti, Dominic explains. Mixed in with them are zebras and different varieties of gazelle that are also making the journey.

'The wildebeest is an animal made from spare parts of others,' he then tells us.

It's certainly a strange and ungainly looking thing.

'It has the face of a locust, the beard of a goat, the body of a cow, the tail of a horse, the brain of a housefly and the legs of Posh Spice.'

He grins in amusement at his own joke and I smile back at him.

We see a herd of elephants traversing across the plains in search of water. There are two babies with them, which causes much oohing and aahing, and the herd gather them in protectively. As well as wildebeest, babies of any kind are vulnerable to attacks from the many predators. Then we drive down to the water's edge and stand in the bus, roof open again, to watch dozens of crocodiles marshalling as the ditzy wildebeest dither about whether to make the dangerous journey across the river or not.

'The water is full of crocodiles waiting to eat them,' Dominic says, 'but the wildebeest are willing to risk life itself to get to the green pastures on the other side.'

An hour later and there's still a stand-off between hesitant snack and hungry croc, so Dominic turns the bus away and finds us a quiet picnic spot beside the river, far away from the crocodiles, where we can have our breakfast.

Below us, however, there are around a hundred happy hippos all cuddled up together, snoozing in the water, their pink tummies turned to the sun. Sean and Maura snap away at them

126

while I help Dominic to unload our picnic box. Breakfast in the bush consists of warm pancakes, fresh fruit, yoghurt, and there's a huge thermos of coffee and one of orange juice. Along the scrubby trees by the water's edge, pretty yellow and green bee-eaters dart about searching for their own morning meal.

We spread out the fare on a Maasai blanket that's woven with blue and red checks. 'This is a tartan *kanga*,' Dominic says, 'from the McMaasai.'

Obligingly, I laugh at his silly joke and that makes him giggle more.

Then, as we wait for our companions, Dominic says, 'Look!' He puts his strong hands on my shoulders and turns me towards an acacia tree in the middle distance. 'A lilac-breasted roller.'

A strikingly beautiful bird with lilac, blue and gold plumage sings back at us. 'Oh my.'

But while I try hard to concentrate on the stunning bird, I can't help but notice how small I am against Dominic's tall rangy frame, or how taut his body is. There's not an inch of spare flesh over his powerful muscles and his strong hands on my shoulders burn through my T-shirt.

'It is very lovely, is it not?'

'Oh, yes.' I think I'm still talking about the bird.

'Lovely jubbly!'

Then Sean and Maura join us and the lilac-breasted roller flies away. 'Oh, it's gone!'

'We will see many more beautiful things, Just Janie,' he says. He squeezes my arms lightly. 'Do not worry.'

Dominic takes his hands from my shoulders and turns his attention back to our picnic. While Pat and John tuck into their breakfast, I take a photograph of Sean and Maura, arms entwined, sitting on the edge of the blanket, smiling into the lens. For the first time, I feel a pang of jealousy at their obvious happiness and I wonder whether I am destined to be alone and why I can't find someone to love who loves me in return.

We all eat while Dominic pours us coffee and orange juice. He fusses over John and Pat, helping them fill their plates. When he's seen that everyone else is catered for, he comes to join me on a convenient rock that I've found under the shade of an acacia tree, squatting down beside me. He slips his blanket from his shoulders and lays it down for me to sit on and I shift over to it. His constant small kindnesses are reassuring and heartwarming, something that you rarely see in men at home now.

'Do you have a Maasai name?' I ask.

Dominic nods. 'Lemasolai,' he says. 'It means "proud one". My family name is Ole Nangon. Dominic was the name given to me by the Christian brothers at the mission school I attended.' My guide looks into the distance. 'I was a very lucky boy. Every family had to send one child to school by law. It should have been my older brother, but he did not want to go. My daddy sent me instead.'

'Did you like it?'

'Oh, yes, Just Janie. I learned many things. I played football and now I support Arsenal.'

I laugh. 'You're teasing me.'

'No, no. They are my favourite team. Arsène Wenger, Theo Walcott. Come on, you Gunners!' He laughs uproariously and I join him. It seems so incongruous to be sitting out in the African plains with a Maasai warrior who's a staunch Arsenal supporter.

Then Dominic is serious again. 'My family made a big sacrifice to send me to the boarding school in Nakuru. Four cows. That is a lot of money to a Maasai.'

'I think it was worth it, Dominic,' I say. 'You are a lovely man.'

'Now it is my turn to say thank you. *Asante*, Just Janie.' He smiles shyly.

Sean pops up in front of us. 'Photo?'

Dominic nods and slings his arm around my shoulders, pulling me into his body with a laugh. Sean takes our photo and records, for posterity, Dominic Lemasolai Ole Nangon, the proud Maasai warrior, and Janie Johnson, the very ordinary hairdresser, under the shade of an acacia tree, sheltering from the blistering African sun.

Chapter 28

Back in the camp and I let my very welcome bucket-shower wash a pound of sandy dirt from the Maasai Mara plains out of my hair and from my body. Every muscle and bone is aching from being jolted around the bus all day, but every fibre of me is zinging and for the first time in years I feel truly, wonderfully alive.

Not that I have the ability to plug in my hair straighteners here as Nina had hoped, but I do wish that I was able to spruce myself up a bit more. Then I realise that I want to look my best for Dominic and my heart flips as I recognise the significance.

Dinner is served outside again and we have a tender goat curry in a creamy coconut sauce with big bowls of fluffy rice and hot chapattis. Dominic doesn't eat again, but sits and watches us all with that big happy smile of his firmly in place. Every now and again, I catch him looking at me along the table, over the light of the hurricane lamps, and his grin broadens. Despite the fact that everyone can see him, I feel as if it's a secret smile, just for me – not for Sean and Maura or Pat and John, but for me alone. Butterflies start fluttering in my stomach, not the butterflies of job interviews or driving tests but the sort that reserve themselves only for blossoming love.

After our meal, we sit around the campfire again. The sparks fly into the air and the heat from the flames warms our toes. Not that it's a cold night, but after the relentless sun of the day, it's a cooler and more welcome temperature. We all laugh together, talking about our day's drive and the animals we have seen, from huge buffalo to tiny bee-eating birds. Dominic has proved himself, once again, to be a skilled and knowledgeable guide. But then this is his home, where he grew up, all he knows, and he is a man in total synchronicity with his land.

It's a habit that we seem to be sliding into, but the others leave us after about half an hour of pleasant chit-chat and left to our own devices, Dominic and I settle down in our chairs and I notice that he moves his closer to mine. He pours me a glass of Amarula, a creamy liqueur made of marula fruit, which I sip, savouring the taste.

'This is lovely,' I say with a contented sigh. 'The day has been exhausting but just brilliant.' I let my head drop back and gaze up at the black glittering sky.

Dominic reaches out and takes my hand in his. I turn to look at him. The fire has died down and it's hard to make out his expression in the darkness.

'We are from very different lands,' he says softly, 'from very different cultures, but I feel that your heart sings to me, Janie Johnson, and I believe that my heart sings to you too.'

My breath catches in my throat as together we watch the fire-light flicker, flare and fade.

'Am I wrong to think this?' Concern laces his voice.

'No,' I say. 'Not at all.' Tears spring to my eyes. 'I wasn't looking for love, Dominic. I thought that it wasn't for me. And never, not in a million years, did I expect to find it here in Africa.'

'I was not looking for love either, Just Janie.' He grins at me. 'But I think we may have found it.'

We both laugh, hesitantly.

'It is a game,' he continues, 'like looking for the wild animals. When you want to see them most, they hide away! Love is the same. You can look and look and look and find nothing. Then, when you are not looking, suddenly it springs out at you or creeps up from behind!'

A breeze ruffles the acacia trees and fans the flames of the fire. We bask in its glow. Dominic pulls the warm Maasai *kanga* tighter around my shoulders.

'What do we do now?' I want to know.

'We must be very respectful of our companions,' he says seriously. 'I do not want them to think that I neglect my duty to them.'

'No, no. Of course not.'

'Then we will look at my country together and I will show you wonderful things.'

But with a secret between us, an extra special bond. 'I can't wait.'

'Now you must go to bed, Just Janie. We have a long day again tomorrow.'

'I don't want to leave you.'

'I will be outside your tent all night and every night,' he assures me, 'for as long as you need me.' With that, he stands and says, 'Come, Janie.' He escorts me away from the fire and back to my tent, his arm slung casually around my shoulders.

There, in the pitch darkness on the veranda, he takes me into his arms and holds me tight and I let my soft body mould against his.

'Maasai men do not kiss women,' he says softly as he strokes my cheek. 'I think that this is a mistake.'

Dominic lifts my face to his and his lips find mine and it is so different to anything I've ever experienced before. He tastes of Africa, of the wild, of the untamed, which is at odds with the full, gentle sensuality of his mouth, the tenderness of his kiss. I lose myself in the moment, letting the night, the sensations, overwhelm me. If I were to die now, I would die a very happy woman.

Then I remember the lions prowling around the camp and think that perhaps I'd rather not die at all. Perhaps I'd rather just stay here in his arms for ever, miles away from the hairdressing salon, from my twee little village of Nashley, from the life that I have known.

Slowly unwinding me from our embrace, Dominic then zips open my tent for me and I step inside. A lion roars in the darkness and is answered by the trumpet of an elephant. This time I don't quiver with fear, but that's because Dominic is here.

I reach out and touch his arm. 'You'll be here?'

'Always.' He lays his blanket on the floor across the opening to my tent. 'Right here. Tonight you will not be afraid.'

'No, I won't be.' I stand on tiptoe to kiss him again. 'Good night, Dominic.'

'*Usiku mwema*. Good night, Just Janie. Sleep tight,' he says with a grin on his face. 'Don't let the lions bite.'

And, inside my tent, I lie down in the dark next to him.

Chapter 29

So, as it always is when you want time to pass slowly, the rest of the week positively races by. A week is such a tiny amount of time and I'm wishing now that I could stay longer – weeks, months, perhaps never go home to Buckinghamshire again.

Each day we go out on game drives. Once early in the morning when the daytime animals are stirring and the night-time prowlers are going home to bed, then again in the late afternoon when the sun is lower and the heat is slowly seeping out of the day. That's the time when the predators are up and about and ready to feed. We bump around in the van, thanking God for digital cameras that allow us to take more photographs than we'd ever planned for: lions, cheetahs, buffalo, zebras, rhinos, hippos, giraffes, monkeys, baboons, warthogs, jackals, a dozen different type of antelope and more weird and wonderful birds than I'll ever be able to remember. Dominic, as he promised, has shown us all some wonderful sights.

Now it is our very last evening here at the Kiihu camp. Tomorrow, the other driver takes over again and escorts us on the long dusty drive back to Nairobi. Already it feels like my heart might break.

After dinner, we all linger around the campfire, wanting to make our last evening stretch and stretch, prolonging the agony of departure. For me, more than the others, I never want this night to end. Perhaps they're going back to full and enjoyable lives and the wrench won't seem too difficult. Perhaps they want to be back in their own bed, with their own cup of tea, back to loved ones, to a job they adore. All I can think of is that I'll be going home without Dominic.

We've had a great week together and I think the growing tenderness between us has been hard to hide from our travelling companions. They've all smiled indulgently at us as we've become welded to each other's sides or he has slung his arm around my shoulders, helped me more tenderly from the bus than anyone else. Whenever we've been able to, we've spent time alone together talking, laughing, learning about each other's lives and I know that I've never felt so at ease with anyone before. I have forgotten all that is familiar, all that is waiting for me at home, and have lived just for the here and now. However, as much as I want to deny and delay it, the time for parting is almost upon us.

When the embers die down and the sounds of the night grow louder – the whoop of the hyenas, the low menacing roar of the lions, the grunting of the warthogs – we all take leave of each other, bracing ourselves for the early start in the morning. In silence, Dominic walks me back to my tent and in the darkness, he holds me in his arms.

'What will we do?' I ask him.

'You will go back to your life, Just Janie, and you will very soon forget me.'

'No,' I protest. 'Never.'

'We have different lives. What else can we do?'

135

'Is that what you want? That I just go home and forget you?'

'No.' He strokes my face with his long elegant fingers. 'I do not.'

'We'll work something out,' I promise. 'Some way to stay in touch. Can you get access to a computer?'

'Yes,' he says. 'There is one in the nearest town, just a fifteen-kilometre walk.'

'Fifteen kilometres to get to a computer?'

Dominic nods as if this is not a problem.

'We could do that then, at the very least.' I realise that I'm clutching at straws. How often are we going to be able to coordinate an instant chat? Dominic is going to have to walk all that way just to pick up a message from me or an email. Will he soon tire of doing that? I can call him. Even in the plains of Africa, there's excellent mobile phone coverage and Dominic has a phone for work, but he can't afford to call me or to text me. It's a ridiculous amount of money and I'd struggle to find the cash for regular calls too. Why does the only man that I've ever fallen in love with have to be on the other side of the world, living in a time warp?

'You must sleep.'

'No,' I say, 'not yet. I want to stay awake all night with you. I want to lie in your arms.'

I would never normally consider doing this, but I have to face the fact that Dominic and I might never get another chance to be together and I can't let this moment slip through my fingers.

'Stay with me,' I beg, unable to help myself. 'Stay with me tonight.'

In the darkness, I see him nod. We unzip the tent and, together, step inside.

Falling into each other's arms for the first time, we kiss passionately and with total abandon. Slowly we undress each other, Dominic shrugging off his red tunic, *shuka*, to stand naked before me. His body is like carved teak and I tremble as I run my fingers over his skin. I lift the strands of beads, his wedding band, from around his neck and lay them carefully on his *shuka*. He lifts me onto the bed and we lie in each other's arms. The scent of his skin is intoxicating, alien, and I want to breathe him in for ever. My love smells of musk and spices and the Maasai Mara.

We make love, which is insane, but my body, my heart, can't help it. I want this man inside me, body and soul. I gasp with pleasure as we join together and I see the answering joy in his eyes. Dominic moves above me in the black night and never before have I felt so fulfilled, so complete as a woman. I had no idea that it was possible to feel like this. Tears roll from my eyes.

He kisses them away. 'Do not cry, Janie. You must be happy.'

Lying in his arms, my fingers trace the scars on Dominic's body. 'Where are these from?'

'Lions,' he says. He shows me a livid scar on his thigh. 'This is where a big lion had its jaws around me. My brother, Joseph, saved me.'

'You were attacked by a lion?'

My lover shrugs. 'I hunted a lion,' he tells me. 'It was part of the ritual to become *ilmoran* – a warrior, a man. A way to show your strength.'

'Wasn't it terrifying?'

'Oh, yes,' he laughs, 'but you are not allowed to show it. If you show fear then your family will not speak to you for many, many years. It is unforgivable for a Maasai to be weak. People must respect you or the shame is too much to bear.' Dominic slings his arm above his head. 'Our customs are changing. We do not hunt lions any more. Now we treat the lion as a brother. If we do not look after the lion then the tourists will not come to see him and the Maasai can no longer live just by their cattle.' He smiles at me. 'We need you to come to Kiihu camp.'

'I wish you could see my world,' I say to him wistfully. 'Our lives are so easy compared to yours.'

'That is the way of life, Just Janie. We must accept it.' His dark fingers travel my body. 'I see you have no scars from wild animals.'

'No. No scars at all.' Only on my heart, I think, and I've just sustained one that will never fade.

We lie together, me fighting sleep all the way, until the first light of dawn creeps over the horizon and it's time for me to go.

Chapter 30

It's pouring down with rain and it's seven degrees. I shiver with cold. Mike is waiting at the barrier in the arrivals hall at Heathrow with a handwritten sign saying, WELCOME HOME JANIE! I force a smile when I see him, though my heart feels as heavy as lead.

Mike is beaming, solicitous. He pats me on the back, saying, 'Well, well, well,' and immediately takes my case from me. 'You look fabulous. That African sun has given you a healthy glow and some freckles.' Together, we march out of the airport and towards the car park, Mike's hand under my elbow, guiding me.

I feel shell-shocked, like a woman who has awoken from a dream – a lovely dream. Every mile I travel away from Dominic, it seems that another little piece of my heart splinters away. The greyness, the icy needles of rain, the press of people – these seem more remote to me now than the colour and heat of the African plains. Do I really live here? Is this dirty, noisy, freezing place my home?

'Archie's been missing you.'

'Has he?' I realise that I really want to see my curmudgeonly cat, and risk life and limb by giving him a big cuddle.

'Well, you know Archie,' Mike admits, meaning that as long as someone has been opening a tin for him, he's been fine. 'Did you have a great trip? I thought of you all the time,' Mike gabbles on. 'I was very jealous.'

'It was marvellous,' I manage, hardly able to find my voice.

'Better than you expected?'

'Yes, more than I could ever have imagined.' How true is that?

'What did you see? The Big Five?'

'Yes,' I say. 'Yes, we did.'

We dodge the traffic on the perimeter road and even though we had to contend with the legendary rush of traffic in Nairobi, it seems like nothing compared with this. Mike nips nimbly through the cars while I lag behind him, moving like a sloth. How ridiculously cramped England seems compared to the vast openness of the Maasai Mara.

'Everything all right?' Mike asks, a frown of concern on his brow.

'Yes, yes,' I say. 'I'm fine. I'm sorry I'm a bit quiet. It's just been a very long journey back.' I raise a tired smile. 'All I want now is a cup of tea and a hot bath.'

Mike throws my case in the back and then we slip into the car. Can it only be a week since we were last here? So much has happened that I don't think my brain can process it.

'Thank you, Mike. This is so kind of you to pick me up.'

'Nonsense,' he says, 'no thanks necessary. It's my pleasure.'

My friend, my neighbour, seems ludicrously pleased to see me and in other circumstances, I'm sure that would give me the lift I need. But since our kiss, I feel that things have changed between us and then, since Dominic, I feel my whole world has shifted on its axis and it's taking some getting used to.

140

'I know you're tired,' Mike steers the car out of the airport and onto the motorway, 'but I've sort of made a casserole, if you're up for it. Thought you wouldn't feel like cooking.'

'That's very thoughtful.' He's right, I don't feel like cooking. I don't feel like going back to work. I don't feel like myself at all.

I sink into the seat and let the thrum of motorway traffic lull me into a trance. The rain and the grey sky blur away and all I can see is the wide blue African sky and the vast open Mara stretching ahead of me.

'You really are OK?' Mike can sense that something is wrong. 'You weren't mugged or anything like that?'

'No, no,' I assure him. 'Nothing like that.'

My heart was stolen, that's all, I want to say to him. I know exactly who has taken it. It's out there on the African plains with Dominic Ole Nangon, Maasai warrior and wonderful man. And I have no idea how I might get it back.

Chapter 31

Mike carries my case into the cottage and then fusses around me for no particular purpose. Archie comes to wind himself around my legs and I bend to stroke him, burying my face in his neck, which he tolerates benignly for a few seconds before scooting away, homecoming ritual completed. Now he heads to the kitchen and the cupboard where his food is kept and feigns hunger, acting out that he hasn't been fed at all for the week I've been away and that Mike, a poor substitute, has totally neglected him.

On the table is a small box of groceries. 'Oh, Mike. Thank you.' *Asante.* 'That's very kind of you.'

'Just a few things to tide you over until you can go shopping. Wouldn't want our boy to starve.' He flicks a look at Archie's Oscar-worthy performance. 'I'll go and put the casserole on to warm,' my neighbour says. 'See you in an hour?'

'That will be lovely.'

And with that, Mike takes his leave.

I look around my tiny cottage and it seems like an alien place. There's a weird sense of disconnect that I can't begin to explain. My twee little knick-knacks, my floral curtains. Did I really choose these? I hardly recognise my own home. How can that have happened in so short a time? It seems so unutterably English. Ridiculously so. This is a million miles away from the Maasai Mara. A fiddly little watercolour compared to big, bold brushstrokes. I wonder what Dominic would think of it here? He'd bang his head a lot, that's for sure.

It's five in the afternoon and already I need the lights on. The cottage feels chilly as no one has been here for the week and I click the central heating up a notch or two and the pipes clang into life. No campfire to snuggle up to around here.

I feed Archie, who then turns his back on me to eat – cupboard love – and I go upstairs, heaving my suitcase behind me. In the bedroom, I plonk it onto the bed and open it. On top of the case is Dominic's *kanga*, his Maasai blanket which he gave me as a keepsake. I hold the bright red and orange striped fabric to me and inhale deeply. The scent of Dominic, of Africa, comes flooding back and tears rush to my eyes.

Part of me should be happy to be back at Little Cottage. Isn't there usually a sense of relief when you land on home turf once again? The going away is marvellous and, usually, the coming back is even better. Your own bed, your own pillow, your own cup of tea made exactly as you like it. But not this time. This time I don't care about these things. This time a part of me has stayed in Africa and I wonder how long it will take for me to feel whole again.

The red light on the answerphone is flashing and I flick it on to play back the messages. One is from Nina hoping that I'm back safely. All of the others are from Lewis 'The Moron' Moran, wondering when we'll be able to 'hook up' again. Never, I think. Not in my lifetime nor the next. Not until Jimmy Carr tells clean jokes. Not until Terry Wogan stops waffling. Not until Simon Cowell needs to claim Jobseeker's Allowance.

I wrap Dominic's *kanga* around my shoulders and sit on the bed, thinking about where I was just the night before last, on the plains of Africa, lying happily in his arms.

After a few moments, I realise that I'm going to have to move myself, otherwise Mike's casserole will be burnt and I'll still be sitting here, pining. In the bathroom, I run the hottest bath you've ever known while thinking guiltily of a people to whom water is the most precious commodity. I strip off my travel-worn clothes and sink into it, letting the water soothe my weary bones and my weary heart.

Half an hour later and the water is cold and the colour of caramel. It seems as if I brought half of the Maasai Mara home with me on my body. I wash the dust from my hair and it feels strange using my hairdryer and straighteners again.

I slip on an old Juicy Couture velour tracksuit – I can hardly *stand* up, let alone *posh* up. And it's only Mike, for goodness' sake. He won't expect me to make an effort. Then I root in the bottom of my carry-on bag for the presents I bought for my neighbour – a hastily purchased bottle of Amarula and two CDs of African music at Nairobi airport. Downstairs, I also grab a bottle of wine from the rack.

Kissing Archie, I say, 'I won't be long, just going next door,' and he looks at me reproachfully as if to say, 'You're back *five minutes* and you're going *again?*'

Knocking at Mike's door, I feel nervous and I don't know why. He's all smiles as he lets me in.

'Perfect timing,' he says. 'It's just ready.' There are wonderful aromas coming from the direction of the kitchen.

'Here.' I hand over my presents and the bottle of wine.

'You shouldn't have.'

'Just a little thank you for my lift.'

'I wouldn't have it any other way, Janie,' he insists. 'You know that.'

'Thanks, anyway.'

'I'll put this on.' He takes the CDs, slots one into his player and the sounds of rhythmic African music fill the room. It seems strangely out of context here in swinging, ringing Nashley.

Mike's cottage is much bigger than mine, but still has a homely feel. He has three bedrooms to my single one and a much larger living room and kitchen. It's a lovely place, but I have to say that a lot of it remains a shrine to Tania. The telly is bigger now and there's also a Wii and a selection of boys' shoot-'em-up-type games, but little else has changed. I don't think that his wife took very much with her when she left. Though today, I note that the dozens of photographs of them doing coupley things have been removed from the windowsill. Another sign, perhaps, that Mike is keen to move on?

'Ready for dinner?' he asks.

I nod and we go through to the kitchen where the table is set for two. A candle flickers in the middle. I've been to dinner here a million times and a candle has never featured before.

'Can I help?'

'No, no,' he insists. 'All under control.' Then he looks slightly bashful as I take my seat.

Mike dishes up and places a beautifully prepared plate of food in front of me. Among his other attributes, Mike is an excellent cook.

He pops the cork and pours me a glass of hearty red before he sits down opposite me. Lifting his glass to mine, he says, 'It's good to have you home.'

I want to say, 'It's good to be home,' but the words just won't come. Is it good to be home? I think the jury's out on that one. Instead, I swig my wine and nod like a loon.

So we eat dinner together and listen to the African music and soon the wine makes me relax. If I try very hard I can go minutes without thinking about Dominic. Perhaps the African music was a mistake.

Before nine o'clock, I'm yawning and sinking lower in my chair.

'You need an early night, young lady,' Mike advises.

I laugh but I'm glad to have the excuse to take my leave. 'I am very tired,' I say. 'Dinner was wonderful, very thoughtful.'

'You know that you're welcome anytime, Janie.'

'I'll reciprocate during the week,' I promise.

'I'll hold you to that,' Mike warns and then he moves towards me, but before he can do whatever he thinks he might be about to do, I sidestep away from him and head for the door. Was Mike planning to kiss me then? I think he might have been.

'Good night,' I say. 'Thanks again.' Then I tiptoe down my path in the dark and let myself back into my own cottage.

I get ready for bed and Archie, having done several rounds of the bed, comes to settle by my pillow. Before I slip under the duvet, I pull Dominic's *kanga* around my shoulders and go to the window. I look out to the patch of cloudy sky that's visible between the towering oak trees and think of the endless span of African sky laden with stars and wonder where my love is now. He is out there, somewhere, under the same sky as me.

'Good night, Dominic,' I offer up to the universe. *'Usiku mwema.* Good night.'

146

Chapter 32

Monday morning. Eight o' clock. Back at work. Meh!

Nina is already in the staffroom. 'My God,' she says when she sees me. 'Look at you. A week in the Mexican sun has done you a world of good.'

'African,' I remind her as I shrug off my winter coat. 'I went to Africa.'

'Mexico, Africa,' she says. 'Is it not all the same place? Did you have a good time.'

'Fabulous,' I say with a sigh.

'Hmm,' my friend says. 'So why the long face?'

I sit down next to her. My first client isn't due for another twenty minutes, so there's time for a coffee to try to revive me. I was awake at four o'clock this morning and now, just as I start my working day, I'm already on my knees with tiredness. 'I don't really want to be back,' I confess.

'That good?'

I nod.

'You should have had another week.'

'I don't even think that would have done it.'

My friend nudges me. 'Was there a man involved?'

147

Trust Nina to cut to the chase. 'Yes. There was.'

'Glad you took those condoms?' she laughs.

'Yes, I am, but do you know, I wouldn't care if I was pregnant,' I say rather rashly. Perhaps I shouldn't have been my usual sensible self. Perhaps I should have thrown caution to the wind and let fate run its course. 'Actually, I'd rather like to be pregnant with his baby.' At least I would have brought part of Dominic home with me from Africa.

'Woaw,' Nina says. 'Are you mad?' She looks at me as if she's never seen me before. 'That's a bit random. What happened to cautious Janie "I'm not looking for love" Johnson? Who is this strange woman before me?'

'I hardly know myself,' I admit.

'Coffee,' Nina declares. 'Strong coffee. That's what you need.' She clatters about doing the honours. When she hands me my cup, she asks, 'Have you had a blow to the head on this holiday, perhaps?'

A blow to the heart, I think.

'Has the sun scrambled your brain?'

'I don't know,' I tell her. 'But if it has, it feels great.'

'So,' Nina says, 'more about this guy that seems to have knocked you sideways, please. Photos?'

'He's called Dominic,' I tell her and feel the smile returning to my face. 'And he's wonderful. For the first time in my life, my *whole* life, I feel . . . ' Dare I even say it aloud? ' . . . I feel as if I'm in love.'

Nina looks taken aback. 'Love?'

I shrug. 'What more can I say?'

'Love?' she repeats, nonplussed. 'Does he feel the same?'

'Yes, I think so.'

'Wow.' She digs into her daily carrier bag of fruit. Clearly this news cannot be stomached without the aid of an apple or two. 'When are you going to see him again?'

'I don't know,' I admit. 'That's the tricky part.'

'Where does he live?'

I look at her as if she's mad. 'In Africa. In Kenya. In the Maasai Mara.'

'Oh,' my friend says. 'I thought that he was someone that you'd met on your trip, but that he was from England.'

'No. He was our guide. He lives out in the Mara.'

'You do know how to pick them,' she sighs. 'I might have known that you wouldn't fall in love with someone who lives at the end of your road.'

I don't remind my friend that when she thought 'Miserable' Mike and I were getting a bit too cosy, she wasn't in favour of that either.

'I've still had a dozen calls from Lewis while I've been away,' I tell Nina. 'I hoped he would have given up while I've been gone. Can you have another word with Gerry?'

'Ah,' Nina says, 'that might be a bit tricky.'

I wait for her to explain.

'Gerry and I aren't really speaking at the moment,' she says, avoiding my eyes. 'He's going through one of his funny phases.'

That means he's disappearing without explanation, staying out late, coming home boozed up and smelling of other women's perfume – and worse.

'Oh, Nina.'

'I'm sure he's seeing someone else,' she confides. 'He swears blind that he isn't but . . . you know how it is.'

This does seem to be a regular occurrence with Gerry. For as long as Nina and Gerry have been together, it's been the same pattern, recurring with increasing regularity. With the passing years, he's showing no signs of becoming a one-woman man.

'Are you at home?'

My friend nods. 'Had a couple of nights at my mum's while you were away, but I'm back there now. Things are a bit tense though.' Nina chews furiously on her Golden Delicious. Sometimes I wish my friend would just take up smoking again.

'You can't go on like this,' I point out.

'What else do you suggest I do? Leave him? And go where? Do what?'

'I don't know.'

'He's been my life, Janie. He's the only man I've known since I was a teenager. How do you turn your back on that?'

It's probably best that I don't point out that it seems to be no trouble for Gerry.

'Has your new man got a fit brother? Perhaps that would give me the impetus I need.' She laughs at her own suggestion. 'Anyway, no more of my woes. Have you got a picture of this bloke?'

'Not yet,' I say. 'I haven't had time to look at my photos. I got home quite late and then Mike had cooked dinner for us both.'

'Good God,' Nina says. 'He's more like a husband to you than Paul ever was.'

We giggle together, but I don't tell her about the kissing incident at Heathrow or Mike's hesitant suggestion that we might take our friendship further. At the moment, the less Nina knows about that the better.

Cristal pokes her head around the door. 'Your clients are here.'

'Oh, joy,' Nina says. 'The tousled hair of Buckinghamshire awaits us.'

My holiday is now officially well and truly over. I push all thoughts of Dominic aside and prepare to pick up my scissors once more.

Chapter 33

When I get home that night, Sean has kindly sent me an email with the photograph of Dominic and me under the acacia tree as an attachment. I stare at it for a long, long time, transfixed, my emotions whirling. Eventually, I go and borrow some photographic paper from Mike so that I can print it out.

'Fancy a film tonight?' my neighbour asks.

'Maybe I'll give it a miss,' I say. 'I'm still really tired.'

I daren't admit to him that on the way home from work, I popped into the DVD shop and rented *Out of Africa* and *The Lion King* and that my plan for this evening is to watch them back-to-back. But as I might well cry, I also plan to view them alone.

'Perhaps another night,' he suggests. 'Or maybe we could go out for that dinner I promised you. At the end of the week. When you're feeling up to it.'

Ah, so he hadn't forgotten.

'Let's see how it goes.'

Mike is clearly disappointed, but is trying not to show it. 'Are things OK between us?'

'Yes, of course they are.' Would this be a good time to tell him about Dominic? But then I think, what's the point when the chances are that I'll never, ever in my entire life see Dominic again? I'll get over him. In time I'll get over him and then, who knows, perhaps I'll be able to see Mike in a different light. Goodness knows, he ticks all the right boxes for enough women. Me included.

It's just that, at this moment, I've fallen for someone with dark eyes and chocolate brown skin, with a smile that would rival the sun and who counts lion wrestling as one of his skills. That's a lot to compete with.

'Don't worry about me,' I reassure him when his frown fails to go away. 'I'm just a bit ... out of sorts.' Ridiculously, hopelessly lovesick, I mean, but fail to say.

I thank him for the photographic paper and hotfoot it back to my little house. There, in my utility-room-cum-office, where my washing machine and my computer nestle cosily side by side, I seek refuge. The pile of washing from my holiday is still there and seems rather reproachful, a little scattering of dust from the Maasai Mara has settled on my tiled floor. I'll get to it just as soon as I've done this. I sit at the tiny desk and print out the picture. After a bit of whirring and chugging, it's in my hot little hands. Dominic's smile beams out and I'm looking up at him, quite clearly, even to the untrained eye, totally besotted.

I log onto Facebook. I don't harbour much hope that Dominic will have made the long arduous walk to the nearest village with a computer to try to make contact. But when I pull up my profile page I'm shocked to see that there, right in front of me, is a friend request from one Dominic Ole Nangon.

My heart flips with joy. There's a message attached and I read it and re-read it and then I read it again. There are some pleasantries. He hopes that I had a safe journey home. He tells me that there has still been no rain. This week, he recounts, his new group saw a leopard up a tree – a very rare sighting. Then I see what I was hoping for. He's missing me, it says. He's missing me very much. I sit back in my chair. It wasn't my imagination, Dominic cares for me just as much as I care for him.

I type him an effusive note. I tell him that my journey was safe. That I hope there will soon be rain. Then I tell him that I'm missing him too, missing him very much. I'm sure that my heart is sighing with relief. I'm just so glad that we've managed to make contact. I've got the sum total of about twenty friends on Facebook – a couple of girls from the salon, a few old school friends – I hardly ever use it, could never much see the point in it. Now I'm sure I'll be checking it every night to see whether there's something from Dominic for me.

I don't let the thoughts of how on earth we can possibly progress this relationship mar my happiness at hearing from him. How will I ever get to see him again? *When* will I get to see him again? Is there hope for us? I wonder. Is there hope that we could, against all the odds, make this work?

In the kitchen, I open a bottle of wine, give Archie an impromptu hug that makes him howl in protest, then I throw the washing into the machine. Dominic's message has given me a spring in my step and a song in my heart.

Taking the bottle and glass through to the living room, I put on the first of the DVDs. Archie curls up on my lap and I pull Dominic's *kanga* over us both – my new security blanket. Its vivid colours are out of place in my pastel, flowery cottage and that makes me love it all the more. Together, without Mike, Archie and I watch *Out of Africa* and *The Lion King* and I cry and cry and cry, but I'm not sure whether it's because I'm sad or because I'm deliriously happy.

Chapter 34

Tuesday morning. Eight o'clock. Second day back at work. Meh!

The Christmas rush has started in earnest and my book is virtually full for the day. Then Nina phones in sick, citing a cold, and some of her clients are pushed in with me, which means that I won't even get a lunch break and my feet and legs will be throbbing in agony by the time I get home. The rest of Nina's appointments are dished out between the other stylists.

I worry that Nina is having more problems with Gerry as she's rarely ill and, if she was planning a sneaky day off, then she would have told me in advance so that I knew I'd need to cover for her. I text her to see whether everything is OK and ten minutes later she replies that no, she isn't all right, and can I go to her house on my way home from work.

All I want to do is sit in the staffroom all day and gaze at my photograph of Dominic and think about the sights and sounds of Africa, but that's obviously been thwarted. I'm so busy that I don't even have time to show him to my regulars who are whipped in and out with alarming speed to accommodate Nina's appointments. Anyone who came here today seeking a relaxing experience will have been sadly disappointed.

155

I'm sure I catch a glimpse of Lewis skulking outside the salon, but I'm too rushed off my feet to even think about him. Cristal is in a foul mood all day because she thinks she's overworked and the boys have another round of bitch-slapping because Tyrone has to do one of Nina's clients who Clinton is convinced fancies him. The clients do nothing but whine all day long. Kelly's in a foul mood too because she likes everything to run smoothly and it's a long way from that today. By home time, I could joyfully kill the lot of them. Huh, and they think the struggle for survival is tough in the Maasai Mara!

So at six o'clock, I swing into Nina's driveway when I would really rather be heading straight home to lie down in a darkened room. The salon was absolutely manic and, if Nina is away again, tomorrow is going to be even worse.

My friend opens the door without me needing to knock and I can tell from her puffy eyes and face that she's spent the whole day crying. In the hallway, I take her into my arms. 'Honey, honey, honey,' I say as I rock her. 'What's the matter, hey? Tell Auntie Janie all about it.'

'He's seeing someone else,' Nina sniffs. 'I know he is.'

'Let me put the kettle on.' I steer my friend towards the kitchen, sit her down at the table and flick the kettle on. I hand her the kitchen roll and, gratefully, she rips off a piece and sniffles into it. 'Have you eaten?'

My friend shakes her head.

'Chicken soup,' I instruct and then rummage in her cupboards until I find a tin of said chicken soup.

'I think it's supposed to be mother's homemade,' Nina notes.

'Beggars can't be choosers,' I point out and that makes her laugh.

'He was away at the weekend,' Nina says while I open the

soup and tip it into a saucepan. 'Supposedly on a business conference, but I found a bill yesterday in his pocket. Double room
at some posh spa. I called them to ask if there'd been a conference there for his work and not a sausage. It was just him and
her. Lying bastard.'

'Oh, Nina.' I pour the soup into a bowl for her and put it
down on the table, sliding it in front of her. Then I hand her a
spoon. My friend toys with the surface of the soup, picking out
bits of the chicken and letting them fall back in the bowl.

'This is not how marriage is supposed to be,' she complains.
'It's supposed to be about trust and growing old together and
shared history. All we have is secrets and hurt and uncertainty.'

'You have to talk to Gerry.'

'Don't you think that I've tried? Even faced with this,' she
waves the offending receipt at me, 'he denies everything. He just
thinks that I'm stupid. We argued all last night about it, that's
why I couldn't face coming into work this morning. I'm
exhausted, Janie.' Nina starts crying again. 'Now he's gone off
and I haven't seen him all day. He's not answering his mobile
and I don't know where he is.'

'He'll come back,' I promise her. 'He always does.'

'I don't know,' Nina whispers. 'Maybe this time it's for good.'

'What you have to decide, my love, is whether you want him
back or not.'

'Of course I do,' she says. 'I love him. Do you think that I
want some other bitch waltzing off with him?'

Why can't love always be the nice, grinny, happy love? Why
does it always come with heartache and pain attached? I think
of the photograph of Dominic in my handbag that I'm so desperate to show Nina, but how can I waffle on happily about my
love when hers seems to be crumbling down about her ears?

Chapter 35

The week goes by in a blur and already my holiday seems like a million years ago. I log on to Facebook without much hope in my heart but when my page comes up, there's a message in my inbox from Dominic. Just a few lines, but nevertheless they make my weary heart soar. When I've replied and pressed 'send', Mike's knock comes at my door.

'Hey,' he says when I open up. 'Thought we might be able to fix up that dinner date.'

'Oh, Mike, I've had a terrible week,' I tell him. 'Nina's been off and I've been doing her appointments too. I can hardly string a sentence together, let alone promise to be interesting dinner company.'

'There's a new restaurant opened in Cranway, right by the canal, The Barge Brasserie.' Mike pulls an apologetic face as he perches on the edge of the sofa. 'I've already made a booking for tomorrow night. I didn't think you'd be doing anything.'

Is that how dull my life is? Mike is so convinced that I'll be sitting alone on a Saturday night that he doesn't even need to check with me first? The sad thing is that he's right.

'Is that OK?' He picks up the DVDs of *Out of Africa* and *The Lion King* and fiddles with them.

How can I say no now? My resolve and my heart soften. I know that Mike has really been looking forward to this. Plus I look at the DVDs in his hands and wonder how much more *Out of Africa* and *The Lion King* I can watch. Pining for something that I can't have isn't doing me any good at all.

'That'll be fine,' I say. 'What time?'

'Pick you up at seven-thirty?'

'Seven-thirty it is.' I won't be home from work until at least six-thirty so that'll be a quick turnaround. But it's just Mike so he won't be expecting me to look like Nicole Kidman on a red carpet night.

The Barge Brasserie used to be a ratty old canal-side pub, serving stale sandwiches and drinks that tasted of cleaning fluid. Now it's had a multimillion-pound revamp and is unrecognisable. The dining room is warm, cosy and a stainless-steel fire slap-bang in the middle is a stunning and functional centrepiece. The tables and chairs are thrown together eclectically, no chain uniformity here, and the effect is very pleasing.

The menu, too, is appealing and Mike orders a steak and I order a prawn curry. My neighbour and I have eaten out together dozens of times, but usually it's a pizza-and-glass-of-plonk sort of dinner. This is altogether different. Tonight, Mike is wearing a very smart shirt that I haven't seen before and I'm worried that he's bought it specially for the occasion, so I don't comment on it at all. Thankfully, I have thrown on a frock, so I don't feel underdressed.

'This is nice,' he says, surveying the restaurant.

'Lovely.'

'I've heard very good things about it.'

Our table is by the window and due to judiciously placed lighting, the canal is beautifully illuminated. In summer this will be a wonderful spot, popular with families, I'm sure. Tonight, it seems to be the haunt of romantic couples. Damn.

'It's a long time since we've done this,' Mike remarks as we settle ourselves in seats facing each other.

I'm not sure that we've ever done it at all.

A bottle of champagne turns up. 'Oh,' I say. 'For us?'

'I took the liberty,' Mike admits. 'No harm in pushing the boat out every now and again. Besides, we've not had a chance to celebrate your return from Africa.'

'I only went for a week, Mike,' I protest.

The waiter pours our champagne into tall flutes.

'A week too long,' Mike says as he lifts his glass to mine. We clink them together and then sip at the bubbles. 'You haven't really said much about it,' he notes. 'Was it all you hoped it would be?'

More, I want to say, so much more. And I want to tell him about Dominic, but how can I in this situation? Clearly Mike thinks that this is more than two mates having a rare night out together and I don't want to burst his bubble, so I keep quiet about my Maasai warrior and say, 'It's a lovely country and the camp was excellent. I'd love to go back one day.'

Oh, how I'd love to, I think. How I'd love to pack a bag and go back there next week.

Dinner arrives and it's every bit as excellent as Mike had been led to hope.

'That was very lovely,' I say when I've finished my crème brûlée for dessert. 'An excellent meal.'

'And excellent company,' Mike says.

I flush. 'Thank you.' *Asante*. Even when I'm not trying, the smattering of African words that Dominic taught me still spring to mind.

Gazing across the table, I drag my thoughts back from the Maasai Mara and think instead of Mike, this kind man, and how much nicer he is than the likes of that hideous Lewis Moran. I wonder why I haven't fallen for him before now. If Dominic hadn't arrived on the scene, would this evening have made me feel differently about Mike? How can I tell? How can anyone tell? If fate hadn't played its fickle hand who knows how things might have turned out.

Mike drives us home. He had just one glass of fizz which means that I've knocked back the rest myself. In the car, in the warmth, my resistance feels very low. Now that I've had a taste of love and I know what I'm missing, I want to feel strong arms around me, holding me, loving me. My body is pining for Dominic, but Dominic isn't here. It's raining and the rhythmic clack of the windscreen wipers is making me deliciously drowsy.

I know what the other girls – and boys – at the salon would do. They'd take Mike in and spend the night with him. That's what they'd do. Steph, in particular, would have had him as a 'maintenance man' years ago. Their motto is most definitely, 'If you can't be with the one you love, then love the one you're with.' Could it be mine too?

Mike pulls up to the cottages, turns to me and smiles. 'OK?'

This could be my moment. I could invite him in for coffee and see where that would take us.

'I've had a lovely evening,' I say. And truly, I have. Mike is nice, steady, kind – all of those things that we women say we value most. 'But I'm very tired now. Do you mind if we call it a night?'

If Mike is disappointed then it doesn't register on his face. 'Of course not,' he says. 'Thanks for being such great company.'

Then he leans towards me in the car and kisses me on the cheek, but so tenderly that I could cry.

'You're a very nice man, Mike Perry. Did anyone ever tell you that?'

'Yes,' Mike says. 'Lots of women. Just before they jump out of my car and rush into their houses alone.'

We both giggle at that.

'You really don't mind?'

'No,' he says. 'I'll catch you some time tomorrow.'

'Yeah,' I say. 'See you tomorrow.' Then I jump out of his car and rush into my house alone.

Archie looks at me disdainfully as I throw my bag down.

'I couldn't bring him in,' I protest to my sour-faced puss. 'How could I? He would have got the wrong message.'

Peeking out of the curtains, I watch Mike go up his own path, listen to the bang of his door behind him. Loneliness gnaws at me. It would be so easy to call Mike and ask him to come back. All I have to do is pick up my mobile and ring his number. He'd be here in seconds, I know he would. He'd be a caring, considerate lover and I wouldn't have to wake up alone. I stare at the phone long and hard for five minutes, maybe more. Then I turn and head upstairs.

I crawl into my bed and for company, I have a bad-tempered cat jammed behind my knees. I wrap Dominic's *kanga* around me, pretending that it's his arms, and within minutes I fall into a deep, drink-induced sleep.

Chapter 36

Another normal Monday morning in the salon. Cristal is crying because yet one more man ran out on her after her usual Saturday night shagathon. She is currently being comforted by Steph. Tyrone and Clinton are sitting at opposite ends of the staffroom as they've had a spat at the weekend and are still huffy with each other. God help us if any good-looking men turn up wanting a haircut today – World War Three could well break out.

Nina, on the other hand, is back at work. They may not be love's young dream in the Dalton household, but Gerry is home again, promising to forsake all others for the umpteenth time and, therefore, all is relatively quiet on the Western Front. At least Nina is smiling thinly and chain-eating grapes once more.

Despite all the doom and gloom among the staff, Kelly is putting up the Christmas decorations. To get in the mood, she's wearing flashing reindeer antlers. Our boss is festooning the stations with tinsel, hanging baubles from the lights, sticking snowflakes on the window. As she fusses and fiddles, she's singing along to the chirpy songs on the 'Now That's What I Call Christmas' album that she's got belting out. At least someone's happy.

Nina nods in her direction. 'She'll be handing out the bloody Santa hats soon.'

I roll my eyes. 'Not again.'

All the staff are required to suffer the humiliation of Santa hats throughout December. Our indifference, or even outright hostility to them, does nothing to curb Kelly's enthusiasm for the festive season.

'How was your dinner with Miserable Mike?' Nina wants to know.

'He's not *miserable*!' we then say together.

'It was lovely,' I tell her. 'Really lovely. In any other circumstances, it might well have turned my head.'

What I *don't* tell her is that I was a hair's breadth away from calling Mike and asking him to spend the night with me. It would have been a terrible mistake. For me and for Mike. Though admittedly, Mike may not have seen it that way. I love Dominic and can't believe that I could have even thought about doing that to him.

'But you're still in love with this bloke in Mexico.'

'Africa.'

'That's the one.' Nina isn't known for her attention to detail.

'Oh, yes.' I reach for my handbag. 'I've got his photograph here,' I say, excitement rising at the chance to show Dominic off. 'You haven't even seen him yet.'

My friend has been so engrossed in her own misery that my happiness has taken a bit of a backseat, but that's fine. Needs must. But I've been dying to show her this for days. I rescue Dominic's picture from the depths of my bag. It's already well-worn as I don't miss an opportunity to have a sneaky look at it. Smiling, I hand over the photograph of us sitting together beneath the acacia tree under the brilliant African sun looking totally blissed out.

Nina snatches at it. 'Let me get a look at this hunk,' she says. Then her mouth drops open as her eyes frantically scan the picture. 'He's ... he's ... he's ... ' My friend stares back at me.

'He's a Maasai warrior,' I confirm.

'Bloody hell,' Nina says and gapes at the photo again. 'This is the man you've fallen in love with?'

I nod. 'He's so lovely, Nina. Like no one I've ever met before.'

'Jesus Christ, Janie. That's an understatement. You're hardly likely to meet a bloody Maasai warrior down at Oceana nightclub, are you? Eh? Of course he's not like anyone you've met before.'

'I mean the way he is, not the way he looks. He's kind and proud and ... ' I go weak at the knees just thinking about him.

'Have you heard from him since?'

'Yes,' I say. 'He's messaged me a few times on Facebook already.'

'He hasn't asked you for money?'

'Money?' I frown. 'No. Why?'

Nina puckers her mouth in concern. 'That's what they do, Janie.'

'What who do?'

She nods at Dominic's image. 'This sort of man. You know, they get in with the rich white woman, promise her the earth, make you feel it's all for real ... '

'It is all for real,' I insist. 'Dominic isn't like that.'

By now our conversation has attracted the attention of the others in the staffroom. Even the boys patch up their differences for long enough to come and have a peep.

Over Nina's shoulder, Steph says, 'Hmm, I would.'

And I think, Oh no, you wouldn't. He's mine!

'Let's have a look,' Cristal says. 'Is this your holiday romance?'

'It's not a holiday romance,' I counter. 'We're in love.'

Nina and Cristal exchange a glance that I don't much care for.

'It's not like you think,' I find myself objecting.

'He's fit,' Cristal concedes. 'I can see why you were taken in.'

'I haven't been "taken in". Dominic's a lovely man. If there's any way that we can be together then I'm going to find it.' At that, I pull up short. I hadn't even admitted that to myself and now I'm announcing it aloud to the entire staffroom.

'Just be careful, Janie,' Nina warns. 'I don't want to see you hurt.'

'The only way it's going to hurt is if I can't see him again.' I take my photograph back.

'I'm just saying.' Nina slips her arm around me. 'You've got to watch these blokes.'

'My mate went to Turkey last year and met a guy,' Steph chips in. 'He led her a right merry dance. Shagged her ragged, then took her for a load of cash. Turns out he had a dozen different women on the go.'

'Dominic's not like that.'

'My friend got done in Egypt like that,' Cristal adds.

'I'm not "getting done" by anyone,' I protest.

They all give me a sympathetic look.

'A few weeks ago you were all urging me to go out and find love,' I remind them. 'Now that I have, you don't like it.'

Nina looks around for backup but realises that she is the chief spokesperson for Janie Johnson's Unofficial Love Life Committee. 'We're just saying that this is a bit more ... *complicated* ... than the average relationship, hun. That's all.'

They all nod vehemently behind her.

'Is it?' I ask. 'Is it really?'

I don't like to raise all of *their* relationship issues at this point but if I'm pressed, I will. One-night stands, commitment-phobes, green-eyed monsters, unfaithful husbands. I'd rather take on Dominic any day than any of their lot and I don't give a damn what my friends think about it.

Chapter 37

The rest of the week is ridiculously tense. Clearly the word about my relationship with Dominic has spread around the salon. Clients, before I've even said anything to them about my holiday, are giving me pitying looks. I feel as if I'm the subject of gossip because whenever I emerge from the staffroom or walk into it, everyone else shuts up.

I know that there are a lot of stories about women who go abroad looking for love and come a cropper, but this is different. I just know it is. Dominic would never dream of doing anything like that, and though I haven't known him long at all – by anyone's standards – I just know that it's not in his nature to be deceptive. With Dominic, what you see is what you get, and I very much liked what I saw. I'm not some silly impressionable girl or some desperately lonely divorcee. Apart from the odd moment of regret, I would have been quite content on my own, but Dominic has turned my world upside down. I want to be with this man and if I have a chance of future happiness with him, then I'm going to make sure that I grab it with both hands.

Nina has been very cool with me this week and I don't know whether it's simply that she's finding it hard to come to terms with the fact that I've found love while she is watching hers slip away. I haven't said a single word about Dominic in days, and I feel it's somehow unfair that I can't talk to her about him when I've always been there to listen to her unloading all her worries about Gerry.

My phone buzzes again and there's another text from Lewis asking me for a date. I press 'delete'. If only I could delete him as easily as his messages.

The salon is full this Friday morning – every station is busy. It will be like this from now until Christmas.

Mrs Norman is here, ready and waiting in my chair, for her ten o'clock appointment. Cristal has already washed her hair and combed it through for me.

I plaster a smile on my face to greet one of my favourite clients. 'How are you today then, Mrs N?'

'I'm fine, lass.'

'Same as usual?'

'Yes,' she says with a pat of her hair. 'Nice and tight. Got to last me the weekend.'

Sectioning her hair, I start to wind in the pink rollers.

Then, as she does week in, week out, Mrs Norman asks, 'How's your love life then, young Janie?'

'It's wonderful, Mrs Norman,' I say too loudly. 'My love life is very wonderful.'

Everyone else in the salon stops what they're doing and looks up. In the mirror, Mrs Norman looks particularly shocked as this is not the usual mumbled response of, 'Same old, same old.'

'I met a wonderful man on holiday,' I continue for the benefit of everyone within earshot. 'He's kind. He's funny. He's handsome.'

The photograph of Dominic is in my pocket and I slap it down in front of Mrs Norman, making her jump.

'That's him.'

While I wind more rollers into her hair, Mrs Norman puts on her glasses and peers at my picture.

'Is that him in the red dress?' she asks. Given that there are only two of us in the photo and one of us is me, I think it's a safe assumption.

'Yes,' I say. 'That's him.'

'He's as fit as a butcher's dog,' is Mrs Norman's verdict.

'He certainly is!'

'I'm not deaf,' Mrs Norman points out. 'There's no need to shout, Janie, love.'

But I think there *is* a need to shout. I think there's a need to shout this from the rooftops.

'He makes me feel like no one has ever made me feel before,' I say at top volume. 'When I'm in his arms, I lose myself. I lose myself until I'm no longer Janie Johnson, bloody boring hairdresser from Buckingham, but I'm anything that I want to be. And if this isn't love, then I don't know what is.'

'That's nice.' Mrs Norman is now looking worried.

'I love him,' I announce. 'And I don't care whether that suits anyone else or not. It's my life and I'll do with it as I choose.'

I've finished putting Mrs Norman's rollers in and I tie a pink hairnet tightly around them. I find myself breathing heavily. You could hear a pin drop in the salon. Scissors are poised mid-snip. If I'm not mistaken, there are people outside who've stopped to look in the window.

'Cup of tea?' I say into the voluminous silence.

'Yes, please,' Mrs Norman says meekly.

'Right!' I clap my hands together. 'One cup of tea and two of your favourite caramel biscuits coming up!'

170

Chapter 38

For the rest of that day and the next day, everyone pussyfoots around me. Cristal does everything that I request without fuss or complaint. She even sweeps the hair from the floor before I have the chance to ask her. Clearly, they all feel as if they are dealing with a scary unhinged woman. As well they might.

At lunchtime, I can stand it no longer and in an effort at conciliation, I offer to do the sandwich run. I stand with pen poised.

'Fruit,' Nina says. 'Anything.'

'Ham and cheese with salad. No mayo.' Cristal hardly dares to look at me in case I go off on one again.

'Smoked salmon,' Tyrone ventures, clutching at Clinton's hand for support. 'Please.'

'Anything with that?'

He shakes his head as I jot it down.

'On brown?'

Nodding.

'Clinton?'

'Cranberry and brie baguette please, Janie.'

'Very festive.'

'Yes,' he says weakly. 'Trying to get in the mood.'

'Steph?'

'I'll have a coronation chicken on brown with salad.'

I survey them all. 'That it?'

Much nodding.

Kelly, our boss, is on reception. She's filing her nails.

'Want anything from Deli Delights?'

She holds up an exciting diet bar in response. 'Everything OK today?'

'Yeah,' I say. 'Normal service resumed.'

'You must really like this guy.'

'I do.' That's something of an understatement but the sentiment's there. 'Sure I can't get you anything?'

'No thanks, hun. Phil doesn't like me getting too fat.'

For the record, Kelly is probably about eight stone when wet through. And her tub-of-lard boyfriend is a twat.

Armed with the order, I sweep out of the salon and head purposefully towards Deli Delights. The Christmas lights are on in the courtyard and the wind is whipping at them, making them swing giddily. Head down, mission-mode on, I'm about to stride across the alley when someone grabs my arm and pulls me back.

Two inches from my face is Lewis Moran. 'Hey, baby,' he says.

Really, he does. I'm not joking.

'You don't answer my calls,' he whines. 'I'd hate to think you're avoiding me.'

'I *am* avoiding you,' I tell him. 'I went to Africa to avoid you, which in my book is a whole step worse than jumping out of a toilet window into the arms of waiting lesbians to avoid you.'

He laughs at that.

'Visiting another continent could be classed as a serious avoidance technique,' I point out.

'I don't give up easily,' Lewis offers.

'Now I'm back and I'm in love with someone else.' I detect a slight wince in his countenance.

'You and I were made for each other,' Lewis tells me.

'No, we weren't. Not on any level.'

'If you'd just give me a chance.'

'I did,' I remind him. 'You were awful, truly awful. If you had any idea what your competition was like, then you'd give up. You'd just give up now.'

He points a finger at me and grins. 'You will be mine, I promise you.'

'And I promise you, I won't.' I hold up my sandwich list. 'Now if you'll excuse me, I have important business to attend to.'

Lewis backs away and I try to cross the road again. 'I won't give up,' he says. 'Just watch me.'

I'm not frightened of him now, I think. He's just a short, fat, deluded man and I have a new courage inside of me. I could squash Lewis Moran like the unwanted fly that he is. After all, I am the woman of a Maasai warrior.

173

Chapter 39

Mrs Silverton is in for a blow-dry. 'Now then,' she says, 'how did the holiday go?'

There's a collective sharp intake of breath in the salon, conversation ceases and I feel scissors freeze in frightened fingers.

'It was lovely,' I say sweetly. 'Really lovely.'

The breath is exhaled. Conversation and snipping resumes.

'I told you.' Mrs Silverton gives me a wink. 'I knew you'd love it.'

'It was all I could have hoped for.'

'We're going back,' my client says. 'Can't stay away from the place now. I've booked us a quick trip over Christmas. Just me and the hubby. Arm and a leg, mind you, but we're flying direct to the Mara from Nairobi so it's just about doable for a weekend.'

'You're flying direct?'

She nods. 'Adds a few grand, but it's well worth it. Cuts out that interminably long drive. Nearly shattered my kidneys, that did ...' Mrs Silverton pauses for breath and looks up. 'What are you doing for Christmas, Janie?'

'I, er, me? Er ... nothing.' Same old story. While my client will be having festive fun a stone's throw away from my loved one, I will be home alone. Just me and my grumpy cat. I will have turkey dinner for one and a Christmas pudding in a cheerless single-sized pot. You can't even pull a flipping cracker if you're by yourself. Suddenly, that seems unbearably sad. I don't even know if I can face putting up a tree this year, let alone anything else.

'We can't wait,' Mrs Silverton carries on.

Then I hear nothing else that she says. My client is twittering on about where she's staying and what they're doing, but all I can think of is that it doesn't have to be like this. I don't have to be miserable and by myself. I too could be going to the Maasai Mara for the holidays. I could see Dominic for a few days. I could fly straight to him. All I'd have to do is raise the money.

I finish Mrs Silverton and, clearly, she didn't notice that I was off in my own world as she gives me a very big and very welcome tip.

At the desk, I book her next appointment and then turn to Kelly. 'I've still got a week's holiday left,' I tell her. 'Any chance that I can take the days off between Christmas and New Year?'

My boss flicks through the appointments screen on the computer with a well-manicured finger. 'There's not much in your book yet,' she concedes. 'Will any of your clients be desperate?'

'I've got most of them booked in for the twenty-third.' We don't work Christmas Eve any longer as we used to get so many cancellations from people who'd got distracted down the pub that it wasn't really worth it. I'm thinking that if Kelly says yes, then I could perhaps get a flight on Christmas Eve.

'Is this about you chasing after this man?'

'I'd like to go out to see him again,' I correct.

Kelly sighs. 'You can go, Janie, of course you can. But be careful. Take it slowly.'

This is from a girl whose boyfriend is a petty crook, thirty years older than her and thinks she's fat to boot. Who is she to tell me to take it slowly? Did anyone say that to her when she hooked up with her wholly unsuitable man? Or did she think then that love comes in many shapes and forms? Does she still love him now? I guess she must do to live on diet bars rather than real food at his behest.

That night, I get on the internet. There are trips available to the Maasai Mara over Christmas but as Mrs Silverton so rightly prophesied, they cost an arm and a leg. I look at the meagre balance of my savings account and realise that there's no way that will cover it. If I'm serious about going to see Dominic again so soon then I'm going to have to sell something to raise the cash.

How long would I have to wait if I simply saved up my spare money every month? He might have forgotten me by the time I could go out there again. But what can I sell? There's very little that I have of value that I could bear to part with.

Nevertheless, my heart's pounding when I access my Facebook page and type a message to Dominic:

I'd love to see you at Christmas. Do you want me to come?

I sit back. All I can do now is wait for his reply.

Chapter 40

Four days later, a message comes back:

> Yes, Janie Johnson. I would very much like to see you
> again. I miss you.
> All my love, Dominic.

That's enough for me. I'm going to book the trip right away. While I've been waiting for Dominic's reply, I put my mind to what I could sell and I've dredged up every scrap of jewellery that I can lay my hands on. Gold, so they say, is at an all-time high and surely I could get the price of my ticket for this lot.

I tip my stash out on the bed. A couple of bracelets that look dated now. Some broken chains that I've never got round to having mended. There's a ring that Paul bought me – not an engagement ring, but a nice dress ring. It was expensive and I loved it when he bought it, but now I never wear it. It may seem harsh to be selling presents that my former love bought me, but is it better to live with memories or to put it towards investment in a brighter future? That day when he came to the salon to tell me that he's getting married and is about to become a father, he said that he would do anything to help me. Surely this would count? I'd like to think that it would.

There's a load of other stuff here too, some of which will be much harder to sell. I have some of my mother's jewellery that I inherited when she died of cancer some years ago now. I've put two pieces aside that I could never part with – Mum's wedding ring and a sapphire pendant that she was particularly fond of – but the rest of it? There's a brooch set with pearls and diamonds – not one of Mum's favourites, I hardly ever saw her wear it, but could I sell it? Could I cut that emotional link and let it go to a stranger in return for a fistful of cash? Would my mother turn in her grave at the thought of me doing this or would she give me her blessing and encourage me to follow my dream?

I'll have to decide soon. I've organised a gold party at my house tonight with the organisation All That Glitters. Everyone from work is coming along, most of them hoping to raise a few extra pounds for their Christmas funds. Me, I have a very different reason for doing this.

While I'm still contemplating my small pile of jewellery, I hear Mike's knock at the door and I abandon it to go and let him in.

'Hey,' he says. 'Wondered what you were up to tonight?'

I haven't seen Mike since our dinner 'date' last week and I'm happy to see that there's no awkwardness between us. It seems as if we're back to where we were.

'I've got the girls and guys from the salon coming round tonight,' I explain. 'I'm having a gold party.'

'A gold party? That's a new one on me.'

'Selling off some old jewellery. You're more than welcome to join us if you've got something to get rid of.'

'Hmm.' Mike scratches his chin. 'The temptation to flog off the remaining contents of Tania's jewellery box is very strong.'

'You wicked man,' I laugh.

'Maybe I'll give this one a miss.' He holds up a hand. As he turns to leave he says, 'Oh, there was one other thing, Janie.'

'Yes?'

'I meant to talk to you about this last week.' Now he hesitates. 'I wondered what you were doing for Christmas? Whether you've made any plans yet?'

Ah.

'Well . . . ' Is this the time to come clean and tell Mike about Dominic? 'That's partly why I'm having this gold party.' I know that I'm sounding cagey and Mike's looking at me with a puzzled stare too. 'I'm planning to go back to the Maasai Mara for Christmas, just for a few days. I fly out on Christmas Eve, but it's a fortune. I'm having to flog off some of the family silver . . . well, gold.'

'Oh,' Mike says. It's fair to say that he looks dumbfounded by my revelation. As well he might. I'm a bit shocked by it myself.

There's another knock on the door and glancing out of the window – a necessary habit since the introduction of Lewis Moran into my life – I see that Nina has arrived with a car full.

'They're here,' I say to Mike apologetically.

'I'll be off then.'

'No need to rush away. Stay and have a glass of plonk.'

'Things to do,' he insists. 'Have fun.'

I open the door.

'About bloody time,' Nina complains. 'It's freezing out here. Oh, hello, Mike.'

'Nice to see you again, Nina.'

'Not stopping?' she asks.

Mike shakes his head. Another car pulls up and the boys jump out.

'I'll catch you later, Mike,' I promise as he makes for the door.

My neighbour holds up a hand in a wave as he hastily retreats.

Meanwhile, Nina has disappeared into the kitchen and is already pulling glasses from the cupboard and pouring wine. 'Mike's looking a bit fit,' she says over her shoulder.

'He's always looked like that.'

'Really?' She gives the wine a trial sip and pouts appreciatively. 'I've never noticed before.'

I wonder whether she really thinks he looks fit or if she's just trying to point out his charms to me in the hope it will deflect my attention from Dominic.

I've put out some nibbles on the kitchen table – crisps, some cocktail sausages, a platter of cheese and biscuits. The girls fall on them.

Another knock at the door signals the arrival of the man from All That Glitters. He looks just like a gold dealer should do, in his pinstripe suit and with his comb-over. Oh, I'd love to get my scissors on that.

I settle him in the corner of the living room by the stairs. All he asked for was a little table and I've duly obliged. On it, he puts a machine which, he tells me, will check whether the jewellery is gold or not, and some scales for weighing it.

'Would you like a glass of wine?'

'Tea,' he says, 'if that's no trouble.'

So I make him a tea and then he gets to work. All of the girls are clutching a handful of gold jewellery, but the boys seem to have more chains, bracelets, earrings and watches between them than all of us put together.

Cristal goes first and is delighted to come away with nearly a hundred pounds for the bits of jewellery she's brought along. The boys go next and they too are delighted to offload their haul in exchange for a wedge of cash.

Nina is sitting next to me. 'That Gerry is lucky that I don't sell these as well,' she says, looking down at her wedding and engagement rings.

'Things no better?'

She shrugs. 'Will they ever be?'

'It's your turn next.' I nudge her, indicating the table.

'Feels like going to the bloody dentist,' she mutters and heaves herself off the sofa.

But she's smiling when she comes back to me. 'Seven hundred quid for that lot,' she beams as she high-fives me. 'Cheers, Janie. This was a great idea.'

'There's only Steph, then me.' Moment of truth.

'I've noticed some of the stuff you've got there, hun,' Nina says, suddenly serious. 'That's your mum's.'

'I know. I'm keeping a couple of bits of the important stuff. These are just trinkets.'

'Yeah, but they're your *mum's* trinkets.'

'I need to see him, Nina.'

My friend takes my hands. 'This worries me, Janie. It's not like you to be silly. He's just a bloke. They come, they go. Don't pin all your hopes on him. Chances are, he'll let you down.'

I lay my head on her shoulder. 'I have to believe otherwise, Nina.'

Then the gold dealer nods at me and it seems like it's my turn.

Chapter 41

The dealer gives me fifteen hundred pounds. A not inconsiderable sum. At any other time, I'd be running around the room doing a happy dance. The piece that turned out to be the most expensive from my haul was my ring from Paul. It was 24-carat gold and I got five hundred pounds for that alone. I mouth a little prayer of thanks to my ex-boyfriend and hope that he wouldn't be too disappointed to know that I was parting with it. I hope he'd be glad to be helping me in my quest to find true love.

I fidget while the man from All That Glitters goes through the ritual of packing away his equipment and the jewellery he has just purchased into a large briefcase, then with effusive thanks I show him to the door.

When the dealer's gone, I sit back down again next to my friend. The others are in the kitchen tucking into cheese and wine. They are giddy with their success and I can hear talk about going clubbing straight from here. Oh, to be young again.

'That was pretty good,' Nina says.

'Yes.' Then I sigh. 'But it's not enough.'

'Wow,' my friend says, eyes wide. 'That's going to be one expensive Christmas fling.'

Is Nina right? Is it madness, I think, to blow this amount of cash? I quickly tot up how long it would take me to earn that money, how many months' mortgage that would cover. It's a sobering sum. But then, no matter what my friends might think, this isn't a Christmas fling for me. It's about seeing the man I adore at a time of year when it's so important to be with the ones we love. Isn't that worth any amount of money? The worst thing is that even with my unexpected goldrush, I'm still a thousand pounds short. I've booked the holiday now, maxed the credit card. Where else am I going to get that sort of dosh?

'I'll have to do some more home hairdressing,' I say.

'You'll have to cut like flipping Edward Scissorhands to get that sort of money together in the next few weeks.'

'Hmm.'

'Much as it pains me,' Nina says, 'I'll lend you this.' She holds out the seven hundred pounds she's just acquired. 'If it was for a bill, for your car or your house or something, I wouldn't hesitate. But to blow it on a bloke?' My friend whistles through her teeth. 'Lady, I think you're mad.'

I chew at my lip.

'I'll want it back, Janie. Every last penny.'

'I can't take it,' I tell her. 'Thanks for the offer, but I'll work something out.'

'If you don't have it now, then I'll spend it,' Nina warns.

'I'll find some way of making it.'

She shrugs. 'Let's go and join the others, have a top-up and celebrate our good fortune.'

'Sounds good to me.'

When they've gone, I tidy up – who knew that so few people

could use so many wine glasses – and then go upstairs to bed. Archie, very unhappy about having his house invaded for the evening, is sulking. He hooks a single but deadly claw into my thigh and hangs on for grim death while I try to detach him.

'Archie,' I scold, 'play nicely. I have things on my mind.'

With much kitty backchat, he settles on the bed and I pull Dominic's blanket around both of us.

'What am I going to do?' I ask my cat. 'Do you think this is madness? Everyone else seems to think that it is.'

Archie miaows and I wonder if I should interpret that as a 'Yes, of course you're mad, woman. Think of all the cat food you could buy with that money' type of miaow.

Lying here on a cold December night, it seems like madness to me too. Despite my bravado at parting with some of Mum's jewellery, I'm now wracked with guilt and I really hope that she would understand. Chasing my dream is going to be expensive. I cling to the thought that my dear old Mum would have thought that it was great fun to have a Maasai warrior in the family.

The timbers of the house shiver in the cold as they too settle down for the night. Oh, to be back on the African plains right now. To be lying in Dominic's arms. With that thought in mind, I realise that nothing, not even a severe lack of cash, could keep me away from him. I'd rather live on nothing but beans for the rest of the month than not see him at Christmas.

In the morning, I'm running late. My sleep was fitful and splintered by dreams of Dominic, Nina, Mike, jewellery and lions, all jumbled into one big mess that kept me tossing and turning. At three o'clock, I got up and sat in my utility room office for an hour, head in hands, just staring at the trip that I've booked on the internet, trying to convince myself it's the right thing to do. Then I look at the inviting pictures of the plains, the savannah, the animals and my mind calms.

Now though, I'm knackered before I've even started and I know it's going to be a long day as I try to remain bright and cheerful. As always at this time of year, the salon is full of clients getting their hair done in time for office parties and such. Normally, as we're so busy for weeks on end, I just want it all to be over. This year, for once, I have a frisson of excitement about Christmas. I feel a happy glow just thinking about it. If only I could square my finances.

I throw Archie some food in his bowl and he complains about the lack of attention. There's been a heavy frost overnight and the car windscreen is glazed with a thin layer of ice. It's the first time this season that I'm going to have to get the scraper out. Now I'm going to be even more late.

Muttering, I search about on my car floor for the plastic scraper. I know it's in here somewhere under one of the seats. I saw it not two weeks ago and meant to put it in a more prominent place for this very moment. As I'm rummaging about, I hear Mike's voice.

'Here,' he says, 'let me do the honours.'

'Can't find my flipping scraper,' I grumble.

My neighbour, despite the turn in the weather, is smiling as he sets about scraping my windscreen for me.

'Thank you,' I say. 'Thank you so much.' Then, I grin at him. 'Why am I always in your debt?'

'I'm a handy guy to have around.' Mike shrugs. 'How did the party go last night?'

'Good.' Now it's my turn to shrug. 'I didn't raise quite as much money as I wanted to,' I confide. 'I'm still short if I want to make my trip.'

Mike feigns interest in his scraping. 'How much?'

There's no point hiding it from him. 'A grand.'

'Ouch.'

'My thoughts exactly.' Saying it aloud suddenly makes reality hit home. I can't do this. I simply can't. Where am I going to get that sort of money? Anxiety twists my stomach. 'I'm thinking that I might even have to cancel.' This is despite my nocturnal vow to go at any price. 'To be honest, it was a bit rash of me to book it.'

'I'll say,' he agrees. Mike stops scraping and looks at me. 'I could lend you the money. I've got some put away. Tania didn't clean me out completely.' He laughs. 'I don't need it for anything. Hell, I could even come with you this time. I'm not doing anything else over Christmas.'

Oh.

'Well . . . ' I study the ground. 'That's kind of you. Very kind. But there's something that I haven't told you, Mike.'

He stares straight at me and he knows, he already knows before I even have to say anything.

'I see.'

'I have to go back to see him,' I say.

'Right.'

'So thanks very much for your kind offer, but you understand why I can't accept.'

'Of course. Of course.' Mike blows out a breath and it hangs in the chilly air. 'Didn't really see that coming,' he admits.

'I'm sorry, Mike. I should have told you earlier. It was stupid of me not to have said anything.'

'No worries.' He says it brightly. Too brightly.

'*Hakuna matata*,' I blurt out inappropriately. 'It means no worries.'

'Right.' He flicks a thumb at my windscreen and I never knew that thumbs could be embarrassed until now. 'I'll just finish this up and then I'd better get a move on. Oh, is that the time. My, my.' He scrapes with a renewed frenzy.

'Mike, you are my best friend,' I tell him. 'I don't know what I'd do without you.'

'You've sold your jewellery and everything to get back to him?'

'Yes.' I don't tell him that I have sold my own mother's too.

He looks at me, eyes bleak. 'You must really love him.'

'Yes,' I agree. 'I think I do.'

Chapter 42

I'm exhausted when I get home. It's been relentlessly busy today and – how crazy is this? – I've asked Kelly if I can come in on my day off to earn some extra money over the next few weeks and she's more than happy for me to do so. Am I a sucker for punishment or what? By the time I get myself out to Africa, I'll hardly be fit to stand up.

I'm just making an omelette for my dinner tonight and I wonder if Mike would like to join me. I felt terrible about the way I broke the news to him about Dominic this morning. It was bad, bad, bad and I should have done it any other way than that way.

I've got a couple of DVDs that we could watch together too – *The Pursuit of Happyness* and *Slumdog Millionaire* – see if we can't patch this up between us.

'Shall we ask Mike round for dinner?' I ask Archie, who mews his indifference.

Then there's Mike's signature knock on the door except it lacks its usual perkiness. I check the spyhole just in case it's not him. But, sure enough, it is.

'Hey,' I say as cheerfully as I can muster. 'Perfect timing. I was just thinking about you. Want to come round for dinner tonight? Thought I could knock us together some omelettes?'

Mike shakes his head. 'I'm not staying, Janie,' he says. 'Things to do.'

'Oh.'

'I came to give you this.' He holds out a bulky brown envelope and I take it from him.

'Don't stand at the door, Mike. Come on in. We could do wine? We could do tea?'

'I won't,' he says, holding up a hand.

So while my neighbour stands there looking uncomfortable, I open the envelope and find that it's stuffed full of money.

'What's this?'

'A thousand pounds.'

The money I need to take me back to Africa, to Dominic. 'I can't accept this.'

'View it as a loan. You can pay me back whenever.'

I stare, bewildered, at the money.

'Why?' I ask. 'Why would you do this?'

'You deserve to be happy,' my friend says. 'If I'm honest with you, Janie, I had hoped that it would be me who could do that for you. I thought ... well, it doesn't matter now.' Mike can barely meet my eyes. 'If this helps you, then take it.'

Oh, bloody hell. What do I do now?

'Come in,' I beg. 'Let's talk about this. Let me at least explain what happened.'

He shakes his head. 'I don't need to know.'

I look at the money again and although every fibre of me says that, morally, I should, I simply can't afford to turn it down.

'I'll pay every single penny back,' I promise him. 'Can I do something for you? A chore? Anything?'

'You already cut my hair for nothing.'

'That takes me two minutes flat,' I remind him. 'Hardly a huge effort. What about your ironing? Let me iron your shirts for you every week – you know you hate it. I could do that.'

Mike assembles a laugh. 'There's no need.'

'Let me do *something* to thank you.'

He studies the floor. 'Just promise that you'll always be my friend.'

'Of course I will. Christ, Mike, that goes without saying.'

'Good,' he says. 'I'll be off then. Catch you later.'

I don't want to see him go like this, to walk away from me, hurt. But there's nothing else I can say and a moment later, he's back in his own cottage and I go to make an omelette for myself.

190

Chapter 43

Mike avoids me for three weeks. *The Pursuit of Happyness* and *Slumdog Millionaire* go unwatched. Our cosy nights on the sofa together stop completely. When I call his mobile or his house phone, it always goes straight to voicemail and I'm not brave enough to march around there and knock on his door. I should give him space, let him work it out for himself, even though it pains me to do so. He's become such an intrinsic part of my life, always there in the background. I can't believe how much I've missed him. It's been hell not seeing him every day.

We're so busy at the salon that I barely have time to think about my impending trip. I've worked my day off every week and have stayed late in the evening every day and have upped my late nights to two rather than one. I'm shattered, looking every bit as droopy as the salon's Christmas decorations now do and, quite frankly, I never want to cut another head of hair ever again. However, I'm sure that when I get paid in January, the very welcome extra money will definitely be worth the effort.

Now it's the twenty-third of December and I'm flying out tomorrow afternoon. It's snowing outside. Looks like I'll be leaving behind a white Christmas. Tonight, I need to fling my things in a case and make arrangements to get to the airport. Because of the snow, I'm worried about driving myself. It's not bad, but the roads are getting a bit slithery. I'd be happier if I could organise a taxi to pick me up.

I've booked Archie into a cattery for the first time and I haven't had the nerve to break that news to him yet. He will not be a happy puss.

I take off the Santa hat I've been wearing all day – and every working hour for the last few weeks – to help engender festive spirit in the salon and hug Nina as I get ready to leave.

'Be careful,' Nina warns. 'Don't do anything stupid.'

'Is that the same as "have a lovely holiday"?'

'You know what I mean,' my friend scolds. 'I just hope this works out OK for you, that this bloke is worth it.'

'I think he is.'

'I'll worry about you,' she adds.

I'll worry about her too. Christmas is always a fraught time in the Dalton home, as I suspect it is in many homes.

'Text me,' my friend instructs.

'I will. Have a happy Christmas, Nina.'

'You too, babe.'

We all kiss each other – Cristal, Steph, Kelly, the boys. I'm getting quite tearful now. I've never spent Christmas out of this country before and nerves are beginning to set in. All my recent Christmases have been spent with Paul and his family doing the usual stuff that Christmas brings – eating too much, drinking too much and watching too much rubbish television – and now I'm feeling well out of my comfort zone. Would I have been better to have accepted Mike's invitation to spend it with him instead of chasing halfway around the world for another man?

Driving home, I listen to Christmas carols on the radio and wonder if they have them in Africa. I also wonder how Dominic is feeling now, whether he's looking forward to seeing me, whether he's as anxious as I am. It's been weeks since we were last together and communication, in the interim, has been at best sporadic – mainly Facebook messages when he can get the time to walk all the way to the next village.

When I pull up outside the cottage, there's a dark shadow standing in the snow by the front door and for a moment my heart stops as I think it might be Lewis. He sent an enormous Christmassy basket to my house last week, packed with poinsettias and glittery leaves, and I took it into the salon and left it there. Kelly thought that it looked pretty on reception. But when the figure moves from the shadows and is caught by my security light, I see that it's Mike and a wave of relief washes over me. By the time I get out of the car, he's leaning against the doorframe.

'Hi.' My smile is warm, genuine. It's all I can do not to grab him in a great big bear hug.

'Hey,' he says softly. 'I've missed you.'

'Me too,' I admit.

'I wanted to wish you all the best for your trip and if you want me to take you to the airport, then I'm around tomorrow. I've got nothing else to do.'

'You're not spending Christmas alone are you, Mike?'

'Well ... ' he says, 'I could do with a bit of peace and quiet.'

'Oh, Mike.' Now I feel even more guilty.

I open the door and he follows me inside. Archie greets me with complaints about the dark, the cold, his hunger.

'What are you doing with this little fellow?'

'*Cattery*,' I mouth.

'Cancel it,' Mike says. 'He'll hate it. You know that I'll always look after him. Why didn't you ask?'

'Mike,' I let my hand rest on his arm, 'I didn't think that things were right between us. How could I ask you to have Archie?'

'I'm over my sulk,' he says, trying to sound light. 'I'll be pleased to have some company.'

My heart goes out to Mike. Fancy having no one but my ill-tempered cat as a companion over the holidays. I can hardly bear to think of him alone here.

'I don't want to impose.'

'Nonsense,' Mike says. 'Just tell me what time I need to pick you up.'

'My flight's at four o'clock. It's a three-hour check-in.'

He does a rough calculation of how long it will take to drive to the airport. 'Then I'll see you just before eleven-thirty.'

I nod.

'Have you packed?'

'Not yet,' I admit.

'Then I'll leave you to it.' He turns towards the door.

'Mike . . .' I step forward and hold open my arms.

He hesitates and then lets me hold him in my embrace. Reluctantly, his arms twine around me and then we stand and hold each other tightly.

'Best friends?' I say.

'Yeah,' he replies. 'Best friends.'

Chapter 44

The tiny plane swoops down over the Maasai Mara and my heart swoops along with it. I can see the small runway come into view and know that in a few moments I'll be touching down on Kenyan soil once more.

All my nerves are jangling and I haven't been able to eat a scrap of food all the way from Heathrow. I haven't slept either, not a wink. I'm as excited as a five-year-old and I haven't looked forward to a Christmas so much in years.

My head's in a spin and I still can't believe I'm here. This is the sort of thing that other people do – the likes of Simon Cowell, Posh Spice, Ivana Trump. Hairdressers from Buckinghamshire don't spend their life savings on a few days in the Maasai Mara. But if I have lost my mind, it feels very nice.

I think about the men I've left behind. I hope that all goes well for Paul and his impending marriage. I sent him a card and a small gift to show that I really am happy for him. When I told him I was going away to Africa at Christmas, I never really imagined that I would be. Now look at me! Then there's Mike and Archie, and I wish there was some way that they could be here with me too, instead of being back in Nashley alone. But most of all I think about Dominic. I can't wait to see him again and I think I might explode with joy, with anticipation, with anxiety, if we don't touch down soon.

The plane turns, my stomach rolls and we drop for our final descent. There are no airport buildings here. In fact, there's nothing much at all apart from a single strip of concrete amidst the miles and miles of scrub. I can see a cluster of minibuses waiting at the side of the runway. One of them is from Kiihu camp and I hope it's just for me.

On the flight there are a dozen other people and we all wait impatiently as the plane touches down and taxis to a halt. Steps are brought to the door and five minutes later, I'm emerging into the brilliant African sunshine – as far away from the usual cold and rain of Christmas Day in Britain as it's possible to be.

I shield my eyes against the brightness as I scan the plains, then I see Dominic's tall frame in the distance, his distinctive red tunic, and I wave to him. His face, anxious, now lights up and he breaks into a run as he comes towards me. I drop my bag on the ground and hold out my arms. Then my Maasai warrior scoops me up and with a triumphant war cry, twirls me in the air.

'You have come back to me, Just Janie,' Dominic says. 'In my heart I knew that you would.'

He lowers me to the ground and we hold each other tightly. Never before have I been able to feel sheer happiness coursing through my veins. It's a heady feeling. Then, when I begin to wonder if we will ever be able to let go of each other, Dominic takes my hand and leads me towards the bus.

'It's only for a few days,' I whisper. 'I wish it could have been longer.'

'Then we will have to make those days very special.'

Together, we jump into the bus and head off towards the camp. Dominic is grinning widely. 'I cannot believe my own eyes,' he says, shaking his head. 'I cannot believe them.'

I'm so glad that I came, so glad that I sacrificed Mum's jewellery, so glad that I accepted Mike's loan. My mind flits again to my lovely neighbour and I hope that Mike is all right at home alone with just Archie. As soon as I'm settled, I'll call him and see how they both are.

'I do not have to work while you are here,' Dominic says. 'We can be together.'

'Oh, Dominic. That's wonderful.'

He smiles again. 'I knew that you would like this, Just Janie. I also have other surprises.'

How can I have ever doubted that this was the right thing to do? My friends, my colleagues who have warned me against Dominic have no idea what he is like.

We head across the open plains and I feel as if I'm in seventh heaven as I see the zebras and the giraffes and the wildebeest once more. The vast blue sky is unchanged and I feel that everything has been waiting here just for me, exactly as I left it.

As we drive into the camp, instead of parking at the main entrance, we drive around to the far side. There, on its own, just on the edge of the camp, is a solitary tent.

'This is the honeymoon suite,' he teases.

'It's lovely. Perfect.'

'This will be our home,' Dominic says.

'We'll stay here together?'

'Oh, yes.' He picks up my bag. 'And you will not be frightened of the lions.'

'No,' I say. 'I'll never be frightened of the lions again.'

He takes my hand and leads me inside. Our tent is much bigger than the one I had before, and the furnishings more lavish. A double bed is dressed in cream with a red and pink *kanga* across the bottom, the dressing area has a wardrobe, the shower will comfortably fit two. But the best thing of all is that, this time, I'll be sharing it with Dominic.

'You are tired?' he asks.

'No,' I say, 'not tired at all.' Despite not having slept, I'm completely hyper and I don't want to waste a minute of the precious time we have together by sleeping.

'I have made the shower ready for you.'

'That's lovely. Thank you. *Asante.*'

'*Karibu.* You are welcome, my love.' He looks at me with such tenderness that my heart melts. My love, I think. He called me my love. 'When you have showered, we will have lunch.'

'You've thought of everything,' I say gratefully. There could be no better reunion than this. I had expected our time together to be snatched, surrounded by other tourists. I had no idea that Dominic had this planned for us and I'm touched by his thoughtfulness.

'I'll take a shower then.' Shyly, I start to undo the buttons of my shirt.

'Here,' Dominic says. 'I think that you need help with this.'

He undoes my shirt, slowly, slowly, one frustrating button at a time, and strips it from my body. Then he kisses me deeply. I shiver with anticipation even though the temperature outside must be pushing eighty degrees. Inside the tent, it is a cool dark sanctuary.

Together we undress each other and then go to stand under the shower. As we kiss, we drench each other with the warm water. Dominic soaps my body tenderly, massaging his firm hands all over me. All my tension leaves me and Dominic holds me against him as the water cascades over us once more.

Making love on the double bed, our bodies move together as if they've done so a thousand times before. Outside the tent, a gazelle passes by and casually glances in. I curl into Dominic and he strokes my hair.

'My Janie,' he murmurs. 'My own Janie.'

We lie entwined for an hour or more, until Dominic says, 'I think it is time for you to eat.'

He shrugs on his red tunic and then disappears from the tent. While he's gone, I change into some fresh clothes. A few minutes later, two more Maasai men appear with a small table that they set up on the veranda. They bring a dish of barbecued meats and some rice and then quietly melt away into the bush. Dominic grins as he opens a bottle of champagne that's been chilling in an ice bucket.

'How have you managed all this?' I ask him.

He shrugs. 'Some people, they owe me favours,' he explains. 'I say that this is a special occasion for me. Now I ask for them to be returned.'

Dominic pours me a glass of champagne and he pours himself some milk from a jug that's also appeared on the table. We toast each other.

'Bottoms up,' Dominic says with a cheeky grin.

I laugh. 'To us,' I tell him. 'This toast should be to us.'

'To us,' he echoes. 'To us, Just Janie.'

Chapter 45

Believe me, listening to lions roar in the dead of night while you're lying in the arms of a Maasai warrior holds no terror. None whatsoever. Whenever I wake, Dominic is there next to me, awake, watching over me and I've never felt so cared for or so protected in all my life. It is, however, still pitch black when he rouses me from a deep and dreamless sleep.

'You must get up now, Janie,' he says, gently stroking my cheek.

'Now?' I think my eyes are open, but I can see nothing.

'There is something we must do.'

I prop myself up. 'What time is it?'

'It is very early.'

You don't say.

'Come,' Dominic urges. 'We must go now.'

Reluctantly, I leave his arms and slide out of bed. On autopilot, I find my way into my clothes. Dominic hands me my warm fleece as the morning air is chilly and then, as I stumble about sleepily, he leads me outside and towards the minibus.

This better be worth it, I'm thinking as I fight the urge to nod off again. A hippo is grazing by the van and he turns tail and trots off into the bush as we emerge. In the darkness, we bump across the plains. I have no idea how Dominic is even finding his way as the headlights only throw a tiny pool of light into the night.

When my eyes are focused enough, I manage to look at my watch. 'It's four o'clock,' I say to Dominic, eyebrows raised.

'It is the early bird that catches the worm, Just Janie,' he informs me.

'Ah, you and your old Maasai sayings,' I tease.

'Look.' Dominic points through the windscreen. 'A spring hare.'

There's just enough light to pick out a tiny thing, like a miniature kangaroo, that hops across in front of us at break-neck speed and then bounds away, consumed by the darkness once more.

'We will be there very soon,' he says with a grin and, sure enough, a few minutes later we stop, seemingly in the middle of nowhere.

'Here?'

'You must trust me,' my Maasai warrior says.

We get out of the bus – no matter that there are wild animals all over the place – and walk into the darkness. I suddenly realise there are other people here and it's only when there's a blast of flame ahead of us that I see the enormous hot-air bal-loon filling the sky.

'Wow,' I say in awe. 'This is for us?'

'Yes.' Dominic nods. 'To take a balloon flight over the Maasai Mara is one of the things that you must do in your life.' He grins at me.

'Omigod. Omigod!' I shriek and do a happy dance. 'I can't believe it.'

My lover grins. 'Happy Christmas, my Janie.'

'Happy Christmas, Dominic.' I kiss him warmly. 'I'll never forget this for as long as I live.'

To think that I could be shivering at home in Buckinghamshire in front of my fire with Archie and a Christmas dinner for one. My mind turns to Mike and I hope that he's doing OK. How can I ever thank him enough for helping make this happen for me?

Dominic shakes hands and exchanges a few words with the man who I assume is our pilot. Then, while the crew prepare the balloon, filling it with dramatic blasts of golden-blue fire, we stand and watch.

'We need to get going,' the pilot says and with the briefest of briefings, we're helped into the large wicker basket that's still pegged to the ground.

'There's just the two of us?'

'Just the two of us.'

And so we take off, whooshed into the clear starlit sky above the Maasai Mara. Higher and higher we go until we're travelling way above the treetops. The sun starts to peep over the horizon, flooding the plains with a soft golden light. It's warm in the balloon and we drift serenely at the whim of the wind, and the only sound is the intermittent noise of the burner.

Dominic puts his arm around me and points to the ground. 'Hyena.'

Below us, a pack of six spotted hyena run along, keeping pace with the balloon. Herds of wildebeest do their ungainly gallop across the plains and skittish gazelles dart to and fro as we pass overhead. The sun climbs higher and the land is transformed. The Maasai Mara stretches as far as the eye can see, banded only on one side by the massive Oloololo escarpment. Three lions wander below us in search of a daytime sleeping spot, giving us an indifferent gaze as they go. In the distance, a male ostrich does his very best strutting dance to a seated female who seems terminally uninterested.

We brush the trees where a group of giraffes are having breakfast, but they carry on chewing, unworried by our presence.

'This is magical,' I say to Dominic, tears in my eyes. 'Truly magical. Thank you so much.'

We drift quietly above the landscape until the sun is high in the sky. Already the temperature is climbing.

'Look like a good place for breakfast?' the pilot asks as he points ahead of himself.

There's a lone acacia tree with nothing around it for miles. Beneath it is a table set for two.

'Oh, Dominic,' I cry. 'It looks wonderful.'

We come down, skimming the ground until the balloon comes gently to rest. Dominic helps me out and then takes me to the table. There's a van parked a discreet distance from us and at the back of it, a man in chef's whites with a gas range is preparing to rustle us up a cooked breakfast.

Beneath the dappled shade of the acacia, I'm served fresh fluffy pancakes with maple syrup and then a full English of bacon and eggs and proper British sausages. The toast is bucks fizz for me and milk for Dominic.

What would my friends think if they could see me now? Would they realise that Dominic is sincere? That this isn't about him fleecing some gullible tourist? Would they be jealous that the men in their lives aren't so thoughtful?

'Thank you for making this happen,' I say. 'This is the most perfect Christmas I've ever had. Thank you so much.'

'Nothing is too much trouble for my Janie,' Dominic says.

'Dominic,' my mouth is dry despite the bucks fizz, 'I must tell you this.'

He waits patiently while I find the unfamiliar words.

'I love you,' I say.

'That is good,' Dominic says, 'because, Just Janie, I love you too.'

Chapter 46

On Boxing Day, we go out together on a long game drive. We take picnic lunches out on the plains, dinner at the camp under the stars. My world is Dominic and his world is mine. He tells me of his life as a Maasai warrior and I tell him what it's like to be a hairdresser in Buckingham. I tell him about my village of Nashley and my house, Little Cottage, and of Archibald the Aggressive. I tell him about Mike and then I call my neighbour to see how he and Archie are faring. Our conversation is brief as the line is bad and keeps cutting out, but I think that both of my men are bearing up well without me.

When I hang up, Dominic says, 'We must go to my village tomorrow. My Daddy and Mummy would like to meet you.'

Wow. Meeting the parents. This is a big deal.

'Are you sure?' So soon? is what I really mean.

'Yes. Yes. You must see my home, my family.'

So the next day, my last day – how quickly the time has flown – we set off for Dominic's village. In deference to a lazy Brit, we don't walk what Dominic sees as a measly ten kilometres, but take the camp minibus instead. Plus I feel it wouldn't do to get eaten on the way to the in-laws.

The village – *manyatta* – is completely surrounded by a circular fence of thorny acacia branches to keep out the lions, Dominic tells me. When we pull up, the gate swings open and it's clear that we are expected.

Two lines of Maasai people come out to greet us, one of men, one of women. They're dressed in the most amazing colourful clothes. The men are in the traditional red *shukas* and carry hefty sticks, the women are in pink and blue and orange tunics, wrapped with bright cotton blankets and heavily adorned with beaded necklaces, some of which fall all the way to the ground. They're singing joyfully and they dance towards us, hips swaying.

'This is a song of greeting,' Dominic explains as we stand and wait for them to approach us.

'What shall I do?' I ask anxiously. 'What shall I say?'

'Be your own person, Just Janie,' is his only advice.

But I'm as thrilled as I am struck with terror. This is as far away from Nashley as it's possible to be. The Maasai people come close, bumping against me, the level of the singing increasing. They're all distinctively tall with the most striking facial features and elegant bearing. Then a girl smiles shyly at me and takes my hand, easing me into the dance.

'My sister,' Dominic says and he slips into the line of men beside me and we make our way, chanting, into the village.

I stumble along with her, unsure what to do. Dominic's sister emphasises the words of the song for me and I try to copy but from the hysterical giggling that ensues, I'm not sure that I make the best stab at it.

The spectacle of these people coming to meet me is remarkable but to be honest, I'm stunned at how basic the village is. A half-dozen mud huts are formed in a rough circle inside the walls and that's it, there's nothing else here. This is where

Dominic lives and, suddenly, here in his own domain, I see in shocking contrast how very different our lives are. The dancers surround us and I cling to Dominic in the middle of the circle.

'Our songs are about our lives,' he explains, while they mill around us, chanting. 'They are very important to us. Songs tell of nature, of love, the struggle between good and bad. This one tells how the women build the houses, milk the cows and care for the children.'

'What do the men do?'

'The young boys look after the cattle until they become warriors,' he says, 'and the rest of the men, we jump.'

'Jump?'

'It is very important to jump.' His face is serious. 'It is how we show that we are good men, good husbands. If you can jump well, you do not pay for your wife.'

'You're kidding me.'

'No,' he says, 'I am not.'

The women dance, another song now, and I'm urged to join in, which I do to the best of my ability, but it still causes hilarity. Their rhythm is so alien to me, a person who is used only to dancing around her handbag at weddings or nightclubs. The Maasai movement ripples through their bodies from head to toe. Then the ladies stop dancing and just chant while we stand and watch the men show off their jumping skills. Each one comes forward separately and shows his prowess.

'I am the best jumper,' Dominic tells me proudly and then he steps forward to show me.

And as jumping goes, he certainly does look like he knows what he's doing. Repeatedly and rhythmically, he leaps gracefully into the air, higher and higher. Much higher than any of the others have done.

But in truth, I'm quite frightened by this. It's the first time I've seen Dominic away from the Kiihu camp, the tourists, among the things that are familiar to me. Now, in this raw primitive setting I see who he truly is, where he really comes from. I am in awe of these people who are still trying to cling to traditions that don't appear to have changed for hundreds and hundreds of years, but I also realise that I don't know where to begin to understand them. I hate to admit this, but I wonder whether my friends are right to be worried for me. Are our cultures just too far apart for us to be able to form a relationship on middle ground? He's a man who lives entirely on milk and blood, doesn't sleep and thinks that fighting lions is no big deal. What exactly is the middle ground between my twee Nashley village and Dominic's harsh Spartan homestead? Or between my comfortable modern life and his ancient tribal customs?

The chants reach a crescendo and then we all applaud Dominic's skill. He comes over to me, not even out of breath despite his exertion.

'Do you have a dance, Just Janie? My people would consider it a great honour to see it.'

'A dance?'

'Yes.'

'Er . . . er . . . not really.' I wrack my brains. Do we even have any traditional British dances? Other than morris dancing, of course. And no one sane would want to be seen doing that in public.

'It is important,' Dominic whispers.

'Oh, right.' Wish he'd given me some warning about this. Then it hits me. 'Yes,' I say. 'I know one.'

'If you start, the women will follow you.'

'Right.' Taking a deep and disturbingly wobbly breath, I step

208

forward. This is the best I can come up with so I might as well give it my all.

'Oh. Oh. Oh,' I begin nervously. Then thinking what the hell, I kick into Beyoncé's excellent hit tune, 'Single Ladies', and the accompanying dance. How many times have I done this on the SingStar with the guys from the salon? It'll be a piece of cake. 'All the single ladies,' I intone. 'All the single ladies!'

The Maasai women look slightly bemused as they watch me, but after a few verses and when I'm getting into my stride, they gamely join in. We all smack our rumps in unison and wiggle around in a circle.

Dominic laughs heartily at my efforts – as well he might do – particularly when I advise him that if he liked it, he should have put a ring on it.

'Oh. Oh. Oh,' the Maasai ladies chant as they copy my strutting.

And I think, Oh. Oh. Oh. What have you started, Janie Johnson? What have you started with this relationship? And how exactly are you going to finish it?

Chapter 47

I meet Dominic's father and his mother and then the other three wives in the family. There seem to be dozens of children in a wide range of ages who are all Ole Nangon offspring – some who look older than Dominic, some who are still babes in arms.

My greeting is warm and enthusiastic and I feel very humble to be welcomed into their home. Instantly, my heart is captured by their sunny disposition and open manner. But inside the hut, things are even more basic. Even at my height, I can't stand up and all it consists of are a couple of sparsely furnished spaces that serve as the living room and communal bedroom. The beds are wooden pallets on the floor covered with traditional woollen *kangas*. Cooking is done on an open fire, which is smouldering in the centre of the room. There's no window or chimney and the air is stifling, hot and heavy with smoke. A few pottery dishes grace the single shelf that is fashioned from mud and there's a curved tubular jug, a calabash, in which, Dominic tells me, the milk is fermented before drinking. But that's pretty much it. No microwave, no fridge, no state-of-the-art range cooker. Just a few pots and some spare fire wood. And I know straight away, in my heart of hearts, that never, no matter how much I love Dominic, could I ever contemplate living here.

'They think you are strange,' Dominic says with a smile, 'because I tell them your family has no cattle.'

'They're very kind to have me here,' I say. 'Very kind, indeed. *Asante. Asante.*'

His whole family grin broadly at me.

'Come,' Dominic urges, 'I will show you our school.' He leads me out of the hut and to the far side of the *manyatta*.

Under an acacia tree, there's a range of wooden benches. Children, tiny ones from the age of two, up to self-conscious teenagers, crowd on to them. Their attention is held rapturously by an elderly gentleman wearing an orange *kanga* and leaning heavily on a stick. On the tree, a piece of paper is pinned. It has the days of the week and the months of the year both in Swahili and English. A young girl, about eight years old, is pointing out the words and the rest of the children are chanting them musically.

'No schoolroom?'

'We are hoping one day that the village will have enough money,' Dominic says. 'It is difficult for the children to sit still in the heat and harder when the rains come. If they come.'

He waves to the teacher and indicates that we wish to stay. With his blessing, we then sit down at the back of the class on a spare bench and listen to the lesson. The children twist and turn in their seats to get a glimpse of me and then giggle into their hands.

'Is this how you started your learning?' I lower my voice.

'Yes,' he says. 'Then I was very lucky to go to the mission school. We want to keep our customs, Just Janie, but we also see that we need to be an educated people. The Maasai cannot live by cattle alone now. Times have changed and so must we. I have encouraged my people to invite tourists into our *manyatta* as visitors. We cannot manage without them.'

Is that how they view me? I wonder. As simply another goggle-eyed tourist? Do they know that I am with Dominic as a partner? That I want to be with him for a long time?

I watch the children eager to learn, shouting out their language lesson. How on earth they manage to concentrate under the baking hot sun is beyond me. Plus it strikes me that there's no two-week Christmas break for these kids like there is at home.

'The problem is that when our young people go to school and to university, then they do not want to come back to the village any more,' Dominic tells me.

'What about you, Dominic? You see such comfort, an easiness of life at the camp. How do you then come back to your village and cope with such a hard existence?'

'I will not lie, Janie. It is a difficult thing.' He shakes his head sadly. 'I do not know if I am now Maasai warrior or Western man.'

'Do you think you could live anywhere else?'

Dominic shrugs. 'I talk to the people who come to Kiihu camp and they tell me how beautiful their own countries are. England, America, France, many, many places. I think one day that I would like to see them. I would like to see the world. But I have never been in a plane. The only time I have been in the sky is in the balloon yesterday.'

'Really?'

'Oh yes.' Dominic sighs. 'This is the land that I love. My home. How would I leave Kenya?'

I place my hand on his arm and we look into each other's eyes. How indeed? I think.

212

Chapter 48

Too quickly, the time comes for me to leave. With a heavy heart, I pack my bag and say goodbye to the camp. It has been a wonderful few days with Dominic, the best Christmas holiday ever, well worth the extortionate expense. But, I ask myself, will I ever come back here again?

Last night I lay in Dominic's arms, but we both avoided talking about what might happen next. It seems impossible that Dominic could leave here and come to England. His ties, his people, are in this land and yet I know that I could never make my permanent home in the Maasai Mara either. So where does that leave us?

Never before have I felt like this about a man, yet the barriers, the distances, the differences between us seem insurmountable. What do we do? Do I simply come back here as often as I can manage? When will that be – once, twice a year? If I save every single penny that I can, I could just about do that. Will the relationship, the love between us gradually dwindle so that my every waking moment isn't spent dreaming of Africa? Perhaps I'll move on, find someone else to love, someone like Mike who will always be there for me, kind and caring.

Dominic drives me to the airstrip in the bus and our mood is sombre. He parks up and then we watch the sky, waiting for the plane to arrive to deposit the next lucky band of tourists.

My Maasai warrior takes my hand.

'OK?' I ask.

'I do not have the words to tell you how I feel,' he says. 'It is as if you are taking my heart away with you.'

'And I feel as if I am leaving my heart here.'

'It is very sad for us, Just Janie.'

'Oh, Dominic.'

He musters one of his trademark grins. 'Oh, Just Janie,' he mimics.

'I'll phone you,' I say. Hang the expense. 'And we'll talk on Facebook.'

He nods but his expression says that it's not enough and in reality, I know that's the case too.

Then we see the plane appear on the horizon and its drone gets louder and louder, until moments later it touches down in front of us. The turnaround is amazingly quick and soon it will be time for me to go. This little plane will take me back to Nairobi and then my connecting flight to Heathrow is later this evening. The tourists pour off the plane and join their safari groups, kicking up the dust as they disappear.

'I want to teach you one more Maasai saying before you leave,' Dominic tells me. '*Aanyor pii.*'

'*Aanyor pii,*' I repeat.

'It means, I love you with all of my heart,' he says.

'*Aanyor pii,* Dominic.'

He lifts my fingers to his mouth and kisses them.

Sadly, we both know that our time has run out and we climb out of the bus. Dominic lifts my bag from the back. Now, we who have shared so much these last few days stand awkwardly together, uncertain what to say, what to do.

'I do not want you to leave,' Dominic says.

My eyes fill with tears. 'I don't want to go.'

'When will I see you again?'

'I don't know,' I say truthfully. 'When I have the money.'

'It may be a long time?'

I nod miserably. Does he realise, I wonder, that at home I'm near the bottom rung of the financial ladder and that trips like these don't come easily?

'These few days have been wonderful,' I tell him. An unforgettable Christmas and a memory that will be etched on my soul for a lifetime. Dominic wraps me in his arms and we hold each other tightly.

'*Aanyor pii*,' he says. 'Do not forget that.'

I cry as I pull away from him and head to the plane.

'You may be a long way from me, Just Janie,' he shouts after me. 'But my heart will always be with you.'

Is that enough? I want Dominic's heart to be with me always, no doubt about that. But at this moment, I desperately want the rest of him too.

Chapter 49

Wouldn't it be easier if I could just forget Dominic and fall in love with someone close to hand, someone who clearly has feelings for me? Someone like Mike?

Together, Mike and I stand in Nina's kitchen, glasses in hand. Kings of Leon blast out from the living room. Gerry bursts into the room. He has a silver conical party hat on his head, complete with pink streamers. In one hand he has a brimming glass, in the other a party trumpet, both of which he's putting to good use.

'Wooooah, wooooah!' he shouts out at the top of his voice. 'Your sex is on fire!' He thrusts his hips lasciviously at the nearest woman. Mike and I exchange a weary glance.

It's New Year's Eve and the celebration at Nina's house is in full swing. I brought Mike along for company as I knew he'd be happy to stand quietly in the corner with me, and I was right. That's exactly what we're doing.

'OK?' he asks. 'Need a top-up?'

The temptation to get blindly and roaringly drunk is very appealing, but sense prevails. 'I'm fine with this,' I assure him.

'I'm just going to get another beer,' Mike tells me. 'Don't go away.'

I don't plan on leaving this corner of the kitchen until there comes a time when I can politely go home.

Mike sets off, fighting his way to the other side of the kitchen in search of alcohol. When he's gone, Nina appears by my side. She's wearing a very short dress all covered in white and grey sequins. One of the juniors did her hair this afternoon and her bare limbs are freshly spray-tanned. There's plenty of make-up in evidence and I can tell that my friend has gone all out to look her best tonight.

'Are you going to stand here all night looking miserable?' she asks.

'I'm just a bit down,' I explain. Nina is fully aware of that.

'Sorry we can't compete with the African plains,' she says snippily. It's clear that my friend has started on the vodka early as she's already swaying in front of me.

'I can't help it, Nina,' I say, 'but I'm having a nice time just watching everyone else. Maybe I'll perk up a bit later.'

'Love isn't supposed to make you this bloody miserable,' she advises.

I don't like to point out that she's spent most of her marriage being 'bloody miserable' and for very good reason.

Out of the corner of my eye, I can see Gerry flirting with one of their neighbours. His hand is travelling slowly up and down the woman's hip, caressing it. I wonder if he has done that to her before. The neighbour certainly looks quite comfortable with it. If my friend catches him at it, then Nina will no doubt be 'bloody miserable' once more.

'I just wish Dominic was here,' I say. 'That's all.'

'Well, he's not,' my friend needlessly reminds me. 'You need something to put a smile back on your face. Can't you just get off with Mike instead?'

And, of course, that's the very moment that Mike chooses to return and stand behind her.

I incline my head slightly to try to inform my friend that the object of her derision has heard this and very clearly. But Nina is oblivious.

'He's as fit as you like, Janie. You should get in there instead of mooning over someone a million miles away. The bloke looks as if he needs a bloody good shag,' she decides. 'If you're not going to give him one, then I just might.'

Mike grins good-naturedly at me over her shoulder. 'I'll look forward to that, Nina.'

My friend splutters her vodka back into her glass. 'Oh, God,' she says, hand to head. 'Sorry, Mike. Just joking. I'd better be off. Mingle.' With that, she disappears into the throng.

'I think that was sound advice,' Mike says.

I thump his arm playfully. 'I'm really sorry. She's absolutely trolleyed.'

'She's fun,' Mike says, looking after my friend admiringly. 'Ballsy.'

'Mouthy,' I add.

'Look,' he studies his glass, 'I know how you feel about this guy. It's pants when you can't be with the one you love.'

'Yes,' I agree, 'it is.'

'Sometimes a bit of moping can be very therapeutic,' he continues. 'Goodness knows, Janie, you helped me enough when I was going through the mill after Tania left.'

'That's what friends are for.'

'Let me know if you want to slope away,' Mike says. 'I know how hard these situations can be.'

'I'll stay. For Nina's sake.'

'Let's go in the other room,' Mike suggests. 'There's a bit of boogieing going on. I'll show you some of my new dance moves.'

I laugh. 'Been practising in front of the mirror?'

'You'd better believe it.'

He takes my hand and together we weave through the crowd and into the living room. It's fast approaching midnight and the revellers are losing any inhibitions they might have had.

Rug rolled back, the team from the salon have commandeered the middle of the room as the dance floor. They're currently pogoing, arms around each other, to Prince's '1999'. Our boss, Kelly, is in the thick of the fray, pointedly enjoying herself while her older boyfriend sits and watches from the sofa looking distinctly unhappy.

'I don't think I'm that energetic,' I whisper to Mike.

'Me neither.'

Someone switches on the television and there on the screen is Big Ben. The minutes of this year tick steadily away. This year when I never expected to find love and have.

Then suddenly we're on the countdown to midnight. 'Ten! Nine! Eight! Seven! Six!' the crowd chant. 'Five! Four! Three! Two! One!' Big Ben chimes out. 'Happy new year!'

Mike takes me in his arms and kisses me softly. 'Happy new year, neighbour,' he says. 'May it bring you all that you hope for.'

'I wish the same for you too, Mike.'

He smiles at me sadly. 'I'm not sure that's going to happen.'

'You never know,' I say. 'Look at me. I never expected love to find me, but it did.'

We join in a robust chorus of 'Auld Lang Syne'. Nina works her way over to us and kisses both me and Mike, even though she seems to be having trouble focusing her eyes. Her kiss with

Mike lingers longer than it needs to, in my opinion. And when she comes up for air, she's wearing an expression of pleasant surprise. As is Mike. Hmm, feeling a bit of a gooseberry for a minute or two there. Then they look at each other and go down for another session. Oooh. I'm definitely not sure where to put myself now.

Tyrone and Clinton are snogging passionately in the corner – but not quite as passionately as Nina's husband, Gerry, and their neighbour. Steph and Cristal seem to have bagged themselves spare men and it looks like some festive spirit may well be exchanged later. I hope Cristal remembers to get the name and number of this one.

I'm smiling at the drunken scene and then, unbidden, an overwhelming wave of sadness crashes over me and I bite back a tear. No one should be alone on New Year's Eve. It's a time for being with loved ones, and mine isn't here. He's thousands of miles away under the African sky. I wonder exactly where Dominic is now. Is he working at the camp? Or is he at home in the *manyatta* with his family? I do hope so. What do the Maasai people do to bring in the new year?

'Phone him,' Mike says in my ear. Clearly he has finished snogging my friend for the time being. 'Go into the garden and phone him.'

'I've no credit left on my mobile. I should have topped it up today, but we were so busy at the salon, I clean forgot.'

'Here.' He hands his phone to me. 'My new year present to you.'

My eyes widen. 'Are you sure? It'll cost a fortune.'

'I don't like to see you sad.'

My smile comes back instantly. 'Thanks, Mike.' I peck him on the cheek and dash outside.

I punch in Dominic's number – already I know it by heart. Since I got back from Africa, I've been phoning him from my landline two or three times a week, even though I know my bill will give me a heart attack when it arrives.

Tapping my foot, I wait for the number to connect. The snow has all but gone now, but the night is cold and there's going to be a hard frost. I wish I'd thought to bring out my coat as, already, I'm shivering. Then I hear Dominic's phone ring and a second later, he picks up.

'Dominic?'

I hear the smile, the warmth, the love in his voice when he says, as if he can't believe his ears, 'Just Janie?'

I hug Mike's phone as if that will bring my Maasai warrior closer to me. 'Happy new year, darling,' I say. 'Happy new year.'

Chapter 50

So it's a new year and I've made a whole list of resolutions. This year they extend beyond not swearing and losing half a stone. This year they will involve going all out for what I want. Oh, yeah.

The salon is quiet, business slack. All the Christmas decorations are down now and everywhere looks as dull as dishwater. But perhaps that's just in comparison with the African plains. The sky is grey and baggy. Darkness falls at three o'clock and the evenings stretch interminably, but long nights alone have given me plenty of time to plan.

'You're mad,' Nina says as she gnashes on a Granny Smith. 'Stark raving bloody mad.'

'I sent him a message last night,' I continue as calmly as I can, 'on Facebook.'

My friend tuts again. 'Can't you get it back? How do I talk you out of this?'

'It's what I want,' I tell her. 'It's what he wants.'

'Is it?'

'I believe so.'

She runs her hands through her hair. 'It's the most ridiculous thing I've ever heard.'

Last night I wrote to Dominic and asked, begged, him to come to live here – with me, in Nashley. I've thought long and hard about it and know it's the right thing to do. We should be together and if we can, then we should give it all we've got.

I imparted that knowledge to Nina as we were having our morning coffee together in the staffroom of the salon and now she's in a complete strop with me.

I don't know what to say to Nina's comment. Is it so wrong of me to want to be with my loved one? I can't understand why Nina is being so hostile.

'This is a once-in-a-lifetime love,' I point out. I'm absolutely sure of it. 'I can't let that slip through my fingers.'

'What nonsense,' she scoffs.

But is it? Thirty is well behind me and yet it's the first time I've ever felt like this. If I don't make it with Dominic, what are the chances of me finding someone who makes me feel like this again? Does it sound ridiculous to say that I feel we were destined to meet? That against all the odds, we should be together? They say that there is someone for everyone and I feel, most definitely, as if I have found my soulmate. How many people can say that with absolute conviction?

'What will he do?' Nina asks. 'For work? Will they even let him in?'

'We let *everyone* in, don't we?'

'How's he going to pay for his fare?' my friend wants to know. 'Are you going to send him the money?'

That was my plan.

Nina rolls her eyes without me having to say anything.

Since New Year's Eve, I've been missing Dominic desperately. I think the days we spent together over Christmas have only served to intensify our love for each other.

'He hasn't said yes yet,' I point out. But he will. I'm sure he will.

'This is what they all do, Janie,' Nina goes on. 'If he comes over here, he'll go through your bank account in no time.'

'There's nothing in my bank account for him to go through,' I remind her.

I'm also still in debt to Mike to the tune of a thousand pounds. I will, however, be paying that back the minute I get my salary this month, which will be any day now. As well as all the extra hours I worked in the weeks before the holiday, I was on a product-selling frenzy that Alan Sugar would have been proud of. If it was in my power, no one went out of the salon without a bottle of shampoo or conditioner or some essential hair grooming requisite. With all the overtime I did before Christmas and my extra commission on sales, I'm hoping that I'll be able to clear my debt to my neighbour completely. I haven't told Mike yet about my plan to bring Dominic to come and live here and I'm praying that he'll be far more supportive than Nina has been so far.

Cristal, Steph and the boys arrive in the staffroom, all wrapped up against the cold weather outside.

'Have you heard this?' Nina says to them as they're still stripping off their outer layers. There's a distinct snort in her voice that I take exception to. 'Janie wants her Maasai bloke to come and live here.'

They all look very sceptical.

'Can't you find a nice English fella?' Cristal asks.

'Can you?' I retort.

Cristal shrugs her defeat. 'Fair point.'

Steph says, 'Sounds like a bag full of trouble to me.'

Kelly puts her head around the door. 'First customer's here, Janie. Mrs Silverton.'

'Thanks.'

'She's only gone and asked this bloody Maasai warrior to live with her,' Nina informs our boss with a flick of her thumb that I read as disdainful.

'Really?'

I nod my confirmation, fuming silently at the way my friend is bandying my news about.

'Oh, Janie,' Kelly intones. 'Do be careful. Are you sure it's the right thing to do?'

'I think so.'

Kelly and Nina exchange a doubtful look. Do I tell them how to live their lives? Do I? Do I ever tell Kelly that she and her ageing, petty criminal boyfriend are terminally unsuited? Do I ever mention to Nina that her lecherous husband takes every opportunity to feel up any woman who gives him half a chance? Do I ever tell Cristal that she should stop indiscriminately shagging around every weekend with any knobhead who asks her? Do I tell Steph that there's no such thing as a stress-free 'fuck buddy' and that someone will get hurt in the end and it's more likely to be her than the bloke involved? Do I tell Tyrone and Clinton that they should stop playing around and just settle down together?

No, I don't.

Why, then, do they all feel free to comment on my love life, my choice of man? Is that what love, what chemistry is all about? It doesn't matter how little you have in common or how little suited you are, when that stupid cupid strikes there's no ignoring those arrows that get under your skin.

They don't see that this is not poor old Janie Johnson being gullible or taken advantage of. It's me asking Dominic to make a huge sacrifice and leave the land that he loves, where he is

225

most at home, and to trust me enough to come and live my life here with me.

I stand up. 'I'd better not keep Mrs Silverton waiting.' I march out into the salon, quietly grinding my teeth as I go.

Mrs Silverton is already gowned up and waiting. Just a wash and blow-dry today. Another posh do must be in the offing.

'Janie, love,' she says when she sees me. 'How's the big romance?'

'It's fine,' I say.

'I think you should keep him at arm's length,' she warns. 'My friend brought a bloke over from Egypt last year. Nightmare.' My client shakes her head. 'Worst thing she ever did. He asked her to marry him, quite forgetting he already had a wife back home.'

'It doesn't always have to be like that,' I start to say and then I give up. I just give up. Wait until Dominic's here, I think. Wait until he's here and they can all see what he's like. Then they'll understand.

226

Chapter 51

Dominic has said yes. His message came just two days – and no fingernails – later. I stare at the screen in front of me. He's coming. My Maasai warrior is coming. He's packing all his worldly goods, placing his utmost trust in me and is travelling halfway around the world to live in Nashley.

Archie is on my lap. 'We're going to have someone else live with us,' I tell my cat.

His miaow tells me that he is distinctly unimpressed. Even if one of the neighbourhood dogs accidentally strays onto his territory, Archie is all for kicking its head in. He only tolerates Mike because he's good at opening cans. How will he feel when there's another man in my bed?

'You'll love him,' I reassure Archie while crossing my fingers. 'I do.'

Dominic's note tells me that he has to apply for a visa to be able to visit. It will involve an arduous three-day journey to Nairobi and back on a dozen different public buses as he has to appear at the embassy in person. I hope there are no hitches there. I check how much the air fare might be and gulp. I'll have to work some more overtime, sell some more stuff – possibly my body – in order to get the money together to send to Dominic. There are plenty of excess ornaments in Little Cottage that I could get rid of at a car boot sale, surely?

Downstairs, in an envelope, I have a thousand pounds in cash to give to Mike. I'm going to pop round there later to watch a film with him and I hope that I can surprise him by returning his money so soon. What might be more of a surprise for him though is when I tell him that he will soon have a new neighbour in Nashley.

I sit at my kitchen table and eat a bowl of pasta and pesto sauce for my dinner. How strange will it feel to have someone else in the cottage after so much time on my own? I can hardly picture Dominic sitting here opposite me and, at the same time, I can hardly wait.

When I've cleared up, I clutch my envelope and take it round to Mike's house. He beams as he lets me in the door and I hold out my hand to him.

'What's this?'

'Debt repayment,' I say. 'Thanks so much.'

He takes the envelope. 'Are you sure? I don't need it yet.'

'You should have it while I've got it,' I advise. 'I might need to borrow it again soon.'

Mike cocks an eyebrow.

Launching in without preamble, I say, 'I've asked Dominic to come and live here.'

The other eyebrow joins it.

I wait for him to tell me what a bad idea this is, how stupid I am, how I don't know the man. All of these things and possibly some more that I haven't even thought of, but Mike says nothing. It's fair to say that he looks a little bit stunned by my announcement.

228

'Are you paying for him to come here?'

'Yes.' Now the stern warnings will follow.

'You'll be needing this then.' Mike offers the envelope back to me.

I hold up a hand. 'I'm going to try to raise it with overtime and I'm thinking about doing a car boot sale.'

'I'll help you,' Mike says. 'I've got a load of old sports stuff in the loft that I could do with getting rid of: squash racquets, cricket bats, ski gear that I'm never likely to use again.'

I sigh gratefully at Mike. 'You're so good to me.'

He takes my hand and kisses my fingers to his lips. 'That's because I love you.'

Right. Where can I take this conversation? 'Mike . . .'

My neighbour holds a finger to my lips. 'And I want you to be happy, Janie. I've said that before. If there's anything I can do,' Mike continues, 'you only have to ask. Remember that.' He squeezes my hand. 'Always remember that. Promise me.'

'I will.'

'I'm going to open a bottle of wine and we can toast Dominic's arrival. Pick a film,' he says and spreads out a selection of DVDs on his coffee table.

'Anything in particular you fancy?'

'As long as it's not *Out of Africa* or *The Lion King*, I don't mind,' he teases.

I can't believe how kind this man is and I'm feeling very emotional. I think I'll steer clear of anything too slushy or romantic that will make me blub. Instead, I'll go for something with a high body count or lots of gratuitous violence.

Chapter 52

Barely two weeks later and I hear that Dominic's visa has come through. He took the bus all the way to Nairobi and back without a hitch and flying in the face of the normal pace of bureaucracy, his application sailed through. He texted me the news. That has to be a good omen, right? I feel sick and elated in equal measure. There's no going back now. This is really going to happen. I gave Dominic my credit card details and he walked to the next village to book his flight on the internet. He messages me to let me know the date. In another week's time, he'll be here. Maniacally, I start to tidy the house and try to make space in a crammed wardrobe for Dominic's things.

At the salon, there's an underlying tension in the air that's not very pleasant. They're all talking about me behind my back, I can just tell, and I'm sure it's not me being paranoid. It seems to be led by my supposedly closest friend, Nina, and that makes me very sad. Why can't she simply be happy for me?

At the allotted time on the allotted day, I set out for the airport to meet Dominic from his plane. Mike had offered to drive me, but how could I do that to him? I would have liked Nina to come along with me, but she didn't offer and I didn't feel that I could ask her. Relations between us aren't that good and I can tell that she's having problems with Gerry again, but she's not confiding in me. I hope that when Dominic is finally here she'll grow to like him. How could she not?

This morning, I spent my time running around like a headless chicken making the cottage look like a show home. Now every surface is gleaming. The place hasn't been this tidy since the day I moved in.

Now, driving round the M25, my palms are sweating and I'm all in a lather. The air-conditioning is on full-tilt even though the temperature outside is near zero degrees.

It's just over a month since I last saw Dominic but, stupidly, I'm worried that he won't recognise me. I worry too how he's got on with the long plane journey as his only previous experience of flying was on the balloon flight we took over the Maasai Mara.

Leaving the car in the Short Stay car park, I head into the terminal building at Heathrow. Checking the board, it seems that Dominic's plane is on time and with good luck and a following wind, he should be coming out of the arrivals gate at any moment.

I stand at the barrier, taking up my place amid the relatives, the taxi drivers, the crush waiting for people to arrive, be it business colleagues, loved ones or Maasai warriors. I'm barely able to keep still. Excitement is even making my toes twitch.

A steady flow of people emerge through the automatic doors and I look over the heads in front of me, trying to pick out Dominic. Minutes pass, then more. Nothing. I should have got him to text me to let me know that he'd actually got on the plane. Anything could have gone wrong. The bus to Nairobi could have broken down. What if it took Dominic longer than usual to walk the ten kilometres to meet it? What if he was eaten by a lion on the way?

Then my breath catches in my throat.

The doors open and there, standing tall in his traditional red *shuka* is Dominic. His shoulders are back, his head up, but he looks anxious and confused, lost. I push my way to the front of the barriers.

'Dominic!' I shout. 'Dominic! Over here!'

He turns and sees me and the whole of his face lights up, and I can't stand it any longer. With superhuman strength, I climb up the barrier, jump over and run into Dominic's arms. He picks me up and twirls me around.

'You made it,' I say. 'Thank God. You made it.'

He lowers me to the ground. 'Janie,' he says. 'My Janie.'

We kiss, oblivious to the crowds around us. Then we pull away from each other, shy now.

'Come on, let's get you home.' I slip my hand into his. 'The car's just across the way. How was the flight?'

Dominic shrugs. 'I think it was a good flight, but I did not feel as if I was in the sky at all.'

'I know. Boring as hell,' I agree. 'Did you watch movies?'

'No,' he says. 'I did not know how it worked and I did not like to ask.'

As we leave the concourse and hit the street, Dominic recoils. The temperature out here is hovering just above freezing and Dominic is only wearing his tunic and a blanket. On his feet are open leather sandals. He is, quite probably, going to die of hypothermia before I manage to get him back to Nashley. It must be like stepping straight out of a sauna and into a freezer for him. How I wish I'd thought to borrow a coat from Mike for Dominic. And trousers. Some socks wouldn't have gone

232

amiss either. How stupid of me not to think of it. I just assumed that Dominic would be in Western clothes, but then I know that he has nothing else. As I take him to the car, he looks around in awe at all the vehicles in the multi-storey car park.

'It's much nicer than this once we get away from the airport,' I assure him.

He nods uncertainly. My heart goes out to him and it suddenly hits me just how much trust he has put in me, in our relationship, to come here. Everyone is warning me about how awful it is going to be for me and no one – not even me, if I'm brutally honest – has thought about how different and difficult it will be for Dominic.

All his worldly goods are in one tiny case, which I put on the back seat. In the car, I whack the heater up as high as it will go, but Dominic is already shivering.

'We'll get you some clothes,' I promise. 'Tomorrow. Some warm things.'

'I would like that, Janie,' he says.

'We'll be home before you know it and my cottage is lovely and warm.'

He smiles at me and I see the relief in his eyes.

Before I pull away, I turn to him. 'Thank you,' I say. 'Thank you for coming to me.'

'I am very pleased to see you, Miss Janie Johnson. Very pleased indeed.'

I lean towards him and we wrap our arms around each other again.

'Everything will be all right,' I whisper against his neck. 'Just you wait and see.'

233

Chapter 53

We drive down the narrow winding lanes to Nashley, past the ancient church and manor house, past the duckpond where the ducks have, quite sensibly, settled down for the night. When I pull up outside Little Cottage, I turn to Dominic and say, 'Your new home.'

Dominic, it has to be said, looks more than a bit shell-shocked. 'Your village,' he says, 'is not like my village.'

'No,' I say. 'But you'll love it here. I'm sure you will.'

He looks reluctant to leave the warmth of the car, which is quite understandable.

'The house will be warm,' I assure him. 'I'll get you some clothes from my friend, Mike, who lives next door. He'll help us out until we can get to the shops.'

Dominic nods.

'The only thing I need to warn you about is my cat, Archie. He's a nightmare. His favourite game is to pounce on strangers and part them from their flesh. Just watch him.'

My Maasai warrior laughs. 'I should be frightened of a cat?'

I shrug. 'You've been warned.'

We brave the cold and rush to the front door. 'Watch your head,' I advise as I open up.

Dominic has to stoop to get inside and in the living room, there's just about enough headroom for him in between the low beams. I flick the lights on and my appropriately named little cottage is shown off in its full glory.

'This is your home?'

'And yours now,' I remind him. 'Do you like it?'

'I have never seen anywhere like this before,' Dominic admits.

'Do you think you can live here?'

'Oh, yes,' he says. 'I am sure.'

Then he whacks his head on a beam.

As Dominic rubs his forehead, Archie pads nonchalantly down the stairs. Then his hackles rise and he spits at the new member of our family.

'Don't be naughty, Archie,' I admonish. 'Come and say hello.'

But before Archie can move, Dominic picks up the cat by the scruff of the neck and holds him aloft. '*Jambo*. Come, cat,' he says gently. 'We are to be friends.'

Archie's eyes bulge and I'm not sure whether that's surprise or terror registering on my feline friend's face. Dominic drops Archie around his neck like a shawl and much to my surprise, the cat settles there without protest – even though his eyes are still agog.

'I'll show you the kitchen. It's nice and warm in there as the range is always on.'

'This is very nice,' Dominic says as he follows me through, ducking as he does.

'Can I get you a drink? Tea? Coffee? Something to warm you up?'

'Milk,' he says. 'Just milk.'

'I can heat it in the microwave.'

He nods uncertainly.

'Sit, sit,' I say. 'Make yourself comfortable.'

Dominic does as he's told and sits at the kitchen table, cat still draped about his shoulders. I do believe that Archibald the Aggressive is purring contentedly. Dominic strokes one of his dangling paws, which would signal imminent danger for most, but Archie simply blows out a happy bubble of spit. My Maasai warrior looks so out of place in my tiny kitchen – the darkness of his skin, the brightness of his clothes, the sheer size of him.

I fuss with the cups and the milk and the microwave. What I want to do is take Dominic in my arms again and tell him how grateful I am he came into my life, that I will do my best to make everything all right for him and how much I appreciate him turning his life upside down for me. Instead, I say, 'Are you hungry? Can I get you something to eat?'

'I could not eat the food on the plane,' he explains.

'So you haven't eaten since yesterday?'

He shakes his head.

I wrack my brain to think of something that Dominic would like. A lasagne ready meal is probably out of the question. 'Porridge?' I say. 'What about some porridge?'

'If you think so.'

I pull a packet of Oatso Simple out of the cupboard and fling it in the microwave.

'I'll just call Mike. See if he can bring some clothes round for you. I don't want you to die of cold.'

'*Hakuna matata*, Janie. I will get used to it.'

'We can go and get you some Western clothes tomorrow.'

236

Dominic looks as if he hadn't considered this possibility. He looks embarrassed. 'I have no money to buy clothes.'

'Don't worry about that,' I admonish. I don't want him to worry about anything. Kneeling in front of Dominic, I rest my head in his lap. 'Everything I have is yours now. Do you understand that?'

He strokes my head and I hear him sigh shakily. '*Asante*, Janie.'

The microwave pings and I bring him his bowl of Oatso Simple. He peers at it suspiciously.

'It's good,' I assure him. 'You have to eat something.'

He picks up the spoon and tastes it tentatively. His face relaxes into a smile. 'It is good,' he says. 'Very good.'

Sitting down next to him, I stroke my hand over the dark smoothness of his shaved head. I will do everything in my power to make this man happy.

'We'll be OK. I promise you, Dominic. We'll be OK.'

Chapter 54

Half an hour later and Mike knocks on the door, bringing the clothes I requested for Dominic.

'Just a few bits,' Mike says. 'Jumper and jeans, a coat, some socks. I brought a pair of shoes, but I only take a size nine so I'm not sure that they'll fit.'

My God, I hadn't even considered half of these things. We're going to need a serious shopping trip as soon as possible. I gratefully take the clothes from Mike. 'This is brilliant.'

'If there's anything else you need . . .'

'Come through,' I say excitedly. 'Meet Dominic.'

Mike looks uncertain.

'Please . . .'

With a tired smile, he follows me through to the kitchen. Dominic stands as we enter. He hits his head on a beam again.

'I'm going to have to cover all the beams in foam, if you keep doing that.'

Dominic grins.

I turn to Mike to introduce him and find that my neighbour is standing, staring open-mouthed at my lover.

'Mike,' I say. 'This is Dominic Ole Nangon.'

Mike keeps staring.

'Mike?'

'Sorry, sorry.' He snaps himself out of his trance and holds out his hand. 'I'm Mike. From next door. Very pleased to meet you.'

Dominic shakes his hand and I see Mike wince at his grip. 'Thank you, Mike. I am very happy to be here.'

'I brought some clothes,' Mike says, 'to help you out. But, bloody hell, I don't think you'll get anywhere near them, man.' He looks Dominic up and down. 'How tall are you?'

'Very tall,' Dominic says.

That breaks the ice and we all laugh together.

'Look, if you need anything,' Mike says to Dominic, 'I'm just next door. You only have to ask.'

'Thank you, Mike.'

They shake hands again.

'I hope you'll be happy here.' Then Mike says, 'I won't stay. I'm sure you've got things to do. To get settled in.' He's embarrassed now and I don't want him to feel like that. 'I'll be off.'

'We'll catch up with you in the week, Mike. Come round for dinner one night.'

'I'd like that.'

As I show him to the door, Mike turns to me, a concerned frown on his face. 'I think he's going to need some help settling in, Janie,' he says. 'He's a bit like a fish out of water here.'

Bristling slightly, I say, 'He'll be fine.'

'It wasn't a criticism,' Mike adds hastily. 'I just want you to know that I'm here for you. For both of you.'

I relax at that and kiss him on the cheek. 'Thanks, Mike. Catch you later.'

Back in the kitchen, I make Dominic some more hot milk and

239

another packet of Oatso Simple. I'm going to have to stock the cupboard up with this, I can see.

'Well,' I say to Dominic as he eats, 'what would you be doing at home now?'

'There are no guests in the camp,' he tells me, 'so I would be practising my jumping with my friends.'

'Oh.' I'd forgotten about the jumping thing. 'You can do that here if you want to, out in the back garden.'

Then the doorbell rings and, through the spyhole, I see Nina standing there.

'Hey, lady,' she says when I open the door. 'Thought I'd just drop by and see if everything's OK.'

Nina never just drops by. She's either come by way of apology or she simply can't wait to see what Dominic's like. Whatever the reason, I'm happy to see her as things haven't been right between us for weeks.

'It's fine,' I tell her. 'Dominic's flight was on time. Come through and meet him, he's in the kitchen. Poor thing is half frozen to death here. He's left twenty-nine degrees in the Maasai Mara.'

Dominic stands as Nina comes into the kitchen. This time, he doesn't bang his head. His broad grin spreads over his face.

'This is Nina,' I say. 'My best friend. I've told you all about her.'

'Yes,' Dominic says. 'I am very pleased to meet you.'

My friend stares at him too, but not in a good way. She takes in his height, his red *shuka*, his colourful blanket, his bare feet and it's clear that she doesn't like what she sees.

'Tea,' I say. 'I'll make tea.' I nudge my friend in the ribs. 'You sit and talk to Dominic.'

Lowering herself into the chair opposite him, Nina says, 'HELLO. HOW. ARE. YOU?'

'Dominic's not deaf, Nina,' I snap as I make a cup of tea. 'He speaks perfectly good English.'

'WHAT. DO. YOU. THINK. OF. OUR. COUNTRY?'

'I. THINK. IT. IS. VERY. NICE,' he shouts back and I can see the mischievous twinkle in his eye.

'There's no need to talk to him like a Spanish waiter.'

'SORRY,' she says.

I hand her a cup of tea and we all sit in awkward silence.

'I. HAVE. TO. GO,' Nina says, quickly downing her tea. 'THINGS. TO. DO. SEE. YOU. AGAIN. DOMINIC.'

'YES,' he says. 'HASTA. LA. VISTA. BABY.'

My friend recoils in shock. She flicks her head, indicating that I should go to the door with her, which I do. In the living room, she grabs my arm tightly. 'Have you lost your mind?' she hisses.

'Why?'

'This is him? The love of your life?'

'Yes.'

'What do you think you're playing at?' My friend shakes her head, bewildered. 'How can you love a man like that?'

'Like what? He's handsome, he's funny, he's interesting.'

'Pah,' Nina says.

'Are you being racist?'

'Racist? Don't be ridiculous. I'm being sensible, whereas you seem to have lost your marbles. Take a look in the mirror, Janie. Have you seen how different you are? What have you got in common? You can't create a relationship out of this.'

At this point, I could mention to her that I'd rather be with Dominic any day than a lecherous, smarmy man like her husband who hits on all my friends. Or, even worse, someone like Lewis The Moron who she was quite happy to fix me up with.

But, of course, I don't. I take all her venom about Dominic on the chin. I know she will come to love him in time.

'This time you really have lost the plot, Janie.' My friend wags a finger in my face. 'And when it all goes horribly wrong, don't say that I didn't warn you.' With that she flounces out, leaving me open-mouthed and fuming.

Back in the kitchen, Dominic is sitting at the table, still grinning.

'That went well,' I say.

My proud Maasai warrior comes and puts his arms around me. 'Some we will win and some we will lose, Just Janie,' he says sagely. 'I think we will count that as a lose.'

At that, we both burst out laughing and Dominic hugs me tighter. My heart overflows with love for him. He kisses me and as I melt all over again, I think that this is where I'm happiest, wrapped in his warm embrace. I don't care whether my friends like or loathe my choice of man. Sod them, I think. Sod the lot of them.

Chapter 55

In the bedroom, Dominic lays his case on the bed and opens it. Archie sticks his nose in for a quick examination. Suddenly this room seems a lot smaller with Dominic in it. I look at my standard double bed and wonder exactly how Dominic's long frame will fit into it. There is very little in his case, but there *is* a very big machete.

'How on earth did you get that through security?' I ask.

'Security?' Dominic shrugs. 'I do not know.' He draws it from the case.

'Wow.' That looks like it could do a lot of damage. 'We're a bit funny about knives here,' I explain. 'You'd better leave that in the house.'

'How will I kill our food? How will I cut through the bush?'

'We don't do a lot of that here either.' I take the knife from him and slip it in the drawer I've cleared for him. 'You'll see. You'll be able to manage just fine without it.'

He doesn't look convinced but I think that if I take him to Asda tomorrow and show him that all our food comes already dead and in plastic packaging, he might understand. He'll also soon realise that the worst he will come across in Nashley is a seriously overgrown clematis.

'I have already left my spear behind,' he says. 'My shield, my spear and my knife are my Maasai badges of honour. We do not go anywhere without them.'

His shield is small, oval-shaped, and made of goatskin, I'd guess. He holds it proudly to him.

Can't see him needing that here either, but I decide not to say anything.

Dominic puts a few other items of clothing in the drawer – it seems he has taken the art of travelling light to extremes. He lifts two strings of beads from his case. 'One day I hope that we will be married, Just Janie,' he says, 'but until then, I have brought these.'

He holds up the necklaces. They're both intricately worked with thousands of tiny glass beads.

'Will you accept this gift from me?'

'Yes,' I say rather breathlessly.

Dominic places the circle of beads over my head. It sits on my jumper like a flat collar and the strings hang down to my feet. 'It's beautiful.'

'It is the necklace of a married woman.'

'And this is for you?'

He nods and hands me the other necklace which I place over his head. This is much shorter, but no less stunning.

'Now we are engaged,' I tell him.

'Engaged?'

'It means we have promised each other that one day we will be married.'

My Maasai warrior smiles. 'Then we are engaged, Just Janie.'

Dominic is allowed to live in this country on a temporary

244

basis for six months on his visa. After that, he has to leave or we can apply to get married. The other slight problem is that he's not allowed to work here for the initial six-month period, which is going to put a strain on the finances. But we'll manage. I'm sure we will. Dominic is hardly high-maintenance. There's just going to be some initial outlay for clothes for him, and my oats bill is going to rise considerably. Not much more.

'Would you like a nice hot bath before we go to bed?'

'Yes, Janie.' His eyes shine. 'That is a luxury I have never had. At home, we must walk to collect water from the river and we would not waste firewood to heat the water just to wash.'

'I'll go and run it.'

I fill the bath and pour in some foaming gel. Instead of the bright overhead light, I burn some fragrant candles.

Dominic comes to stand at the door, watching me.

'Want to try to squeeze in together?'

'In there?' Dominic laughs.

'We could give it a go.'

In a second, Dominic shrugs out of his *shuka* and lets it fall to the floor. He steps into the bath and, shyly, I undress and get in with him.

His long limbs fill every space as I sit between his legs with my back against his chest and we slide down into the water, letting the bubbles cover us.

'This is a very civilised country, my Janie,' Dominic says with a sigh.

'I hope you'll be very happy here.'

'If I am with you, then I will be,' he says.

Afterwards, damp skin against damp skin, we make love tenderly on top of the bed, with Archie complaining vociferously from the floor where he's been banished to. Already, it seems he is jealous of my place in Dominic's affections.

We slide under the duvet and I notice with a smile that Dominic's feet stick out of the bottom and hang over the edge of the bed. A king-size bed won't even fit in this room, so we'll have to manage. I think of the wooden pallet that was Dominic's bed on the hard floor and hope that even this is better for him.

'How did your parents feel about you coming here?' I ask quietly in the darkness.

'They are pleased that I will have a new life,' Dominic replies softly, 'but they are sad that I leave their home. They knew too that the Maasai ways were not always my ways.'

'I'll do my best to look after their son,' I promise.

'Then they can ask no more.'

'We should send them some money,' I say. 'When we've got a little bit to spare, we should send some to them. Would that help?'

'Most certainly. When they can, they use Maasai medicine but sometimes it is not enough and they need to buy Western drugs, antibiotics. My family always need money for that.'

And here's me thinking that it would provide a few extra treats for them.

'Then we'll do it,' I assure him. 'Just as soon as we can.' I snuggle against him.

Dominic clicks his fingers and says, 'Come, cat.'

I hear Archie as he thumps gently onto the bed and curls up against Dominic's shoulder. I can hardly bear to take my eyes off my lover for one single minute and don't want to go to sleep, but I curl into Dominic's side and very soon tiredness overtakes me. As I sink into sleep, I hear Dominic whisper against my hair.

246

'I will watch over you, Janie Johnson, every day of my life,' he says.

As I fall deeper and deeper, I know that I have never felt more loved or more protected.

Chapter 56

In the morning I wake up and Dominic isn't by my side. Neither is Archie. I have a momentary panic and then I reason that he can't have gone far. Slipping on my dressing gown, I pad downstairs and hit the kitchen. There's no sign of Dominic or Archie here. I glance out into the back garden, but they're not there either. I flick on the kettle and start to make a cup of tea, when there's a knock on the door.

Checking the spyhole, I see Dominic standing there with Archie around his neck. But he's not alone. I fling open the door.

On either side of my lover and my cat there is a burly uniformed policeman. A squad car is parked next to mine.

'Dominic!' I throw my arms around him. 'Are you OK? Are you hurt?'

'I am fine, Just Janie,' he assures me. 'These nice men have told me that I have been bad.'

'Bad?'

One of the officers steps forward. 'We had a complaint from several of your neighbours. Apparently they spotted this gentleman, Mr Ole Nangon, jumping over their fences and wandering around in their back gardens.'

I turn to him. 'Dominic?'

'I am a Maasai warrior,' he says proudly. 'It is my job to protect the village. That is what I was doing.'

The policemen raise their eyebrows.

'He is,' I confirm sheepishly. 'He only arrived in England yesterday. I haven't had a chance to explain the official Neighbourhood Watch Scheme to him yet.'

'It quite startled one of the ladies in particular,' one of the policemen says. He checks his notebook. 'Mrs Peterman. Gave her a bit of a turn.'

'I'm sorry,' I say to him. 'I'll take Dominic around the village today, introduce him to people.'

'I think by now they'll already know who he is,' the policeman offers.

I'm sure if Mrs Peterman was involved then she will have made sure that they do. I can just imagine Dominic hopping over her yew hedge in his red *shuka* and not much else. That'll be a tale that spreads like wildfire.

'I have apologised to the lady, Janie,' he says. 'A Maasai warrior must dedicate his life to achieving harmony with his people. I thought that I was doing a good thing.'

'I'm sure you were.'

'Once the local villains hear that there's a Maasai warrior protecting your village, I'm sure the burglary rate will drop off quite significantly,' the policeman observes. 'Well, Miss, Mr Ole Nangon, we'll be leaving you.'

'You're not charging Dominic with anything?'

'No,' the officer says. 'No charge. Mrs Peterman was happy to see it all as a simple misunderstanding. We're just very happy to have a good story to take back to the station on a quiet Sunday morning.' He laughs in spite of himself. 'Wait 'til we tell the lads.'

'Thank you.'

'Don't go frightening the villagers, young man,' the policeman warns. He tips his hat to us and then they both head back down the garden path, leaving Dominic in my tender loving care.

'Oh, Dominic,' I say when we've waved them away. 'I'll have to instruct you in the niceties of *our* village life. I don't want you getting arrested.'

'I just want to belong,' Dominic says. 'I want to be an English gentleman and to make you proud of me.'

'I'm very proud of you just as you are,' I tell him.

'I think that I frightened the policemen just a little bit,' he confides.

'I'm not surprised.' Then, 'You don't need to protect us here. There are no lions in Nashley, Dominic. No wild animals at all.'

'No?'

'Not unless you count Archie.'

We burst into laughter and giggle like children until tears run from our eyes.

Chapter 57

I shoehorn Dominic into Mike's clothes. It's a bit of a disaster. Despite Mike having a fairly average frame, the sleeves of the jumper stop halfway down Dominic's forearms. The jeans could nearly accommodate another person around the waist and they also stop way short of his ankles. The shoes go nowhere near his feet, neither do the socks. He looks like some terrible mutation of a trainspotter.

It's almost ten o'clock and the shops will be opening soon. If we dash into the city there's a shop called Tall Boys there and I'm sure they'll be able to cater for Dominic's clothing requirements. Plus it would be better if no one saw him dressed like this, but if he goes just in his *shuka* not only is he likely to die of cold, he could well frighten people too.

'Let's go,' I say to Dominic when he's finished his second bowl of porridge. As we head to the door, I notice that we're not alone. 'Archie can't come with us.'

'No?' Dominic lifts him from his shoulders. 'Stay, cat.'

Archie backchats in protest and slinks off to shred the sofa in revenge.

'I'm going to have to change this cat's name to Archibald the

Affable. He's a reformed character since you arrived. I can't believe how he's taken to you. He normally doesn't like anyone,' I say. 'Really, he doesn't. Even the post office have given him an ASBO because he claws the postman through the letterbox.'

'ASBO?'

'Anti-Social Behaviour Order. If he keeps doing it, they won't deliver my post any more.'

'They are frightened of a *cat*?' Dominic finds this hilarious.

'He only just tolerates Mike because he spends so much time at my house and also looks after Archie when I'm away.'

'You and Mike are very close,' Dominic notes.

'As friends,' I say. 'That's all.'

'I think that Mike would like it to be more.'

'You're right,' I admit. 'But he knows it would never happen. He's been very good to me and I'm sure he'll be a good friend to you. I couldn't have come out to see you at Christmas if Mike hadn't lent me the money.'

'Then he is a very kind man.'

'Yes.' I decide to fess up about Lewis Moran as well. 'There is another man.'

His eyebrow raises.

'There's nothing in it. He's been pestering me,' I tell Dominic. 'I had one disastrous date with him before I met you and now he won't leave me alone. Every now and again he turns up at the house. I just wanted you to know in case he does that and I'm not here. I'll put the word out that you're living here now and hopefully that will get the message through to him. If it doesn't, then you have my enthusiastic permission to scare him off.'

Dominic nods thoughtfully.

'Come on. We need to go before the shopping centre gets busy.' We leave the house and jump into the car.

'Can I drive the car, Janie?'

'Do you have a driving licence?'

He shrugs that he doesn't.

'Then maybe not.' Though having seen the way Dominic can throw a vehicle around the African plains, I'm sure the roundabouts of Milton Keynes would hold no fear for him. 'We'll have to organise for you to take a test here.'

Dominic smiles at me. 'I cannot believe that I live here now.'

'Me neither.'

In the shopping centre, Dominic stands and stares in awe. 'These are all shops?'

'Yes.'

'I have never been in a place like this,' he says. 'How can people need to buy so many things?'

'I don't know. It's just the way we are here.'

'I am a Maasai warrior,' he continues. 'I should not be afraid, yet my heart is pounding in my chest.'

'That's a normal bloke's response,' I assure him.

'Are you being serious?'

'Yes. Most men are terrified of shopping. We'll be in and out like a flash,' I promise.

'There are so many people. This is a very busy place,' Dominic remarks.

It's true that the shopping centre is filling up now and the crowds mill up and down the aisles, but it's still early. 'This is nothing. You should come here on a Saturday.'

'I do not think I wish to do that.'

'Probably a good idea.' Even I try to avoid coming here on a

Saturday, when retail frenzy is at its peak. For Dominic it must be utterly mind-blowing. His nearest shop in the Mara – a mud hut with a few dozen items for sale – was a ten-kilometre walk or more. This must seem like shopping heaven – or hell, depending on your perspective.

In Tall Boys, the middle-aged lady who comes to assist us goes all silly at the sight of Dominic. She clucks around him like a mother hen, helping him as he struggles with the buttons of the shirt he's trying on.

'Oh my,' she keeps saying. 'Oh my, oh my.'

But in no time, she finds him jeans that not only fit him on the waist, but also go all the way down to the floor. We buy a couple of shirts and sweaters, the jeans and a pair of smart trousers and a warm coat. They have shoes here too and we discover that Dominic is a size fourteen. It's the first time he's ever worn full shoes rather than sandals and he's walking as if he's got flippers on his feet. I get him a pair of smart shoes, and trainers too.

'I will not need all these things,' Dominic protests.

'Oh, you will, lovely,' the attentive assistant assures him. 'You will.'

'My whole family does not have this amount of clothing.'

It's hard to remember that Dominic has nothing more to his name than a couple of red *shukas*, a blanket and a pair of sandals, that the things we take so much for granted are completely alien to him. When we send his family some money, I should also put a parcel together of my surplus T-shirts for his mother and his sisters.

'This is a land of plenty,' he says. 'You have it all. Food, clothing, money.'

It's a land of profligate consumerism and waste, I think,

though I don't correct Dominic. Already seeing how little he has compared with how much we have has left me feeling slightly ashamed. I've always been quite careful, but ever since meeting Dominic I've made sure that I don't throw any food away and all my old clothes go to Oxfam. They're small things, but it's a start.

An hour after we arrive, Mike's clothes go into a carrier bag and we leave with Dominic looking absolutely gorgeous in his Western outfit.

'Thank you, Just Janie. *Asante*. One day I will repay all of this money to you. When I have a job.'

'Well, you can't do that yet,' I remind him, 'so let's not worry about it. This is my gift to you.' I tuck my arm in his. 'We can't have you freezing to death.'

He keeps staring at himself in amazement as we pass by the shop windows, drawn by his own unfamiliar reflection. 'Now no one will know that I am not an English gentleman,' he says proudly as he strokes his shirt.

'No,' I agree fondly, gazing up at all six foot several of him. 'They certainly wouldn't.'

Chapter 58

Back at Little Cottage, I call Mike who comes straight over to collect his clothes, which are surplus to requirements now that we've kitted out Dominic in things that actually fit.

'Look at you, dude,' Mike says, his voice full of genuine admiration. 'I hardly recognised you.'

Dominic beams with pride and strokes the front of his shirt again. Mike holds up his hand and they high-five each other.

'What did you think of Milton Keynes, mate?' he asks as I hand over the cup of tea I've made for him.

'It was a very frightening place,' Dominic admits.

'Then you really are a Western bloke,' Mike assures him. 'We're all frightened of shopping centres.'

Dominic laughs at that. 'Janie told me that but I thought she was just teasing me.' He sips at his glass of warm milk.

'No way.'

'Then I do not feel like less of a man now.'

'Settling in? Other than the shopping thing?'

'Yes,' Dominic says. 'I think that I will like it here.'

'You'll have to do some male bonding stuff,' I suggest. 'Mike can take you down to the pub and to a football match.'

'I support Arsenal,' Dominic informs him.

'No accounting for taste,' Mike says. 'I'm a Spurs man, myself.'

'Tottenham Hotspur. Robbie Keane. Peter Crouch,' Dominic says, showing off his knowledge of English teams.

'We'll have to catch a game together.'

Dominic beams. 'I would like that very much, Mike.'

A spit of rain starts to hit the windows in fat splats. 'Oh, look at that,' I complain. 'Did they forecast rain?'

'All week,' Mike says.

'Bloody weather,' I mutter. 'I was going to walk around the village with Dominic this afternoon.'

Dominic walks to the window and presses his hand against the glass. 'I have not seen rain in many years,' he breathes. 'How I wish that I could send some home to my family. They are in terrible need of it.'

Now I feel guilty about complaining.

'I would like to go out in it,' Dominic says, looking for my agreement.

'Of course,' I say. 'If you want to. Put your coat on so you don't catch your death of cold.'

'No. I will take off my fine clothes,' he says. 'I do not want them to spoil.'

'A bit of rain won't hurt them ...'

But he's already climbing the stairs and moments later he comes down in his *shuka* and bare feet. The rain is heavy now, coming down sideways, helped along by a steady wind.

'You can't go out like that,' I protest.

'I would like to feel the rain on my skin,' he says and a second later he's out of the back door and in the garden.

Mike and I stand at the window and watch him.

Dominic, in the middle of my small patch of lawn, holds his hands up to the rain and starts to chant a high-pitched song that he offers up to the sky. The rain pours down. He starts to dance around in a circle, stamping his feet. The smile on his face is ecstatic.

I chew at my fingernail. 'I think I should go out there with him,' I say to my friend.

'Maybe it wouldn't be good to leave him alone,' Mike agrees.

Question is, do I wrap up or strip off?

'I'll get out of your hair.'

'Don't fancy joining us?'

'I'll do a lot for you, Janie, but getting piss-wet through in the middle of winter isn't at the top of my list. I'll give it a miss, thanks.'

'Coward.'

Mike laughs and heads for the door. 'I'll see myself out.'

'Thanks, Mike.'

'*Hakuna* whatever it is,' he throws back.

'*Hakuna matata!*' I shout out.

In the kitchen, I strip down to my undies and then wrap myself in a big fluffy towel that I grab from the utility room. I also slip on the Crocs that I keep in there for trogging about in the garden.

'Bloody hell,' I mutter to myself. Then, bravely, I step out into the garden and join Dominic in the rain.

He breaks off from his song. 'This is beautiful, Just Janie. Very beautiful.' Dominic takes me in his arms. 'I am singing a song of thanks. A song for my family. I am hoping that I will send the rain to them.'

'Teach me the song,' I say.

He starts to sing again in his gentle lilting voice and I try to copy him. We dance around the garden as the rain pours down on us. I throw off my towel with a reckless 'woo hoo' and I can safely say that this is the first time that I've been in my garden in just my bra and pants. Instantly, my skin and my underwear are soaked. Dominic is beaming and his smile is so infectious that despite the cold, the rain, the wind, I start to laugh. We twirl around the garden, entwined together. I throw my head back and let the rain course down my face and I feel cleansed, liberated, and very much in love.

'I love you,' I shout out to Dominic. 'I love you so much.'

And he picks me up in his strong arms, spinning me around and around.

Chapter 59

After a fabulous weekend of Dominic and me getting to know each other again, I'm very reluctant to go back to work. I'd much rather stay in bed with him. Plus I'm worried about leaving Dominic alone all day while I go to the salon so I issue him a list of instructions.

I've shown him how to work the microwave so he can make himself some porridge for lunch. He still hasn't been tempted to eat anything else since he's been here, but perhaps he will in time. I've shown him how to work the television and he's currently mesmerised by BBC *Breakfast*, which is showing what the fashions will be for the coming season. I'm not sure that exaggerated shoulder pads and nipped-in waists would suit my Maasai warrior, but he seems transfixed nevertheless. I think he's missing his songs from home, but he absolutely loves Radio Two and is already starting to sing along to some of the more jaunty pop songs. Cheryl Cole's 'Fight For This Love' seems to be a particular favourite – but I think the irony of the lyrics may be lost on him.

'You will be OK?' I ask for the tenth time.

'Yes, Just Janie. Do not worry about me.'

But worry, I do. With all my fussing over Dominic, it's later than normal when I get to work, so I don't have time for my usual coffee with Nina. It seems this is just as well because when I walk into the staffroom an uncomfortable silence falls over everyone. It looks like Nina has already shared her opinion about Dominic with the rest of the staff. So much for friendship. I thought she would be happy that I've finally found love, whatever shape, size, colour or culture that it came in. But no, it seems that's not the case.

Somehow I get through the day, cutting and perming and setting and straightening. At lunchtime I go out and wander up and down the High Street rather than sit in the staffroom, even though the day is bitterly cold. Buckingham is a nice town that's retained a lot of its old charm. In the middle is an ancient gaol that's now a museum and there's a smattering of half-timbered buildings that escaped the sixties massacre. Normally a bit of a walk around lifts my spirits, but today it singularly fails to do so.

I ring the cottage at lunchtime and Dominic assures me that he is OK. I'm worried that he hasn't eaten since this morning, but he convinces me that he doesn't need to have anything else until this evening. How can someone eat so little? I'm half the size of him and eat twice as much. I ring off, promising that I won't be home late. If everyone is avoiding talking to me in the salon, then there'll be no temptation to hang around and chat. It will be so much better when Dominic is properly domiciled here and he can work. I imagine that it's no fun for him being stuck at home all day in the cold with nothing very much to do other than watch crap telly and listen to vacuous pop songs. I'll have to think about if there's some way I can help him to pass the time.

At six o'clock I grab up my things and I'm out of the door. Nina and I have barely exchanged two words all day and it pains me that in finding love, I seem to have lost my best friend.

I drive home like a thing possessed, unable to wait to see Dominic again. My stomach is literally fluttering with joy and it's worth putting up with all the tittering behind hands to have this feeling.

Pulling up outside Little Cottage, I'm slightly alarmed to see that there are no lights on inside. Is Dominic sitting in the dark in there? I can't even see the flicker of the television. Surely he knows how to work the lights?

I'm out of the car like greased lightning and fumble with my key as I open the door. Sure enough, the whole house is in darkness. 'Dominic!' I shout out. 'Dominic! Are you home?'

There's no reply. It strikes me that there's no sign of Archie either and there's no way that the cat would be out in this cold by choice.

'Dominic! Dominic!' Panic is rising now in my chest. I fly out of the house and go next door to Mike's place. But there's no one home. His cottage, too, is in darkness. 'Jesus Christ,' I mutter. 'What now?'

I go back to Little Cottage and get a torch. I'm going to have to look around the village to see if Dominic is anywhere to be found. I'm worried to see that his new coat is still on the peg by the door.

Out in the darkness in the lane, I switch on the torch. 'Dominic!' I pace towards the centre of the village, shouting as I go. Fear has gripped me. Where can he be? Where can he have gone? I even try my Maasai noise and whistle the 24 ringtone as I walk, even though my mouth is dry. Nothing. It might be of some use in the wide open plains of Africa, but here, where everyone is shut in their own little homes, it seems pointless.

As I get to the post-office-cum-village-store, Mrs Appleby is just closing up for the night. 'All right, dearie?' she asks.

'I'm looking for someone,' I pant breathlessly.

'Dominic?'

I take a step back. 'You know Dominic?'

'Yes,' she says. 'What a lovely man. I'm so pleased for you.' She smiles as she touches my arm, then notes my puzzled face. 'He came into the shop today and introduced himself. Caused a bit of a stir yesterday going through the gardens in the wee small hours. I don't think Mrs Peterman will ever be quite the same again.' Mrs Appleby giggles. 'He's the source of a lot of gossip.'

'I'm sure he is.'

'Is he not at home?'

'No,' I say. 'I'm really worried about him.'

Mrs Appleby purses her lips. 'I did see him going off arm-in-arm with Mrs Duston, but that was hours ago.'

Arm-in-arm with Mrs Duston? She's the rather frosty lady who heads up the Nashley Church Flower Committee, one of the top positions of power in the village. What the hell is she doing with Dominic?

'I'd check her house, dearie,' Mrs Appleby advises. 'He might still be there.'

With renewed energy and armed with Mrs Appleby's information, I head off to the neat cottage where Mrs Duston lives. I open the gate in her immaculate white picket fence then, in the darkness, I rap on her front door. A moment later she opens it to me, all smiles.

'I'm looking for Dominic,' I say, anxiously. 'Mrs Appleby says you might have seen him.'

'Oh, yes,' she says. 'Come on in.'

'He's here?'

'Yes, yes. Your young man has kept us entertained all afternoon.'

'He has?'

'Oh, yes.' Mrs Duston titters girlishly. 'He's quite the one.'

Bemused, I step through the neat porch and into the living room. There, in the middle of half a dozen elderly ladies, my loved one is holding court. He's wearing his traditional clothing and has a glass of milk in his hand. In front of the fire, Archie is stretched out, sleeping contentedly on the rug.

'Just Janie.' He stands up when he sees me and whacks his head on a beam.

'I was worried about you,' I tell him.

'You should not be.' He surveys the room. 'These very nice ladies have made me feel at home.'

There's more girly tittering from women who are, quite patently, old enough to know better. These are the ladies of the village who have lost their husbands, the elderly widows who have replaced the loves of their lives with carnations and chrysanthemums and cut roses. The love and attention that they would have lavished on their men folk now go on the flowers for the church. But how can that hole in your life ever be filled by a few pretty floral arrangements? It's no wonder that they're keen to embrace my handsome Maasai warrior.

'Dominic has agreed to do a talk in the village hall,' Mrs Stevens says, hands fluttering to her throat excitedly. 'All about his life in the Maasai Mara, and the wild animals he has wrestled.'

I raise my eyebrows at him, but he does nothing but grin. You flirt, I think.

'He's going to look after us all,' says Mrs Peterman, the woman who complained about him to the police. 'I'll sleep happier in my bed knowing that Dominic is around.'

I swear that she bats her eyelashes at him.

'Oh, really.' I give him a look, but his face is completely guileless. 'Well, thank you for looking after him, ladies. That was very kind of you.'

'Oh, no trouble,' Mrs Duston assures me. 'No trouble at all.' Then to Dominic, 'Drop by any afternoon, dearie. I'm usually here. It's so lovely to have you.'

He drains his glass of milk, hands it back to her and then slings a startled Archie round his shoulders. 'Thank you, good lady.' Dominic bows to her and she nearly swoons. I usher him to the door before all this adoration goes to his head.

As I do, Mrs Duston whispers in my ear. 'You are a very lucky lady, Janie. Very lucky, indeed. He's such a poppet.'

'Thank you.'

All the ladies come to the door and wave Dominic goodbye, giggling as they do. We duly wave in return. I march back down the road towards Little Cottage in the darkness, Dominic in step beside me.

'A poppet?' I say when we turn the corner and are out of sight. It's only then that we both burst out laughing.

Chapter 60

So the weeks continue in the same sort of way. I'm pretty much snubbed at work and every afternoon Dominic works his charm on the impressionable ladies of Nashley. Most days when I get home, neither he nor the cat are there so I go and fish them both out of some elderly lady's cottage. Dominic has usually been chopping wood or gardening or fixing things that need repairing or sitting in front of the fire telling stories of Africa and his own village while they, in turn, ply him with hot milk and porridge. Dominic, it seems, is settling in nicely – at least in Nashley. And he's stopped banging his head on the low cottage beams now. So that must be a good sign, right?

At night, it's a different matter. He finds it difficult to lie in bed and exists on two to three hours of sleep at the most. So in the wee small hours, he gets up and patrols around the village. The only concession to the cold is that he wears his new coat over his *shuka* and slips on his trainers. Archie is slung around his shoulders like a scarf.

'We'll do something today,' I promise him as we finish breakfast. 'I'll take you out to look at some of the countryside round here.'

'I would like that,' he says. 'It is important for me to know my new home, the nature, so I can be in harmony with it.'

'Right.' I wonder how much use I'll be to him there, as I'm not first and foremost known as a nature lover.

'Before that I must practise my jumping,' Dominic says. 'I cannot be happy if I do not jump.'

'You could do something else now you're here,' I suggest. 'Take up another sport, perhaps.'

He looks at me as if I am mad. 'But I am a Maasai warrior,' he reminds me. 'Jumping is very important. I cannot be content if I do not jump.'

'OK,' I say with a shrug. Jumping it is. 'I'll clean up here and then I need to pop down to the post office with a couple of things.' We're sending a few T-shirts and other bits back to Dominic's family. 'You go out and jump to your heart's content.'

'I would like a stick,' Dominic says. 'A tall stick.'

A stick? Where am I going to find a stick? Then a light bulb pings in my brain and I trot off to the utility room. I unscrew the head on my outdoor broom and hand him the stout wooden handle. 'This do?'

'This is a good stick,' he says happily, and then takes himself outside.

The day is cold and there was a hard frost early this morning. When Dominic and Archie returned from their dawn patrol, my reformed cat had frosty whiskers. But now it's sunny and bright, the sky a sharp summery blue.

I lean on the windowsill and watch as Dominic starts to jump, springing high into the air. He chants as he does. There are worse habits to contend with, I think with a smile. Though I wonder idly whether we'll have rows in the future about how much time he spends jumping when he should be taking the bins out and that sort of thing. Is it a novelty that will wear off? It takes me all my time to do half an hour on the Wii Fit but jumping, it seems, is as necessary to Dominic as breathing is.

Dominic seems to be settling in well, but he still refuses to eat anything but porridge or drink anything other than milk. Will he ever, I ponder, be able to spend more than a couple of hours at a time in bed, or be comfortable in Western clothes? He's only been here for a few weeks so I can't expect too much and I sincerely hope that, in time, he will be completely at home in Nashley, that we will always have a full and happy relationship. Occasionally, when I catch glimpses of Dominic's culture that are embedded so deeply in him, I wonder if I have done the right thing in bringing him here. No doubt it's the right thing for me, but is it the right thing for him?

I don't want to interrupt him, so I turn away from the window, pick up my shopping bag and the parcel that I need to weigh and set out for the post office. As I open the door, an unwelcome visitor is standing there.

'Ah!' he says.

When I've recovered from my fright, I reply with a weary sigh, 'Hello, Lewis.'

His face is black. 'Gerry tells me that there's a new man in your life,' he says without any other introduction.

'Yes,' I tell him, 'there is.'

'Is this why you're not answering any of my texts?'

'Of course it is.'

'I don't think you've given us a fair chance,' he spits.

'Lewis, I'm sorry but you're deluded. There never was an *us*. We had one horrible date that ended prematurely. That's it.'

'Is he here?' Lewis says. 'Gerry says he's moved in. Already. I'd like to give him a piece of my mind.'

'I don't think that's really appropriate.' But before I can do anything to dissuade him otherwise, I find that Dominic is standing by my side. He towers over my dating disaster and looks very fearsome in his traditional dress. Lewis's jaw drops open and stays there.

'This is my new man,' I inform Lewis. 'Meet Dominic Ole Nangon, Maasai warrior.'

'How do you do?' Lewis offers.

'Who is this?' Dominic asks sternly.

'This is the man I was telling you about.'

'Then I must challenge you, friend,' he says darkly. 'You are my rival.'

'Well,' Lewis says weakly, 'I wouldn't put it quite like that.'

'I must challenge you.' Dominic bangs his stick on the ground and both Lewis and I jump.

'All right, all right, mate.' Lewis is visibly shaken. 'Keep your hair on.'

'We must have a competition.'

'I don't think so,' Lewis says and goes to head up the path.

'It is the Maasai way.'

'I'm out of here.' Lewis turns on his heels.

Dominic gets hold of his collar and prevents him from leaving. 'You cannot refuse the challenge of a Maasai.'

'I can't?'

Dominic shakes his head and folds his arms. 'I must challenge you to jumping.'

'Jumping?'

My lover barely inclines his head. 'Jumping.'

'Jumping it is then,' Lewis concedes with a resigned huff of breath. Then, chest puffed out with bravado, he reluctantly follows Dominic through to the back garden. I trail after them, interest piqued.

They stand, Lewis breathing heavily, face-to-face, ready for the jump-off. Dominic lets out a blood-curdling scream and leaps high into the air again and again, getting higher and higher.

'Jump,' he instructs Lewis.

In response, Lewis lets out a terrified squeak and launches his not inconsiderable bulk into the air. He clears the grass by about three inches.

'Jump! Jump!' Dominic insists.

Lewis bounces again and his fat sets up a counter-wobble. After a few leaps, he gives up and wipes a hand over his sweaty brow.

'That is it?' Dominic demands fiercely.

Lewis looks puffed out already. He cowers away from Dominic. 'Do what you have to do, mate,' he concedes. 'I'm done.'

Dominic throws down his stick. 'Then I win.'

Now it's Lewis's turn to say, 'That's it?' He looks astonished. 'You're not going to flatten me, beat me to a pulp now?'

'No. My honour is served.'

'Thank Christ.' Lewis sags to his knees on the grass. 'Thank Christ for that.'

'But only if you leave my lady alone.'

'I will,' Lewis promises. 'I will.'

Dominic leans close to him. 'If you do not,' he says softly, 'I will strip your skin from your body and eat it all.'

'Right,' Lewis says, struggling up. 'Right.' His voice hardly dares come out. 'Can I go now?'

Dominic nods.

Before I can show him to the door, Lewis is through my house and out in a flash. His car roars off down the lane.

I turn to Dominic and say, 'You terrible man.'

'Yes,' Dominic agrees with a broad grin, 'but it was very much fun, Just Janie.'

Chapter 61

On Monday, Nina is in the staffroom when I arrive. 'Hey,' she says.

'Hey,' I reply somewhat cagily.

'Heard all about Lewis.' Her face breaks into a smile.

I return it. 'Dominic was pretty impressive,' I venture. 'I don't think that Lewis will be bothering me again.'

'I only heard the story second-hand,' she admits. 'But I think the man pooped himself.' Nina starts to laugh.

I do too. 'Well, you shouldn't mess with the woman of a Maasai warrior.'

She sighs at me. 'How's it going?'

'With Dominic? Excellent. Everyone in the village loves him.' I don't mention the unfortunate police incident.

'I'm sorry I've been funny about it,' my friend says. 'I don't know why. I just want to see you happy.'

Sitting down next to her, I take her hand. 'I am happy with him, Nina. Very. I don't want our friendship to suffer because of it.'

'We should get to know him better. Gerry and I. We could do things as a couple then.'

At the moment, I can't think of anything worse. But if Nina is willing to make the effort to get to know Dominic then I should make the effort with Gerry too.

'Everything all right there?'

'Oh yeah,' she says breezily. 'You know Gerry and me. One minute I want to smash his car up with a golf club, the next minute we're all over each other again.'

I don't remind her that the 'smashing' phases tend to last significantly longer than the 'all over each other' ones – but I hope that will change for her too. If Nina thinks that Gerry is The One, then who am I to argue otherwise?

'Clients are here,' Cristal says. 'Showtime.'

My first lady today is Linda Turner, a woman with five children by five different men. Frankly, as a single mum with five children, I don't know how she finds time to have her hair done at all.

As I start her cut and finish, I wonder if she started out on each relationship thinking that she'd finally found her soulmate. After five failed partnerships, I wonder if she's given up on love completely or whether she still remains optimistic in the face of all the contrary evidence. How could she find the energy not once, not twice, but five times, to start all over again with someone new? Did she set out with blind optimism each time or by the time number five came along, did she have every expectation that it would be a fleeting union?

'Heard you've got yourself a new man,' Linda says as I'm snipping away.

Nothing stays quiet in this place.

'Cristal told me while she was shampooing me.'

She'll probably get a bigger tip for that bit of gossip too.

'Maasai warrior, eh?'

'Yes.'

'I thought she was joking at first.'

I bristle at that. 'No.'

'Good for you, girl,' she says. 'About time you had some fun.'

'Yes,' I agree. But I want to tell her that this isn't about fun – it's about love. Is that where Linda has gone wrong? Has she chosen her life partners on the basis of how much fun they are? How do any of us choose who we love and who we don't? Why can we look at some people and feel absolutely unmoved by them and yet the mere sight of someone else will make us shake like a leaf?

'Just make sure that you don't start sending money and stuff to his family.'

I don't tell her that in my handbag there's an envelope containing fifty pounds in cash to send to Dominic's family. I don't tell her that, comparatively, we have so much and they have so very little. Would she understand that I begrudge them nothing? We couldn't even send the money in a more secure way. Dominic's family don't have a bank account, they couldn't change a money order without a two-day round trip into Narok – so cash it had to be. But this small sum will ease their lives for months to come. It's not going to buy designer shoes or iPods or UGG boots. It's more likely to go on antibiotics or food than fripperies. It will also go some small way towards assuaging my guilt at taking their son away from them and the money they had from his job as a tour guide, which will be hard, if not impossible, to replace. If we can send them something to help them out every month, then I'm more than happy to do so. And before anyone suggests otherwise, it wasn't even Dominic's idea to send money to them – it was mine. All mine.

'Well, enjoy it while it lasts,' she advises before she returns to her magazine. 'These things never do.'

But this *has* to last. I can't imagine life without Dominic now, whatever our difficulties. I want him as my partner, my husband, and the sooner everyone else gets used to that the better.

I have to do something so that they all get to know Dominic and see him through my eyes. Once they see how kind, funny and hot he is, then they'll be able to see why I am utterly enchanted by him. But what?

Back in the staffroom and Nina is already tucking into her fruit for the day.

'I'm starving,' she says. 'Couldn't wait for lunch. This is second breakfast.'

That's what I could do, I think. Cook for them all. She's still mid-peel of an orange when I say, in a rush of bonhomie, 'Come to dinner. At the weekend. Everyone from the salon.' I'll have to squash them all into my little dining room, but it can be done.

'I'll get Mike in too. Has Steph got a man on the go at the moment?'

'Two or three, I think, but I'm sure another one wouldn't go amiss. If you're thinking of matchmaking though, Miserable Mike might be single but he's *so* not her type.'

'You don't think so?'

'Noooooo way!' Nina decides.

'But he's lovely.'

'I'd agree with that now,' my friend says a bit cagily.

'I've always told you so.' I don't dare remind her that she didn't seem too reluctant to get close to him on New Year's Eve.

She gives me a sideways glance. 'Then why didn't you snap him up?'

I have no answer to that.

'Steph would eat him alive,' Nina continues. 'You couldn't do that to him.'

'Maybe not.' She has a point. Still, it would be nice to see Mike fixed up with a girlfriend and other than Steph – or the sex-starved ladies of the Nashley Church Flower Committee – I can't think of any other single women that might suit him.

'Do you think the boys would like to come?'

'Not speaking,' Nina fills me in. 'They had a big bust-up at the weekend. Tyrone texted me. He caught Clinton getting jiggy with another bloke at some nightclub.'

'When are they next in?'

'Clinton's in tomorrow. Ty's not in until Wednesday. We've got two quiet days before the fireworks start.'

If it's as it usually is, they'll be sulking at either end of the salon, interspersed with bitch-slapping episodes. Cristal won't want to come as she'd rather be out trying to pick up some Johnny No Stars bloke to shag.

'I'll see what I can do.' I get a warm fuzzy feeling inside. 'I'd really like you all to meet Dominic properly.'

Then you will love him, I think. Then you will love him. Just like I do.

Chapter 62

I've put on my LBD and I've ironed and laid out on the bed some of the new clothes we bought for Dominic: a fitted black shirt and some bootcut jeans.

I wrap my arms around him tightly. 'I want you to look fabulous tonight,' I tell him with a kiss. 'I want them all to see what a handsome man you are and what a lucky woman I am.'

He grins. 'I will try my best for you, Just Janie.'

As I'm wondering if we'd have time for an extra-quick quickie, the doorbell rings. I check my watch. Whoever it is, they're early. 'Get your finery on and come down as soon as you can,' I instruct. Then, giving Dominic a quick kiss, I disappear downstairs to let the first of our guests in.

As I might have suspected, it's Mike who arrives first for our dinner party.

'Hey,' he says and pecks my cheek shyly.

His hair is freshly washed and there may well be a smidgen of gel in evidence. He's tried with his clothes too – black jeans, Ted Baker grey shirt. And he looks pretty hot. Despite Nina's warning, I'm so hoping that he likes Steph and that she likes him. I've told her that she has to be on her best behaviour and be nice to him and view him as potential date material even though he's not married.

'You look lovely,' he ventures.

'Not too shabby yourself, Mr Perry,' I tease as I take the proffered bottle of champagne from him. 'Wow. You're flash.'

'I thought we might celebrate Dominic's arrival in style.'

'I'll drink to that. Thanks, Mike.'

Tyrone and Clinton are talking once again and so are coming along together tonight. Kelly and Phil couldn't make it – busy, she said. But to be honest, I think Phil hates socialising with the minions from the salon, sees it as beneath him. He'd rather be out with the movers and shakers, not the cutters and blow-driers. Can't say that I'm too disappointed and it's enough of a crush in my dining room as it is. Out of all of them, I'm most nervous about Nina and Gerry as I really want them to see how great Dominic is.

Cooking isn't my natural forte, but I've made an effort with the food tonight: a spicy leg of lamb with pilaff rice and a Greek-style salad of tomatoes, cucumber, olives and feta cheese. For afters, I've whipped up the speciality of the house – a chocolate bread and butter pudding. I'm only slightly disappointed that despite the delicious smells wafting from the kitchen, Dominic has requested just a bowl of porridge. It sounds ridiculous, but I wanted them to know that he can blend in perfectly well and there's nothing weird or unusual about him, that he's exactly the same as everyone else. I'm worried that if he just eats porridge they'll think he's funny.

The boys arrive hand-in-hand and it's clear they're loved up again. While I'm fixing drinks for them and wondering what's keeping Dominic, Nina and Gerry turn up in a taxi. It's also clear that they're not having a 'love's young dream' day. Black looks are being exchanged before they're through the door.

'Good to see you both,' I say too brightly.

Nina plasters a smile on her face as she kisses me. 'Sorry we're late.' Another look at Gerry.

'My fault.' Her husband kisses me. 'As usual.'

'You're not late,' I say as I take their coats. 'No worries. *Hakuna matata*.'

'What?' she asks, distracted.

'It's Swahili,' I supply, 'for "no worries".'

'Oh.' My multilingual skills fail to pique her interest. 'Where is the guest of honour then?'

'I'm sure he'll be down in a minute.'

'Dinner smells great,' Gerry says, rubbing his hands together. 'What have we got?'

'Lamb,' I say.

'Oh.' Disappointment clouds his face.

Not at the top of his list of favourites, obviously.

Steph arrives and I leave the rest of them in the kitchen to let her in. She's on her mobile as I open the door. I stand there while she finishes her list of expletives and then hangs up. 'Fucking men,' she says with a tut. 'Fuck the lot of them. Tossers.'

My heart sinks. Poor Mike is going to have his work cut out tonight if he's going to be able to impress Steph. I might as well give up on my matchmaking career before it has started.

She kisses me, also distractedly, and holds out a box of chocs and some wine. 'I need a drink,' she says, 'and fast.'

'Problems?'

'Isn't everything with a cock trouble?' she mutters as she shrugs her jacket off and dumps it on the sofa.

'Er ...' I say. 'Let's get you that drink.'

Mike has already opened the bottle of champagne and soon we all have a glass in hand.

'Shall we wait until Dominic arrives before we propose a toast?' Mike suggests.

'I need this now,' Steph points out and necks the glass while he stares, open-mouthed, at her. She holds out her flute for a refill and, though gobsmacked, Mike duly obliges.

'You're one glass short,' Nina points out.

'Dominic doesn't drink,' I explain as I pour him a tumbler of milk.

Nina raises her eyebrows at that. 'Not at all?'

'No. He just likes milk.'

'Strange,' she remarks in an off-handed way that riles me.

'Not really.' Some people don't have to be pissed to have a good time, I think.

Then a voice says, 'Good evening, everyone.'

As one, we turn to see Dominic standing in the doorway. A silence falls over the party. Steph drops her glass, which shatters on the tile floor.

'Bloody hell,' Nina manages.

This is not the reaction I'd hoped for, I think bitterly. Not the reaction I'd hoped for at all.

Chapter 63

'My goodness.' Mike is the first to rally. 'You look magnificent, Dominic. Truly magnificent.'

The others are still speechless.

Dominic, instead of wearing the clothes I had put out for him, has chosen his own costume.

Over his usual red *shuka*, he's wearing an orange skirt slung around his hips that is encrusted with beads and dozens of little circular mirrors that catch the light. There's a fringe of multi-coloured beading at the hem and his machete is tucked into the waistband. He's barefoot and is wearing his wedding necklace and a dozen other strings of beads are strung across his body. His arms and ankles are also adorned with bracelets. On his cheeks, there are streaks of ochre war paint and he's wearing an elaborate headdress of brown feathers fanned out in a circle around his face. Archie, in repose around Dominic's shoulders, completes the outfit.

His tall willowy frame looks utterly terrifying in my tiny cottage and everyone – myself included, if I'm honest – just gawps.

Mike, again, is the first to move. He hands Dominic his glass of milk.

'Shall we drink a toast, Janie?'

'Yes, yes.' I'm coming out of my own shock now. 'Yes. Of course.'

Everyone else starts to return to normal, only Dominic is looking uncertain now.

'To Dominic,' Mike proposes, champagne aloft.

'To Dominic,' we echo and we all drink from our glasses, some of us more gratefully than others. Nina downs hers in one.

'It is very nice to be here,' my lover says hesitantly. 'It is very nice to meet you. I hope that friends of Janie will be friends of mine.'

Nina stares fixedly at the floor.

'We most certainly will.' Mike again. 'Anyone need a top-up?'

My best friend thrusts out her glass.

'Dinner's nearly ready,' I say, anxiety rising. I wanted this all to go so well and now, before it's even properly started, it feels like it's going horribly wrong. 'Mike, why don't you lead everyone through to the dining room and get them seated while I fiddle about here?' My voice is an octave higher than I'd like it to be.

'Will do,' he says.

Dominic stands aside and, without fuss, Mike leads the others out to the living room.

'I'll follow you in just a minute.'

Dominic hangs back. His handsome face is troubled. 'I have done wrong,' he says. 'You meant for me to wear the clothes you put on the bed for me.'

'No, no. It doesn't matter.'

He shrugs apologetically. 'I put those away in the cupboard,' he explains. Dominic looks down at his dress. 'These are my best clothes. My finery. The outfit I wore for my *ilmoran*, my warrior ceremony. I misunderstood you.'

I put my arms around him. 'You look fabulous,' I say. Instantly, I start to relax in Dominic's embrace. 'It was wrong of me. I wanted you to fit in with my friends, but I am most proud of you when you are being you. Just you.'

'I think that I have frightened them.'

I laugh. 'Perhaps you have,' I admit. 'Just a little bit.'

'I will go to change immediately.'

'No. Stay as you are,' I insist. 'This is you. This is why I love you. They'll just have to get used to it. This is our home.' How dare they make Dominic feel uncomfortable here, in his own domain. 'Now, I must lift this lamb out, otherwise it will be like serving them a piece of charcoal. Can you be a darling and quickly make yourself some porridge while I do it?'

'I will eat lamb,' Dominic says.

I look up. 'Sure?'

'Yes.'

I abandon all thoughts of the burning lamb and give Dominic a cuddle again.

'I love you,' I say. '*Aanyor pii*. I love you with all of my heart. Don't ever forget that. Just as you are.' Then I grin at him. 'However, you might want to take that off,' I nod at his head-dress, 'otherwise you'll never clear the beams.'

He pulls off his headdress and kisses me passionately, branding me with his ochre war paint.

'Is it a bad thing to wish they'd all go home right now so that we can go straight to bed?' I whisper breathlessly.

'Yes,' Dominic says as he kisses me again. 'There will be time for that later, Just Janie. Much time. Now,' he takes my hand, 'we will go and be charming hosts to our friends.'

283

Chapter 64

With Dominic's help, I serve the lamb. Thankfully, it's not too dried up. He keeps smiling at me reassuringly, but I can tell that conversation around the dinner table is stilted. If this was an episode of *Come Dine With Me*, I would get nil points and someone else would walk off with the thousand-pound prize money.

Nina is getting more and more drunk. As is Gerry. In fact, it seems to be something of a competition for them to see who can slog back the most wine in the shortest space of time. My friend is slumping further and further towards the table and, surreptitiously, I try to move the bottle of wine out of her reach, but she snatches it back.

Steph is morose. Whatever the conversation was about on her mobile phone when she arrived, it clearly wasn't good news. Has she finally fallen for one of the married men she's so keen to count as 'fuck buddies' and he's refusing to leave his wife? Pure speculation on my part, but not beyond the realms of possibility. I don't know what I was thinking of when I decided she might be a suitable date for my Mike. She's nowhere near good enough.

Thankfully, the boys are proving to be as chatty as always. Tyrone is currently admiring Dominic's beads and Clinton looks like he might well have a crush on him, which could be the source of a row later this evening if things take their usual course.

But out of all of them, it is Mike who proves to be the stalwart – laughing in the right places, coming up with silly anecdotes to keep us from awkward silences. I have no idea what Dominic makes of all this. He's trying his hardest, I can tell that, but I can also tell that it's not easy for him. Sitting there in his tribal costume, picking at a plate of meat and drinking his milk, he does look like an alien creature. But I wish they would look at him properly, I wish they could see his heart. I want them to fall in love with him, to be entranced by him as I am. Instead, my work colleagues are all gossiping about clients and *I'm a Celebrity ... Get Me Out of Here!* and *The X Factor* and Dominic clearly hasn't got a clue what they're talking about. Normally, I find their shallow chit-chat entertaining but right now, it's irritating me and I don't want them to be rude to my lover and I think they are being. Nina has just ignored him completely. She's not spoken one word to him, not even in her shouty way. Mike tries to steer the conversation back to Dominic and asks about his life and what he thinks of England but, clearly, that's not as interesting to them as Z-list television personalities and wannabe pop stars.

When we've eaten the main course, I stand to clear up.

'I'll help you with that,' Gerry volunteers. So far, my friend's husband has been suspiciously quiet. He's usually loud after a few drinks, telling inappropriate bad-taste jokes, but not tonight. Not yet.

I take the plates and he brings the decimated platter of lamb, following me through the living room and into the kitchen. 'Just there would be great,' I say, indicating the one clear spot on the work surface.

Gerry brushes close to me as he puts the platter down and then lingers at my shoulder, saying, 'Anything else you want me to do?'

His voice is loaded with innuendo.

'No, no. That's fine.' I conjure up a smile.

'You only have to say the word, Janie.' More sleazy smirking.

Twat. The chocolate bread and butter pudding is just finishing off in the oven, filling the kitchen with the usually delicious scent of chocolate, but the cloying smell of it is overpowering and is making me feel sick. 'I'll be through in a few minutes with dessert.'

Instead of taking the hint and disappearing, Gerry decides to stand and loiter. He leaves my side and wrings the dregs from the champagne bottle into a glass, drinking it while he eyes me up and down from the other side of the kitchen.

'You're a good-looking woman, you know,' he says after a few moments' contemplation on the matter.

What am supposed to say to that? I mumble, 'Thanks.'

'You could do a lot better than him.'

I spin around. 'Than Dominic?'

Gerry has a lecherous grin on his face. Clearly, he's one over the eight as he's not entirely steady on his feet. He drains his glass, searches around for something else to fill it with, but is unsuccessful and puts it down, knocking it over as he does.

'I'll pretend I didn't hear that.'

'It's true,' he continues with a slur. 'What you need is a real man.'

'You think so?' All my hackles are up now. I can't stay here and listen to this nonsense. I need to get away from this idiot now. 'I'm going to see how the others are getting on.'

'I could show you a good time, Janie,' he says.

'I don't think so.'

As I go to pass Gerry, he grabs hold of my wrist. He strokes the inside of it with his thumb.

'Pretty girl like you needs a proper English bloke.' He licks his lips lasciviously.

'Like you?'

A slow and, presumably, seductive nod. Gerry might be good-looking on the outside – though not quite as good-looking as *he* thinks he is – but he's as ugly as you can get on the inside.

'A proper English bloke like you who propositions his wife's best friend?'

He reaches out his other hand and rubs it over my breast. I recoil back from his touch, but Gerry merely laughs. Before I can think better of it, I slap his face. A resounding slap. His face darkens and then the mark where my hand connected reddens.

A moment later, Mike pops his head around the door, frowning. 'Everything OK in here?'

'Fine,' I say, though I'm breathing heavily.

He glances from me to Gerry and takes in the stand-off between us. 'Sure?'

'Yes.'

'Can I take anything through?'

'There's some cream in the fridge. White jug. The dessert's ready now.' If it isn't, we'll just have to eat it as it is. I'm not staying in the kitchen a second longer with this idiot.

Mike, as instructed, gets the cream and lingers in the doorway. He knows enough about Gerry by now to make a good stab at guessing what's going on.

'I'm following you,' I assure him.

Reluctantly, he leaves. When he does, I turn back to Gerry. 'If you ever do that again, if you ever even *think* it, I will tell her,' I threaten him. 'I *will* tell her.'

'Look at him,' Gerry sneers. 'Look at him properly. He's barely domesticated.'

'You know nothing,' I retort. 'Dominic is a better man than you'll ever be.'

He laughs at that.

What does my friend see in this oily plonker? How dare she question my choice of man when she stays married to *him*?

'Now I want you to drink up,' I say as calmly as I can manage. 'I'm going to call you a taxi and the minute you've eaten this dessert –' which I currently have an overwhelming desire to push into his smug, fat face '– you're going to make your excuses and leave and you'll never come back to this house again. Understand me?'

'Loud and clear,' Gerry says and with that, he leaves me in the kitchen shaking with anger.

Chapter 65

After that, my heart isn't in it. My guests ooh and aah over my pudding, but there's a tension in the atmosphere that's palpable. Only Nina, who is now three sheets to the wind, is oblivious. Gerry, his eye firmly on mine, keeps topping up her glass in a kind of petty defiance. How I'd like to whack that man over the head with a bottle. It's just a shame that Nina doesn't feel the same way.

Mike is studying me intently, but I try to breeze through my duties as hostess. It's midnight when they all go and, frankly, it's not a moment too soon.

As I wave the last of them away, Mike hangs back. 'I'll help you to clear up,' he says.

'No need.' I lay my hand on his arm. 'I've got it covered.'

Dominic is already clattering about, stacking the dishwasher like I've shown him.

'What happened in there?' He nods towards the kitchen.

'Gerry was being a complete arse.' I lower my voice as I confide. 'Did he make a play for you?'

'Yeah. Pillock.' I shake my head. 'I have no idea why Nina stays with him.'

'He'd just had too much pop,' Mike says. 'Don't let it worry you.'

It's not that easy though, is it? It does worry me. I worry that he's changed my friend over the years and not for the better. She used to be so much fun, now she's becoming embittered, jealous of anyone else's happiness and just as opinionated as her damn husband.

Dominic comes to the kitchen door and leans his rangy frame against it.

'Look, I'll catch up with you both tomorrow.' Mike kisses my cheek and then goes to shake Dominic's hand. My neighbour claps my lover on the back. 'See you, Dominic.'

'Thank you, Mike.'

I show him to the door and he gives us a wave as he disappears. It's freezing out there and it's starting to spit with rain. Mike hurries to his own cottage.

Closing the door, I lean against it. 'That was terrible,' I say with a weary sigh. 'I'm so sorry for putting you through that.'

Dominic shrugs and I go to him and we wrap our arms around each other. I wanted us all to have great fun together and for everyone to love Dominic. But you know what they say about the best laid plans of mice and men.

'You and me against the world,' I say, 'hey?'

'And Mike,' Dominic adds. 'I think that Mike is on our side.'

'Yes,' I agree, 'he's a good man.'

I flop down onto the sofa and pull Dominic down with me. We sprawl out together, the warmth from the log burner easing my mood.

Dominic is unusually quiet.

'Don't take it to heart,' I tell him.

He takes a deep breath. 'For the first time in my life, I am afraid, Janie,' he admits. 'Your friends, they do not know who I am and yet they think that I am not a good man. I try to do good in the village and a policeman has to bring me home. I do not know my place in this life, in your life.'

Panic rises in me. 'Don't think like that.' I stroke Dominic's handsome ebony face. 'We'll work it out. You're different. It will take time for some people to get used to you, to us.'

'I will take a walk in the village.'

'It's cold out there. It was starting to rain when Mike left.'

'I am Maasai,' he says softly. 'I am nothing if my village does not need me.'

He stands up and makes his high-pitched Maasai noise. I do hope it doesn't wake the neighbours. Archie comes thumping down the stairs.

'That's a good party trick,' I say, trying to add some levity.

'Come, cat.' Dominic lifts the adoring Archie onto his shoulders. 'I will not be long.'

'Put your coat on,' I beg. 'What about your shoes? You'll freeze.'

'You forget how much I appreciate the rain, Just Janie. I will be fine.'

'*We'll* be fine,' I reiterate.

'Yes.' There's a sadness in his voice that breaks my heart. 'We'll be fine.'

Barefoot and dressed just in his *shuka*, Dominic steps out into the night.

Chapter 66

I hear the slow horror-film creak of the ancient front door as Dominic lets himself in. Peering at the clock on the mantelpiece, I see that it's four o'clock in the morning. The wood in the stove has burned away and it's chilly in the cottage. My bones are aching from falling asleep on the sofa. I hear Archie grumble as he's lowered to the floor and then Dominic comes to kneel next to me.

'Hey,' I say, trying to focus my eyes.

'You should have gone to bed, Janie.' He kisses my forehead. 'I did not mean for you to wait for me.'

'I dozed off here.' I give a shiver. 'I didn't realise the time.'

'Come to bed.'

We both stand up and I put my arms around Dominic's neck. His skin is ice-cold to touch. He lifts me into his arms and carries me up the stairs, not even faltering when Archie weaves in and out of his legs.

He undresses me, then strips off his thin *shuka* – hardly adequate protection from the worst of the British winter. Together we slide under the duvet and press our chilled bodies together.

'Brrr,' I murmur. 'I wonder if we can think of any way to warm us up quickly?'

Dominic isn't slow on the uptake. 'I think there might be a way.' He moves above me, kissing me deeply.

If it was just me and Dominic, alone together in our own little world, then everything would be idyllic. I hear Archie complain from the bottom of the bed, our movement clearly disturbing his sleep. If it were just me, Dominic and Archie, I correct, then everything would be idyllic.

In the morning, we're late to rise and I pad around the cottage in my dressing gown and slippers, drinking tea and eating toast. Dominic sits at the kitchen table and eats his porridge.

'I promised Mrs Duston that I would chop wood for her,' Dominic says. 'We will go now.'

Giving him a cuddle, I stroke his chest. 'Feeling OK this morning?'

'Yes,' he says with an assuring nod.

But he's quiet and it worries me.

'Come, cat.' He lifts Archie from the warmth of the hearthrug and still my fickle feline doesn't complain.

'Will you get a newspaper while you're out? From the village shop?'

'Yes.'

A quick scrabble in my purse and I hand over the money. 'That'll be a nice treat.'

I watch from the doorway as Dominic heads out through the village, his long loping stride taking him towards the duck pond. I notice that Mike is washing his car in his drive – the favourite Sunday morning pursuit of most male villagers.

'Kettle's just boiled,' I shout to him.

'I'll be there in five,' he says, acknowledging my offer with a friendly wave.

Sure enough, I've only just had time to dig some chocolate digestives out of the cupboard when Mike's face appears around the kitchen door.

'Recovered from last night?'

'Sort of,' I say. 'Coffee?'

'Mmm.'

When I've made us two cups of instant, I proffer the biscuits. Mike accepts gratefully.

'Dominic OK?'

A shrug from me. 'I don't know,' I admit. 'He seems quiet. He's just gone off to see Mrs Duston to chop some wood for her.'

'He's certainly made himself popular with the good ladies of the village. Something I've never managed to do.'

I laugh at that. 'You need to go and offer them your household DIY skills. That's what pleases women of a certain age. Wearing less clothing seems to work too.'

'I haven't quite got the body for it that Dominic has,' Mike says ruefully. 'I'd be more likely to scare them off than attract marriage proposals.'

Distractedly, I nibble on a digestive. 'I'm worried about him,' I confide in Mike. 'He has no friends here. I think he could do with a bit of male bonding.' My eyes meet Mike's. 'Are you up for it?'

'What do you want me to do?'

'I don't know. What do blokes do?'

'I could take him to a footie match.'

'He'd like that. But I'm also worried that he's kicking around here all day with nothing to do. He's a proud man, Mike. He needs a purpose. It's six months before he can apply for a work permit. If he doesn't find something to do, I think he'll go stir crazy by then.'

Mike fails to meet my eyes when he asks, 'Do you think he'll stay here permanently?'

'I can't even contemplate the thought that he might go home. He's my life, Mike.'

My friend, my neighbour, my steadfast rock, sighs at me. 'Let me get alongside him,' he suggests. 'We can do "man" stuff together.' Mike pounds his chest in the style of Tarzan, teasing.

'I'd really appreciate that.'

'If you don't mind me saying, I thought your work colleagues were very rude last night.'

'Yes, they were. But what can I say? They're young, self-absorbed, a generation who think of no one but themselves. Why would it even have occurred to them that Dominic might need some friends? It was my fault, I should have realised that. I was too keen to show him off.'

'It's understandable.' Mike covers my hand with his. 'He's a great bloke, Janie. I mean that sincerely.'

'I know you do.'

Then we hear Dominic's key in the lock – something else he can't quite get used to having to do.

'In here!' I shout and seconds later, he appears in the kitchen.

'*Jambo*. Hello.' He nods to Mike and I'm glad to see that his trademark grin is back in place. 'I have bought the newspaper.' The *Sunday Times* is tucked under his arm. He seems pleased by this small achievement and I hope it's because he feels as if he's becoming integrated in the village. 'Mrs Appleby told me that this is the best one.' He puts it on the table.

'Great,' I say.

'Also, I have brought gifts from Mrs Duston.'

Dominic is carrying a wicker basket and there's a red and white gingham cloth draped over the top of it. I peek inside. 'Home-baked?'

'Oh, yes.'

In the basket there's a crusty loaf, still warm, and half a dozen muffins. It's nice of her to think to recompense Dominic for his time and his kindness.

'Ooo, they look delish. The smell is making me hungry again.'

'Why don't I stay and cook us lunch?' Mike offers. 'Dominic and I could do it together for you.'

'I'm liking that idea.'

'Are you up for that, Dominic?'

My lover looks uncertain.

'Janie can sit and read the paper in peace while you and I knock something together? What have you got in the fridge?'

'I was going to do a spag bol.' No complicated cuisine in this house. Last night's dinner exhausted my domestic goddess skills for the next six months.

'I'm game.' Mike looks encouragingly at Dominic.

My Maasai warrior shrugs his acceptance, but I sense a reluctance in his demeanour. I'm sure Mike will sort him out.

'I'll just go and throw some clothes on then,' I say as cheerily as I can manage and then I leave the two men in my life to it.

Chapter 67

'Ever eaten spaghetti bolognese, mate?'

Dominic shakes his head. 'No. The cook used to make it in Kiihu camp for the tourists so I have seen it. But I have not tasted it.'

It seems so long ago that Dominic and I were there together that I let out an involuntary sigh. They both turn to look at me.

'Sorry,' I say. 'Just daydreaming.' I return to the paper and all the doom and gloom contained in its pages.

'We'll stick to the Mike Perry classic recipe if that's OK with you.'

While I was upstairs getting dressed, Mike emptied the contents of my fridge out onto the work surface. There's a pack of mince, one of bacon, some mushrooms, onions and a red pepper.

Dominic smiles his agreement.

'We'll get some herbs from the garden,' Mike says as he picks up the scissors. He ushers Dominic to the door and out into the garden. 'The selection isn't brilliant at this time of year, but you can't beat fresh herbs. I grow some myself.'

My herbs grow in an old stone trough that sits along the

back wall of the house, a place that catches the best of the sun in the summer. They leave the door open and I should get up and close it, but the temptation to listen to their conversation is too strong. I'm trying not to watch either, but I can't help it.

Mike hands over the kitchen scissors. Dominic stares at them, mesmerised. 'This is thyme. You might know some of these. This is rosemary.'

I see Dominic lean close to Mike, but I have to strain to hear what he's saying.

'Mike,' Dominic murmurs. 'I am very worried.'

My neighbour raises his eyebrows.

'Cooking, collecting the herbs, this is considered woman's work,' he continues quietly. 'I do not want Janie Johnson to think that I am not a man.'

Mike sits on the low wall that separates the garden from the patio and beckons Dominic to join him, which he does. I bury my head in the newspaper and strain to listen.

'It's not the same here, mate,' Mike says. 'Women like a man who can cook. They go mad for them.'

Dominic laughs at that. 'Then why have you not got a lovely wife?'

'Well, not always,' Mike concedes. 'But in all honesty, there's not much difference here between what a man does and what a woman does. Having said that, men tend to wash the cars and put petrol in them and take out the bins. Women usually do the washing and maybe the ironing, but that's not always the case.'

'You would wash and iron?'

'Yeah. Can't stand ironing, mind you. I live alone so I haven't got anyone else to do my shirts.'

I think of when I offered to do Mike's ironing for him when

he had lent me the money to go and visit Dominic and my heart goes out to this kind man.

'You have to find your own way, work out which chores suit you both,' Mike adds.

Dominic shakes his head. 'With the Maasai way, everyone knows what their role is. Here, it is all mixed up.'

'Who knows whether that's better or worse,' Mike admits. 'That's just the way it is.'

'Janie goes to work all day, while I must stay at home.'

'Your situation is temporary,' Mike points out. 'Hopefully you'll get your work permit, then you can find a job. But it's not unusual here now for the woman to be the main breadwinner.'

'Breadwinner?'

'The one that earns the money,' he explains. 'Then, the man tends to take on the lion's share of the household stuff. It's no big deal.'

'I have a lot to learn,' Dominic says.

'You're doing great, mate,' Mike assures him. 'It'll all come right. Just give it time.'

Dominic nods as he contemplates this. Then, as he stands, 'Which herbs would you like me to cut, mate?'

Mike claps him on the back. 'Let's have a bit of this.' He points to the herbs. 'A bit of that too.'

'I like to use the herbs as medicines,' Dominic says and he wields the scissors at the thyme, holding them awkwardly.

'Don't know much about that,' Mike admits. 'Swear by Nurofen and red wine myself, but I like to whack them in my cooking.'

In the kitchen, I quickly turn my attention back to the newspaper – though I haven't read a word of it – as the two men come back inside.

'Right,' Mike says. 'Now we can prepare the veg.' He peels the onion and chops half of it. Then, along with the paring knife and the chopping board, he hands the other half over to his attentive student. 'Here. Why don't you chop this up for me?'

Dominic frowns at the tiny knife and at the onion and there's a bit of an uncomfortable pause. A moment later he draws his large machete from the waistband of his tunic. 'This is the Maasai way.' And with more vigour than style, he hacks the onion into little pieces.

When he's finished, Dominic stands back and admires his handiwork.

Mike high-fives him and laughs as he says, 'That works too, mate.'

Chapter 68

We all eat the lunch that the boys have prepared together at the kitchen table. Mike cracks open a bottle of red wine, which he and I demolish. Dominic, quite wisely, sticks to his milk.

'What do you think of Dominic Ole Nangon's home-cooked pasta extravaganza?' I ask. 'Prepared meticulously to the Mike Perry special recipe, of course.'

Dominic toys with the spicy minced beef. 'It is quite good,' he says with a shy grin.

Secretly, I think he's rather proud of himself and the first meal he's produced. After we've cleared up, we go and flake out on the sofas in the living room. We split the various sections of the newspaper between us and Mike and I squeeze in bites of Mrs Duston's excellent muffins.

'This is a traditional English Sunday afternoon,' I tell Dominic. 'Eat too much, drink too much, flake out for the rest of the day with papers. Except we should have had a roast dinner instead of spag bol.'

'That could be our next project, Dominic,' Mike ventures. 'Full roast dinner.' He rubs his stomach. 'Although I'm going to have to do some more exercise if I keep eating all this good food.'

'Jump with me,' Dominic offers.

That clearly takes Mike by surprise and I stifle a smile.

'Jump?'

'In my village, every day the men jump together. It is a good thing to do.'

Mike puts his newspaper down and says gamely, 'I'll give jumping a go.'

'This I've got to see.' That's me.

'Come on then.' Mike drags himself from the depths of the sofa. 'Before it gets dark.'

'You might want to *wait* until it gets dark,' I suggest.

But before Mike has the chance to ruminate on this fine idea, Dominic is on his feet and halfway out of the door.

'Looks like jumping is on the cards *now*,' Mike says with a wry smile at me.

'Just make sure that you don't see your dinner again,' I warn.

Putting down the paper, I follow the men out into the garden. The dampness of a winter evening is settling now, the watery sun low on the horizon.

'You need the stick,' Dominic instructs.

I perch on the cold wall and watch.

Mike takes the broom handle.

'Now jump,' Dominic says. 'Be light like a cheetah. Be strong like a lion.'

My neighbour gives a little jump and I burst out laughing. 'That was hefty like a hippo.'

'Shut your face, Johnson,' he says affably and jumps some more.

Now I fall about, giggling until my sides hurt.

Dominic soars gracefully into the air, a good two feet or maybe more from the ground, and he chants and whoops as he does. Mike huffs and puffs along with him good-naturedly, clutching his stick and risking the occasional strangulated yelp.

'Very good,' Dominic says encouragingly. 'You are very good.'

'This feels great,' Mike admits. 'Makes me wish I'd been a punk rocker.' Puff, puff. 'All that pogoing.' Puff, puff.

Frankly, I'd love to join in, but I want something that just Dominic and Mike do together, something that will cement their friendship. If it proves to be cooking or jumping, then so be it.

While I watch and clap along, Dominic and Mike jump together, bouncing on the grass, chanting, whooping. The sun drops behind the fence and the night begins to creep in over the hedges. Lights start to come on in the cottages around us.

I think that Dominic could jump for ever but Mike is going redder and redder in the face. Sweat pours from his brow. Before my friend has a heart attack, Dominic quite wisely brings the jumping session to a halt.

'That was brilliant,' Mike enthuses as he gets his breath back. 'I feel quite liberated. Quite carefree.'

He looks like he needs another lie-down on the sofa.

'I've not had so much exercise in years,' he pants as he mops his brow with his handkerchief.

'I'll make us some tea,' I say and move my chilled bottom off the wall.

'We should do that again,' Mike says, still breathing heavily.

'I jump every day,' Dominic informs him. 'I would consider it to be an honour if you would join me.'

'If you can wait until I get back from work then, yes, I'd love to.'

'Enjoy that?' I ask Dominic.

'Very much, thank you.'

'Good. Because if you are happy, then I am happy.'

Dominic's beautiful smile beams back at me. 'I am happy, Just Janie.'

And you don't know how relieved I am to hear that.

Chapter 69

On Monday, I'm back to work. As I'm rushing around to get out of the house on time, Dominic is eating his porridge while watching his favourite BBC *Breakfast*, learning how to blend pastel shades to modernise the living room. His eyes are wide in disbelief.

'I have to go,' I say, pecking his cheek. As I head for the door, the telephone rings. Out of habit, I pick up. 'Janie Johnson.'

On the other end of the phone is Mr Codling-Bentham – the closest we have to a village squire. 'Wonder if it would be possible for Dominic to help us out in the gardens?' he asks. 'Our gardener's gone off sick and we're a bit stuck. There's some leaf clearing to get on with, a bit of cutting back. We'd be frightfully grateful.'

'I'll ask him,' I say and cover the phone with my hand. 'Fancy a bit of gardening?'

He tears his eyes away from the tempting palettes of pale heather, mink, pistachio and duck-egg blue. 'Yes.'

'It's for the Codling-Benthams.'

'The big house?'

I nod. 'They can't pay you,' I remind him. 'It would have to be on a voluntary basis.'

'I like to be busy,' he says. 'I will go there right away.'

Turning back to the phone, I say, 'Dominic will be with you very shortly, if that's all right.'

'Champion.' Mr Codling-Bentham sounds thrilled.

'You can't pay him though. He's not allowed to work legally until he's been here for six months.'

'I'm sure we can sort something out,' Mr Codling-Bentham assures me.

I hang up. 'There you go. A job for the day. Now I really must run.' I kiss Dominic again and fly out of the door.

When I get to work, there's no time for a sociable coffee in the staffroom, which is perhaps just as well. At the moment, I'm still pissed off with my colleagues and I'm not in the mood to play nicely with them.

I get straight to work on my first client. 'Hi,' I say. 'How are you?'

'I'm fine,' Mrs Yates says. She looks knackered.

'The twins?'

'I survived the terrible twos,' she says with a careworn sigh. 'No one told me that three was ten times worse.'

Winona Yates got married later in life. She'd been a career woman well into her forties before she met the man of her dreams. They spent a couple of years travelling and generally having a lot of fun, as a couple with a high income and no responsibilities can. When they finally decided to add children to their list of acquisitions it was, of course, way too late. Low sperm for him – believe me, I know all about Ian Yates's sperm count in every last detail – and no eggs for her.

They went through two years of hell and high expense with a million different IVF procedures until they finally produced twin girls. She even invited me to the baby shower. Three months after the babies were born, they split up. Ian Yates found he had a penchant for lap dancing clubs and met a twenty-two-year-old Thai girl there – complete with two children of her own – and left Winona high and dry.

She hasn't seen him since, or any of his money. So now she's left alone trying to hold down a full-time job and juggle demanding twins. The glossy groomed woman I used to know is long gone. She used to come in every week for me to wash and straighten her hair. Now I'm lucky if I see her once every six months for a trim. When I do, she wears the permanently harassed look of a woman who longs for her old life back.

It's lunchtime before I go anywhere near the staffroom. If I've had a spare minute I've just hung around the reception desk and talked to Kelly. The truth of the matter is that I'm finding it increasingly hard to fit in here. All the silly banter that I used to enjoy leaves me cold now. What do I care about *Britain's Got Talent* or *The Apprentice* or *Coronation Street*? The soaps now seem to be full of self-indulgent shouty people and it makes me think of Dominic and his family, how hard their life has been, how every day it's a struggle just to find enough food to eat. Here, all we're concerned about is nonsense. I'm even starting to find the amount that people spend just on grooming their hair quite offensive when previously, I would have said there was nothing more important than having good-looking hair.

Being with Dominic is making me think more deeply about my life. No longer do I sit and watch mindless television all night, but now we talk together for hours on end and I lie on the sofa with my head on his lap as he reads to me. Dominic says he wants to improve his English, even though it sounds pretty flawless to me. He borrows Shakespeare's plays and the novels of Jane Austen from the ladies of the Nashley Church

Flower Committee. I'm learning something too as my reading taste has been stuck on Jackie Collins and Jilly Cooper for far too long.

Whenever I do venture into the staffroom, everyone looks a bit sheepish.

'Thanks for a nice evening,' Tyrone says. 'Clint and I really enjoyed it.'

I could make a sarcastic comment at this juncture, but what's the point? I have to keep working with these people so it's better that I try to keep the atmosphere genial. Nina is quiet. Her carrier bag of fruit sits next to her, as yet untouched.

'OK?' I ask.

She shrugs non-committally. I can tell by the look of her that she didn't get much sleep last night and I wonder what has gone on in the Dalton household since Saturday.

'Hey,' Cristal interrupts. 'We've all decided to go snowboarding on Friday night. Up for it?'

'Nah, I don't think so.'

'You love it,' Cristal whines.

It's true. I do enjoy it. As a group, we all had snowboarding lessons last year at the big indoor Sno!Zone in Milton Keynes. It's a brilliant place and we normally have such a good time. I love the exhilaration of whizzing down the slopes and for someone not normally enamoured by exercise, that's really saying something.

'Come on.' She cajoles me some more. 'Bring whatshisname too.'

'Dominic.'

'Bet he's never been snowboarding before.'

No, I don't suppose he has. He probably hasn't even seen snow and I think he'd be delighted by it. But is that a good enough reason to subject him to my colleagues again?

'You should come,' Nina ventures.

Is this an olive branch?

'Is Gerry coming?' It's out before I can think better of it.

My friend shakes her head. 'No. Away at some business conference.'

I'll bet.

'That doesn't mean you can't bring Dominic.'

No, but it does mean that I can actually consider going now that I know that twat won't be there.

Kelly pops her head around the door. 'Your client's here, Ty. Cristal, can you sweep the floor please?'

They all disappear, leaving Nina and me alone.

'Sorry about Saturday,' she says. 'Gerry and I had been arguing before we arrived.'

'I gathered something was wrong.'

'Another suspicious text on his phone. I picked it up while he was driving. He's explained it away, but I don't know if I believe him this time.'

I wonder how bad it would have to be for Nina to believe it. Is this the point where I tell her that her darling husband has even made a pass at me, her best mate? She should know exactly what he's like by now.

Taking a deep breath, I start, 'Nina . . .' But she cuts me off.

'Despite everything, I still love him,' she says, sounding as if it's the worst thing in the world. My friend looks at me, eyes bleak. 'How can that be?'

I keep quiet. Sometimes things are better left unsaid.

Chapter 70

All the way home, I wonder whether Dominic and I should risk the snowboarding outing. I'm sure that Dominic would be amazed to see the Sno!Zone and I shouldn't let one bad experience put me off taking him out ever again. Dominic needs to integrate into life here and to form friendships if he's not going to feel like an outsider.

As I pull up outside my cottage, I get a rush of love for Dominic. The lights are on and my home is giving out an inviting glow. It's a heartwarming feeling to know that there's someone waiting there for you.

Once inside, I shout out a 'hello!' to Dominic. There's an incredible smell coming from the kitchen and I wander through to find out what it is. I lean on the door and laugh out loud.

In the kitchen Dominic is wearing my apron over his red *shuka*. He's just lifted a golden roasted chicken out of the oven supervised, to my surprise, by Mrs Duston.

'My secret weapon,' Dominic says with a grin.

'Hello, dear,' Mrs Duston says. 'Dominic asked me to give him a hand and everything's just about ready.' She flutters around him. 'He's a very good cook.'

Another item to add to his list of charms. I smile to myself. I'm sure if Nina came home and found another woman in her kitchen, it wouldn't be the likes of Mrs Duston.

'You can take it from here, Dominic,' Nashley's answer to Nigella says. 'I'll be off then.'

'Stay,' I suggest. 'Looks like there's plenty there.' I don't want her going home to an empty house.

She holds up a hand. 'I have flower committee,' she says. 'Important decisions about the Easter display to be discussed.'

'Oh. Right.'

'I'll see you tomorrow, Dominic?'

'Most certainly, Mrs Duston. *Asante*.'

'*Karibu*,' she says proudly as she flutters her eyelashes girlishly.

I follow her to the door. 'Thank you,' I say. 'Thank you for helping Dominic.'

'Oh, the pleasure's *all* mine,' she insists. 'He's a *darling*.'

Promoted from a poppet to a darling, I think. Dominic certainly does have these ladies eating out of his hand.

Back in the kitchen, I throw my bag down on a chair, then go and wind my arms around Dominic's waist. He's tasting his gravy.

'Where did this lot come from?'

'Mr and Mrs Codling-Bentham,' he supplies. 'I worked all day in their garden. They gave me a chicken and vegetables. The apple pie is from Mrs Duston.'

'I'm going to get as fat as a house.' The trouble with all these culinary delights that Dominic seems to attract is that he doesn't eat any of them. So it's left to me to do the polite thing and wolf them down. 'I think I'll put the pie in the freezer for another time.' Though I'm sure Mike might like a slice of it later.

'I did not know what to do with the chicken or the vegetables and Mike was at work, so I asked Mrs Duston what to do. She insisted that she come to help.'

'I bet she did.'

Dominic laughs at that.

'You'll have the entire female population of Buckingham at your feet soon.'

'Not all of them,' he says. 'Your friend, Nina, she still does not like me.'

'She'll come round,' I say confidently. 'We've been asked to go snowboarding with everyone from the salon on Friday night. Do you fancy that?'

'I do not know what snowboarding is,' he says, perplexed.

'It would be fun. Something different for you.'

'If you think it is a good thing, then I would like to try it,' he shrugs.

'Hey. We'd better not let this dinner burn. Mrs Duston would have your guts for garters.'

'My *what*?'

'Figure of speech. Let me just go and change while you dish up.'

I race upstairs and fling on my tracksuit, promising that I'll hang up my work clothes after I've eaten dinner.

Dominic is already putting the meal on the table when I return. On my plate, there's a succulent chicken breast, crispy roast potatoes, buttered carrots and a heap of cabbage. All my lover has are some slices of chicken and a spoonful of his own gravy.

'You should taste the rest of it,' I say as I tuck in. 'Mrs Duston's right, you're a very good cook.'

'I forgot this,' Dominic says. He jumps up from the table and goes to the fridge. 'Mr Codling-Bentham gave me this.'

He puts a bottle of Bollinger on the table.

'Wow, champagne. Very good champagne.' I suddenly feel light and reckless. 'Shall we open it?'

Dominic nods.

'Have you opened fizz before?'

'No. Never.'

'Here, let me show you.' I stand next to him as I strip the foil, unscrew the wire and then wiggle the cork to the edge of the bottle, where it releases with a satisfying pop. 'That's how you do it. None of this denting the ceiling business.' I grab two glasses and pour it out. 'Just a taste,' I tell him. 'A tiny taste won't hurt.'

Dominic, unsure, lifts his glass to his nose. 'The bubbles tickle.'

'We should toast something.'

I put my glass against his. 'To us,' I say.

'To us, Just Janie,' he echoes.

Then, as I sip the chilled bubbles, I come over all light-headed. 'Let's get married,' I say. 'As soon as we can. Let's get married.'

'Mike told me that ladies like men who can cook,' he teases, 'but I did not think that it would work so quickly.'

I think of Mike and wonder what he'd make of me proposing to Dominic like this. I'm sure he'll be happy for us. Absolutely sure.

'Shall we do it? Will you make an honest woman of me?'

Dominic laughs. 'Yes, Just Janie. I will.'

Chapter 71

My last three clients disappear on Wednesday afternoon. A perm, a cut and colour, and a wash and finish. All cancelled. Kelly decides to let me go home early. Business is still flat in the salon after Christmas and Steph is here and has gaps in her appointments in case there are any walk-ins. I also think that Kelly appreciates how many extra hours I worked before Christmas, even though it was for purely selfish reasons.

I used to love the perfumed fug of the salon but these days I'm finding it quite claustrophobic and I can't wait to escape into the fresh air again. Today is a perfect day and it makes me believe that Spring is just around the corner. The sun is bright, doing its best to warm the air but just unable to take that last sharp nip out of it. The pale blue sky is dotted with wisps of milky cloud.

It's nearly three o'clock as I turn into Nashley and although Dominic isn't at home, I know exactly where he'll be. I put on my walking boots and warm coat and head out straight away to find him. Marching through the village warms me up and by the time I get to the Codling-Benthams' home, I'm panting from the exertion.

I find Dominic in the garden, lifting piles of leaves into a huge wheelbarrow. There's a battered old radio by his feet and he's singing along to 'I Predict a Riot' while he works. Not quite the same as the songs of love and nature that he's used to, but he seems to enjoy it nevertheless. Archie is flat out, fast asleep under the barrow.

'Hey,' I say as I come up behind him and kiss his cheek. 'Got off work early. Think you can get away?'

My lover pulls off his gardening gloves. 'I have been very busy.' Together we survey his handiwork. 'I am sure they will not mind.'

He's probably done ten times more work in a day than the ancient gentleman who usually potters about here.

'Thought we'd go for a little walk,' I tell him. 'Show you some more of the area.'

Dominic gazes around him. 'I would like to know more about the trees and plants and birds,' he says. 'It is important to me. In the Mara, I would know every bird, every animal, all the trees. Here, I do not know any of them.'

'I'm not sure I know that many of them either,' I admit, 'but I'll give it a go. We'd better tell the Codling-Benthams that you're leaving for the day and we can see if we can borrow a wildlife book from them.'

Dominic hefts a slightly startled Archie from his resting place and slings him around his shoulders. He picks up his stick too and then we go up to the house and wait patiently while Mrs Codling-Bentham fusses over Dominic and searches for a suitable book for us to take on our walk. She presses a rich fruit cake in a tartan tin into Dominic's arms and Mr Codling-Bentham supplies a bottle of fine port to accompany it.

'If Dominic needs anyone to speak for him,' Mr Codling-

315

Bentham says, 'to the authorities or whatever, then I'm happy to give a reference. Sterling chap. Top drawer.'

He shakes Dominic's hand warmly and he beams at the fulsome praise.

'Thanks.' Who knows, I think, maybe that will come in handy when we make Dominic's application for him to stay here.

With that, we thank them for the gifts and the loan of the book and head off before we lose the light for the day.

I hide the cake and port behind one of the Codling-Benthams' thick yew hedges, thinking that we mustn't forget to collect it on the way back, then Dominic and I stride out to the top of the village, through the woods and into the open fields that stretch behind it. Just five minutes out of the centre of Nashley, we come to the start point of a circular walk near the neighbouring village of Thornborough. It's not a long loop, just a few miles, but I haven't done it for years and certainly not since moving into the village, which is a crime. Perhaps if I had a dog rather than a lazy cat, I'd walk more.

It's muddy underfoot and I'm glad to see that Dominic is wearing his trainers if not his coat. He takes up his stick and armed with our borrowed nature book, we set out across the fields and I'm no longer fazed that Archie accompanies us wherever we go. And neither, it seems, is he.

The fields are dotted with sheep and as we pass by, I say, 'I don't need a book for those. They're sheep.'

'We do not have sheep at home. Not in the Mara,' Dominic says. 'Cattle. Goats. No sheep. This is nice for me.'

'Birds are more difficult,' I say.

'And trees?'

'Hmm.' I gaze around the field as we walk. Apart from being

316

able to pick out an oak or a copper beech, my knowledge of trees is completely rubbish. Must have missed that lesson at school if, indeed, we ever had one. 'It's trickier in the winter as most of the leaves are missing. We might have to wait until the summer for tree identification.'

'You should be able to tell from the shape, the bark, Just Janie.'

'I don't really look at trees.'

'You should.'

'When do I have time?'

'You come all the way to Africa to see the animals, the birds, but you do not see your own?'

'That's different.'

'No. Your animals are as exotic to me as lions and cheetahs are to you.'

'Sheep?'

Dominic laughs and takes my hand. 'Perhaps not sheep.'

We crest the hill and then dip down into the valley. Using a small wooden bridge we cross the stream – Dominic lifts me easily over the stile at either end – and then follow the river as it twists and turns through the meadow.

'There's a heron,' I say. The slender grey bird is walking in the shallows looking for dinner.

Archie, on Dominic's shoulders, cackles his interest.

'Sssh, cat,' Dominic says. 'Do not frighten him away.'

'I always think they look out of place in England,' I whisper. 'They look as if they should be Chinese or something.'

As we're watching the heron, there's a dart of blue that speeds low along the water.

'A kingfisher!' I squeal. 'I haven't seen one of those in years. They're gorgeous. Did you see it?'

'Beautiful,' my lover agrees.

We wait but aren't rewarded with another glimpse, so we press on before it gets dark.

The route follows a disused arm of the canal. The brick walls and the lock gates are still in place, but the rest of it is dry now, overgrown. I explain to Dominic, badly, what little I know about our network of canals.

We pass by and the walk comes to an open stretch of water, a teardrop-shaped lake that's maintained as a nature reserve. There's a bench strategically placed by the edge of the water and we take a moment to sit. The sun is hanging low now, the shadows stretching. The water is busy with activity. Tiny blue tits flit backwards and forwards and some other little, brown jobs. I get out the nature book and flick through the pages.

'Chaffinches,' I tell Dominic as I point. 'And they're moorhens. Those are coots.'

How sad that I don't know any of these things without having to consult a reference guide. If Dominic already knows any of these birds then he doesn't tell me.

Overhead, a flock of starlings is massing, swooping back and forth, splitting and regrouping until there's a huge synchronised group that fills the sky above us. It moves back and forth, drawing patterns in the sky, shape-shifting. One minute it's a whale, the next a bird with its wings outspread. Then, the next minute, the thousands of birds form a heart-shape.

'Oh!' I say.

Dominic slips his arm around my shoulder. 'Tell me that is not beautiful, Just Janie.'

'It's beautiful.' And it has taken this wonderful man from another continent to show me just how spectacular my own country can be.

318

Chapter 72

Even as you approach the entrance to the Sno!Zone, the temperature starts to drop. As a local and a regular visitor, this space looks amazing, but to Dominic who has never seen snow before, it's like a miracle. His eyes are out on stalks.

The Sno!Zone houses one of the biggest indoor ski slopes in Europe and we can see it in all its glory from the wall of windows that flanks one side of it. There are two drag lifts that go to the top of the steep man-made slope and both are already busy with skiers and snowboarders in colourful clothing being carried to the top.

'This is snow?' Dominic says, pressing his hands against the window.

'Yes.' Since Christmas it's just been raining and cold. No late snow this year, thank goodness.

'You have it *inside*?'

'You can practise for skiing holidays and stuff. Or people like us just come along because it's fun.'

Dominic looks as if he can't quite grasp this concept.

'We need to get kitted out,' I tell him and tug him away from the mesmerising sight to join the rest of the group.

'HELLO. DOMINIC,' Nina shouts at him.

'Hello,' he replies politely. 'How are you?'

'FAB. LOOKING. FORWARD. TO. SNOWBOARDING?'

'Yes. Very much so.'

I'm disappointed to see that my friend has brought Gerry along after all. I thought he was supposed to be on some 'business conference'. Perhaps his married lover couldn't get away from her partner and had to cancel at the last minute. Grrr. As we queue up to pay and get our salopettes and snowboards, I nod a curt 'hello' at him and he graces me with one of his smug smiles in return. It's going to be difficult giving him a wide berth for the whole evening, but I'm damn well going to try. Why did Nina have to bring him? I think. Why couldn't she have left him at home for once?

While I'm muttering away to myself in my head, we shuffle forward to the desk and the equipment is doled out to us all. Dominic looks bemused by the whole process, but accepts whatever the girl behind the desk gives him.

This man learns quickly. Tonight he abandoned his *shuka* and came out in the clothes I bought for him without me even having to mention it. He's already sussed that although the villagers have readily accepted him in his traditional clothes, the great unwashed public of Milton Keynes may not be quite ready for him. I only hope that the salopettes they've given him fit, otherwise they'll be flapping around his ankles.

'No feathery headdress tonight, mate?' Gerry says and then adds a guffaw.

'That is only for very special occasions.' Again, Dominic's response is immaculately polite.

I'd like to beat Gerry to a pulp on Dominic's behalf. I'm anxious that we have to split off into separate changing rooms, as that will leave Dominic at the mercy of Gerry, and that's something I'm not keen on at all. I don't want him out of my sight for a second. It's just a shame that Mike wasn't able to come along, but he's going to be late home from work tonight after taking a client out to dinner. I could really do with him here now.

Instead, pulling Tyrone close to me, I whisper, 'Look after Dominic for me. Make sure he knows how to get dressed properly.'

'Sure,' he says. 'No worries.'

'*Hakuna matata.*'

'What?'

'Swahili. It means no worries.'

'Cool,' Tyrone says.

I'm thinking now – somewhat too late – that I should have booked Dominic into some group lessons before I brought him along to the Sno!Zone with everyone else. That's what we all had to do to get our certificate of competence or whatever they call it. Perhaps Dominic can just fiddle about at the bottom of the slope and I can help him with some tips. Ty and Clinton have both picked this up well and scoot down the slopes like pros, so they can maybe show him what to do too.

It takes for ever for us all to be kitted out and then we make our separate ways to the changing rooms.

'Will you be OK?' I ask Dominic anxiously.

'Yes, Just Janie,' he replies with a smile. 'Do not worry.'

But I watch nervously as he disappears out of my sight.

Gerry comes alongside me. 'Bit different for him than wrestling lions, eh?' He laughs and moves on, following Dominic into the changing rooms.

Which is a shame, because my friend's husband doesn't then hear me tell him to shove his flipping snowboard where the sun doesn't shine.

Chapter 73

Every time I come here, it always amazes me how cold it is. Dominic, I think, has gone into full-on shock. This is probably the first time he's had experience of sub-zero temperatures and I bet he's glad now that he's wrapped up in salopettes and a thick jacket rather than his usual thin cotton *shuka*.

He stands shivering at the bottom of the slope, staring up awe-struck, clutching his snowboard. My heart goes out to him as I watch him. He seems so far away from home now and I wonder if that's what he's thinking too.

I put my arms around him and kiss him. 'Fancy giving it a go?'

'Oh, yes.' He watches the skiers and the snowboarders intently.

The others head to the drag lift and Ty comes over. 'Want a few tips, Dominic?'

'Yes, please.'

Tyrone shows him how to fit his helmet so that it's snug, clip on his bindings and how to stand on the board. Then he shows Dominic how to shift his weight from the front to the back of the board, lowering and raising his heels and toes. Dominic stands watching Ty's every move and certainly looks as if he's taking it all in.

'Try it,' Ty suggests. 'Just take it easy.'

Dominic tries a few moves and does surprisingly well, considering that I spent most of my beginners' lessons flat on my butt.

'Cool,' Ty says and then he shows Dominic how to shift his body weight to make the board turn left and right, and how to steer it.

'Want to go a bit further up the slope?' Ty asks and leads the way.

There's a small nursery lift – a magic carpet – that carries them a fraction of the way up the main slope. I tag behind and we all get off at the same spot together.

'OK,' Ty says. 'Let's go for it.'

Dominic clips on the board as he's been shown and stands, unsteadily, on his feet. 'Woaw,' he says as he starts to slither down the slope.

Out of the corner of my eye I can see the others have stopped boarding and are now watching him from the other side of the slope. Gerry is pointing and sniggering. He's been doing this for years and has clearly forgotten what it's like to start. But all credit to Dominic, he gets to the bottom in one piece, still smiling, and with a certain amount of style and a minimum amount of flailing. I slither down behind them feeling more than a bit rusty as I carve my turns. It's months since we've all been to the Sno!Zone together.

'Nice one, mate!' Ty says and high-fives Dominic. 'Let's go again.'

So up we go and time after time, Dominic – with increasing grace – reaches the bottom intact.

'You've nailed it,' Ty says. 'Let's go for the drag lift.'

'Oh, no, no.' I stay Dominic's arm. 'I think it's a bit too soon for that.'

'I am enjoying this, Janie,' Dominic says. His face is flushed, his eyes bright with excitement. 'I want to go higher.'

'Don't feel that you have anything to prove to these guys.' Particularly, that total prat Gerry, I want to add. 'It's not a competition.'

It might be all very well that Dominic is the best jumper in his Maasai village, but I'm not sure how that will translate to the slopes. He's looking a bit over-confident to me, and pride, particularly on snow, always comes before a fall. Still, despite my misgivings, we follow Ty to the drag lift and he quickly shows Dominic how to unclip his rear leg and jump on. We watch other people for a few minutes and then Gerry pushes into the queue in front of us.

'Last one to the top is a sissy,' he jeers.

'Wanker,' I mutter under my breath.

'Hook the button round your leg. Scoot the board along. Keep sideways.' Ty keeps issuing instructions to Dominic as we inch closer. 'Don't try to go straight or you'll catch an edge and go out of the front door. Ready?'

Dominic nods and, seconds later, we're on the lift and following the rest of the group up the slope. Despite my own shaking knees, we're carried higher and higher without incident. At the top we make our way along the summit of the slope. Dominic looks down.

'You don't have to do this,' I say. 'We can unclip and walk down part of it.'

Dominic turns to me, eyes bright. 'This looks like fun,' he says and before I can offer any more sage advice, he's off. I watch, heart in my mouth, as he hurtles down the slope, twisting and turning. Ty and I turn to look at each other.

'Fuck,' Ty says.

'Exactly what I was thinking. Either you're a brilliant teacher or that's one hell of a quick learner.'

'Let's get after him,' my friend suggests and we too hit the slope, serpentining down in Dominic's wake.

Chapter 74

We've booked for two hours and after just one of them, Dominic is snowboarding as if he's been doing it all his life. The rest of the group are cheering him on and only Gerry is hanging back, scowling.

I hug Dominic as he whizzes to the bottom of the slope again. 'You're brilliant,' I tell him.

He's laughing excitedly. 'I have never had fun like this, Janie. Thank you for bringing me here.'

Ty high-fives him. 'Top boarder, mate!'

Gerry comes forward. 'Let's up the ante a bit,' he says. 'Up for a kicker?'

Dominic shrugs. 'I do not know what this is.'

I do. In the middle of the slope, there's a huge ramp of snow and the idea is that you launch yourself from it, getting as much air between you and the snow as possible. The danger of falling on your head, breaking your arm, busting up a leg, is very high.

There's a sly grin on Gerry's face when he says, 'I'll show you.'

I step forward. 'I don't think so.'

'Frightened your boyfriend can't cut it?' he sneers.

'Dominic's doing brilliantly. Leave him alone.'

'Oh, well,' Gerry says, holding up a hand, 'if you don't think he's man enough for it . . .'

'Oh, grow up,' I say.

'I would like to try it.' Dominic moves towards the lift.

Gerry grins. 'You're on.'

'Be careful, Dom,' Ty warns. He looks at me concerned, as well he might.

Unable to help myself, I grab Dominic's arm. 'He's taunting you. There's no need to do this.' Again, I wish that Mike was here. As the voice of reason, I'm sure he'd be able to talk Dominic out of this madness. 'You hadn't even seen snow before today and you've done brilliantly. Don't spoil it. You could really hurt yourself. Quit while you're ahead.'

'I will be OK, Just Janie,' he assures me. 'Just watch.'

I don't know if he realises exactly what Gerry is trying to do, or perhaps he does but feels that he has to rise to the challenge. Whichever it is, naivety or bravado, I only know that it's making me feel sick.

'Gerry,' Nina says, 'don't do this.' Even she, for once, can see that her husband is being a complete knobhead.

All he does is laugh at her, then he and Dominic move away to join the queue for the lift.

'This is stupid.' My anger is rising. 'Utterly stupid.'

We watch them travel to the top of the slope on the drag lift. A minute later, Gerry sets off at high speed and heads straight for the kicker. Dominic swoops down behind him.

'I can't watch,' I say and as the rest of the group stare, open-mouthed, I put my hands over my eyes and peek between my fingers.

Gerry hits the kicker, expertly, and flies through the air before landing safely at the bottom of the slope once more.

'Air,' Ty says with admiration.

Then, before we have time to breathe, Dominic shouts out his high-pitched noise as he hits the kicker. Everyone in the place stops to watch him. My heart leaps into my mouth as he launches off. I turn away, unable to bear it, then I hear everyone else cheering and clapping.

When I turn back, I just catch sight of Dominic coming down from a great height to execute a perfect landing.

Ty, much like myself, is wide-eyed, stunned. 'Big air,' he says, gobsmacked. '*Big*, big air.'

'Really?' I lower my hands and risk a proper look.

'Omigod. Are you kidding me? Can that dude jump!'

I'm guessing all his hours spent practising Maasai jumping have proven to be useful in other areas.

'He's ten times better than Gerry,' Ty says and pulls a happy face.

Dominic is laughing his head off as he comes to a stop in front of the group. Everyone mills around him, delighted at his success, clapping him on the back. The other skiers burst into spontaneous applause. Gerry, to one side, looks less pleased. I glance over and catch his eye.

'Lucky,' he mouths at me.

'Go fuck yourself,' I mouth back.

Gerry slinks away to the changing rooms by himself and I go over to Dominic and crush him in my relieved embrace.

'NICE. ONE,' Nina says in the shouty voice she reserves for my loved one.

'I will stop now,' Dominic says, his arm around my shoulders. 'That was very amazing.'

'We have to come back here,' Ty says. 'You're a star, man.'

'I would like that.'

Again, he high-fives his coach.

'I'm just glad that you landed in one piece,' I tell him as the others move out of earshot.

As Dominic unclips his snowboard, he winks at me. 'Me too,' he says.

Chapter 75

I go into the changing room with Nina. I feel giddy with euphoria. Not only did Dominic rise to the challenge, but he smashed it and now I'm walking on air. I feel at least as tall as Dominic and can't stop myself from grinning madly. He's a crazy, snowboarding Maasai warrior and I love him for it!

My friend and I both flop down on a bench and pull off our boots with a grateful sigh. In comparison to the slope, it's like a sauna in here and I strip off my jacket as quickly as I can.

'Dominic nailed that,' Nina says, reluctantly impressed. 'Certainly wiped the smile off Gerry's face.'

I don't tell her that I'm still cross that her twat of a husband led Dominic into that situation in the first place. It was very lucky that due to some innate ability and supreme balance skills, he survived it, unhurt.

Nina stops what she's doing and looks at me. 'He's certainly got what it takes,' she says, even though it sounds somewhat grudging. She might not be falling all over my lover but, at last, she seems to be accepting Dominic.

'I'm glad you think so.' I peel off my salopettes, fish my jeans out of my locker and tug them on.

'Think he'll stick around?'

As we're having a period of *entente cordiale*, Nina might as well know my news. I take a deep breath. 'We're going to get married,' I say.

At that, she sits bolt upright. 'What?'

'We're going to get married,' I repeat. 'As soon as we can.'

She stares at me, mouth agape. 'How stupid are you?'

I bite down on my lip and curl my fingernails into my palm. 'The usual response is congratulations and much hugging ensues,' I retort crisply. Now I'm cross. More than cross. I'm furious. 'I thought you just said you like him.'

'I do. But he's not marriage material, is he? Let's face it.'

She's sounding more like her stupid husband by the minute. 'Why not?'

Nina sighs as she too pulls off her salopettes in a world-weary manner. 'He's after one thing, Janie. Not five minutes after you're married, he'll be suing for divorce. You mark my words, he might be all sweetness and light now, but he'll be trying to take you for half of your home, half of everything you've got.'

'Dominic's not like that.'

'Why can't you see it?' Nina shrugs off her jacket. 'It's what everyone thinks.'

'Everyone who?' Certainly no one who knows Dominic properly.

'They might pretend to like him to your face, Janie, but they all think like I do. Wait and see. It'll start off innocently enough with you sending money here and there to his family to help them out ...'

The look on my face must give me away.

Nina looks smug. 'There you are,' she says. 'Looks like it's happening already.'

'We've sent them a few things, a bit of money,' I counter, 'at my suggestion. It wasn't Dominic's idea at all. Most of it will be spent on medicine. I begrudge them nothing, Nina. If you saw how little they have, you'd feel the same.'

She shrugs away my explanation. 'I'm just saying, this is how it starts out.'

'You're wrong,' I tell her firmly. 'Very wrong. Just look at him. Can you not see what I see in him?'

'So the bloke looks great, in a different kind of way,' my friend continues, her tone more petulant than I'd like. 'If you want something a little *unusual* there are plenty of websites for that, Janie. You don't need to go this far. You don't need to think about *keeping* Dominic. You don't need to think about *marrying* him.'

'I can't believe you actually said that.' I slam my locker, barely holding my temper, and wrench out the key.

'Just because he's a natural snowboarder, that hardly makes him the perfect husband.'

'So what does make the perfect husband, Nina? One who can't stay faithful for more than ten minutes at a time? One who chats up all of your friends' – even your best friend – 'the minute your back is turned? Sometimes he doesn't even offer that courtesy, Nina. He does it right in front of your face. Is Gerry the perfect husband?' I'm breathing heavily now. 'How dare you criticise Dominic. He's kind, considerate, funny and charming, and I would trust him with my life. Can you say that about your own partner?'

'You can't compare him to Gerry, for heaven's sake.'

'No, I can't,' I agree. 'Gerry is a cheating philanderer.' He might have a certain charm, I want to shout, but that's not enough to compensate for him being a complete bastard. 'What do you see in him?'

'At least he works,' Nina says. 'He holds down a job. He's not living off me, sending money back to some needy family in some dodgy country. He'll be gone, Janie. You won't see Dominic for dust. The minute he's fleeced you, he'll be gone. Everyone thinks so.'

Behind me, I hear the changing room door close quietly. Instinctively, I know who it is and I fly to the door and rush out into the corridor. Sure enough, Dominic is standing there.

'Dominic …'

'I heard what she said, Just Janie.' His eyes are filled with sadness. 'I heard it all.'

Chapter 76

'Please,' I beg him. 'Don't take any notice of her. She's being vindictive. Jealous.'

I retrieved my gear, completely ignoring Nina, and then I marched Dominic out of the Sno!Zone, holding tightly to his arm, avoiding the others too. My blood is boiling. I can't ever recall a time in my life when I've felt so very, very angry.

During the drive home, Dominic is virtually silent. He stares out of the window, a bewildered, hurt look on his face.

I'm so upset myself that I can hardly concentrate and if I'm not careful, I'll end up in a ditch. It's raining now and the irritating clack-clack of the windscreen wipers is making me grit my teeth. I try to focus on the road, but I could weep. I could weep and then I could scream.

'She didn't mean it,' I tell him as I crunch the gears.

'I think that she did,' Dominic counters.

'She might well have done,' I concede, 'but she's wrong. None of what she said is true. I know that. You know that. That's all that matters.'

'In my village at home, I was a man of good standing. The elders respected my opinions. They were proud that I had been to school. All of the community looked up to me. As a Maasai warrior, an educated one, I was a person to be admired, envied. Here,' he says, 'I do not know my place.'

'But the people in the village love you,' I remind him. 'Look at all the old ladies clucking around you like mother hens. They don't think that you're here to take me for all of my money.'

Goodness only knows, there's hardly anything left of it for Dominic to take.

He looks devastated and it's such a shame when we'd had a great evening and Dominic had proved to be the star of the show.

'This brings great shame on me. If this happened in my home, if my reputation was so tarnished, I would be forced to go out and live on the plains alone.'

'It's not the same here. It's not like that at all. Here we just think "fuck it" and carry on. Really we do.'

'My family, my loved ones, would want me to leave. They would be happy for me to take my humiliation from their door.'

How can I make Dominic see that this is a storm in a teacup and that I really don't care what my friends think of him, whether they like him or not? But I can see that it is weighing heavily on his mind, on his heart, and that nothing I have to say will ease this blow.

'If I bring shame on myself, then I will bring shame on you too. The villagers, your friends, will not love you any more.'

'I don't care what anyone else thinks. Please don't dwell on this. I don't want it to spoil what we have. I'll leave my job and do something else,' I tell him. 'I've been thinking about it anyway. They all drive me nuts. Then I won't have to see Nina or any of the others. We can make new friends, friends in the village. When you start to work, you'll make friends there.'

'What if they all think that I am a bad man? What if they all think that I want to take your home and your money away from you? Will they always look at my skin, at my clothes, and treat me with suspicion?'

'They won't.' I grab his hand and squeeze it. 'They won't.' He doesn't look convinced.

'Nina has issues. That's all. She can't trust Gerry and her relationship is breaking down. She just can't bear to see anyone else happy.'

'She is your best friend.'

'*Was* my best friend. If she's going to be like this then I don't want anything more to do with her.'

'You should not break friendships.'

'I'm not the one breaking it, Dominic. She is. By being a complete cow.'

I pull up outside Little Cottage. The rain is lashing down now and I'm just grateful to be home in one piece.

'I'll make you some warm milk,' I cajole Dominic. 'Then we can cuddle up by the fire and talk about this. I don't want you to worry about it.'

Hesitantly, he opens the car door and steps out into the rain. 'I must think about this,' he says. 'I must think what is the best thing to do.'

I let us into the cottage as I say, 'There's nothing *to* do.' Archie comes running down the stairs and twines himself around our feet, purring happily.

Turning, I wrap my arms around my lover. 'We just carry on as we are, being in love, making plans for our wedding.'

'In the village, I would talk to the elders about my fears. Here, I have no one.'

'You have me. And Mike. Should I get Mike? Do you feel that you can talk to him?'

'No. He is a Western man. He will say the same things as you do. I must think about this alone. I will sit in the garden.'

'You can't sit in the garden. It's pouring down out there. You'll catch your death. Please come to bed.'

He shakes his head. 'I must be alone to think.'

'No,' I beg. 'Think with me. We'll think together. Don't go out in the rain, Dominic.'

But he goes upstairs and a moment later comes down in his *shuka*.

'Dominic, you can't go out like that, in *this*!' I gesture to the rain pouring in rivulets down the windows. 'Have a bath. A nice warm bath. That will help you to relax.'

'Go to bed, Janie,' he says. 'I will be in soon.'

'You're frightening me, Dominic. This is just one of my friends being spiteful. We can do without her. We can do without everyone. The only person I can't live without is you.'

'Maybe you would be better without me. They all seem to think so.'

'*I* don't. I don't think that. All that matters is what *we* want.'

'Go to bed,' Dominic says. 'I will be in soon.'

I watch him go out into the night, the freezing rain, in nothing but a cotton tunic. Archie, giving a reluctant backwards glance to the warmth of the kitchen, follows him outside. Even the cat is going to get soaked through.

Dominic closes the door softly behind them and, out of the rain-streaked window, I see him walk up the sodden garden, the thin cotton of his *shuka* darkening with water as he goes. In the far corner, there's a bench under the arching branches of a tree – possibly a willow – and I see Dominic settle himself there. Archie hops up beside him and I hope that the tree is providing

337

them both with a bit of shelter. They could have taken an umbrella, I think. Or a coat.

'Bloody men,' I mutter. 'They're all more trouble than they're worth.'

But I don't mean it. I don't mean it at all.

Chapter 77

I sit on the sofa and watch some rubbish on television, even though I should go to bed. I've got work in the morning and will be fit for nothing at this rate.

At two o'clock in the morning, I wake up and find that I'm slumped down in among the cushions. One of my legs is numb and both of my arms. I struggle to sit upright and then I try to massage some life into my limbs. The heating has gone off and the log burner has smouldered away, so the cottage is chilly. Pulling the throw around me, I pad out to the kitchen and peer through the window. The rain is still pouring down and Dominic is still sitting in the garden. I can just make out the red of his tunic through the torrent.

I sigh to myself and pour a cup of milk and ping it in the microwave. Then I go into the utility room and pull on my wellies and big jacket. Finding the umbrella amid the detritus, I head outside, putting it up as I do. The rain patters on the fabric. Dominic looks up as I approach.

I crouch down in front of him. Smiling, I say, 'You must have done enough thinking by now.'

He returns my smile and says, 'Yes. You are right.'

'You'll come inside now?'

He nods.

'I've just warmed some milk for you.'

Archie, curled up, paws tucked tightly under the front of his body, looks thoroughly relieved that his nocturnal outdoor ordeal is over.

Dominic stands and stretches. When I touch his arm, his skin is frozen like ice.

'You'll be lucky if you don't catch a cold,' I tell him.

He says nothing.

'Feeling better?'

'Yes. I know what I must do.'

'Want to share?'

Dominic shakes his head. Then, 'You must know that I love you, Just Janie,' he says. '*Aanyor pii*. With all of my heart, for all time.'

I hold him to me, looking into his eyes. '*Aanyor pii*.' Resting my head on his chest, I say, 'Come and have that milk now and then we can both go to bed. I've got to get up at seven o'clock.'

'I am sorry to disturb your sleep.'

'Don't be silly,' I chide. 'I'm worried about you. I don't want you to struggle with problems by yourself. If we're going to make a life together, then we need to sort out our problems together.'

Taking his hand, I gently pull him inside and into the warmth. In the kitchen, I make him strip off his *shuka* and I rub him down with a warm towel. I trace the contours of his firm muscular body, marvelling at just how very beautiful it is. I plant kisses where I've dried and sigh with pleasure when I think that I could be doing this for the rest of my life. The reaction from Dominic's body tells me that he's enjoying it too.

Archie, at Dominic's broad bare feet, complains jealously about his own lack of attention. When I've finished with Dominic, I towel my cat down too while he miaows pitifully.

We all go upstairs and I curl against Dominic's body. 'You're cold,' I whisper. 'How can I warm you up?'

His face is soft in the darkness and he moves above me and we make love, long and languorously. Even though I should have one eye on the clock, I don't, as I never ever want this to end.

Afterwards, I lie in his arms and feel that I am in heaven, truly in heaven. Whatever anyone else says about this man, I know that his love is steadfast, unwavering, that he would never do anything to hurt me and that I would not, for one moment, ever doubt him.

'I love you,' I murmur against his neck. 'I love you so much.'

Dominic strokes my hair from my face. 'I love you too,' he says. 'Whatever happens. I love you too.'

That's the last thing I hear as I sink into deep contented sleep.

Chapter 78

LeAnn Rimes singing 'How Do I Live' wakes me up on the radio alarm. I stretch out my arm for Dominic, but my hand just finds more bed. Forcing my eyes open, I see that he's gone. It must have been three in the morning or even later by the time we finally went to sleep and now I feel not unlike death warmed up. I lie on my back and stretch. My body shivers when I think of our lovemaking last night. In my mind, I can still feel Dominic inside me, his body pressed against mine, and I want him all over again. I know that never in my life have I felt this satisfied, this loved as a woman, and I don't care what anyone else says. If this is not real love, then I have no idea what is.

When the sad song finishes, I make myself sit up. No luxuriating in bed this morning for me. At nine on the dot, I have a cut and blow-dry to do and then a full appointment book all day – not a single gap, not even lunch.

Dominic, I expect, is out doing his rounds of the village, checking on his old ladies, and that makes me smile to myself. Then I notice that Archie is still curled up at the bottom of the bed and I'm jolted wide awake in an instant. If the cat is still here but Dominic isn't, then there's something seriously amiss. My heart hits the bottom of my stomach and I know, instinctively, without a shadow of a doubt, that Dominic has gone.

Jumping out of bed, I pull on my dressing gown. My cat stirs reluctantly.

'Where is he?' I ask his favoured feline friend. 'Do you know where he's gone?'

But Archie looks as bemused as I do that our man is missing.

I fly downstairs and, pointlessly, check all the rooms. I know. I know in my heart that he's no longer here. In the kitchen his *shuka* is gone and my broom handle isn't in its usual place in the utility room. I should have picked up on it last night when he was talking about having to quit the village to live in exile if he was shamed. Oh, bloody hell. Stupid, stupid me. Why didn't I understand what he was talking about?

Then I notice that next to my purse, which has been taken out of my handbag, there's a note. All it says is, '*Aanyor pii*. Dominic.'

Oh, Christ. I hold on to the worksurface to stop me from collapsing to the floor.

Running outside into the lane, I call out his name. 'Dominic! Dominic!' I chase up and down like a headless chicken, dressing gown flapping, but I can't see him anywhere. How long has he been gone? I wonder. When did he leave? I heard nothing. My love was leaving me and I slept on, blissful in my dreams, and heard nothing at all.

When I reach the post office, there's half a dozen people collecting their morning paper as I barge in. 'Has anyone seen Dominic?'

Much head shaking from the queue.

'No,' Mrs Appleby says from behind the counter. 'Is everything all right?'

'No,' I tell her. 'No, it's not.'

'Anything I can help with, lovey?' She frowns, concerned.

'Dominic's missing. If you see him, send him home,' I say. 'Please send him straight home.'

Sprinting back to the house, I keep shouting and shouting but wherever Dominic is, he's long gone from Nashley. What do I do? What do I do now? How am I going to find him? How can I get him to come back?

As I dash breathlessly back to Little Cottage, Mike is coming out of his house, getting ready to start his day's work.

'Mike!' I shout out.

He rocks back in shock when he sees me. 'What are you doing out in your dressing gown in this weather, woman? Is everything OK?'

I shake my head as I run up to him. 'Dominic,' I say. I fall, panting, against him, tears flowing now. 'He's gone.'

Mike holds me away from him and looks into my face. 'Dominic? Where?'

'I don't know,' I admit. 'I have no idea. As far as he can away from me. That's all I know.'

'Have you had an argument?' my neighbour asks.

'More than that.'

He waits patiently for my explanation.

'We went to the Sno!Zone last night. A whole group from work. It was brilliant. *Dominic* was brilliant. You should have seen him.' I sigh with frustration. 'Then I was talking to Nina in the changing rooms afterwards and I told her that Dominic and I were planning to get married ...'

Now it's my neighbour's turn to look taken aback. 'You're getting married?' His expression changes to hurt. 'And you didn't tell me?'

'Don't be cross. Please don't be cross,' I say. 'I would normally tell you first, of course I would, but Nina was being nice for once so I thought that I'd let her into our secret. It just slipped out. I didn't plan it. Oh, Mike, she was awful, said the most terrible things. Her view is that Dominic is just marrying me for my money, that he'll divorce me and take me for half of everything as soon as he can. She said everyone thought so. You don't think that, do you?'

'No,' Mike says. 'Of course I don't. I think Dominic's a great bloke. I'm pleased for you, Janie. Really I am. I'm pleased for Dominic too.' He smiles at me, but there's a sadness behind his eyes. 'I'm just a little bit upset for me. That's all.'

'Oh, Mike.' Tears well. What else can I say to him? That if it wasn't Dominic I was crazy in love with, then it might well be him? Would that make him feel better or worse? 'The thing is,' I continue, 'Dominic heard it all. He said that it would shame him in the eyes of the village and that he had to leave. Except I didn't understand him at the time. It's some Maasai thing. He was effectively saying that if he stayed when people thought that about him, then I would be shunned too. He's trying in his own silly way to save me from that. When I woke up, he'd gone.'

'Any idea where he might be?'

I wrack my brains, but all my thinking is veiled in a thick fog. 'He said something about having to go out onto the plains and live alone if you're a Maasai who's been shamed. It might be clutching at straws, but he could just be in the fields around here somewhere. He has nowhere else to go.'

'Has he got any money with him?'

'No,' I say. Not that I've checked. 'I don't think so.'

'Have you phoned in to work yet?' he asks.

I shake my head. 'I came out as soon as I realised he was gone.'

'Do it,' he instructs. 'There's no way you can go in today. They'll have to cope without you. I'll phone my office too, tell them that I'm not coming in, then we can jump in my car and go and look for him. He can't have gone far, not without any cash. Let's not waste any time.'

The tears roll down my cheeks. 'Thank you. Thank you so much.'

'No worries.' He takes hold of my arms. 'We'll find him, Janie. We'll find him and bring him back home.'

No worries. *Hakuna matata*. We'll find Dominic and bring him back home. I can only hope with all my heart that Mike is right.

Chapter 79

I call the salon and speak to Kelly. 'I'm not going to be in today,'
I tell her. 'Dominic's gone missing. I have to look for him.'

'Janie, you have a full book,' my boss says, somewhat
sharply.

What do I care about cut and blow-dries and touching up
roots when my loved one is missing? 'Did you not hear me?
Dominic's missing,' I repeat. 'I have to find him.'

'Missing? How? What's happened?' she wants to know.

'Ask Nina,' I reply tartly. 'Ask Nina what happened.'

Then I hang up. If she sacks me, so what? I could care less.
Let Nina fit in my clients today, as I've done for her so many
times in the past when she's been having problems with Gerry
and has been unable or unwilling to turn up for work.

Still steaming, I throw on some clothes. A quick check in the
wardrobe tells me that Dominic has taken very little. His small
case is still here and so is his shield and his machete. Thankfully,
his passport is still in the drawer too and I hug it to me. Not
that he would have had the money to, but at least I know for
sure that he can't leave the country. All the clothes I bought him
are hanging from the rails. His trainers are missing but other

than that, he hasn't taken any other clothing with him. Not even his warm coat – in this weather – and even the thought of that chills me to the bone. Does that mean he's not planning to be gone for long?

When I check my purse, I can see that all he has taken is a ten-pound note. Ten quid. That's not going to get him very far. He's left another twenty-five behind and I don't know whether I'm relieved or not. How will he manage out there on his own?

Mike and I have to find him. We just have to.

As I leave, Archie is sitting on the doorstep, miaowing pathetically. I give the fur behind his ear a reassuring rub.

'We'll bring him back,' I promise. My cat doesn't look convinced.

Mike is already in the car, engine running. It's warm when I slide inside, but I still feel frozen.

'Where to?'

I look blankly at him. 'I don't know.'

'If you think he might be in the fields, then let's just drive around,' Mike suggests. 'We'll cover the local area as best we can.'

'He doesn't know anywhere.' That makes me wonder if I've tried hard enough to fully integrate Dominic into my life. I've never taken him into Buckingham or to the salon. But then my life is small. All there is to it is work and Archie and Mike. Without Dominic in it, my life was extraordinarily dull.

'Then he must still be round here.' Mike pulls out of the drive while I, in the passenger seat, chew frantically on my nails.

We tour the lanes around Nashley, Mike driving at a steady speed, both of us with our eyes peeled for a tell-tale flash of red from Dominic's *shuka*. It's becoming light now, but the temperature is still barely above freezing and there are pockets of fog hanging in the dips in the road.

'He'll die out here,' I say and I don't think I'm being melo-dramatic. I'm genuinely worried for his health. He was out half of the night in pouring rain and now this. I know that Maasai warriors are supposed to be tough, but he's not used to this at all.

'He'll be fine,' Mike counters. 'Dominic isn't stupid. He won't put himself at risk.'

Inside I can feel my hysteria rising and, for the rest of the day, I struggle to fight it down. When we've covered as much of the countryside as we possibly can, Mike and I turn our attention to the town.

'Let's try Milton Keynes first,' Mike says, and we trawl up and down the main roads, hoping to get a sight of him. He should stand out like a sore thumb here.

But nothing.

It's getting dark and my eyes are dry from staring. We haven't eaten anything all day. We haven't had so much as a cup of tea and now we're both flagging.

'Let's stop,' Mike suggests. 'Get a sandwich and a drink. We're no good like this.'

He pulls up at a garage and we buy plastic cheese sandwiches and get putrid coffee from a machine. But I'm just grateful for something and we sit in the warmth of the car and force them down.

I turn away from Mike and stare out of the window as I can't stop the tears from falling. Where is Dominic now? Is he cold? Is he hungry? Is he missing me? Has he thought better of his actions and has now gone back to Little Cottage and is waiting there for me, wondering where I am?

Taking out my mobile, I dial the house number and let it ring until the answerphone cuts in. Looks like there's no one home.

I should have kitted Dominic out with a mobile, but I just hadn't got round to it. To be honest, in the short time he's been here, we've hardly been apart at all, so the need hasn't arisen. How I wish he had one now. But, I wonder, if he can walk away like this, would he answer my calls at all? Does this self-imposed exile, if that's what it is, last for a few days or a few weeks or is it for ever? I have no idea. I know so little about the ins and outs of Dominic's traditional customs.

'Don't worry,' Mike says for the millionth time, but the strain is showing in his voice. He, too, is as worried about Dominic as I am.

'I'm frantic, Mike.' My words are choked with emotion. 'Where can he be? I don't want him to spend a night outside.'

'We'll go to the police station,' my neighbour says decisively. 'See if we can enlist their help. Goodness only knows he should be easy enough to spot. Perhaps we could try to get something on the local television news or the radio.'

That thought brightens me up considerably. 'Let's do it.'

'OK.' Mike crushes his sandwich packet and then takes mine and does the same. 'Drink up.'

He waits until I drain the dregs out of my paper cup and then takes that too. Hopping out of the car, he throws our rubbish in the nearby bin and his reliable, steady kindnesses almost have me undone again.

'You don't know how much I appreciate this. You're a good man, Mike.'

His hand squeezes mine. 'That's what friends are for.'

Then we're off again, working our way through the build-up of traffic on the rush hour streets of Milton Keynes in search of the police station.

You may think that I've had a sheltered life, but I've never been into a police station before. I've never had a reason to. I've never had so much as a parking ticket in my thirty-odd years. I am a careful, law-abiding citizen.

When we eventually locate the police station, Mike steers me inside while I plod along like a zombie. The officer at the desk is high above us. 'I'd like to report a missing person,' I say in a tremulous voice.

The officer seems reasonably sympathetic, at least he makes all the right noises. He takes down all of Dominic's details, asks for a photograph, which, of course, I don't have on me, then tells me that they'll circulate the details via computer to all of the other forces' missing persons listings.

'Right,' he says. 'That's all for now.' He leans on the counter in front of him. 'They usually come back, Miss. By the time you get home, he might well be there. Or in the morning. One night of this weather and they don't stay away for long.'

He exchanges a glance with Mike. Clearly the policeman thinks that this is some sort of petty domestic spat that will resolve itself.

'If he's not at home?' I ask.

'Then call us. We'll get someone to come round, collect a photograph from you, and take a few more details.'

'I'm worried about him,' I say. What I want is people out there with tracker dogs, hundreds of them, and helicopters and that kind of thing. I don't want to fill in forms and sit and wait. 'He's vulnerable. There's no one else.' I've already told him this in my report. 'He's got nowhere else to go.'

'Most people turn up,' he assures me. 'You mark my words.'

There's nothing else to do, but go home.

Mike and I drive in silence and I stare out of the window, willing myself to catch sight of Dominic trudging home. When we pull up outside the cottages, there are no lights on in either of them. He cuts the engine and we sit in the darkness, the complete quiet.

'He's not back,' I say.

Beside me, my neighbour, my friend, my rock, sighs. 'We'll look for him again tomorrow,' he says.

'Thank you.'

'He can't be far.'

I feel sick inside. The temperature is dropping. If the British weather can be relied on, it will soon hail, rain, or snow, or all three. Does Dominic realise just how bad it can be?

Where is he? I wrack my brains to think where he might have gone, what he might have done. Where would I go in his situation? He hasn't been here long enough to establish a favourite place. How will he manage without me? But the most pertinent and pressing question is, what on earth can I do to get him back?

Mike insists on bringing me into the house and feeding me tea and toast until my stomach is roiling. We check the answerphone, but the only messages are from me. From Dominic, nothing.

Now Mike, reluctantly, departs for his own home leaving me with the promise of an early start again tomorrow to look for my loved one. Archie is mooching about looking miserable and Little Cottage feels horribly empty without Dominic.

I should go to bed but I can't bring myself to sleep there alone. In the wardrobe I find the *kanga* that Dominic gave me on my very first holiday in the Maasai Mara. Its cheery colours fail to lift my spirits, but the scent of Dominic on it somehow gives me hope.

Wrapping myself up, I go out into the garden and sit on the

bench where Dominic sat last night, brooding. Knives of empty pain stab at me and I don't know whether I want to curl into a ball or stand and howl at the sky. I want to be cold enough to feel Dominic's pain. Where is he bedding down for the night? I wonder. Is he sleeping in a hedgerow? Maybe he's found a hut of some sort or an abandoned barn. God, I do hope so. The tiny amount of money he's taken isn't going to find him anywhere comfortable, that's for sure. It might, however, buy him a cup of tea and something to eat. Will that be enough to stop him from getting hypothermia?

The thought of being without him now is unbearable. He's only been in my life for a relatively short amount of time, but I don't know how I'll manage without him, his innate charm, his infectious smile, his dry wit, his calm manner, his elegance, his strength, his fabulous body. I could go on and on.

On the bench beside me, Archie complains.

'Let's go in,' I suggest. 'There's nothing more we can do tonight.'

So Archie pads into the kitchen after me. I give him some cat treats as I don't know what else to do to ease his pain.

After that, I lie down on the sofa still wrapped in Dominic's *kanga* and will the morning to come quickly.

Chapter 80

The next day follows the same pattern. Mike comes to collect me and as he marks out our route for the day on an Ordnance Survey map of the area, he forces me to eat breakfast before we leave the house. Then, as soon as we turn out of the village, he has to stop in the nearest lay-by so that I can throw it all back up again.

While I'm cleaning myself up with a tissue, he calls the local radio station and explains our situation. They take down the details and say they might run something later. Then he tries the regional television company who broadcast to our area. In polite and measured tones, Mike begs them for help. I'd be screaming down the line by now. They instantly dismiss it, saying that they only cover important stories. One man lost in a sea of many isn't even on their radar.

We criss-cross the country lanes again. Every now and then we park up and trudge about in the fields, checking the hedgerows. Nothing. Nothing. Nothing. It's as if Dominic has simply vanished off the face of the earth.

Once more, we visit the police station. I drop off Dominic's photograph and fill in another form. The officer behind the desk offers more platitudes.

When it gets dark we decide to go home, have a quick bite to eat, and then do another couple of hours searching tonight. Mike has one of those ridiculous torches that have 'the power of a million candles'. I always teased him about it. Who knew that it would come in so horribly handy one day?

I'm just letting us into Little Cottage, when I see a delegation of the ladies of the Nashley Church Flower Committee coming along the lane. They're all wearing heavy coats, stout boots, and hats that look like tea cosies.

'Hello, ladies,' I say tiredly as they approach.

'Janie.' Mrs Duston, their self-appointed spokesman, puts her hand on my arm and addresses me. 'We heard about Dominic from Mrs Appleby in the post office. I'm sorry. So terribly sorry. We can't believe it.'

Me neither.

They all huddle together. 'We've been out searching,' Mrs Duston continues. 'Can't have our best boy catching a cold.' Under the streetlight, tears sparkle in her eyes. They spring to mine too. I'm humbled by their concern for Dominic. I wish he was here to see how much they love him. 'We walked the fields behind the village.' Her demeanour tells me that, like us, they found nothing.

'That's very kind of you,' I say gratefully. 'Very kind indeed.'

'Nonsense,' she counters. 'It's the least we can do, isn't it, ladies?'

All the other elderly women nod earnestly.

'Thank you. I really appreciate it.'

'We'll do it again tomorrow. Won't we, girls?'

'Oh, yes,' they all say in unison.

'And the day after,' she adds. 'And every day, for as long as it takes.'

Much nodding in agreement.

'He'll be back, Janie,' she assures me. 'He'll definitely be back.'

I hope that this statement is based on some wise, old wives' intuition and isn't just blind hope like my own. My own fear is that if Dominic wants to stay disappeared, then he is resourceful enough to do so.

'Mr Codling-Bentham is going to go out on that dratted quad bike of his to look too,' Mrs Duston then tells us. 'It's the first time in my life that I've ever been grateful that he has it.'

'Tell him thank you from me,' I say. 'That's very kind.'

'I've some soup on the stove,' Mrs Duston continues. 'My lovely homemade cream of chicken. Dominic's favourite.' Her voice catches. 'That will perk you up. You both look all in.'

We are, I think. We are exhausted, on our knees.

'I'll run back with a flask in just a moment. I don't even suppose you've had time to think about eating.'

'No,' I agree. Food is the last thing on my mind.

Yet, a few minutes later, Mike and I are sitting with trays on our laps in my living room eating Mrs Duston's chicken soup – which is, indeed, lovely – while she is busy making us a cup of tea in the kitchen. I could weep at her motherly kindness. As soon as we've eaten this, then Mike and I will go out again. The million-candle-power torch is at the ready and, somehow, I don't find that funny any more.

For something to do, I switch on the television and flick to the local news programme. Their headline story tells us that a celebrity, one of many who are famous only for getting their breasts out and sleeping with footballers at every opportunity, has been signing copies of her autobiography at a city centre bookshop. There are lots of pictures of her pouting and preening for the camera. Is this a news story? Is this what matters more in our lives these days? Are people really more interested in that than they are in the plight of a missing man?

Sadly, I guess they are.

Chapter 81

Minutes turn into hours. Hours turn into days. Days, of course, turn into weeks. I would that it were different, but it isn't. Time goes on, no respecter of heartache.

A month has gone by now, and there's still no sign of Dominic. I'm back at work, going through the motions of normal life. What else could I do? Every time my phone rings I'm sick with anticipation, but it's never him. It's usually someone worried about me and I want to tell them all to stop phoning, stop torturing me further. The only person I want at the end of the line is my missing loved one.

I put Dominic's picture on all the UK missing persons websites I could find on the internet. They're peopled mainly by parents estranged by bitter divorces, one of whom has abducted their own child or children and has spirited them away to hotter or colder climes. The others are more often than not teenagers who seem to have left home after one too many rows and never came back. One lot of children loved too much and another lot perhaps not loved enough.

Every night I scour the web pages, tracing my fingers over the on-screen photograph of Dominic Lemasolai Ole Nangon. At least I had the forethought to scan the picture of Dominic and me under the acacia tree in the Maasai Mara. It's the only one that I have of him and I had to give the police the original. Uploading the half with just Dominic on it seemed too sad for words.

In all the time he's been gone from my world I've hardly slept, I've hardly eaten. When I do eat, it rarely stays down for long. Mrs Duston has kept me in chicken soup, as it's all I seem able to manage. All my nights are spent curled up on the sofa in Dominic's blanket. And I still have no idea where he might be.

Absently combing my client's hair, I lift up my brush with bleach on it.

'It's not for me,' the woman says and, suddenly, I snap back to the present.

'What?'

'It's not for me,' she repeats, looking at me in the mirror. 'The bleach.'

That stops me in my tracks.

She nods her head towards Mrs Hitchley, who is sitting in the seat at the next station. 'That's your client.'

'Oh, God,' I say. 'I'm sorry. So sorry.'

'No harm done.' She and Mrs Hitchley exchange a worried glance.

Mrs Hitchley has been coming in to get her roots done every six weeks for the last ten years. How on earth could I mistake her for another client? Sheepishly, I wheel my trolley to the next chair.

'Are you all right today, Janie?' my proper client, the one I should be making into a blonde, asks over the top of her magazine.

'Dominic's gone missing,' I tell her. By now everyone knows

359

about Dominic and the minutiae of our relationship. 'I'm out of my mind with worry.'

She pulls a sympathetic face but I already know what's coming next. 'Oh dear. You poor thing.'

'Yes.'

Then, not a moment later, 'It's not unusual, you know.' A knowing shake of the head, even though I'm still trying to slap bleach on. 'Happened to a friend of my sister. Had a bloke in the Dominican Republic. Thought she was the only one. Spent all her money visiting him. What she didn't buy him wasn't worth having. Found out he had a dozen other women on the go.'

It's not like that, I want to tell her. You haven't met Dominic. He's different. He wouldn't do that to me. But everyone, it seems, was fully expecting him to do the dirty on me. Everyone except me.

I um and ah my way through the next half hour, barely listening to what Mrs Hitchley has to say, as I put the foil packets on her hair and smooth on the bleach on autopilot. After I set the timer for the bleach, I retreat, gladly, to the staffroom. I feel as if I'm constantly on the verge of hyperventilating and I fall into the nearest seat and breathe deeply.

A moment later, and Kelly comes through to the staffroom. She sits down next to me. Everyone else makes themselves scarce. No one here really knows what to say to me, anyway. Nina and I are barely speaking except to exchange clipped sentences concerning work. She hasn't apologised to me or broached the matter of Dominic's disappearance at all. The subject has swallowed up our friendship like a gaping cavern. All the warnings and the gossip about Dominic leaving me, betraying me, have come true and they're all feeling righteous now.

360

Like a robot, I go through the motions of my job and ignore them all.

My boss sighs before she starts speaking. 'Janie,' she says gently. 'We need to talk about this.'

'About what?'

'You're making too many mistakes. I just watched you nearly put bleach on the wrong client.'

'But I didn't.'

'Because *she* stopped you,' she points out, quite correctly. 'We've had a number of complaints about services in the last two weeks since you've been back. You lopped a good two inches off Mrs Palmer's hair on Tuesday and she only came in for a trim.'

Did I? But if I'm honest, I don't even remember seeing Mrs Palmer. That's bad, right? I might be here in body, but it's fair to say that my mind isn't. It's also fair to say that I'm not coping very well with my situation.

The first week after Dominic went, I was a complete mess. I was as sick as a dog every single morning after a long and wakeful night. There was no way that I could have considered coming into work at all, so I agreed with Kelly that I should take the time off as holiday. Mike did the same and we spent every day trawling around the local areas just hoping for a glimpse of Dominic. My friend tracked down the names of all the homeless charities in the area and we visited them all. In the evenings, we'd hang around where the homeless people sleep – partly praying that Dominic would be there and partly praying that he wouldn't. We saw nothing to give us hope. Nothing at all. It's as if he has completely disappeared. We managed to get a mention for him on the local radio news for one day. One day only. Then everyone had lost interest.

I check in with the police on a regular basis, but they have no news for me and I feel there's not a great deal of interest in just another man who's gone missing – even though he is here on a temporary visa. I think they suspect that he conned me to get over here and now, in the pattern I'm used to, believe he has simply absconded and that's the last that I'll ever see of him.

No matter how much I say it – Dominic isn't like that, he wouldn't do that – no one wants to believe me. No one wants to see the good in him, that he wouldn't have done this without reason. Only Mike.

If Dominic would just call. If he would just call and tell me that he was OK, then I might at least be able to sleep at night. If he did just decide that he didn't want to be with me any longer – even the thought of that makes my chest hurt – then he should have told me. He should have been straight with me. But in my heart, I don't think that's the case. He was still trying to put my best interests first. Deluded as he might be, he thought he was doing it for my benefit: taking the shame from my door, to protect me from a few people's biased and incorrect opinion of him.

As it is, I haven't had a decent night's sleep since he disappeared. I sleep on the sofa, unable to face the comfort, the loneliness, of my bed. At most, I might catch a few hours out of sheer exhaustion. Now, back at work full-time, I can hardly stand on my feet all day let alone remember, or care, who should have bleach and who shouldn't.

I realise that Kelly's still poised, waiting for me to speak. 'I'm sorry,' I say. 'I can only apologise.'

'Go home,' she says. 'Steph can cover your appointments. Get some rest. Those dark shadows under your eyes make you look like one of Edward Cullen's crew.'

That gives me the glimmer of a weak smile.

'And not the good-looking ones,' she adds more gently.

I summon a laugh at that.

'Take a few days off.'

'I'd rather be here than on my own at home.'

'I'd rather my clients didn't go out with dodgy haircuts in colours not of their choosing.'

'I'm sorry,' I say again. It makes me sound pathetic, but that's how I feel so I do nothing to dress it up. 'I'll get my act together.'

'Take today and tomorrow off. Sleep. Rest. Come back on Monday and we'll see how you are then.'

'OK. I'm sure I'll be fine. I probably do just need to catch up on my sleep.' But that's not true. I might be lying to Kelly, but there's no lying to myself. What I need is the hole in my heart to heal, the gaping wound in my life to be filled once more. What I need is Dominic to come back, then I'll be just fine.

Then again, I'll have to be all right, I think. I can't afford to go to pieces. There are bills to pay. I can't afford to lose my home because of this. And although I feel as if the world should have ended as soon as Dominic walked out of the door, it hasn't. I have to carry on but at the moment, I can't for the life of me see why.

Chapter 82

It's Saturday and a bright Spring day. It's the kind of day when I should be watching the leaves unfurl from the trees, see the green shoots of early daffodils poking through the soil, see the first flush of colour coming back to the land after the long months of winter. Instead, I just think that it's the ideal type of day for looking for Dominic. Mike and I have searched day in, day out, in rain, hail and sleet for weeks. Even though we're both working again, we still go out together in the evenings and scour the streets.

A day like this is a bonus. I'm all wrapped up and ready and waiting for my neighbour, peeping anxiously out of the front window of the cottage until I see him. I've now lost count of how many times we have toured the roads laid out on our map during the painful period that Dominic has been missing – ten, fifteen, twenty? And we'll still keep doing it until he turns up.

When I finally spy my neighbour, I've got the door open before he knocks.

'Ready,' I say, snatching up my gloves.

Mike steps into the living room and he takes my gloves from my hands.

'This is it,' he says sadly. 'We can't keep searching for him, Janie. It's been well over a month now.'

I don't need reminding how long it's been, I think. 'We can't give up now,' I protest.

'We've found nothing,' Mikes continues. 'Not even a tiny clue. If Dominic's going to come home, then maybe he needs to do it in his own time.'

Tears fill my eyes. 'I'm worried for him.'

Mike takes me into his arms. 'I know.' He pats my back like you would an upset child. 'I know, but this isn't doing you any good, Janie. Look at you. All these hours and hours of searching have really taken it out of you. You need to look after yourself ...'

Or you're going to have some kind of breakdown, is what remains unsaid.

The reality of the situation hits me like a low punch to the stomach. We've failed to locate even a trace of Dominic, despite our best efforts. I have to accept that, as time passes, he might be going further and further out of our reach. All hope ebbs out of me and I sob in Mike's arms. I let the tears flow for the man who has so suddenly departed from my life. It's as if Dominic has died and the grief consumes me.

'What if he just doesn't want me any more?' I cry. 'What if he's never going to come back? What if it's like everyone said?'

'Ssh, ssh,' he soothes. 'You know that's not true, Janie.' Mike strokes my hair as he reassures me. 'But I don't know what else to do. We've searched high and low and it's been utterly futile. Enough is enough.'

Deep inside, I'm partly relieved that Mike has taken control, taken the decision out of my hands and I'm partly distraught that we are just going to stop looking, leave Dominic out there all by himself.

Eventually, when the tears are drying up, I have a moment of clarity and I admit, 'You're right. I haven't the strength to do this.' It's like trying to find the proverbial needle in a haystack and I feel as if I've exhausted all my emotional resources. For the last few weeks, I've been tired beyond belief. Kelly has temporarily booted me out of the salon for my own good, and for the good of her customers' hair. Now my best friend, who has so far done everything in his power to help me, is telling me that I need to stop. Perhaps I should heed his advice.

'Why don't we work in the gardens together today?' Mike suggests. 'They're both looking a bit ragged.'

I must look dubious as my neighbour insists, 'It would be very therapeutic. A change is as good as a rest, they say.'

Reluctantly, I nod. I feel as weak as a kitten, probably due to the lack of food and sleep. I know that I can't keep putting Mike through this every day and yet I also know that I don't have the wherewithal to continue alone. Mike has been so good, so tireless in his support, but I can see that even he has reached his limit. He makes me a cup of tea and I sit at the table and cry some more. Then he sits with me, quietly, until both the tea and the tears have gone.

His hand covers mine. 'OK?'

'Yes.' I muster a ghost of a smile and wonder if I'll ever feel truly happy again. Dominic is out there somewhere. All this thinking makes my head hurt and I can see that Mike might well be right. Some fresh air and exercise would do me no harm at all. 'Let's give that garden what for,' I say decisively.

I pull on my boots and we head outside. So instead of clocking up futile miles together searching for my lost love, we're working in my garden this morning and are planning to do the same in Mike's this afternoon, if the weather holds.

Archie sits on the wall like a statue and watches us, feigning a lack of interest. Even the damn cat hasn't been the same since Dominic disappeared. Archie has gone off his food and nothing puts this animal off his grub. He's listless, as opposed to his usual lazy, and even a rare treat of prawns can't muster any enthusiasm in him.

I'm raking up leaves that have gone black and slimy in the rain and cold, heaping them into piles to be taken to the Tidy Tip. Mike is doing the heavy manly lifting. The things that Dominic should have been doing with me. He's pruning branches, even though it's probably the wrong time of year to be doing that. My garden has to survive on a blend of inexpert maintenance and sheer neglect.

My mind drifts as I work. What more could we do? I wonder. Cover the same old ground that has yet to yield anything? I still have no clue where Dominic is and it seems that scouring the countryside isn't going to offer one up. This feels too much like admitting defeat, but I have to accept, perhaps for my own sanity, that Dominic might not be coming back. Can I ever move on if he never comes home to me? Has he found somewhere to live? Has someone else, some other woman, taken him in? What might he be doing now? I wonder if he has found a job. If he has, perhaps he has saved enough money for a ticket home. I still have his passport in the drawer, but could he have reported it lost or stolen and simply got another one? Maybe he could buy a fake. Who knows, these days? If he could, would he go home? Forget about our love, marry a Maasai woman? Would that make Dominic's life easier? Is that what he wishes he'd done all along?

I wonder if I could have read him so wrong to believe that we would be together for ever, that he would always be here by my side, but my heart won't allow me to accept it. If it hadn't been for other people's opinions then Dominic would still be here, I'm sure of it. Now I'm concerned that he's come to some terrible harm and I feel powerless, utterly powerless, unable to do anything to help him. He could have been lying hurt or suffering from hypothermia in one of the thousands of ditches or hedgerows that Mike and I passed and we would have been none the wiser. We could have driven by him, feet away, and never have seen him.

Yesterday, I dozed on the sofa, on and off all day. I even slept for part of the night until I woke up soaked with sweat and aching with wanting at three in the morning. Archie and I roved the house and channel-surfed until dawn when it was time to pretend to eat some breakfast. But part of me is frightened that I'm starting to forget Dominic. I have to look constantly at his photograph to remind me of the lean outlines of his handsome face. I'm scared that, as times goes by, the lilting tones of his voice will leave me, that the feel of his hard body against mine will become a distant and blurry memory.

'Brrr,' Mike says, breaking into my thoughts as he comes to check on my progress.

I stand back from my raking.

'You've got on well.'

Have I? Looking at the pile of leaves in front of me, I see that he's probably right although I have no idea what I've been doing for the last hour. My thoughts are still entirely with Dominic. I've been reliving our times together in Kenya, the morning he took me on the balloon ride, the nights we spent in my tent.

368

Mike claps his hands together to get some warmth into them. 'It's a bit parky out here today.'

His constant support and optimistic outlook have really helped me to survive these last few weeks. I have no idea what I would have done without him.

Smiling at him, I say, 'What about some hot chocolate? Would that work?'

'Hmm. Sounds good to me.'

'I'll go and make some. It's about time we took a break.' I check my watch and to my surprise I see that we've been out here for two hours already, pottering about. Keeping occupied is clearly the answer. 'Coming in for a minute?'

Mike shakes his head. 'I'll stay out. Get me in the warmth of the cottage and I won't want to go out again. I'll load some of these branches into the back of my car.'

Thankfully, there's a gate at the back of the garden and a lane which leads round the side of all the houses, which means that my garden rubbish doesn't have to be carted right through the house.

'I won't be long with the chocolate.' As I pass him, I touch his arm. 'Thank you,' I say. 'Thank you for this.'

Mike smiles at me. 'You know that you don't have to thank me.'

Walking back to the cottage, I strip off my dirty gardening gloves, deep in thought. How would I have managed without this man? What on earth would I do without him now?

Chapter 83

In the kitchen, I bang about with the cups and find my favourite Hotel Chocolat drinking chocolate in the cupboard. Archie comes to look at what I'm doing in case there's anything to eat involved, even though it's all for show at the moment. I wish the days would come back when he was a greedy pig who'd eat anything, rather than have him wandering around like a little lost cat.

If I don't think too deeply, it almost feels like a normal Saturday in some ways. Almost. As the milk is boiling, there's a knock at the front door and I lift the pan from the stove.

As I walk to the door, a wave of nausea comes over me. I can't identify the feeling. It's a familiar one now, but I can never decide whether it's hope or fear or a heady mixture of both. I'm always aware that it could be Dominic standing there at the door. Or a policeman coming to tell me that they have found him first and it's bad news.

Whichever way, if I answer my phone or open my door now, it's always with this sickly sense of dread. To think that my only worry at one point was the pesky and persistent Lewis Moran. I hope that he hasn't heard that Dominic has disappeared and has come back to try his luck again.

But no. This time, it's Nina who's standing there. She's looking sheepish and is holding up a bottle of wine and a bunch of flowers.

'Hey,' she says.

'Hello.'

'Can I come in?'

At one time, she would never have needed to ask this. I stand back and open the door. Nina breezes through to my kitchen and I follow. Archie hisses at her and all the hackles on his neck stand up, proving that animals are, indeed, sensitive to moods.

'Peace offering.' She holds out the flowers and wine.

For a second, I wonder whether I should take them or whether I should tell her that our friendship is over and I'm not interested in what she has to say any more. But then I sigh to myself. Nina and I go back a long way. I shouldn't let this come between us. I'm hoping that she's come to apologise for what she said about Dominic. In her place, I'd feel entirely responsible for Dominic having left.

'Thanks,' I say and relieve her of her gifts. 'I'm just making hot chocolate. Want some?'

'That would be nice.'

Awkwardly, she ensconces herself in my kitchen.

'You look terrible,' she says to me. 'No wonder Kelly was worried about you. Your hair's gone all floppy and lank.'

Has it? I'm a hairdresser, I should notice these things.

'You look exactly like my sister did when she was preg ...' She stares at me, horrified. '... nant.'

I think of all the early morning puking, the tiredness, and although I'd put it down to generally being unwell, I now begin to wonder. Have I missed a period? Frankly, I've no idea. Could it be possible? It had never even occurred to me until now.

Dominic and I both wanted to have children, but I never thought that it might happen so easily, so quickly. I've been so distracted, so busy trying to bring Dominic home that I haven't had time to consider that there might be new life growing inside of me. The thought knocks me sideways. Surely Nina can't be right?

'Mike's in the garden,' I say hurriedly, as a diversion. 'Want to say hi?' Do I see her eyes brighten slightly? 'I was just going to take out some hot chocolate for him too.'

She shrugs. 'Yeah. Why not?'

I pick up Mike's mug and we both go outside. 'We have a visitor,' I announce.

'Oh, hi,' Mike says as he straightens up from his work. If he's surprised to see Nina here, then he doesn't show it. 'How are you?'

'Fine,' Nina says. But her discomfort says that she really isn't.

'I'll drink this down and then take the rubbish up to the tip,' Mike says. 'Give you some time to talk to each other.'

He's well aware that I'm not Nina's biggest fan at the moment.

'Don't run away on my behalf,' she says.

'Good timing,' Mike insists.

They're slightly awkward with each other and I wonder if it's simply because of the situation or whether they're both thinking back to the rather passionate kiss they shared on New Year's Eve. Whatever it is, Mike scuttles off and Nina and I go back inside, retreating to the warmth. We sit at the kitchen table both nursing cups of chocolate.

My friend breaks the silence. 'Kelly said that she had to send you home on Thursday.'

372

'Yes.' There's no point lying about it. Everyone in the salon will know that I messed up, anyway.

'Are you feeling any better now?'

'Yes,' I say. 'A little.' Might as well lie about that one.

'Still no sign of Dominic?'

'No.'

Nina sighs at me. 'You know it's for the best,' she says.

'What is?'

'That Dominic's gone now. Sooner rather than later.'

'How do you work that out?' Like Archie, my hackles are up now too.

'It was bound to happen.'

'So everyone keeps telling me.' It's all I can do to stop my hands from shaking in anger.

'Have you closed your bank accounts?' she asks, concerned. 'Gerry said it would be a good idea. Or at least take all of the cash out of them so that he can't get his hands on it.'

'What cash?' I ask, wishing Nina's lecherous husband would keep his nose out of my business. 'There's hardly anything in the bank for Dominic to take and if there was, I would gladly give him every last penny of it.'

She looks at me as if I'm a hopeless case. Perhaps I am. Hopelessly in love.

'I just think that you should take steps to protect yourself,' she advises sagely. 'Cancel your credit cards and stuff.'

'This isn't about money,' I rail. 'Not for me. I feel sick not knowing where he is and I'd give every last penny that I had simply to get a telephone call from him to say that he's all right. Don't you understand that?'

Her expression says that she doesn't. 'All I'm saying is that you have to watch this type of man.'

'What would you know about that, Nina?' I say bitterly.

'We just all knew that it was going to end like this. The sooner you can accept that and move on, the quicker you'll get back to normal.'

'I don't want to be normal,' I tell her. 'I don't want my old life back. I want Dominic and the life I had with him. Perhaps if he hadn't heard directly from you how badly you thought of him then he might still be here.'

My so-called friend bristles. 'None of this is my fault. I'm the one who's been trying to warn you.'

'Dominic heard exactly what you had to say about him that night at the Sno!Zone. That's why he left. He knew that everyone was against him.'

Now she blanches. 'You never said.'

'How could you not know? He was standing directly outside the door. He heard it all.'

'I had no idea.'

'Oh, don't give me that. Whatever you've come here for, Nina, don't play the innocent with me.'

She stares at me, mouth agape. 'I came here to be your friend again,' she continues when she finds her voice.

'No,' I said. 'You didn't. You only want to be a friend on *your* terms. If you were truly my friend, you'd be distraught for me. Distraught because the only man I've ever truly loved has disappeared from my life. If you were a true friend, you'd be like Mike.' I fling a finger at the garden where my steadfast neighbour has his back to me, picking up logs. 'He's the one who's been searching day and night with me. He's the one who's been round here every day, making sure I'm not alone, that I don't think too much, that I don't do anything stupid. Or you'd be like the people of the village, who have been out walking the fields looking for him. Or you'd bring me little gifts of tasty food to tempt me because you'd know that I'm not eating. That's what friends do. So take your wine and your flowers back, Nina. That's not what I need from you at all.' I take a deep breath. 'And before you start putting *my* house in order, take a long hard look at your own.'

Clearly offended, my friend stands up and heads for the door. Then she turn and says, 'One day, Janie, you'll thank me for this.'

'I don't think so, Nina.'

My friend marches to the front door and bangs it behind her. It shakes on its hinges.

The only day that I'll be giving thanks is the day that Dominic comes back to me.

Chapter 84

In the afternoon, Mike and I work for another two hours on his garden. I don't tell Mike about my argument with Nina, but I think he can tell from my sombre mood that all didn't go well with her.

The temperature is dropping quickly now and I fail to fend off a shiver. My hands go protectively to my tummy. If there's a baby in there, Dominic's baby, then I should make sure that it doesn't catch a chill.

'OK?' Mike says.

'Yes. Yes.' I gather up the last of the leaves and put them into a black sack. We're just finishing off the last bits and Mike is going to make one more run to the Tidy Tip before it closes.

'Want a DVD night?' Mike broaches as he gathers the garden tools together.

'Sure. I'll make dinner,' I offer, 'by way of a thank you. Curry?' I need something to warm me up as I feel frozen through to the bone.

'I never turn down curry,' he says. Which is true enough.

So while Mike trundles off to the Tidy Tip for one last time, I set about making what I call a good old-fashioned 'English' chicken curry, with chopped apples and raisins and livid yellow curry powder.

We sit at the kitchen table and eat. Mike, chatting away happily. Me, brooding in troubled silence. After we've cleared up together, I make us both a coffee and we linger in the warmth of the kitchen.

'What do you fancy watching tonight?' Mike asks.

'I don't mind.' There's a pile of DVDs waiting on the coffee table.

He looks up at me, concerned. 'You're very quiet tonight, Janie. Is everything all right?'

No, I want to say, of course everything isn't all right. I'm missing Dominic more than I ever thought it was possible to miss another human being. Every cell in my body yearns for him. I want to tell Mike that I might be having Dominic's baby and that it's now even more important that I find him, if he's going to be a father. I don't want to bring my child up alone. I want him here with me. I want us to be happy together again. On top of that, I've fallen out with my best friend since school. A friend who, until all this, I'd been through thick and thin with. Unbidden, tears fill my eyes.

Mike reaches out and takes my hand. The warmth of his touch never fails to comfort me and I glance at him gratefully, mustering a tired smile.

'I know that you love Dominic very much,' he starts to say, 'but what if he never comes back, Janie?'

'He will.'

'You can't go on like this.'

'I have to.'

Mike smiles tenderly at me. 'You know that you're very important to me,' he says. 'I'll always look after you. All I want is for you to be happy. I'll do whatever that takes, you know that.'

'I do. Of course I do.'

'Best of friends?'

'Best of friends,' I agree.

Then the phone rings and I go and pick it up, always with that same feeling of sickness and sense of dread that has become familiar to me.

'It's me.' Nina's voice is on the other end of the phone and she sounds completely hyper. 'Are you watching the telly?'

'No,' I say. 'Mike and I are just finishing supper.'

'Put it on,' she urges. 'Put it on now! BBC News. I'll be round in five.' With that, there's a click and she's gone, leaving me looking puzzled on the other end.

Mike frowns. 'Everything OK?'

'No idea. That was Nina. She said to put the news on and then she hung up. For some reason she's on her way round.'

'Let's go and see what all the fuss is about.' Mike follows me through to the living room. I haven't watched the news for weeks so consequently I have no idea what's happening in the world, nor do I care.

On screen, the presenter is wittering on about some EU summit about something or other and I can't think why Nina would be getting all hot under the collar about this. 'Sure this is the BBC?'

Mike checks the channel. 'Yeah.'

I shrug and he shrugs back but, as instructed, we continue to watch. That story wraps up and then the presenter says, 'Coming up.' There is a montage of the next breaking news stories and there, right there on the screen, is an image of Dominic. He looks different, scruffy, unkempt and he's thinner

I think, but there's no doubt that it's him. Whatever has happened to him, wherever he's been, he is still my Dominic and I'd know him anywhere.

'It's him,' I want to say. 'It's Dominic.' But the shock of seeing his handsome face again has taken my voice and all I can do is point wordlessly at the screen.

'Good God,' Mike says in my stead.

The presenter continues smugly, 'Find out why *this* Maasai warrior has been causing a stir.'

I scrabble for the remote and turn up the volume. Now we have to sit through ten interminable minutes of world news. Who cares what's happening in China or Copenhagen or anywhere else for that matter? All I want to know is what's happening to Dominic. I pray that it's good news. If it was bad news surely they would have put it differently? It has to be good. Doesn't it? Mike comes to sit close to me on the sofa and we both perch on the edge of the seat, me squeezing his hand so tightly that the bones might break.

Eventually, the news presenter reads out the headline in measured tones, a wry smile on her lips. 'Today a Maasai warrior, Mr Lemasolai Ole Nangon, also known as Dominic, who has been living homeless on the streets of London, was commended for his bravery after tackling a mugger who attacked an elderly lady.'

The rest of the details blur into white noise as I gape, transfixed. Dominic is in London. He's been sleeping rough on the streets. I feel the colour drain from my face. How has he managed? How has he survived the bitter cold at all? We have searched and searched and searched the countryside, the hedgerows, the fields, tirelessly and, quite possibly, all the time he's been in London. Why did I not consider that? It hadn't even occurred to me. But it doesn't matter now where he's been or how he got there. He's safe. He's alive.

The studio hands over to a reporter for an outside broadcast and the next thing I know, the man is thrusting a microphone into Dominic's face.

'Oh, God,' I cry out and clutch harder at Mike's hand, needing something tangible to anchor me.

Dominic looks tired and gaunt. His beautiful face is dirty and bruised. He's wearing his red *shuka* and his colourful blanket, but both are filthy and ripped. Instead of his shaved head, his hair has grown and there's a halo of ragged afro that alters his features, but still it is unmistakably my Dominic, my love.

Tears pour down my face and I turn to Mike. 'He's alive,' I say. 'Thank God. He's alive.'

It seems that a mugger had snatched a handbag from an old lady at knifepoint and Dominic, seeing what happened and without thought for his own safety, gave chase. He brought down the thief and returned the bag to its rightful owner.

'How does it feel to be a hero, Mr Ole Nangon?' the reporter asks.

Dominic shrugs shyly, obviously discomfited by the presence of the camera, the attention of the press. 'I only did what every English citizen would do.'

'Oh, Dominic,' I sigh. 'Come home.' I turn to Mike again. 'I have to find him.'

Mike nods. 'I'll get the car,' he says.

Chapter 85

Not five minutes later, we're in Mike's car speeding down to London. In the back, Nina is with us and she's holding my hand tightly between the seats, while Mike has his foot flat to the floor.

'I'm sorry,' she says over and over tearfully. Her eyes are red-rimmed and her face puffy. She looks truly awful. 'I've been a complete cow, Janie. Can you ever forgive me?'

Despite my earlier intentions of never speaking to her again for the rest of my life, my heart softens immediately. 'Of course.'

My friend clutches my hand tighter and sobs. 'I've been a rubbish friend,' she says. 'But I'm going to do all I can to make things right between us.'

'Now's not the time for blubbing, woman. We've got to stay strong until we get Dominic back. He's still out there, alive and well. That's all that matters to me.'

'We'll find him,' she promises. 'I'll do all I can to help.'

'Thank you.'

'I've been a right twat,' she admits. Neither Mike nor I disagree but whatever our differences, I'm so glad that she's here with me now.

'Let's see if we can pin down where he might be,' Mike suggests as he drives. 'Phone the BBC.'

My voice shaking, I call the television station and eventually manage to speak to the editor of the news programme. Due to data protection, frustratingly, he can't tell me where Dominic is living, but he does give me the name of the police station where the incident was dealt with. So that's our first port of call.

An hour later and we're at the station. Nina and I shoot out of Mike's car and run inside to explain our plight. Whether the officer on the desk breaks data protection rules or not, I don't care, but he clearly takes pity on me and tells me that Social Services have now found a bed in a homeless persons' hostel for Dominic. Nina scribbles down the address for me, as my hand is shaking too much to be able to hold a pen.

Back in the car and Nina gives the address to Mike, who then keys it into his sat nav and off we go again. The traffic is slow and it takes us half an hour to crawl to King's Cross where the hostel is situated. All the while, I drive myself to distraction by tapping the dashboard impatiently.

Mike, grim-faced next to me, says nothing. Nina, in the back, chews her fingernails. My friend follows the sat nav's well-modulated instructions while I want to scream at the damn thing to get a move on. When I think that I can stand the waiting no longer, we pull up outside a tall austere building that looks like a run-down hotel.

'This is it?'

Mike nods.

Grim. Very grim.

We all get out of the car and I press the buzzer at the door.

Chewing gum is stuck liberally around the metal. The intercom crackles into life. 'I'm looking for Dominic Ole Nangon,' I say. 'The Maasai warrior. I believe he's here.'

On the other end, a man says something unintelligible and I'm just about to ask him to repeat it when I hear the door click and it swings open. I glance nervously at Mike and Nina, then we all go inside.

The reception is sparsely furnished but clean and the man behind the desk stands up when he sees us. 'How can I help?' he says.

'We're looking for Dominic Ole Nangon,' I repeat. 'The police told us he's been brought here.'

'He's not long left,' the man tells us. 'We gave him a hot meal and there's an emergency room available, but he wouldn't stay. He wouldn't take the room in case someone else needed it.' The man shrugs.

'So you let him go?' I'm incredulous.

'We can't detain people if they don't want to be here,' he points out. 'This is temporary accommodation for the homeless. A direct access hostel.'

I have no idea what that means.

'They come here on a voluntary basis.'

I turn to Mike and Nina, eyes bleak. He's gone. We've missed him.

'Any idea where he might be?'

'Anywhere around here is my guess,' the man offers. 'This is cardboard box central.' He looks at me kindly. 'He's only been gone half an hour or so. Not much longer.'

'Thank you.'

A second later and Mike is starting the car engine, pulling away into the night. The temperature is dropping and I can't

383

bear the thought of Dominic spending another night on the streets. Not when we are so close. Not when he is so loved.

'We'll find him,' Nina assures me. 'He can't have gone far.'

In a way that's become so familiar now, Mike drives slowly, scouring the streets, eyes peeled. There are too many unsavoury characters on the street corners for us to be comfortable and Mike clicks on the central locking as we exchange an anxious glance.

'I can't go home without him,' I say.

'We won't,' Nina promises. 'We'll stay here as long as it takes to find him, won't we, Mike?'

'Of course we will,' he agrees.

As we get away from the main road, the streets become narrower, darker, more menacing. I feel myself shrinking into my seat.

'Bloody hell,' Mike mutters. 'How on earth has he managed out here?'

I can't even bear to think about it. When I glance back at Nina, I can see that tears are rolling down her face.

The amount of litter is increasing, paper blowing about the streets, and I cringe as I see a rat scamper along the gutter. We're now alongside the arches provided by the overhead railway track and I see what the man at the homeless hostel meant by this being cardboard city. Boxes and boxes are lining the arches, each one providing a shelter for one or more people huddled inside.

'Do you think we should get out here?'

Mike looks dubious. 'I don't think it's safe.'

'We have to try. He could be down one of these alleys.'

With a resigned sigh, Mike says, 'You're right. Let me park up here.' He pulls up against the one area of roadside that doesn't have double yellow lines. 'I just hope the wheels are still on it when we get back.'

'Safety in numbers,' Nina says with an attempt at bravado. 'If we stick together, we'll be OK.' Though her horrified face gives away how frightened she really is.

As soon as Mike emerges from the car, a couple of scantily clad ladies appear from the shadows, both smoking, eyes narrowed. They're wearing cropped tops, denim jackets and ridiculously short skirts. They're also wearing high boots, but they have bare legs and it's a cold, cold night. When Nina and I also get out, they start to back away.

'Ladies,' I shout. 'Can you help? Please.' They look at me warily, but before they can scarper, I hurry up to them. 'I'm looking for someone. His name's Dominic Ole Nangon. You really can't miss him.' I'm wishing that I'd thought to bring a photograph of Dominic with me. 'He's a Maasai warrior.'

I see recognition spark in their dull eyes.

'What's it worth?' the older one says, leaning against the wall and adopting a couldn't-care-less attitude. 'We don't give out free information, lady.'

'I'm his girlfriend,' I explain as I look in my handbag for my purse to see what money I've got. 'He's been missing from home.'

She shrugs. 'Maybe he don't want anyone to know where he is.'

While I'm still struggling, Nina pulls a twenty out of her purse and hands it over. The younger of the two stubs her cigarette out on the pavement, grinding it down with her heel. 'Yeah, I know him,' she says. 'He's been round here a while.'

My heart starts beating faster. 'Do you know where he is now?'

'No,' she says. 'Haven't seen him tonight. We've only just got here. He often kips down there though.' She flicks a thumb back towards the arches.

It looks like a hellhole.

'Thanks,' I say. 'If you see him, please tell him that Janie's looking for him.'

They both shrug and the older one pockets the twenty.

Mike takes my hand as I head towards the entrance to the tunnel-like arch. 'Sure you want to do this? I'll go by myself while you two stay in the car.'

'No,' I say. 'I'd be happier if we all go together.'

'I second that,' Nina says and she gets hold of Mike's other hand.

So, clinging together, we head into the damp archway, listening to rattling coughs, the occasional dog bark, a man singing 'Danny Boy' into his bottle. Most of the people ignore us. Some call out, asking for money, but in their voices you can tell that there's no hope of success. It's filthy in here and I'm glad that it's dark because there's no telling what might be underfoot. A torch would have been useful, but I didn't think to bring one. We pick our way gingerly through the rubbish, calling out Dominic's name as we go.

'Here,' a voice shouts. 'I'm Dominic.'

Instantly, I can tell by the tone that it's not my Dominic. Another call comes from the other side of the tunnel. 'I'm Dominic.'

That's not him either.

'I'm Dominic.' Followed by hysterical laughter.

'Oh, shut the fuck up, the lot of you,' Nina retorts to no one and everyone.

'Very funny,' I grumble, again to no one and everyone. But

then I think that there must be precious little to laugh about on the streets and you can't blame them for having a joke at our expense. Still, it's not helping our quest and I have to say that I'm very reluctant to venture into the piles of boxes to ask individuals if they've seen a Maasai warrior hanging around here.

'This is useless,' I complain. 'They're all bloody "Dominic". How are we going to find him in here?' Then I have a brainwave. 'Guys,' I say, 'whistle the ringtone from 24.'

'What?' Nina looks perplexed.

'Trust me. It's my Maasai sound. If Dominic's here, he'll recognise it instantly.'

My friend shrugs. 'OK.'

Mike nods his agreement too. He and I have spent enough time together following the trials and tribulations of the indestructible Jack Bauer for Mike to be able to replicate it without any prompting from me.

We all whistle as we go and, strangely, it somehow makes me feel more hopeful, but as the minutes go by and there's no response, the desolation begins to overwhelm me and I too feel as if there's no chance of Dominic being here. Bloody Maasai noise! It might well work on the wide open plains of Africa, but here in the bleakness of this cardboard city, it's holding no truck.

'This is hopeless,' I say to my companions.

'Let's keep going until the end,' Mike says, pointing to the back of the archway where there's a huge pile of boxes. He puts his arm under my elbow and urges me forward.

Then my heart leaps into my mouth as I catch a flash of bright red in the gloom. I put my hands on my friends' arms. 'Mike! Nina!'

They both swivel and focus on where I'm looking. A smile

breaks out on their faces and, as one, we bound forward to the pile of cardboard boxes. Sure enough, inside, Dominic is huddled in his *kanga*, a stick at his side. As on the television, he looks exhausted and dirty, bruised and a bit battle scarred, but otherwise he seems well. His head is tucked down and even though his blanket is pulled up, he's shivering. Even when we stand in front of him, he doesn't acknowledge our presence.

'Dominic,' I say softly.

At that, he starts and his eyes snap open. I drop to my knees in front of him and wrap my arms around him, weeping now. 'We've come to take you home.'

'I do not know where my home is, Just Janie,' he says.

I press my face against his and feel the chill of his cheek at odds with my hot tears. 'With me,' I tell him. 'Your home is with me.'

Chapter 86

With an effort, Dominic raises himself and he holds me to him, tightly. Mike and Nina, standing together to one side, come to join us. Mike pats Dominic on the back and hugs him and I'm sure there's a tear in his eye.

'Glad you're safe, mate,' my friend says. 'You had us worried there.'

'I am sorry.' Dominic hangs his head. 'I did not mean to cause trouble.'

Nina comes forward and hugs him too and now she's crying heartily. If Dominic is surprised to see her, then he doesn't register it. 'I'm sorry,' she says again. 'Really sorry.'

But now is not the time for recriminations. Now is a time for relief, rejoicing.

'We've looked everywhere for you,' I tell him. 'You've had us all out of our minds.'

'I had to leave,' he explains. 'The shame was too much for me to bring on you. Everyone was thinking I was a bad man.'

'Not everyone,' I correct. 'Just a few stupid misguided people.' Nina and I make eye contact. 'And they realise now they were wrong.'

'Completely wrong,' Nina chips in with a sniffle.

'We all love you, Dominic.' I hold his face in my hands, hardly able to believe that we've found him. 'And I love you more than anyone. I've missed you so much.'

'I have missed you too, Just Janie.'

'Let's get you home,' I say and without need for further encouragement, Dominic gathers his blanket and allows himself to be guided towards the car. He's weak and much thinner than he looked on television. But I hope that the scars from his ordeal are mainly skin-deep and that, tough Maasai that he is, mentally he's intact.

Mike helps us both get in the back of his car and, there, I hold Dominic in my arms like a baby. Nina slips into the front with Mike. Dominic's head rests on my shoulder and as we drive home to Nashley, my broken heart is slowly melded back together again. My spirit lifts even more as the cottage comes into sight and Mike pulls up outside my door.

'We're home,' I say to my lover. 'We're home again.'

Mike and Nina help Dominic to the door while I fumble with my keys and let us in. I flick on the lights and, suddenly, the cottage is warm and welcoming.

As soon as we're inside, Archie comes thundering down the stairs and then winds himself around and around Dominic's legs, purring ecstatically. Dominic lifts the cat tenderly and drapes him on his shoulders, where he belongs. Archibald dribbles with delight.

'Sit with him,' Mike instructs. 'Don't move, either of you.'

I don't resist, as I feel that I'll never want to let Dominic go again.

'We'll get the kettle on and make Dominic something to eat,' Nina says.

'Porridge,' I say to her. 'Make him some porridge, please. It's his favourite. That will warm him through.'

'Sure thing.' Nina takes charge and goes into the kitchen, followed by Mike. I want to cry with gratitude as I feel incapable of moving.

My brave Maasai warrior lies back against the sofa and sags with relief. A solitary tear rolls down his cheek and I curl into him. We stay there, unmoving, unspeaking.

A few minutes later, Nina and Mike come back with hot chocolate and porridge for Dominic and tea and toast for me.

'Is there anything else you want?' Mike asks.

'No,' I say to him. 'You have done so much for me, for *us*. More than enough.'

'It's my pleasure.' Self-effacing, as always.

'We should be going now,' Nina says. 'Leave you two alone.'

Nina goes to get her coat and I take the time to have a quiet word with Mike. I stand up and draw him away from where Dominic is resting and hold him to me.

'You're more than a friend, Mike. You're family,' I tell him quietly and I hope with all of my heart that my neighbour, my friend, sees it as the compliment I intend. I might not have been able to love Mike in the way that he had once hoped for us, but I love him deeply nevertheless. I hope that he'll always be here, being steady, in our lives. 'I don't know what I would have done without you.'

He hugs me tightly. 'I'm happy to settle for that,' he whispers so that only I can hear.

'Thank you.' I kiss his cheek tenderly. 'Thank you so much.'

Nina comes back and we break apart.

'I need a stiff drink,' she tells me. 'Too much excitement for me.'

'Thanks for the call,' I say. 'And for coming to find Dominic with us.'

Her eyes well with tears again. 'It's the least I could do.'

'I can provide that stiff drink,' Mike suggests, 'if you want to come back to my place.'

There's a slightly furtive glance between them. 'Why not?' Nina says and she links her arm through his.

Hmm. Why not, indeed?

As they go to leave, Dominic tries to stand too, but Mike holds out a hand.

'You stay right where you are, mate,' he chides. 'Rest and relaxation for you until you get your strength back.'

'*Asante*. Thank you, Mike,' Dominic says, echoing my sentiments. 'You are a very good friend.' He clasps his hand and shakes it.

'I'll pop in tomorrow,' Mike says. 'Check that you're both OK.'

'Me too,' Nina offers.

'I'm sure we'll be fine, but it will be good to see you both anyway.'

I kiss Nina too, and we exchange a look that acknowledges that our differences have been patched up without us needing to talk about them any more.

With that, Mike and Nina leave us to our own devices.

Chapter 87

When they've gone, a peace settles on the house that has been sorely missing. Dominic finishes his porridge and his hot chocolate.

'I feel better already,' he says with a wan smile.

'It was very brave. Bringing down that mugger.'

'It was nothing.' A shrug. 'I have wrestled lions, Just Janie.'

I laugh at that. 'Sometimes I forget.'

Resting my head on his shoulder, much to Archie's chagrin, we sit in companionable silence until my eyes start to roll. I don't want to ask him too much, spoil the quiet rapture of him being home, but there are things I need to know, things he needs to tell me. 'What happened, Dominic? Where did you go?'

'I left because I thought it would be for the best. I did not want to harm your standing in the village. I was thinking like a Maasai warrior and not an English gentleman.' He sighs. 'I walked the fields for two hours and as I crossed the road, a man stopped and asked me if I was lost and could he give me a lift somewhere. I asked him where he was going. He said that he was going to work in London. Then I asked him to take me there.'

As simple as that.

'He drove me to London and dropped me at Euston station. Then I did not know what to do. There were some young men wrapped in blankets by the door and I asked them where I should go. They took me to King's Cross, told me where to get food and showed me how to live on the streets.'

'Did you not want to come home?' I ask him. 'Did you not miss me?'

'Every day.' He hangs his head. 'I did not know what to do. After one week, the pain was so great that I waited by the side of the road for someone to stop and take me home again.' As they would have done so readily in the Maasai Mara. Perhaps, as he got to London so easily, he never considered how he might get back or how hard it would be. Or maybe he just didn't think it through at all. 'But they did not. After two days I had no money and did not know how else to get back.'

'Oh, Dominic.'

'The longer I stayed away, the more I was sure that you would not want me to come back.'

'How did you survive? What did you live on?'

'It was not easy to get work, but sometimes I helped to wash dishes in the kitchen of a restaurant. It was a very hard lesson for my pride, my Janie. There was nothing else I could do. I am used to having nothing. All the things that you have,' he gestures around the cottage, 'you can live without them if you have to. That part was not so difficult.' Dominic smiles sadly at me. 'Living without you was the part I did not like.'

'I thought I might never see you again.'

'I wanted to come home,' he says. 'I wanted to come home so much.'

We hold each other tightly. 'Now you're home,' I tell him,

'where you belong. I don't want you ever running out on me again.'

'No,' he confirms. 'I do not intend to do that.'

I stroke Dominic's face. My love is exhausted, weak. His time on the streets has certainly taken its toll.

'We shouldn't be too late to bed,' I say. 'You need some rest. Come upstairs and I'll run you a nice hot bath.'

'This is one of the luxuries I *have* missed,' Dominic admits. 'Hot water! Already, you have made me soft.'

He hauls himself from the sofa and on wobbly legs, follows me, hand-in-hand, to the bathroom. Reluctantly, Archie allows Dominic to uncurl him from his shoulders and settles himself on the loo seat so that he doesn't miss any of the proceedings.

I let the water run, tipping in some fragranced oils to wash away the smell of the street from him. Dominic gingerly strips off his red robe and his beads, which definitely look more tattered than they did when he left. The sight of his dark muscled body still thrills me to the core, but no more so than the fact that he is just here at all. I'll take him whatever he looks like, whatever state he's in. Dominic is back and safe with me and that's all that matters.

When the bath is drawn, I help Dominic to lower himself into it and he sighs with relief as the water embraces his body. 'It is good to be home, Janie,' he says, a catch in his voice. 'So good.'

He leans back and lets himself sink into the water while I soap the sponge and then gently wash his body all over. I want to wash away all the pain, the hurt. Dominic closes his eyes and lets me minister to him.

'Was it very awful on the streets?' I ask.

He shakes his head. 'Not so bad for me,' he says honestly. 'I only had a short time to become used to the comforts here. But I think it is very bad for others who are used to more.' He opens his eyes and then he holds my gaze. 'I did not think that there were people in your country who live like that. I thought that everyone had all that they need.'

'Not everyone,' I admit.

'I know that now. Sometimes I had to eat the food that other people threw away.' He looks sick at the thought of it and my stomach heaves in sympathy too. 'They were very kind to me, all of the people sleeping rough like myself. They helped me. I think that I helped them.'

'There was no need to go. You should have stayed and talked it through with me, Dominic. We could have sorted it out. You're always going to get one or two people who can't accept our love. It would be the same if I was in your country.'

'Worse,' he admits.

'There you are,' I say softly. 'Running away isn't the answer.'

'I did not want you to live with the shame.'

'It might be the Maasai way to cut yourself off from your loved ones, but we can't do that. We have to stay strong together.'

'I have learned that.' And I see in his eyes that he's sincere.

'The shame isn't yours. It isn't mine either. We've done nothing wrong. It's the people who have been mean to you, to us. Promise me that in the future we'll just sit down and work things through together. No rash moves.'

'I promise.'

'You mustn't think of it again.' I take his hand and wash his fingers, one by one. 'It's all behind us. Now it's just you and me.' Then I smile. 'Well,' I say, 'that might not be *quite* right.'

He looks at me, puzzled.

I take a deep breath before I say, 'I might be having a baby, Dominic.'

His eyes light up and he squeezes my hand tightly.

'I'm not sure yet,' I admit hastily. 'But I might be. All the signs are there.'

'I hope so, Just Janie. I do hope so.'

'Me too.' Perhaps I should have waited to tell Dominic until I was certain, but I can't hold my happiness inside. How badly I want his child. That would be all of my dreams come true. 'I'll find out just as soon as I can.'

Dominic wraps his arms around me and kisses me fiercely. 'A child,' he whispers. 'The mummy is the most important person in Maasai culture. When you are a mummy, Janie Johnson, I will revere you. I will worship you. I will always respect you.'

'That sounds nice.' I toy with his fingers. 'But to be honest, I'll just settle for you sticking around.'

'We must be married.'

'Oh, yes,' I agree. 'Straight away.'

Then, while I'm still fully dressed, he pulls me into the bath, into the foamy water, on top of him. Laughing and blowing the suds from my face, I lie along the full length of him, loving the feel of his body. He holds me tightly.

'I love you, Janie Johnson.'

'And you, Dominic Ole Nangon, are never going anywhere without me ever again.'

'Lovely jubbly,' he says and kisses me once more.

Chapter 88

A steady knocking at the door rouses me from a deep sleep. I glance over at the clock and see that it's nearly noon. Dominic and I are still in bed, arms wrapped around each other. This is the first time that he has slept the whole night through. Normally, he'd be up well before dawn and would be doing his rounds of the village, checking that everything is as it should be. I'm sure after living rough on the streets he deserves a lie-in.

There's another rap at the knocker and I haul myself out of bed, pull on my dressing gown and go to see who's there.

It's Nina and she has a pile of newspapers in her arms. 'I didn't wake you, did I?'

I yawn in response.

'Sorry, sorry. But I couldn't wait any longer.'

'Where's the fire?' I say sleepily, marvelling that all is well in my world again. I wander through to my kitchen and Nina follows. She's looking very bright-eyed and bushy-tailed, whereas I am not.

'Oh, Janie.' Nina flops into a chair. 'I couldn't believe my eyes when I saw these in the shop this morning. Have you seen this? Dominic's everywhere.' She holds up a selection of the newspapers and, sure enough, my lover's handsome face is splashed all over them. The story of him tackling a mugger has hit the headlines with a vengeance. HAVE A GO HERO! and MAASAI MAULS MUGGER! are just two of the colourful banners. I take one from her and scan the story. It's glowing in its praise for him and my heart swells with pride.

'He'll be very embarrassed,' I note.

'He *is* a hero, Janie. Who would do what he did these days? You'd be frightened to death of intervening in case you got knifed.'

'Dominic doesn't think like that,' I tell her.

'Good job too,' Nina says. 'That poor old woman had been pushed to the ground and beaten. I'm glad someone stepped in to save her.'

I'm glad that it was my man, my Maasai warrior, as it has brought him back to me.

'I was only trying to protect you, Janie,' she says earnestly. 'You do know that now? I thought I knew better.' She tries a laugh. 'As you can imagine living with Gerry, I've got a downer on men in general.'

I'm sure that it's Gerry who's been feeding her half of her warped ideas, but I say nothing.

My friend casts a glance at the papers in her hand. 'Looks like I was wrong.'

'Very wrong,' I remind her. Doesn't hurt to rub a bit of salt into the wound. The outcome, thankfully, has been a good one, but anything could have happened to Dominic out there on the streets.

Nina hangs her head, but I won't make her suffer too much as she did come good when I needed her to.

'Come on then.' I kiss the top of her head. 'Let's not dwell on that. I'll get the kettle on. I don't know about you, but I'm starving.' My appetite, which has been missing as long as Dominic has, suddenly comes rushing back and is demanding bacon sandwiches.

She flicks through the papers, reading out snippets of the stories about Dominic to me while I start to fix us some breakfast.

'I've something else to tell you,' Nina says as I slide some bacon under the grill. 'I'm leaving Gerry.'

I stop what I'm doing and stare at her.

'He's seeing someone at work,' she adds. 'Younger, needless to say.'

'Oh, Nina.'

'Cliché, hey?' She gives a brittle laugh. 'But that's the last time he's doing it to me.'

She must see the doubt in my eyes as she adds, 'Definitely. No going back.'

'Sure?'

'Yeah, I'm sure. I'm feeling OK,' Nina insists. 'And I know that you'd tell me that I'm better off without him, anyway.'

'I'm not the one to criticise your choice of man,' I point out.

'No.' She laughs tearfully. 'Once I get over the shock, I'm sure it'll be for the best. I thought it was love we had – the highs, the lows, the passion of making up after yet another bust-up. Now I realise it wasn't love at all. What you have with Dominic, that's real love. Seeing how you felt about him made me wake up to it. This last year, I've been trying to force feelings for Gerry that, if I'm honest, are no longer there. I've just been frightened to be on my own.'

'It's not so bad,' I tell her. 'I managed.'

'You're a different person to me,' she says. 'Stronger.'

'I don't know about that.'

'You wouldn't want to be on your own again.'

'No,' I agree. 'Life is definitely a lot better with someone you love.'

'And someone who loves you in return.' She sighs sadly. 'Gerry's made a fool out of me for years, hasn't he?'

'Yes,' I agree.

'Fucker,' she continues. 'I feel he's had the best years of my life. Would I have had children by now if it wasn't for loving him?'

'There's still plenty of time. You're not over the hill yet.'

'No, but I'm quite near the top of the slope.'

That makes us both giggle.

'Perhaps Dominic has a brother.'

'He's got more brothers than you can shake a stick at, but I think we'll look for a new man for you closer to home.' I raise one eyebrow and flick a nod towards Mike's cottage.

Nina has the grace to blush.

'Exactly what time did you leave Mr Perry's home this morning, Mrs Dalton?'

She laughs. 'That could have something to do with it. Seeing that there are actually nice people out there has made me more determined to leave. I don't have to put up with Gerry's crap any more.' Resting her arms on the table, she sighs rather wistfully. 'Mike is such a great bloke, isn't he?'

'I've been telling you that for years.'

Nina shrugs. 'I'm going to take it easy. The last thing that I want to do is rush into another relationship, but I think there is something there.'

'I'm pleased to hear it.'

Before I have a chance to quiz her further, Dominic appears. He has a clean red robe on and he has shaved his head again, the ragged afro has all gone. He looks brighter, stronger, and much more like his usual self. 'The smell of the cooking woke me up.'

'Are you hungry?'

'Yes. Very.'

'Hello, Dominic,' Nina says and, for once, she doesn't shout at him like he's an imbecile.

'Hello. *Jambo*.'

'*Jambo*,' she echoes tentatively. My friend stands up and offers her hand to Dominic. 'I want to apologise. I'm really, really sorry about what I said. It was me being a bitch. I didn't mean it. I'm just so glad that you've come home safely.'

Dominic nods and then he takes her hand. 'We should be brother and sister,' he tells her earnestly. 'You are Janie's best friend and that is very important. That is just like family.'

'I know,' Nina says. 'Janie and I go back a long way. I don't want anything to come between us.'

'That is not my intention,' Dominic assures her.

'Friends?' Nina offers.

'Friends,' he agrees. And I'm so happy to see that his wide grin is firmly back in place.

'Do you want to try some bacon, Dominic?'

'Yes, I would like that. I have eaten many different things on the street – sandwiches, McDonald's and Flamin' Hot Monster Munch.'

'Great British cuisine then,' I laugh. 'I'll call Mike. I've put some extra bacon in. He won't want to miss a party.'

Nina looks strangely sheepish. 'He's coming round in a minute anyway,' she tells us. 'He's just in the shower.'

'Oh? You didn't go home at all?' No wonder she dodged my question about the hour of her departure.

402

'I spent the night there,' she admits. Now a fierce blush stains her cheeks. 'We shared a bottle or two of wine and then, well, it was so late. I just crashed out on his sofa.'

'Is that all?'

She grins. 'Of course. Mike was the perfect gentleman. What else would you expect from him?'

That's true enough. I know that if they do want to start a relationship, Mike would only consider it if Nina has left Gerry completely.

Ten minutes later and we're all sitting round the table eating breakfast and reading the newspapers, teasing Dominic about his starring role. I sigh with contentment. This is how Sundays should be. Nina and Mike seem very comfortable in each other's company and I'm glad to see it. I really hope that they do hook up permanently as it would be so lovely for us all to get along well together. It's early in the afternoon when they leave, tottering off happily back to Mike's cottage again, and I slump onto the sofa. Pulling Dominic down next to me, we cuddle up.

'Are we OK again?' I ask.

'Yes,' he says sincerely. 'I feel that my heart has settled, Just Janie. I will make my life here with you and eat Flamin' Hot Monster Munch and become a sophisticated Western man.'

'I want you to be exactly as you are and sod the rest of them. Who else would bring the exotic into my life?'

Dominic grins. He takes my hand and is serious again. 'I would like to take some classes, Janie. I think, perhaps, I would like to work in a job that helps homeless people.'

'We can arrange that, I'm sure. You can get access to college courses and a work permit as soon as we're married. Will you feel more like you belong then?'

403

Dominic nods. 'I would very much like to become a relevant part of British society.'

'Christ on a bike, Dominic,' I mutter. 'Don't get carried away. I'm not even sure that *I* am.'

He laughs at that and I snuggle into him.

'I think I will walk around the village,' Dominic says. 'Make sure that all is well.'

'The good ladies of Nashley have been demented without you.'

Dominic smiles.

'They have,' I say. 'They spent hours out in the fields looking for you.'

'Then I must repay them.'

'Yeah,' I say. 'You'll be chopping their wood and fending off their cake for the rest of your life.'

'It is the least that I can do.' But he looks very glad that his ladies have worried about him.

'Would you like me to come with you?'

'That would be very nice.'

So I kiss all thoughts of a cosy afternoon on the sofa goodbye and set out with Dominic to take a tour of our village, our home.

Chapter 89

Of course, everyone in the village is delighted to see Dominic back in the fold. The ladies of the Nashley Church Flower Committee are, as I expected, particularly enthralled and cluck around him like mother hens. They kiss him and pet him and touch his body far more than is strictly necessary as Dominic smiles at them indulgently.

It's decided that a surprise homecoming party is in order and it's going to be held at the village hall this evening. My only job is to keep Dominic in the dark and to get the guest of honour there on time. It has also been decided that there will be an African theme and I've cajoled Mike into burning me copies of the two CDs I bought for him at Nairobi airport to supply suitable music.

'We're going out tonight,' I tell Dominic late in the afternoon. 'And I want you in your full finery.'

He looks doubtful about this, perhaps remembering what went wrong last time he wore his best tribal costume. 'Perhaps I should wear my Western clothes?'

'Hmm,' I say, as if giving it consideration. 'Not tonight.' I lay all his traditional dress out for him and, without objection, he duly puts it on.

Oh, how this takes me back to the disastrous dinner party we had here and now it seems so very long ago. I hope that this party will give Dominic the confidence to believe in himself again and his place in the village.

I help Dominic to get ready. Over the red *shuka*, he slips his orange skirt decorated with beads and tiny mirrors and ties it low on his hips. So as not to frighten the ladies too much, we decide to leave the accompanying machete at home. He slips on his wrist and ankle bracelets, then winds the strings of beads around his body and tops them with his elaborate wedding necklace.

'Can I wear the one you brought for me?'

'No,' he says solemnly. 'That must now wait until our formal wedding day, until you are properly my wife.'

My stomach does an ecstatic backflip at the very thought of it and I give him an impromptu hug.

He daubs his cheeks with ochre war paint and, finally, I help him to tie on his elaborate headdress of brown feathers, which fan out in a graceful circle around his handsome face.

'Beautiful,' I say as I stand and admire him. 'Quite magnificent.'

'Thank you.' He smiles proudly and he lifts his head in a regal Maasai warrior pose.

'Now you have to go downstairs while I get ready.' And as he goes to protest, 'I won't be long.'

Quickly, I slip on a printed batik wraparound skirt that I bought on holiday in Ibiza years ago, which has languished in the bottom of my wardrobe ever since. I'm just delighted that it still fits. I top it with a red T-shirt and then loop some beads that I've bought at minimum expense from Claire's Accessories around my body. I've also got beaded flip-flops from one of my beach holidays and I slip those into my handbag to be put on when I get there. Not desperately African, but I don't think the partygoers at the Nashley Village Hall will be too particular. I only hope that Dominic likes it. My coat goes on top of all of it, so that he can't see how I'm dressed. Then, as it's coming up to the appointed time, I make my way downstairs.

'Ready?' I say to Dominic who is watching an old episode of *Strictly Come Dancing* that's still on the Sky+ box, eyes agog.

'Yes,' he says. Then, 'Come, cat.'

Archie, the spring back in his step, jumps onto the arm of the sofa, then onto the back, where Dominic then lifts him onto his shoulders.

We make our way through the empty streets of the village, my arm tucked into Dominic's, until we come to the village hall.

All the lights are off and Dominic frowns at me. 'I do not think there is anyone at home, Janie.'

'Really? I wonder if I've got the wrong evening? Let's just see.' I try the door and, sure enough, it opens.

Inside the hall is in darkness. Dominic and I stand by the door. Then the lights flick on and the entire population of Nashley shout out, 'Surprise!'

There's a banner across the back of the hall which reads: WELCOME HOME DOMINIC!

He looks at me, bemused, and lowers his voice to ask, 'This is for me?'

'Yes,' I say, 'because they all love you.'

My warrior looks overawed. 'The last party I had in my village like this was when I became *ilmoran*, a warrior, at my circumcision ritual.'

'Maybe don't mention that,' I suggest.

He breaks into his trademark grin, lets out his high-pitched

Maasai whoop and jumps about ten feet into the air. Giving great credit to the villagers of Nashley, none of them look even vaguely startled. Instead, they swarm around Dominic, shaking his hand, patting his back and the ladies of the Nashley Church Flower Committee add to their annual quota of kisses.

I back out of the way, letting Dominic bask in the glory. I'm putting on my flip-flops and slipping off my coat as Nina comes up.

'Ah,' she says. 'Benidorm 1992.'

'Something like that.' But then she can't talk as she's dressed in much the same way, although her hair is elaborately beaded and braided.

'Who did the hair?'

'Cristal. It's a bit more Bo Derek and less Maasai Mara than I would have liked, but she's not done a bad job.'

'It looks great.'

Nina has come along with Mike this evening and when he's back from getting them both drinks, Mike comes up to me and pecks my cheek.

He hands a lurid red-coloured drink to Nina. 'African punch,' he says with a grimace. 'Though I'm not exactly sure how African a drink vodka is.'

Nina shrugs and knocks it back anyway. He holds out another glass.

'Not for me,' I say.

He looks somewhat self-conscious in Dominic's spare red robe and my excess Claire's Accessories beading. Being British, he's teamed it with trainers and socks. Mind you, the other 'African' costumes are equally tenuously assembled. Mr and Mrs Codling-Bentham look like they have walked straight off the set of *Out of Africa* in safari suits and matching old-fashioned safari helmets, complete with mosquito nets. The ladies of the Nashley Church Flower Committee, on the other hand, are clearly big fans of Alexander McCall Smith and have gone down the Mma Precious Ramotswe route and are wearing voluminous floral print dresses and have colourful headscarves wound around their heads.

'Everything OK?' Mike asks.

'Everything's fine,' I say with a smile.

While Nina is distracted, I pull him close to me. 'How's things with Nina?'

'Fine.' He grins self-consciously.

Before I have the chance to quiz him further, someone flicks on the stereo and the thumping tribal beat of African music pounds out into the hall and the crowd parts, leaving Dominic centre stage. He lowers Archie to the floor before he gives a superb demonstration of his Maasai jumping skills while everyone claps and cheers their encouragement. The ladies of the Nashley Church Flower Committee look as if they can hardly contain themselves. Some of them, I think, have their first orgasm in years.

Mike downs his drink. 'Bloody hell,' he says. 'In for a penny, in for a pound.' He goes to join Dominic on the dance floor where they jump together as brothers and I find my eyes filling with tears once more. Must be my hormones, I think, because as I suspected, the pregnancy test I did showed up positive. I'm having a baby. I'm having Dominic's baby.

I haven't told Nina or Mike just yet, but I know they will both be thrilled and that the baby will have a devoted aunt and uncle to dote on him or her. Dominic is already convinced that it will be a boy.

I'm trying not to hold my tummy protectively, when Mrs

Duston sidles up next to me. 'Couldn't really find many recipes from the Maasai Mara on the internet,' she confesses in disappointed tones. 'So we went for lasagne. Is that all right, sweetie?'

'I'm sure it will be lovely,' I assure her. 'It's Dominic's favourite.'

That sends her into a frenzy of delight.

I have no idea whether Dominic likes lasagne or not, but if it makes an old lady happy to think that she's hit the spot with her Italian interpretation of the African theme then who am I to disappoint her? I do know though that Dominic's time on the street has broadened his palate out of necessity and he's now much more willing to try different kinds of food, so I'm sure he'll give the lasagne a good go.

The other men of the village join in the jumping and I wonder if it makes Dominic think of his home, all those miles away. From the broad grin on his face, I don't think that he's feeling homesick right now.

Eventually, Dominic stops jumping – having seen everyone else off – and comes to join me. The African music gives way to Abba and Wham! and the lasagne is served.

'Are you happy?' Dominic asks, his arm protectively around my waist.

'Yes, I'm very happy.' I stand on tiptoe to kiss him.

'Good,' he says proudly. 'Because if you are happy, then I am happy.'

Chapter 90

I'm back at Cutting Edge where I belong. All my clients are very pleased to see me, now that I'm not dyeing people's hair the wrong shade or giving short lesbian-style crops to women who just wanted trims.

Nina hands me my coffee and we sit together in the staffroom surrounded by towels and hair dye and all the stuff that makes the salon tick. Cristal is loading gowns into the washing machine. The boys, Tyrone and Clinton, are huddled together sharing a daily paper and a takeaway latte they've bought from Deli Delights between them. At the moment, they are the picture of happiness.

'I saw the solicitor last night,' Nina tells me as she peels an orange. 'On the way home from work. Getting divorced isn't that difficult, is it?' There's a sadness in her voice.

I lean my head against hers. 'You'll be all right,' I assure her. 'We'll look after you.'

'Long overdue,' she concludes.

'But that doesn't make it any easier, does it?'

'No,' she agrees. 'Gerry might be a bastard, but it's still hard to think that I won't ever need to see him again once we both sign a few bits of paper. They weren't all bad times.'

'Maybe you'll be able to stay friends?' I suggest.

'With him and his fit twenty-year-old on his arm? I don't think so.'

I risk a smile and Nina giggles too. 'Perhaps not.'

'It would be worse if there were kids involved. As it is, we can have a clean break.'

'You're getting custody of the dogs?'

'Yes,' she says. 'One good thing. My girls will be coming with me.'

'You won't be able to stay in your house then?'

'No,' she says. 'Anyway, it's far too big for one person. There's plenty of equity in it by some miracle. Perhaps I'll buy myself a little place in Nashley.'

'That's not as silly as it sounds, Nina. There is a cottage up for sale. One of the younger couples are moving up north somewhere with his job. It's a lovely place. Nice garden. Easy to manage. You'd have people you know around.'

Since Nina and I have become firm friends again she's been spending a lot of time with Mike, Dominic and me. An awful lot of time with Mike, now I come to think about it. Plus Mike has upped his consumption of fruit considerably in the last few weeks. Should that tell me something? I think so. 'You could do worse. It's a nice place.'

Her face brightens. 'Fancy viewing it with me?'

'Why not? Let's fix up an appointment quickly otherwise it will be gone. Properties in Nashley don't hang around for long.'

'Won't you be a bit busy at the weekend?'

I laugh. 'I think everything is pretty much organised. There might be a bit of last-minute running round to do, but most things are in hand.'

'I'm so excited,' Nina trills.

412

'Me too,' I confess.

My wedding to Dominic is on Monday at noon and Kelly is closing the salon especially so that everyone can come along. It's going to be a very low-key affair. The ceremony is at the register office and there'll be just a few friends to help us celebrate. Nina and Mike will be our witnesses. I'm not sure that Dominic can quite understand why we're such a small party. When there's a Maasai wedding, everyone turns out and hundreds of people attend from surrounding villages. This will be yet another culture shock for him to deal with and I'm sure he'll handle it all with his unique brand of charm, as he does everything.

I smile to think of my love, who is at home now already researching college courses and applying for his work permit. He is so keen to make a contribution here and it makes me proud to have met someone as community-minded as he is. Frankly, it puts me to shame.

In the meantime, he's gone back to helping out Mr and Mrs Codling-Bentham in their garden for a few hours every morning and I know that they're thrilled he's returned to them. In the afternoons, he still helps the ladies of the Nashley Church Flower Committee with various chores and they're now delighted that he'll actually eat all the cakes that they bake for him.

Kelly pops her head around the door. 'First clients are here, ladies.'

Without further ado, we down our coffee simultaneously and head out onto the floor.

My first client is my regular, Mrs Norman, who's already been shampooed and is sitting waiting for me.

'How's your love life then, young Janie?' Mrs Norman's

opening gambit every Friday when I do her set. She settles herself in the chair.

'It's going well, thanks.'

'Saw that boyfriend of yours in the paper,' Mrs Norman says, beaming. 'Fine-looking young man.'

'Dominic,' I supply as I start to wind a roller into her hair. 'Yes, he is.'

'And brave too! Oh, my word.'

I smile at her in the mirror. All the people who were firmly against Dominic – my clients, my friends – have now switched sides and are his staunchest supporters. They can't get enough of him now. Just goes to show what a bit of celebrity status can do for a person. Part of me thinks that it's a shame that they didn't see what a good person he was before he was on the television and in the newspapers. That kind nature was there all along. Should I really be grateful to the *Daily Mail* for making sure the world and my friends realised that? Couldn't they have worked it out for themselves? He was a pretty cool guy before he was on the telly, in my mind.

A few of the reporters have beaten a path to our door and Dominic has treated them all in his usual impeccable and polite manner. Even I was persuaded to join him for a few photographs and give them a quote about our impending nuptials. The coverage has slowed down now though and I'm sure once they've published a wedding photograph or two, we'll become yesterday's news.

'I've bought a little gift for you,' Mrs Norman says.

'Oh, thank you.'

She hands me a silver and white wrapped box, topped with a curl of ribbon.

'Just a little token.'

A pile of similar boxes in different shapes and sizes has been growing in the staffroom. Every day this week, I've taken home armfuls of gifts. This will, no doubt, be the first of several today and I'm touched to think that my clients are so thoughtful.

'Make sure you bring some photographs in, Janie.'

'I will.' I've also bought some little boxes so that I can bring all of my regulars a piece of wedding cake.

'I was thinking,' Mrs Norman says, 'maybe I'll have something a little different done to my hair.'

'Really?' It's a good job that I'm sitting down on my stool.

'Next week. Don't want to rush these things.'

'No,' I say, wanting to punch the air. 'No need to rush. We'll have a look at something else next week.' She's had the same hairstyle for ten years; I can wait another seven days.

'Sometimes it's good to embrace something a little bit different.' She beams at me. 'That man of yours hasn't got an older brother who likes ballroom dancing, has he?'

'You're not the first person who's asked.'

'I'm too old for love,' my client says sadly. 'That's for young ones like you.'

'You never know.' I shrug. 'Sometimes when you're not looking for it, then it sneaks up on you.'

'I hope it gets a bloody move on,' she complains. 'I've already got one foot in the grave.'

But Mrs Norman, despite her teasing, knows what it is to be truly loved and, now, so do I.

Chapter 91

Mike is leaning against my kitchen cupboards, drinking a cup of tea. He made one for me too, but that's remained untouched on the table.

'Drink that,' he instructs, 'and then go and get dressed.'

I'm currently still in my slippers and dressing gown, although I've done my make-up and Nina has fixed my hair. 'How long have we got?' I ask anxiously.

'Plenty of time,' Mikes says. 'Stop panicking.'

I nibble at my nail, even though I've just painted them. 'Have I forgotten anything?'

'No,' he assures me. 'Everything is sorted. All you've got to do is put your gladrags on.'

'Is Dominic ready?'

'Just doing the finishing touches.'

'Nina?'

'In the shower.'

'What about Archie?'

'Nearly took my arm off while I tried to attach that damn bow to his collar.' My cat purrs, feigning innocence, on the table.

'Good, good. I mean sorry, sorry.'

'It's all under control.'

'Right.' I try a deep breath, but it doesn't reach my lungs. 'Right.'

'Janie.' Mike lowers his voice. 'Just one last thing. You are sure you're doing the right thing?'

'Oh, Mike . . .'

He puts down his tea and comes to me, resting his hands on my arms.

'Take a minute to think about it?'

I do and a slide show of the last six months with Dominic whizzes through my mind. 'I adore him more than life itself,' I tell my friend. 'And I know that he feels the same way about me.'

He smiles at me. 'That's all I wanted to hear.'

Leaning into him, I rest my head against his shoulder. 'I've something else to tell you.' I sigh contentedly. 'I'm having his baby, Mike.'

'That's fabulous news.' I see tears spring to his eyes. 'And here's me thinking you were just eating too much pasta.'

I punch him in the arm.

'I feel like I'm giving you away,' Mike admits. 'As if I'm your father or something. Never thought I'd be doing that.'

'You have been my rock, Mike. I don't know what I'd do without you. I hope that you'll find someone to love. And soon.' Then I look at him. 'But she'll have to meet with my approval and live close by. I don't want some flighty piece whisking you away from here,' I tease. 'Think anyone might fit the bill?'

'Hmm,' he says enigmatically, although we are both fully aware that the ideal candidate is already on the scene. Nina has looked at the cottage in Nashley and has had an offer on it

417

accepted. I don't think she and Mike have left each other's side all weekend and it's lovely to see their relationship blossoming. 'I'll have to see what I can do.'

Nina pops her head around the door. 'Come and get your frock on, woman. It's nearly time to go.'

I have a few sips of the tea that Mike has prepared and then follow her up the stairs.

In the bedroom, Dominic is admiring himself in the mirror, his full tribal dress in place.

'Hot stuff,' Nina teases. 'Now get out while I dress the bride.'

'You look wonderful,' I say to Dominic. 'I hope that I can do you proud.'

'You will be a beautiful bride,' he tells me.

'Enough of that, you two,' Nina chides. 'Any more slushy stuff and we won't get to the register office on time.'

'I love you,' Dominic says. '*Aanyor pii.*'

'*Aanyor pii.* I love you too.'

Chapter 92

The registrar reads out the vows and Dominic, and then I, repeat them.

'With this ring, I thee wed.' Dominic slips a gold band on my finger. I do the same to him. I see Nina brush away a tear and Mike slips his arm around her shoulders.

The beat of African music fills the room and Dominic places the long wedding necklace around my neck. The beads cascade down to my feet and I've worn a plain white strapless dress of raw silk to show it off at its best. I slip his wedding necklace in place and the registrar says, 'You may now kiss your wife.'

Dominic kisses me long and hard while our friends cheer at our happiness. Archie, sitting at Dominic's feet, miaows his displeasure at being so roundly ignored and Dominic lifts him onto his shoulder to appease him.

Out at the front of the register office and our friends throw confetti over us. If Dominic is bemused by this, he doesn't show it. Instead, he lifts me into his arms and carries me down the steps to Mike's waiting car.

'Your carriage awaits, Mrs Ole Nangon,' he says.

That's me, I think. Mrs Dominic Lemasolai Ole Nangon. Plain old Janie Johnson has gone for ever!

Cristal, Tyrone and Clinton, Steph, Kelly and her man, all in their finery, follow in our wake. As do Mike and Nina, hand-in-hand.

'Throw your bouquet,' Cristal shouts.

'Shall I?' I have a simple bunch of brightly coloured flowers tied together: vibrant orange gerberas, brilliant yellow sunflowers, deep red flamingo flowers and pink lilies. 'Whoever catches this will be the next person to get married,' I explain to Dominic. 'It's just a silly custom.'

With a carefree laugh, I toss the bouquet. It soars through the air and, as it's heading straight for Nina, she drops Mike's hand and lets it fall right into her own.

She looks up at me, stunned. 'I haven't got rid of the last husband yet,' she says. 'Give me a chance!'

Everyone bursts into laughter and I note, again, that Mike takes her into his arms and kisses her. Maybe wedding bouquet predictions aren't quite so silly after all.

'See you at the restaurant.' We're heading now to a local place that we've chosen for a meal with everyone, and then Mike has treated us to a night at a swanky hotel nearby for our honeymoon. On Wednesday, it's back to work.

Dominic and I slip into the back of Mike's car. I snuggle up close to my husband. 'Are you happy?' I ask him.

'I am very happy,' he says. 'Very happy indeed, Just Janie.'

'Good. Because if you are happy, then I am happy too.'

'One day I would like to go back to the Mara and have a Maasai ceremony with all of my family,' my husband adds.

'Is jumping involved?'

Dominic guffaws. 'But of course, Just Janie!'

I bloody knew it.

'We'll save up,' I promise him. 'We'll save up and take you home.'

'Home is here now,' he says softly to me. My husband rests his hand gently on my bump. 'With you and with my child.'

And I know deep in my heart and in my soul, that this truly is real love. Real love that overcomes all obstacles – colour, creed, culture. Real love that lasts until the end of time.

What happens next?

Do Janie and Dominic stay together?

Can a Maasai warrior survive without
the plains of Africa?

And will true love conquer all?

Find out for FREE in an
EXCLUSIVE SHORT STORY from Carole!
Simply visit www.carolematthews.com, sign up to her
newsletter and we'll send you a code to claim your FREE story.

Carole Matthews

Acknowledgements

A big thanks to Gemma, who very kindly helped me with the research into what it's like to have a relationship with a Maasai warrior. To our friends Ann and Ash who, rather rashly, accompanied us on this trip. Also to our lovely guide, Benjamin Waiganjo – in the happy bus – who made our trip to the Maasai Mara so very enjoyable.

To the beautiful people of Kenya – particularly to those in our camp who made us so welcome. Also to the kind people in the Maasai village who shared their homes and their culture with us. I've tried to be as authentic as possible, but sometimes I just had to take liberties. The Mara is such a stunning place to visit and far exceeded our expectations. Everyone should go once in a lifetime.

To Anthony 'Captain Baldy' Kirby for the notes on boats. To Martin Furminger, next door, for the idea about taking Dominic to the Sno!Zone. To Mr and Mrs Codling-Bentham for having a very exciting bonfire party. Albeit unintentionally. And, once again, to the inimitable Mr Owen Earl for supplying the expert snowboarding advice and know-how with the barest minimum of that 'P' word that we now don't mention. You and Sharon are lovely friends. It's not everyone you'd want to sit in hot water with on a regular basis.

Finally, to Lovely Kev, who always gets a mention in dispatches for services above and beyond the call of duty. This time it's for stopping wild animals eating me and for letting me have all the hot water from the bucket shower. They don't make them like you any more, love.

A Christmas Chat with Carole

What is your earliest Christmas memory?
Playing Mary in the nativity play at primary school. The choir was all standing on stacked up benches and Joseph got told off for looking up the girls' skirts. The next year I was down-graded to a robin and wore brown wrinkled tights. I don't think I've ever got over it.

How do you like to spend your Christmases now?
I like to be at home, see friends, cook a mega-Christmas dinner. The best bit for me is when there are impromptu parties or people drop round unannounced and get stuck into the turkey butties and fizz. Flying in the face of popular opinion, I do love it when it snows at Christmas. Everything just seems so much better.

Is there something you'd like to do for Christmas that you've never done before?
I do harbour fantasies of spending it either on a hot beach with a drink involving a colourful umbrella or perhaps in the Arctic on a polar bear safari. But when it comes down to it, I'm far too lazy to organise anything and just like to be at home.

Is there a particular Christmas Day that sticks in your mind?
The first year that Lovely Kev and I got together we rented a windmill in Norfolk. We took the microwave and everything that could be pinged for Christmas dinner. I'd bought a tiny fibre optic tree that we plugged in. We spent Christmas Day in sub-zero temperatures, fully clothed on a nudist the beach, drank two bottles of champagne and pinged the turkey in a cheerful haze. Because I'd forgotten crackers and we had no paper hats, Lovely Kev wore the tea towel and I had the oven mitt on my head. I'm actually surprised that I remember it at all.

What is the best Christmas present you've ever been given? And the worst!?
One year my ex-husband gave me The Twelve Days of Christmas style presents. Every day from Christmas Day onwards I would have a little, appropriate gift – some funny, some romantic. On the eighth day of Christmas, my true love gave to me, a box of After Eight mints that had a beautiful diamond necklace secreted in one of the mint wrappers.

The Christmas before my ex-husband and I split up he gave me a Dyson Vacuum cleaner.

What will you be asking Santa for this year?
For some years now, I have asked Santa for Rupert Penry-Jones every Christmas and he has never yet come through. I'm beginning to believe that Santa doesn't exist. This year I might try asking for UGG boots instead and see how that goes.

If you're feeling the cold this winter, turn your
mind to the sunshine and fun you'll enjoy with

Summer Daydreams

Meet Nell, Olly and their adorable daughter Petal –
and you'll soon find out what happens when your
daydreams start coming true . . .

Read on to enjoy the first two chapters!

Chapter 1

'Two cod and chips?' I look up from the counter.

'Yes please, love.' The man gives me a welcome smile.

It's lunchtime, Friday, and we should be busier than this. Much busier. There's been a steady trickle, but the usual queue at Live and Let Fry has been noticeably missing for some weeks now, maybe even months. I dish out the chips, golden and hot, and top them with two cod, freshly cooked, with crisp batter sizzling.

'Salt? Vinegar?'

'Just as they are,' the customer says. He's licking his lips already. It's certainly not Phil's fish and chips that are putting off the customers.

Wrapping them in white paper, I hand over his package and with a spring in his step, the customer leaves.

Phil Preston, my boss and fish-fryer extraordinaire, looks at his watch. 'How many have been in today, Nell?'

'Not many.' I give a sympathetic grimace. A handful at best.

'The cold weather normally brings in people in droves.' Phil rubs his hands together even though it's as warm as always in here.

As well as the takeaway counter, we also have a small eat-in café too, which is normally very popular. Today, there are just two people enjoying their lunch. Jenny, my co-worker, who is the waitress today, has spent most of her time flicking through *Heat* magazine.

'I could stand outside and waft some chips about,' Jenny offers helpfully as she drags her attention away from the latest celebrity dramas.

'It's going to take a bit more than that.' Phil shakes his head. 'We can't keep blaming everything on the credit crunch.'

'What about up-selling?' Jen continues. 'Like they do in coffee shops. Do you want a pie with that? Mushy peas? Pickled egg? Gherkin?'

We all laugh.

'You have that down to a fine art, Jen,' I tell her.

'I'm going to try it tonight,' she insists. 'You watch me.'

Pinching a chip from the warmer, I nibble it absently. I've worked at the chippy for well over a year now. I do shifts at lunchtime – twelve until two – and then I'm back again in the evening – six through to ten. It means that my boyfriend, Olly, and I can share childcare for our daughter, Petal. I'm not saying it's easy. We could probably both get jobs in the circus with the amount of juggling we have to do to get through the week, but needs must. We're not alone in having to keep a lot of plates in the air these days. Everyone has to do it, right? Petal's just four years old and as much as I don't want to wish her life away, I can't wait for her to start school. I'm hoping that once she does, life won't be quite as frantic as it is now.

'What am I going to do?' Phil asks, rubbing his hand through his hair. 'This is getting dire.'

The unspoken thought is that if it goes on like this then he won't need to keep on so many staff. It's probably only because Jenny and our other colleague, Constance, have been here for so long and that we all get on so well that Phil hasn't let one or more of us go before now. It's a worrying time.

I look round at the café. The tables are glossy orange pine, the walls are painted peach and there's a flowery border at waist-height that's curling up in more places than it's stuck to the wall. 'It does look a bit tired in here, Phil,' I venture. 'If you don't mind me saying.'

'You think so?'

'You're a bloke,' I remind him. 'You never notice these things.'

'It is a bit of an eighties throwback look,' Jenny adds.

'Really?' Phil looks round as if he's seeing the café with new eyes. 'I'm useless with a paintbrush. I could get a decorator in to give us a quote if you think it needs a spruce up.'

'They call it a makeover these days, Phil. And it probably wouldn't hurt,' I say. It's fair to say that it's been a long time since Phil spent any money on the interior of this place.

Phil tuts. 'What do reckon it would cost? Cash is the one thing I haven't got to splash about.'

'Give me some money,' I say before my brain has fully engaged. 'I'll do it for you.'

Phil laughs.

'You said yourself, you can't afford to bring in the pros. I could do it a lot cheaper. We can all muck in to help. After all, it's our jobs that are on the line if this place sinks.'

'Yes, but—'

'I'm a great decorator,' I protest before he lays out his objections. 'You've been to my house.'

'I know. It's . . . what's the word?'

'Unique,' I supply. 'And fun. And all my own work.' My living room has pink candy-stripe wallpaper with matching spotty chairs. I sanded and stained the floorboards myself and whizzed up some cushions that look like big cupcakes. 'We could do something like that here. Jazz the place up.'

Phil brightens. 'You think so?'

I shrug. 'Why not? I'll make a mood board tonight.'

'Mood board?' Jenny and Phil exchange a puzzled look.

'I can start tomorrow after we close up.'

Now Phil looks surprised – and not a little terrified. 'Tomorrow?'

'No time like the present.'

'I'm not doing anything tomorrow night, more's the pity,' Jenny offers.

She is currently man-free – a fairly rare occurrence. My friend is a curvy brunette with ample comely charms and, as such, is a big hit with the gentlemen. Though cads and bounders feature heavily on the menu and none of them ever stay around for long.

'I'm not exactly a dab hand with a paintbrush,' she admits, 'but I can do labouring and make tea.'

'Sounds good to me,' I say.

We both look at Phil expectantly.

'I'm not doing anything either,' he confesses with a shrug.

Phil is in his early sixties, I would think, and his wife left him about five years ago for a younger man who's been giving her the runaround ever since. He doesn't get out much unless we drag him to the pub or for a pizza. Live and Let Fry is pretty much his life. But he looks good for his age. Dapper, I think you'd say. He's a bit portly due to his largely chip-based diet, and we all tease him about his hair being a bit thin on top. But bald's not a bad thing now, is it? Jenny is always trying to fix him up with sundry women, but he doesn't seem very interested. I think secretly he's probably worried that he'd end up with someone just like Jenny. And she's way too much woman for him to handle.

Phil purses his lips in thought. 'How much do you think it would cost?'

'No idea.' I normally have to beg, steal or borrow paint if the decorating urge comes upon me, so I'm somewhat out of touch with B&Q's current price list. Most of our house is painted with leftover half-tins purloined from my parents' garage and all mixed together. I'm thinking that Phil might want a slightly more upmarket approach than this. 'But say you stump up three hundred pounds and we'll see what we can get with that?' I know that paint's expensive now – what isn't? – but the café is only small. 'If we start on Saturday night, we could work all day Sunday and be open for business again on Monday.'

Phil looks a bit teary. 'Did anyone ever tell you that you're a little treasure, Nell McNamara?'

'All the time,' I say, lightly batting the compliment away before Phil gets into full blub-mode and starts me off too.

'You lot might get on my nerves most of the time,' he jokes, 'but you're all like family to me. I don't know what I'd do without you.'

'If we don't get some more customers through the doors you might well be finding out,' I remind him. And I, for one, need this job. So if it means spending my precious weekend slapping a bit of paint on, then that works for me.

Chapter 2

As always when we shut up the chippy, I take great pleasure in liberating my long blonde bob from beneath my utilitarian cap, and then I always steal ten minutes for myself and walk a circuitous route home, passing my favourite shop. Today, the crackle of autumn is in the air and I enjoy being outside, breathing in the scent of coffee that drifts from a dozen different cafés that I pass.

We live in the small market town of Hitchin in the heart of the beautiful county of Hertfordshire. It's a nice enough place to live, though I'm sure some of its charms have been lost on me after living here for so many years. You take things like that for granted, don't you? I think if you came here as a visitor you'd love it, but for me, well, it's just where I live. You don't really stop to look around and think how fab it is.

Olly and I were both born and brought up here and sometimes I think we should move somewhere more obviously cool, more creative, like Brighton or . . . well, wherever else is more happening. Petal would like it by the sea too. Though this place isn't exactly a cultural desert when it comes to style. There are some trendy independent boutiques selling weird, wacky and wonderful stuff, which I love. Olly and I are both mad keen fans of the sixties – music, films, clothes – and one thing I can say about Hitchin is that we're well served here when it comes to our passion.

There's a great market that has been here since time began. I get a lot of our clothes cheaply from the vintage stall that's always there. I run up the rest on my trusty sewing machine and there are a couple of fantastic haberdashery stalls that are brilliant for picking up cheap ribbons, buttons and the like. Olly's favourite pit stop is the second-hand records stall and we have a mountain of vinyl in our spare room. There's a scooter shop run by one of Olly's mates – my dearly beloved's other obsession – and a couple of great retro lifestyle shops that keep us supplied with cheap furnishings.

The chippy is located in one of the small shopping arcades that radiate off from the Market Place. It might be Victorian – I have no idea – but it's decorated with pretty ironwork and has an arched glass roof. Marvellous for pigeons to settle in. But it's quaint and full of character. The place isn't without its fair share of the unsightly 1960s carbuncles that most English towns now harbour, but there's actually a lot of the centre that's managed to survive, untrammelled by council insanity.

I wander away from the Market Place, turning from the rash of chain stores and down through the old part of town where the shops are in small alleys, still packed tightly together in quaint timbered buildings, all higgledy-piggledy. This is where my favourite shop is tucked away. Betty the Bag Lady is an oasis for me. When people are stressed they might go to yoga classes or take a swim or down a good glass of Pinot Grigio. Me, I head for Betty the Bag Lady.

The Betty in question isn't an ageing lady with a blue rinse as her name might suggest. This Betty is young and trendy. She's even smaller than me and I'm not exactly an Amazonian woman. My mum bought me a school blazer with 'room to grow' when I was eleven and it was still way too big for me when I hit sixteen. My mother was clearly overly optimistic about the size I would eventually attain. Betty has her immaculately straightened hair dyed white, whereas mine is a golden blonde and is generally a random mess or tied up so someone doesn't enjoy a portion of it with their chips. Betty is probably about twenty-five, I'm fast approaching thirty: it's fair to say that I'm hideously jealous of her. Fancy having your own shop! Oh, I'd think I'd died and gone to heaven. Clearly Betty paid attention at school and did her homework and went on to do 'good things'. I stared out of the window and daydreamed and wondered how much better our uniform would have been if it wasn't fashioned from nylon and had been in luscious shades of pink rather than bottle-green. I lost my homework on the way home, hung round with boys in the park and, as such, never amounted to much.

I wanted to learn, I really did, I just didn't want to learn about Pythagoras's theorem or Ox-bow lakes or the Tolpuddle Martyrs. I wanted to learn about 'interesting' things, even though I had no clue what they might be. I just know that I felt like a very square peg in a very round hole. So I left school at sixteen, ignoring my parents' despairing pleas and cries of 'university!', and drifted. I worked in Tesco and a shoe shop and a dozen other dead-end jobs before I rocked up at Live and Let Fry. Some days I wish I'd tried harder. Some days I love my work. Let's face it, how many jobs come with free chips?

Betty also runs with the London crowd, whereas I married young and settled down. She 'knows' people. She 'knows' people in the 'know'. I know no one. If I get another turn at life, I think I'd like to come back as Betty.

This afternoon, Betty's is open for business. The shop has been here for about a year and in my humble opinion, it's a welcome addition to the Hitchin shopping experience. At night when I finish my shift and the shop is closed, I actually press my nose against the window and dream of things that might have been.

Betty's handbags are not mere bags but are veritable works of art and, as such, are completely beyond my price range. I might be a regular visitor here but I'm not a very good customer. I'm purely a window-shopper, but Betty doesn't seem to mind too much. I come in to coo and purr at the bags, but I always have to put them back on the shelf.

'Hi, Nell,' Betty says as I push through the door. 'All right?'

'Fine.' The shop is a calm oasis. If I could ever have my own shop one day, this is the atmosphere I'd like to create. It's done out like someone's living room and I can feel myself unwind as soon as I'm over the threshold. The only thing that I'm conscious of is that until I've been in the shower, I bring with me the lingering odour of cod and chips. 'What's new?'

'Get a load of these,' she moons as she strokes a bag I've not seen before. 'New in today. Bought them from a designer up in Manchester.'

The bags are all handmade in felt, vintage-style, and smothered in buttons of all different shapes, sizes and colours. They are luscious and I'm instantly in love. I pick up an oversized one in differing, shimmering rainbow tones – red, yellow, green, blue, orange, purple – and hook it over my arm. It's mesmerising. And it fits me perfectly.

Ever since I was a child, I've loved handbags. My earliest memory is taking my mother's out of her cupboard and parading round the house with each of them in turn. Looks like I inherited the handbag-fiend gene from her. I am hoping to pass it on to my own daughter too.

438

My mum's responsible for all my interest in fashion, even though she had me quite late in life for that era. I never thought of her as an older mother – compared to my friends' parents, mine were a tiny bit bohemian and fun. Every Saturday when I was growing up, we'd go into town and look at what was new in the shops. Even if we couldn't buy, we'd spend hours trying on stuff. She often made my clothes for me so I didn't look like all the other kids and she taught me how to sew and knit, do patchwork and crochet. We'd spend hours together painting in our old, lean-to conservatory – something I'd like to do with Petal if she didn't have the patience of Attila the Hun. It's a shame that I hardly see my mum now that I'm older and she's moved away. Retirement to a small market town in Norfolk was something that I hadn't seen on the cards for her, but she loves it.

My own extensive collection of handbags is in a wardrobe in our spare room, which drives Olly mad as he'd like to take over the entire space for his precious collection of vinyl records. Sometimes I take them all out just to look at them. Occasionally I let Petal play with them, just as my mum did with me. Men just don't get the whole handbag thing, do they? Though they come in surprisingly useful when they want us to carry all their stuff in them. Right? All my handbags are in their own dust bags, each one with happy memories attached. A woman can never have too many handbags.

'I love it,' I breathe, admiring myself this way and that in the full-length mirror.

'Suits you,' Betty agrees.

'I can't even bring myself to ask how much.'

'A hundred,' she says. Then, at my sharp intake of breath, 'I could do you a discount. As a regular.'

I don't point out that I'm a regular who buys nothing.

'Even with a discount, I can't consider it,' I say reluctantly. Even though it's much cheaper than many of her bags, Betty might as well have asked me for a million quid. 'Olly would kill me.' In a particularly painful manner.

My handbag buying has been severely curtailed in recent years. Frankly, I can't even think of the last time I bought one. But I can all too easily bring to mind the mountain of bills sitting on our sideboard: gas, electricity, council tax. The rent is due and, as always, Petal needs more shoes. The very last thing on earth that I can afford to splash money on is a fancy handbag.

'Want me to put it to one side for you?' Betty cajoles. 'I could keep it for a couple of weeks if you put a small deposit on it. A tenner would do it.'

I can feel myself weakening. In my purse is a tenner. My last one. In my wardrobe there is the perfect outfit to go with this bag. If there's a greater temptation than the perfect handbag, then I certainly can't think of it. Running my fingers over the buttons, I chew at my lip. Surely my child wouldn't mind wearing scuffed shoes for a while longer for the greater good?

Then I come to my senses. 'I can't Betty. Much as I'd love to.' Taking the handbag off my shoulder, I reluctantly hand it back to her.

'Another time,' she says.

'Yeah.' I leave the shop, crestfallen. Another time. Another life.